STARTING OVER
on Blackberry Lane

SHEILA ROBERTS

STARTING OVER
on Blackberry Lane

MIRA

MIRA®

ISBN-13: 978-0-7783-3059-2

Starting Over on Blackberry Lane

For questions and comments about the quality of this book, please contact us at CustomerService@Harlequin.com.

www.MIRABooks.com

Printed in U.S.A.

First printing: March 2017
10 9 8 7 6 5 4 3 2 1

For Roberta, who's done such a good job of starting over.

Acknowledgments

I'd like to start by thanking my editor and friend Paula Eykelhof, not just for the work you've put in on this book but for the countless hours you've given me these past years. You have been wonderful to work with! And speaking of wonderful, thanks as always to my agent and friend Paige Wheeler. You've always been there for me and I appreciate it. You're the best! A big thanks to my husband the tool man for helping me with all things construction in this book. A house build and a remodel and we're still together. Yay, us! Finally, a huge thanks to the whole Harlequin team for working so hard on my behalf. An author may write the story but it takes a team to make a book.

Dear Reader,

Thanks so much for taking time from your own busy schedule to spend some of it with me. I hope you'll enjoy this story of restarts and do-overs. I don't know about you, but I've had times in my life where I've taken a wrong turn and had to reboot. I've definitely lived with remodel nightmares just like Stefanie Stahl, hauling slabs of plywood in from the rain, begging workers not to leave, sprouting gray hairs right and left. And I definitely know the pain of losing someone. I also know that somehow, with persistence, we manage to make it over life's hurdles. If you're facing one right now, let me encourage you by saying that you'll make it over that hurdle. Meanwhile, I hope you'll enjoy the latest adventures of some of the residents of Icicle Falls as they work on starting over.

Sheila

STARTING OVER
on Blackberry Lane

SOME OF YOUR FAVORITE ICICLES

Icicle Falls is populated with so many interesting people.
Here are the ones you'll meet most often

Samantha Sterling-Preston: Samantha runs her family's business, The Sweet Dreams Chocolate Company (also known as Sweet Dreams Chocolates or just plain Sweet Dreams).

Cecily Goodman: Cecily is Samantha's sister, and she, too, works at Sweet Dreams. With her gift for knowing who should be with whom, she gives Cupid a run for his money.

Bailey Black: Bailey is Samantha and Cecily's little sister. She owns Tea Time Teashop. Stop in for a cup of tea and some of her lavender cookies!

Charley Masters: Charley owns Zelda's, one of the town's favorite restaurants. She's married to Dan Masters, owner of Masters Construction.

Cass Wilkes: Cass is good friends with the Sterling sisters and Charley. She owns Gingerbread Haus and keeps everyone in town happily supplied with gingerbread houses and gingerbread boys and girls. (If you're wanting something fancy to serve for dinner, try her cream puff swans.)

Muriel Sterling-Wittman: In spite of being widowed twice, Muriel has managed to find a positive outlook on life. With a blossoming career as a writer she is considered the town's wisewoman.

Pat York: Pat owns Mountain Escape Books and she and Muriel have been friends for years.

Olivia Claussen: Olivia is another one of Muriel's close friends and owns the Icicle Creek Lodge. She recently married James Claussen, who now helps her run the lodge.

Dot Morrison: Dot, also a member of Muriel's group of friends, is known for her smart mouth and her goofy sweatshirts. And her big heart. Her restaurant, Pancake Haus, is the place to go for a great breakfast. She's also good friends with Cass Wilkes.

Tilda Black: Tilda the cop helps keep law and order in Icicle Falls. She's a tough cookie but, like her mom, Dot Morrison, she has a good heart.

Stacy Thomas: Stacy owns Timeless Treasures, the perfect place to find a lovely antique or a china teacup.

Beth Mallow: The town's seamstress. For years her mother was a mover and shaker in the community. Beth never had children of her own, but that didn't stop her from taking in foster kids or helping her mom raise her nephew Colin.

Ivy Bohn: Looking for the perfect Christmas decoration or ornament for your tree? Go see Ivy Bohn at Christmas Haus.

Maddy Donaldson: If you need someone to make something happen, talk to Maddy. She is the quintessential volunteer. (Ask anyone who lives on Candy Cane Lane.)

CHAPTER ONE

Cass Wilkes had wanted to liven up her empty-nest existence, but having her dining room ceiling fall in was not on her list of ways to do it. She'd just come home at three in the afternoon from the usual Saturday swamping of customers at her bakery, Gingerbread Haus, with sore feet and a desire for a bubble bath and a cup of chocolate-mint tea. Looking at the water and the soppy chunks of Sheetrock on her dining table and floor, and the white glop everywhere, she now had a desire for something with more of a kick.

Currently there wasn't anything stronger than cooking sherry in the house. That meant there was only one way to deal with this situation. She walked right back out the door and to her car. Destination: Zelda's, one of Icicle Falls' favorite gathering spots, owned by her friend Charley Masters. Charley would give her a Chocolate Kiss, a boozy chocolate number that was one of the restaurant's specialties, and hopefully she'd also dispatch her husband, Dan, owner of Masters Construction, to deal with the ceiling problem.

Back in her car Cass texted her friend. Emergency. Have Chocolate Kiss ready.

You okay? came the concerned reply.

Yeah, but my house isn't.

Uh-oh, Charley texted back. Will have drink ready.

On my way.

The restaurant was empty, set up for the evening rush, which would start around five with the sundowner crowd, seniors taking advantage of the early dinner bargains. By six thirty there wouldn't be an empty seat anywhere, and people would be crowding in, waiting for a table. She was glad it was quiet now. If she had a complete nervous breakdown the only witnesses would be Charley and the staff.

True to her word, Charley was at a booth in the back of the restaurant with a Chocolate Kiss martini set at Cass's place, along with a plate of nachos. "The crisis kit," she said, stealing a cheese-drenched chip. "Chocolate, booze and carbs."

Cass slid into the banquette. "Bless you." She took a sip of her drink and then dived into the nachos. "I so needed this. Well, not my butt." That seemed to be ever expanding. "My soul, for sure."

"What's wrong at your house? Did your rotting deck finally fall in?"

"Worse than that. Half my dining room ceiling is now sitting on the table." Grandma's dining table. Her grandmother had given her that when she first bought her house in Icicle Falls. She only used it on holidays but it had huge sentimental value. If not for the protective pad and a tablecloth it would have been completely ruined.

Good friend that she was, Charley looked properly horrified. "Oh, no."

"Oh, yes," Cass said miserably. "I knew I was going to need

a new roof soon, but I didn't think it was this bad. I didn't go up to the attic to see what that's like. It must be grim, since my dining room is now a war zone. Please tell me Dan can fix this so I don't have to pull out my hair."

"Dan can fix it," Charley assured her. "But count on him telling you that you need a new roof."

Cass glanced out the restaurant window at the rain dumping on the window boxes of the various shops and buildings, bouncing off car roofs and slithering along the street in streams. *April showers bring May flowers*, her mom liked to say. They also brought roof leaks and wrecked mahogany dining room tables. Ugh. How long had that water been collecting in her attic before it crashed through the ceiling? And shouldn't it have given her a warning by dripping a little?

Except when was the last time she'd been in her dining room to notice any drips? Other than hanging out with her pals for their chick-flick nights, she hadn't had much of a social life. Her daily schedule consisted mainly of work, eating takeout from Zelda's or the Safeway deli while watching TV, and sleeping. Repeat. This was alleviated by occasional visits home by the kids, but those visits weren't nearly frequent enough, and mother-child text sessions never lasted long. Afterward it was just her, rattling around in a house that was as much in need of fixing up as she was. This was her life now that the last little chick had left the nest.

She missed those chicks. Sometimes Cass could hardly believe they were grown. The slide into this new phase had felt both gradual and sudden. When her three kids were small the chaos of life as a single parent had seemed never-ending. But now, suddenly, here they were, launched and mostly out of the house. Dani was happily married and a mom herself, and her bakery in Spokane was doing well. Willie was graduating from college with a degree in environmental science and resource management in June and this would be his last summer home, although she knew she wouldn't see much of him. Amber, the baby, was a freshman at Western and was only home during the summer. Between working and hanging out with her friends, she was gone more than she was around.

Even Tiny, the family Saint Bernard, was no longer there to fill the empty spaces. Tiny had gone to doggy heaven a year ago and Cass hadn't been able to bring herself to replace him.

She took a guzzle of her Chocolate Kiss. "My life is driving me to drink."

"Don't worry," Charley said, picking up her cell phone. "Dan will make everything better."

Cass thought of her current existence and muttered, "He won't be able to make everything better."

Charley frowned in concern, but before she could comment, her husband had answered and she was busy dealing with Cass's crisis. "Thanks, babe," she said after explaining the problem. "He's just finishing up the new place on Cedar," she told Cass after she'd ended the call. "He'll be right over."

"Poor guy, having to work on a Saturday."

Charley showed no sympathy. "It's good for him. Keeps him out of trouble. Anyway, it's nice that things are booming here in town. Job security."

"I hate to bug him when he's working so hard," Cass said. "But he was the first one I thought of."

"That's how it should be with friends," Charley said. "Anyway, he doesn't mind." She studied Cass. "So, what else is bothering you? I get the impression the ceiling is just the final straw."

"I don't know," Cass said with a shrug. "I guess I've got a case of empty-nest syndrome. Coupled with getting-olditis," she added. "I'm going to be flippin' forty-six next month." *Eew.* She consoled herself with more of her Chocolate Kiss. "And you know what comes after that?"

"Forty-seven."

"And then fifty-seven and then…" She finished off her drink. "My life is evaporating before my very eyes."

"You're not that old," Charley protested.

"I'm not that young, either. Where am I going? What am I doing with my life?"

"You're kidding, right?"

Cass scowled at her empty glass.

"You've raised three great kids single-handed. You've got a thriving business. Everyone loves you."

But no one in particular loved her. Other than her kids, of course, and they had to. It came with the territory.

Oh, well. You couldn't have everything. "I don't know what my problem is."

"I do," Charley said with an emphatic nod. "You need a man."

"Been there, done that. Maybe I'll get a puppy and call it good." One divorce had been enough. Marriage was risky business.

"Puppies are great," Charley agreed. "Men are even better. Why don't you splurge and get both?"

"Oh, sure."

"Online dating, baby."

Cass shuddered. "You've decided me. I'll get a dog."

They'd just finished the nachos when Dan Masters joined them. At six foot two and with shoulders like a bull, he was a commanding presence, the kind of man you knew could handle any crisis. Wouldn't it be nice to have something like that of her very own?

Yeah, but not likely. The population of Icicle Falls wasn't exactly brimming with men her age. The closest was Dylan Wright, who'd been single for years. Somebody would come along and whip him into shape someday, but considering the lack of chemistry between them whenever he came into the bakery, it wouldn't be her.

"So your roof's leaking, huh?" Dan said, seating himself next to his wife.

He kissed Charley, and Cass felt a tiny stab of envy. She looked wistfully at her empty glass. "It's gone from leak to 'get the ark.' I have a major flood happening at my place."

Dan shook his head. "I warned you that roof was starting to look grim. Up here in the mountains you really need a metal roof."

"I think my place was built before there was such a thing," she said. "Anyway, I'd have to sell a kid to be able to afford a metal roof." Even with Mason pitching in his share for the kids' college, she still had a lot of money going out.

"Well, no worries. We're supposed to have sun tomorrow. I can come over and patch the leak and fix your ceiling."

Thank God.

"Meanwhile, put out a bucket."

"Or a horse trough. I really appreciate it, Dan. I owe you gingerbread boys for life."

"You already give him plenty of gingerbread cookies," Charley said.

"Hey, don't discourage the woman," Dan told her. Then to Cass, "Patching the roof is only a temporary fix. You're bound to have more problems in the future, so you'd better start looking for a roofer."

"And a pot of gold," Cass said. The restaurant window framed a gray, rainy sky. "Where's the darned rainbow when you need it, anyway?"

Stefanie Stahl came home with her son late Saturday afternoon from a visit with her sister in Seattle to find that her husband had been busy in her absence. She was greeted by the whine of a table saw, and where there'd once been a wall between her living and dining rooms, now there were only studs covered with an opaque plastic sheet. A fine film of dust had crept out and was covering the hardwood floor in the living room as well as her furniture. She could see a pile of Sheetrock behind the plastic curtain, and beyond that hung one of those lamps carpenters often used when working at night. In its murky shadow stood a man happily creating chaos.

The day before the bridal shower she was throwing for her best friend.

That did it. She was going to hit Brad over the head with his hammer and bury him in the backyard under the pile of scrounged lumber that had been there since last August.

"Daddy!" their six-year-old son, Petey, called and began pawing at the heavy plastic in an effort to get where the action was.

"You stay right here," Stef commanded. "It's dangerous in there." And it was going to be *really* dangerous for a certain husband when she got to him.

The plastic had been taped in place, but she made her way through and marched over to where Brad stood, happily whipping up sawdust, and tapped him on the shoulder. He just about jumped out of his skin.

"Hey, don't sneak up on a guy like that!" he said. "I could've sawed my hand off."

"You're lucky I don't saw your head off. What are you doing?"

He flipped up his safety goggles. "What do you mean, what am I doing? You said you wanted an open-concept floor plan and an eating bar off the kitchen. That's what I'm doing."

"I said that months ago." And she certainly hadn't meant for *him* to do it.

"So you should be glad I've finally got the time. I'm all caught up at the office and decided I'd start on it. This, by the way, is your eating bar," he informed her, pointing to a pile of boards.

Brad had taken over a lucrative branch of a national insurance company, which was what had brought them to Icicle Falls. He was still a one-man operation with no office help other than the occasional assistance Stef gave him. Surely he had something more to do at work, someone who needed life insurance. Right now he needed plenty of it. She knew she should've left Petey at home with him. Then he would've been too busy with their son to trash the house.

She threw up her hands in disgust. "Now? You had to start on it now?"

"Sure. Why not?" Down went the safety goggles and he reached over to turn on the saw again.

She grabbed his hand to stop him. "Because Griffin's bridal shower is tomorrow. That's why not. How am I supposed to have a bridal shower here with this mess?"

Brad seemed shocked by that. Which showed how much he listened. "Aw, shit. That's tomorrow?"

"I told you that!" Did he have sawdust in his ears? "And now my guests get to look at this…disaster."

She was about to march off when he took her arm. "Sweet Stuff, I'm sorry. I just wanted to surprise you."

"You surprised me, all right," she said with a scowl.

Meanwhile, Petey was bouncing up and down on the other side of the curtain, shouting, "Daddy, Daddy!"

"Just a minute, big guy." He pushed the goggles back up on his head and gave her a pleading smile. "Come on, Stef—don't be mad. I only wanted to make you happy."

Yes, he'd had the best of intentions. He always had the best of intentions. Sadly, he was better at good intentions than he was at finishing projects, as the half-done patio with its pile of paving stones out back could attest. Not to mention the master bathroom with the missing tub. That had been last month's project. When it came to home improvement projects, the man was totally ADD.

"You haven't even finished the bathroom," she reminded him.

"I was going to, but then I remembered you wanted that wall knocked out and I thought you'd like it done for your party.

Which I forgot was tomorrow," he hastily added. "I thought I had time."

He always thought he had time. Bradley Stahl operated on his own unique timetable.

If he operated at all. When they'd first bought the house, they'd talked about ways they could improve it. But they hadn't shared the same vision. Stef had assumed they'd go at it methodically, one project at a time, hiring competent contractors. Brad had envisioned himself as perfectly competent, insisting on doing the work and saving them money. So far this was not working out.

"Da-ad!"

"Coming, big guy," Brad called and beat a hasty retreat before she could say anything more.

With a growl Stef kicked the pile of sawdust. She wished it was Brad's behind. What was she going to do now? She had a dozen women coming the next afternoon. Even if Brad skipped church, he couldn't get rid of this mess before the bridal shower.

Maybe she could get someone else to host, like Cass. Cass Wilkes had taken her and Griffin under her wing when they'd arrived in Icicle Falls a year ago, both new to town, both wondering how to go about fitting in. Cass had connected Griffin with a book club, and when she found out that Stef was a movie buff, she'd included Stef in her weekly chick-flick-night gatherings with her friends. Not only had Cass become a good friend and neighbor, she also was single. No husband underfoot messing things up. She probably wouldn't mind if they switched the party to her house. Stef could bring the eats, and Cass could provide the sawdust-free environment. She put in an SOS call.

"Oh, Stef, I'd do it in a heartbeat but—"

Uh-oh. If there was a *but*, that meant trouble.

"I have Sheetrock all over my dining room."

"On purpose? You didn't tell me you were doing a home improvement project."

"I am now. My roof sprang a leak and my ceiling caved in. I discovered it when I got home from work."

Okay, that was even worse than a Brad breakout. "Oh, no. I'm sorry."

"Oh, well," Cass said philosophically. "It is what it is."

Cass had a dozen years on Stef. Did a woman master that sort of give-me-the-grace-to-accept-the-things-I-can't-change attitude as she got older? Stef needed it now.

"Why do you want to relocate the bridal shower?" Cass asked.

"Bradley."

Cass knew what that meant. "Don't tell me. He's started a new project."

"He's started a new mess. He forgot that the shower's tomorrow and decided this would be a good weekend to pull down the wall between the dining and living rooms. He's got his saw set up and hung a big plastic sheet between the two rooms. A lovely setting for a bridal shower, don't you think?"

Cass chuckled. "It'll be interesting. But don't worry. Everyone on the guest list is either married or has been. We know what men are like."

"Brad is in a class by himself. He'll tear up the floor, too, and then the one in here because it'll all have to match. Then that mess will sit for about a million years while he figures out his next step." He was still figuring out the next step for installing a new tub. Good thing their house had two bathrooms.

"At least he's making an effort," Cass said, obviously trying to help her look on the bright side.

True. But every time Brad made an effort, it wound up an unfinished disaster. She sighed. "This is going to be so...embarrassing. Some of these women haven't even seen my house."

"Trust me, they won't care. It's about being together, and no one's going to judge you. Anyway, like I said, they've all seen men in action. Your plastic curtain will be a conversation piece."

"Yeah, but it's supposed to be about the bride. If this doesn't give Griffin cold feet…" Except lately it seemed she was already getting them.

"I think she's already got them," Cass said, voicing Stef's thought.

In the last few weeks, Griffin had been a little less enamored of her husband-to-be, a little crankier with him. Okay, he didn't help out around the house much, but he could be trained. And yeah, he wasn't a big reader like Stef, but when he was busy gaming she had plenty of free time to read or hang out with friends. He was good-looking and fun-loving, and his sense of humor balanced Griffin's more serious nature.

They both had interesting jobs. Griffin was a food photographer. (She didn't make much, but it was a heck of a lot more fun than Stef's boring part-time job as a teller at the bank.) Steve was a video game tester. (Brad had been extremely jealous when he learned what Steve did for a living…until he learned what Steve made.) Granted, they weren't rich yet, but the earning potential was there. They had no kids, no responsibilities, and Griffin's house wasn't in a state of perpetual disaster. Life on her side of the fence looked pretty good.

"Do you think she's being too picky?" Stef asked.

"I don't know. Having been down the divorce road, I'm wondering if there is such a thing as too picky. Better to be sure than be sorry."

"But her wedding's the first of June."

"That's still several weeks away," Cass pointed out.

"Maybe I should've had the shower closer to the wedding date," Stef mused. "What if she backs out?"

It would be so awkward for her friend if she had to return all the presents. Still, Stef had picked the early date because she knew Griffin's old friends in Oregon were planning a shower for her next month. Starting the celebrations early had seemed like a good idea at the time. Now she wondered if she should've delayed the party.

"Things have a way of working out," Cass said. "Meanwhile, we'll party tomorrow and commiserate with you on the work in progress."

Stef frowned at the ugly plastic sheet and the mess beyond. This was so...subpar. "Maybe I could switch the shower to Zelda's."

"You can try. But I think you'll find the party room already booked. I'm pretty sure Charley said something about a fiftieth wedding anniversary dinner for some people from Wenatchee."

Stef cast wildly about in her mind. Bailey Black's tearoom? Except that was normally closed on Sundays, and she didn't feel comfortable asking Bailey to go to the inconvenience of opening up.

Here came Brad again, Petey skipping along behind him, hauling the old bedroom curtains she'd planned to donate to Kindness Cupboard. *Oh, no. Now what?*

"I'd better go," she said to Cass. "I don't know what Brad's up to, but it doesn't look good."

Cass laughed, then, after assuring her once more that all would be well, let her end the call.

"What's with the drapes?" she asked Brad.

"Camouflage," he replied. "You were getting rid of them anyway, right?"

"Right," she said cautiously.

"So, it won't matter if they get wrecked. I'm going to nail them up in front of the plastic. Then no one will see. Brilliant, huh?"

He was obviously fishing for a compliment, but she was too irritated to admire his manly creativity. Instead she told Petey, "It's bath time."

"I want to help Daddy," Petey whined.

"We'll be done in five minutes. Then I'll give him his bath," Brad said. "You go relax."

"Okay, fine." She'd recorded a mystery on the PBS channel. She'd watch that and imagine her husband as the murder victim.

The corpse had just been discovered when her two boys stopped by the family room on their way to the bathroom (the one that still had a tub). "Take a look," Brad told her. "It's not half-bad."

She cocked an eyebrow. "Yeah?"

"Yeah," he said confidently. But she noticed he took their son and hurried upstairs before she could render a verdict.

The living room now had tan drapes hanging closed on one side. Okay, maybe someone who used her imagination could pretend the drapes were covering a window.

Yes, everyone had a window in the middle of her house between one room and another.

But it beat the plastic curtain. Barely.

"So, not too bad, huh?" Brad prompted after they'd tucked their son in and kissed him good-night.

"It'll have to do," she said grumpily.

He put an arm around her. "Come on, Stef—have a heart. Are you going to punish me all night?"

"I might."

"You wanna just kill me and be done with it?"

With his round face, reddish hair and snub nose, Brad looked like a perpetual teenager. And when he wore that penitent-little-boy expression it was hard to stay mad at him.

But she was still willing to try. "Yeah. And I know where to hide the body."

He frowned. "You'd miss me. Admit it."

She sighed heavily. "Promise me this project will get done before I'm eighty."

He crossed his heart. "Promise."

"Like next weekend?"

"Petey starts T-ball next Saturday. Remember?"

And Brad was the team's coach. "This is never going to get done," Stef groaned.

"Don't worry, Sweet Stuff. It will," he said and pulled her close. "Now, how about we kiss and…" He waggled his eyebrows.

"No makeup sex for you," she said. "Not until I solve my mystery."

He grinned. "I can wait."

And that was the problem. He was never in a hurry to finish anything. Maybe she should make him wait for sex until he got the great room finished. Of course, if she did that, she wouldn't have another orgasm until she was seventy.

Later that night they had some great makeup sex. If only her husband was as good with his other tools. Sigh.

CHAPTER TWO

Griffin James finished straightening her hair, then double-checked her makeup. Okay. Done. She went into the living room of the old Craftsman she shared with her fiancé, Steve Redford, and found him still happily streaming his favorite online video game. Busman's holiday—wasn't that the saying for doing the same thing on your day off that you did during the rest of the week? There was a reason Steve's job was perfect for him. He was a gaming addict.

She stopped by the couch on her way out the door to the shower at Stef's house. "How do I look?"

"Good," he said, never taking his eyes off the TV screen.

"I dyed my hair purple. What do you think?" she asked, flipping her strawberry blond locks.

"Yeah, great."

She glared at him. "Wanna know how you look?"

"Good, yeah." He punched the controls.

Of course he didn't. The avatars didn't care. It was two o'clock on a Sunday afternoon and there he sat in his ratty old T-shirt and pajama bottoms, his hair pulled back in its usual man bun.

He hadn't shaved yet, hadn't even brushed his teeth. Too busy killing imaginary enemies.

"I'm leaving now," she said abruptly. "I'm going to lie down in the bathtub and open a vein."

"Have fun."

"Steve!"

He glanced up with a start. "Hey, babe, you look good."

Nice of him to finally notice. "Thanks."

"See you later," he said, and his head swiveled back to the TV screen.

She should have been an avatar. He'd have paid more attention to her. As she walked down the street to Stef's house, Griffin tried to convince herself that she was excited about this bridal shower, that she was excited about getting married.

She *needed* to be excited. She and Steve had been together for five years, ever since her junior year in college. Now they'd finally be solemnizing their relationship with a wedding, something that had her grandmother very relieved and her mother looking forward to the next step—grandchildren. But lately Griffin found herself wondering if they *should* take this first step. What were they stepping into?

When they were first together they'd actually gone places, like the Grand Illusion Cinema in Seattle's U District to watch foreign and revival films or to Jet City Improv. They'd gone to local pubs with friends and played Trivial Pursuit. Steve had ridden his bike a lot. (The extra forty pounds he was carrying now attested to how much he rode his bike these days.)

He'd also played video games with his buddies back then. He had to do that, considering the fact that he was going to school for a career in the game industry. Then he'd gotten his entry-level job as a QA tester and it was as if he'd found El Dorado. The job was supposed to lead to bigger things, but once he got hooked on testing games, he'd forgotten about bigger things—including a bigger salary.

Living anywhere near Seattle wasn't cheap. Since they could both work from home, they'd opted for small-town life. Living off the land. Blah, blah. The only one living off the land last summer had been her when she'd gone blackberry picking with Stef one Saturday and they'd made jam together. Steve had used it for everything from ice cream topping to PB&Js and then asked when she was going to make some more. She'd said she would if he'd go berry picking with her. He hadn't. There'd been no more jam.

He'd promised to get working on the house, too. Her parents had lent them the money for a down payment on their fixer-upper. The only proviso was that the house had to stay in her name until they were married (Dad's doing). Steve was going to take care of the sweat equity and fix the place up. The house was in need of paint both outside and in and had a broken step on the back porch. In spite of the fact that she'd weeded the flower beds, it was a bit of an eyesore. She was sure most of the neighbors had hoped when they moved in that they'd whip the place into shape. So far there'd been no sweating, other than by her—Steve had been too busy "working," even when he wasn't—and no whipping. But painting was on his to-do list. Come summer, he was going to get out there and get busy.

Dad had his doubts. And not just about the home improvements getting done.

Now Griffin was starting to have doubts, as well. She tried to picture her life with little Steves running all over the house. Or rather, sitting all over the house. Playing video games. While the back porch step got saggier and the paint continued to chip. Her parents had come to visit Thanksgiving weekend, and Steve had been his usual easygoing, jovial self. Dad had looked around the house and frowned a lot.

Dad wasn't the only one frowning these days. Griffin wasn't exactly happy about their life together. Sometimes she felt it had shrunk to the size of a TV screen. Other than a Friday night at

Stef and Brad's, they didn't do much as a couple. If it hadn't been for Stef and the other women who had befriended her, Griffin would have felt completely marooned on a gamer's desert island.

That would change, she'd told herself. Once they had kids, they'd do things as a family—go on picnics, take hikes in the mountains. It was part of why she and Steve had moved here to Icicle Falls, to get out into nature, get moving. So far she was the only one moving. And all that lovely snow last winter, perfect for snowboarding? He'd gone a couple of times, but then, well, there was this new game…

She'd been so excited when they first moved to town. Where was the excitement now?

Through Stef's living room window, she could see several women, all ready to shower her with presents and hear how the wedding plans were coming along. The wedding plans were coming along fine. The invitations were addressed and ready to send. But she hadn't mailed them yet.

As she stepped on the front porch, the burble of voices drifted out to her. Everyone was having fun. She'd be having fun once she got inside. Of course she would. And she and Steve were going to be happy. He'd regain the balance in his life. They'd start doing more stuff together, talk more. He was just going through an adultolescent stage.

She realized she was frowning, just like her dad when he came to visit. She reminded herself to smile as she knocked on the door.

A moment later Stef opened it, looking like her usual put-together self, wearing jeans, great jewelry and a really cute blouse that said, *I'm new.* Stef could afford new clothes. She worked part-time at the bank and her husband made a decent living. She even bought books new at Mountain Escape Books. Griffin bought them used on Amazon and haunted the library.

"You look great," Stef gushed.

She'd had this sweater for three years. The pants had come

from a thrift store outing and the shoes weren't exactly new, either. But classics never went out of style, right?

She walked into the living room and the misplaced drapes immediately jumped out at her. Oh, boy. Stef had to be happy about that. Not.

"Brad's..." Stef stopped, unable to continue.

"He decided to knock out the wall," Griffin finished for her.

"I nearly knocked *him* out when I came home yesterday. I'm sorry things are such a disaster," Stef finished as she led Griffin into the room to a chorus of hellos.

"At least he does something," Griffin said. Stef's husband was trying. Steve was...playing video games.

"We don't care," said Bailey Black, who was within hearing distance. "And it's not that bad."

"Yeah, it is," Stef said, "but thanks."

"It's such a guy thing to do," Bailey's big sister Samantha said. "Blake's favorite trick is to start a project right before we have to go somewhere."

"Yeah, but at least he finishes his projects," Stef muttered. "Here, come into the kitchen and get some punch," she said to Griffin. "We also have lavender cookies from Tea Time, and Cass made an apricot torte."

Griffin followed her out and helped herself to a cup of champagne punch, passing on the other treats.

"I swear, you're not human," Stef said in disgust.

"When you take pictures of food all day, it kind of turns you off," Griffin lied. Actually, she loved food, but she'd been fat when she was a kid and she was never going there again, even if she had to starve herself. Which it seemed she did a lot.

"I was hoping we could move the party to Cass's place," Stef said, "but her ceiling fell in." She nodded at the apricot torte. "You'd better have a bite of that or her feelings will be hurt."

Griffin had a bite of a gingerbread boy every week for the same reason when she met Stef on her day off for coffee. Stef always finished her cookie for her. Stef had to be a witch, because she somehow magically sucked the calories out of stuff before she ate it.

"You got that right," said Cass, who'd joined them.

Griffin cut a sliver and put it on her plate. "Your ceiling fell in?"

"Roof troubles," Cass said with a sigh. "Thank God Charley loaned me her man for the day. He's over there fixing the mess while I bury my sorrows in carbs." She shook her head. "I dug my table out from under all the gook that was on it. Thank God I had a pad covering it, or the whole thing would've been toast."

Stacy Thomas drifted out to the kitchen. "This is fun," she said to Stef. "I love showers."

"We should've had it at your house," Stef said, frowning at the misplaced drapes.

"You should've said something. I would have. But really, Stef, nobody minds. We just all like being together." Stacy took another piece of the apricot torte. "This is addictive," she said to Cass.

It *was* good. Griffin had one bite and set the rest aside.

"You're killing me here," Cass said. "Do you rent out willpower?" She cut a piece from the other end of Griffin's ignored torte and popped it in her mouth. "Never mind. Willpower is overrated."

The doorbell rang, and Stef hurried to let in another guest.

Griffin and the other two women returned to the living room, which was packed with guests and extra folding chairs. Muriel Sterling-Wittman, the town's local celebrity, was entering the room now. She wrote as Muriel Sterling and all her books were prominently displayed in the bookstore window. One of these days Griffin was going to buy one.

Talk turned yet again to the remodel in progress. "Men," Dot Morrison groaned. "If Duncan had done this to me, I'd have beaned him."

Dot's husband had died early. One of the cattier residents of Icicle Falls once joked that he did so to get away from Dot. No one who knew Dot well paid attention to that. She was feisty and a bit of a smart-mouth, but she also had a big heart.

"I was ready to, believe me," said Stef. "Why does he do this? Why can't he finish anything?"

"I'm guessing it's his one besetting sin," Muriel said softly. "Every man has something that makes him human. Just like we do."

"Didn't you say I was perfect?" Samantha joked.

"All my daughters are close to it," Muriel replied with a smile. Her daughters, Samantha, Cecily and Bailey, like their mother, were the uncrowned royalty of Icicle Falls. The family owned Sweet Dreams Chocolate Company. Often referred to as Sweet Dreams Chocolates or simply Sweet Dreams, it was the town's source of both employment and chocolate.

"The problem," Muriel continued, "is that when we consider our men's flaws, we always think we'll be able to fix them."

"But what you see is what you get," Dot added.

Griffin couldn't help recalling what she'd seen before she left the house. Was that what she wanted to get? Okay, he wasn't all that bad. He was nice, fun-loving.

Lazy, inattentive.

"Well, I liked what I saw and I'm glad I got him," Bailey said with a decisive nod.

"Me, too," seconded her sister Cecily.

"Me three," Samantha chimed in.

"I'm keeping mine," said Dot Morrison's daughter, Tilda, the cop.

Stacy laughed. "You're too newly married to get tired of him."

Was Griffin tired of Steve? Was that the problem? And they weren't even married yet.

"Okay, it's time for a game," Stef announced and pulled out

sheets of scrambled words for everyone to puzzle out. "These are all things you find at a wedding. I'll give you two minutes."

Griffin found it hard to concentrate on the game. She kept mulling over what Muriel had said. The mulling didn't end with the game. It continued as she opened presents and Stef put together her "practice wedding bouquet," an arrangement of ribbons and bows mounted on a paper plate.

"A baby for every ribbon you break, kid," Dot teased as Griffin tore a ribbon on a box from Stacy.

How many little Steves did she want, anyway?

She opened the box to find a lovely illustrated wedding memories scrapbook that offered her opportunities to record how he popped the question ("Hey, babe, I'm getting a raise. Let's get hitched.") to where they were honeymooning (they still hadn't decided—he wanted to hang out in Seattle, she wanted Hawaii).

"What a lovely way to store all those happy memories," said Muriel.

Happy memories, happy times—fake happy smile. What was wrong with her? This was her bridal shower, for crying out loud. She and Steve were finally getting married. She should be having fun. She should be ecstatic.

With the presents opened and the loot piled up by her chair, the women agreed it was time for more punch. As they moved back to the kitchen, Griffin found herself next to Muriel.

"Do you know where you're going on your honeymoon?" Muriel asked. "Or is Steve surprising you?"

"We haven't decided," Griffin said.

Muriel nodded as if it was completely normal for people not to know where they were honeymooning in two months.

Griffin gnawed on her lip. Should she fess up here, at her bridal shower, that she was having second thoughts? At least if she did, then everyone could take their gifts back home with them. She wished her mom and grandma had been able to come.

Mom had the flu, and Gram wouldn't drive all the way up from Lake Oswego by herself. If Mom was here…

"Is everything okay?" Muriel asked gently.

Griffin found herself shaking her head. "How did you know your husband was the right one?"

"I had two husbands, and each time I knew."

"But how?"

"By looking at him and seeing us together in the future and feeling happy about it. Each time I could hardly wait to start our new life together."

There was the problem. Griffin *could* wait. They'd already started their new life and she wasn't all that happy. "I don't feel that way. I think I want…more." Once upon a time, when they were younger, Steve had been enough. But now… What did she want? What was she holding out for, anyway? There was no Mr. Darcy. There was no mysterious, passionate Mr. Rochester. There was no Rhett Butler. Most men were Steves.

Except you wouldn't think so to listen to the Sterling sisters. Or Tilda the cop, who'd let Griffin off with a warning a few months back when she slid through a stop sign; Tilda had said married life was making her mellow. Even Stef, although she complained about Brad's unfinished projects, seemed pretty content with her life.

"Then perhaps you should hold out for more," Muriel said. "There's no shame in changing your mind."

"At your bridal shower?"

"At any time before the big day."

Griffin nodded, taking that in. "Thanks, Mrs. Wittman."

She returned to the punch bowl for a refill and tried to assess her situation. She still loved Steve—at least she thought she did—but somehow it was no longer a big love. Was it a good idea to get married when your love had shrunk? Probably not.

She took a sip of punch and tried to screw up her courage to expose her cold feet. Around her everyone was chatting and laughing. The only one not having fun at her bridal shower was her. If that wasn't a sign, what was?

The party was about to break up when Griffin stopped everyone in their tracks. "Thank you all so much for doing this for me. But…" Oh, boy, this was so embarrassing. Some of these women she still didn't know all that well. She felt like a fool.

But after listening to everyone talk, she realized she couldn't go through with her wedding. And she certainly couldn't keep their gifts. "I need you to take back your presents."

"You're kidding, right?" Tilda said, staring at her.

"I can't. I think… Oh, crap," Griffin said and fell onto the nearest folding chair.

Muriel joined her and laid a comforting hand on her arm. "It's a lady's prerogative to change her mind."

"Griff, are you sure?" Stef asked, kneeling in front of her.

"No. I…don't know. This is feeling less and less right," Griffin said and wiped a stray tear from her cheek. "I mean, it's not like I don't love him. But I don't think I *love* him. I mean, I don't know if I want to be with him forever. I just…don't know."

"Not knowing is a pretty big clue that you really do know," said Cass, who'd taken a seat on the other side of her.

"I feel so stupid," Griffin muttered.

"Better to feel stupid now than end up being stupid later, kiddo," Dot put in. "Marriage can be hard enough when you're crazy about the man."

And that was the problem. She wasn't crazy about Steve anymore. Somewhere along the way she'd outgrown him. He was still stuck in college frat boy mode, and she suspected he'd be in that rut for the rest of his life. There had to be more to love than what they had.

"If you're not sure, pull the plug now," advised Tilda. "I don't mind keeping my blender. I needed a new one anyway," she cracked, coaxing a smile from Griffin.

The bridal shower ended up as a communal shrink session, and by the time Griffin got home, she'd resolved what she had to do.

Steve was still planted in front of the TV, killing avatars. "You back?" he said absently.

"Yeah. I returned all the presents."

"Presents. Good."

She walked to the TV and stood in front of it. "I said I *returned* the presents."

He frowned and his fingers stopped moving on the game controls. "What?"

"I can't do this. I can't marry you."

He blinked and set aside the controls. "Griff, what the hell are you saying?"

"I'm saying I don't want to get married."

He sat there a moment, staring at her. "You've been wanting to get married for the last three years."

She shrugged. "Now I don't."

His brows drew together. "You want to just keep living together? Your mom won't like that."

"I don't want to keep living together. I don't want to be together anymore."

"What the...?" He leaned back against the couch cushions, dumbfounded. "What the hell did those women say to you?"

"Nothing. It's what I said to myself." Behind her, something boomed as one of the players on the screen went down. "This has been building for months. I guess I didn't want to admit it."

He shook his head. "You aren't making any sense."

"I'm making sense to me."

He glared at her. "You need to explain how we've gone from being a couple to you coming home from your damn wedding shower not wanting to get married."

She joined him on the couch. "We've been drifting. We're not together for the right reasons anymore. We're just...a habit."

"We're a good habit," he said and slipped an arm around her shoulders.

She pulled away. "No, Steve, we're not. Not really. I don't want this to be the rest of my life."

"This what?" He held out his hands as if waiting for her to drop a better explanation into them.

"This life we've ended up with."

"What's wrong with our life? It's great."

"It's boring."

He shrugged. "Okay, so we'll do more stuff."

She shook her head. "No, we won't. You won't change."

His expression made her think of a kicked puppy. "Sorry I'm so boring."

The apricot torte and punch weren't playing well in her tummy anymore. "It's not you." Well, yes, it was. "It's just that this isn't going to work. I see that now. We don't have enough."

"Enough what? Sex?"

"Enough…anything. We don't talk."

He moved closer again and put his arms around her. "I can talk. What do you want to talk about?"

"Us."

He frowned. "We're fine, Griff. I don't know what those women told you, but they're wrong. We're good together."

"I don't want good. I want better." Okay, that hadn't come out right.

He set his jaw. "So you're breaking up with me after all these years?"

"Yes, I am."

"Because you want someone better." He dropped his arms.

"Just someone better for me."

That hadn't exactly softened the blow. His face turned to stone. "Fine. I'll start packing."

She felt like the rottenest woman on the planet. "Steve, I'm sorry."

"Yeah, right," he snapped and stormed out of the living room.

And now they were over. In less than five minutes. Just like that. He'd hardly fought for what they had, which showed how little they had. She stayed on the couch and stared at the stupid avatars on the screen and wished she'd blown up the TV when they first moved to Icicle Falls.

Steve was packed and gone in two hours, leaving her with the parting words "Keep the ring and have a nice life."

She already had a nice life. And that was the problem. She wanted more. What if she never got it?

What had she done?

CHAPTER THREE

Cass returned home from Griffin's shower to find Dan Masters and Tilda's husband, Devon Black, packing up their tools.

"We can't do much more with the ceiling until it dries out, but we've patched the hole. Don't forget what I told you about that roof."

"I know," Cass said with a sigh. "I've been putting off dealing with it."

"Some things you don't want to put off," Dan warned. "A new roof is one of them."

"The Linds put one on this summer, and it cost them thirty thousand dollars." She didn't have that kind of money in savings. She supposed she could take some out of her retirement fund. Or get a home equity loan. Ugh.

"Ralph's Roofing," Dan said with a knowing nod. "They're not cheap."

Devon shrugged. "At that price it'd be blue tarp city for Tilda and me. Thank God that's not on the list."

Devon and Tilda had a fixer-upper and they'd been putting in a lot of work into it. Lucky girl to have a man to help her with her home repairs.

"I can recommend someone who'll help you," Dan told Cass. "My dad."

"He a roofer?" Cass asked.

"He's an everything. There's nothing he doesn't know about houses. He started Masters Construction."

"So you worked for your old man?" Devon asked.

"Yep. He taught me everything I know. Left me the business when he retired."

Before her pal Charley married Dan Masters, Cass had never heard of Masters Construction. They had worked primarily in Wenatchee and its close environs.

But then Charley had needed her restaurant rebuilt after a fire, and Masters Construction won the bid. After that the construction company was very much in demand in Icicle Falls. They did good work—and they looked good, too. Women came into Gingerbread Haus talking about the "hunky construction guys." Dan fell for Charley and was almost instantly off the market, but his employees were all single. They were also in their twenties and thirties—cougar prey.

Cass wasn't exactly cougar material. Those guys soon all had girlfriends anyway.

"Is your dad gonna come back and work for you?" Devon joked.

"Nope, but he is coming back to work. I knew that whole early-retirement thing wouldn't last."

Cass had met Dan's dad when she went to Las Vegas for Dan and Charley's wedding. Her jaw had dropped at the sight of him. He'd been happily married back then, to a woman who had found her husband's effect on other women more amusing than threatening. Of course, she'd been pretty and obviously secure in herself, sure of his love.

There was no wife now.

A sudden fantasy of herself getting pulled into the arms of a bare-chested man sporting jeans and a tool belt invaded Cass's mind and she felt instantly guilty. The man was a widower, for crying out loud.

How long had his wife been gone? She couldn't remember. It didn't matter anyway. He probably wasn't interested in pudgy bakers.

Oh, well. At least she could now drool over him with a clear conscience.

"He went down to Mexico," Dan continued. "Got tired of it and now he's on his way up from Cabo. Planning on starting a new business—repairs and handyman stuff."

"Repairs?" There was the magic word.

"He'll be more affordable than Ralph," Dan said.

Anyone would be more affordable than Ralph. The big question was, could she afford anyone?

And was Grant Masters seeing anybody?

Oh, stop, she scolded herself. Not gonna happen. Anyway, the man thing hadn't worked the first time around. She didn't need a man to be happy. She had her business, her kids and her friends. And no sex life.

Oh, well. A girl couldn't have everything. Darn.

Griffin woke up Monday morning, still sleeping on the left side of the bed, leaving the right side empty for…the man who wasn't with her anymore. It was weird to wake up alone. She felt a little like an orphan, which was rather silly considering the fact that she'd orphaned herself.

She couldn't help feeling sad. She and Steve had been together for so long, made memories, made plans. She'd crumpled up five years just like that and thrown them away. And she'd hurt him in the process. She hadn't wanted to hurt him.

She was also tired. She hadn't slept well, kept hearing noises, noises she'd never been aware of when there was another body next to her in the bed. Once she'd gone as far as getting up to tiptoe to the bedroom door and peer out. Of course, she'd seen nothing. Burglars were hardly a common occurrence in this town. Anyway, what self-respecting burglar would bother with a place in need of paint and repairs? It didn't exactly scream money.

She went into the bathroom and it seemed naked without Steve's razor and toothbrush in there. She showered and dressed, made her morning mug of coffee. Then she sat down at her old wooden kitchen table, looking out the window at a sunny day. A robin was hopping around in the backyard. The apple tree was beginning to bloom. Very idyllic.

And a little lonely. Still, she knew she'd done the right thing breaking up with Steve. The fact that he hadn't stuck around to fight for her was proof that what they'd had was more habit than grand passion. He'd be fine without her, was probably already ensconced in his parents' basement, absorbed in testing a new video game. And she'd be fine without him.

But they'd been together so long, she couldn't help feeling slightly adrift. What was she going to do now?

For the moment, work, although she certainly wasn't making her fortune as a food photographer. Not for lack of trying, though. She had pictures for sale on a couple of stock-photography websites and was putting a lot of effort into her own website, offering pictures for sale there, as well. She had a food blog and some followers. She'd even managed to sell a couple of pictures to local magazines. But so far the kind of success she'd dreamed about had eluded her.

In the world of pictures, competition was stiff, and trying to stand out in a sea of internet images was no easy feat. It seemed that the most successful food photographers worked with food stylists in New York, where all the big magazines and advertising companies were.

At least she was making enough to live on (or had been until Steve left), and she was slowly developing her own unique brand, which focused on outdoor living and entertaining—things she had easy access to here in this small town.

During the summer, many of her pictures had featured not only local goodies but local people—like Cecily Goodman's daughter in pigtails and coveralls, poised over a bowl of fresh blackberries (plump and perfectly ripened with the help of a few dabs of black shoe polish). And Mia Wright, wearing an old-fashioned apron and holding a harvest of late-August apples (made extra-shiny with glycerin).

She loved taking pictures, always had. She felt more comfortable behind the camera than in front of it, and capturing special moments of life for posterity had quickly gone from a hobby to a passion. She'd started taking photography classes in college, and the next thing she knew, her passion had become her trade.

There wasn't much you could do with a major in literature anyway, not unless you were a writer (which she definitely was not) or you wanted to teach. Standing in front of a room full of high school students trying to pull them away from their cell phones to imagine Ashley Wilkes rather than look him up on the internet didn't appeal to her at all.

Anyway, taking pictures was art. She couldn't tell a story with words but she could with a snapshot. Like the saying went, one picture was worth a thousand words.

Now she was working with Beth Mallow, who had put together a cookbook featuring favorite recipes of her deceased mother, Justine Wright, and wanted to add pictures. Griffin had never met Justine, but from what she'd heard, the old woman had been one of a kind and much loved by everyone in Icicle Falls. She'd certainly known how to cook. So did Beth, who was creating her mother's recipes for Griffin to photograph.

Griffin finished off her coffee and headed out the door to Beth's house. Today they were going to be using natural light, and she wanted to get there while it was still streaming in through Beth's kitchen window. Apple scones were the subject of the day, and when Beth let Griffin in, the aroma that wafted out to her from the kitchen was enough to make every taste bud in Griffin's mouth spring a leak.

"I put out the red-checked tablecloth," Beth said as she led Griffin into the kitchen, which was serving as their work studio. "And I picked up some apples at the store in case we want to use them. I've got three cake stands. You can see if any of those will work. Or, if you prefer, I also have a cute basket we can put them in with a cloth napkin."

Who needed a food stylist when you had Beth? "I'm sure we can come up with something great."

"By the way, I'm sorry I missed the shower."

"Don't worry about it," Griffin said and hoped they could drop the subject.

"I've got a little something for you, though. Did you get lots of nice gifts?"

Okay, there would be no subject-dropping today. "I did, but I didn't keep any of them."

Beth blinked at her. "You didn't?"

"We're not getting married."

Another blink, followed by a cautious "Oh."

"It's okay," Griffin assured her. "We were sort of growing apart."

"Well, better to be sure," Beth said diplomatically.

That was what her mom had said when Griffin called her after Steve left, along with statements like "We never thought he was good enough for you" and "You can always move back home." Yes, that would spell success.

At least they hadn't spent a lot on the wedding. It was going to be in her parents' backyard and she'd planned to wear her grandmother's bridal gown. Maybe someday she'd get to.

Griffin nodded, then moved on. "These look great," she said, checking out the batch of scones fresh out of the oven and sitting all golden brown and lovely on their cooling rack. Good enough to eat. Which was why she never had breakfast before coming over to Beth's. Somehow she always ended up eating.

"I hope you can find a hero somewhere in this batch," Beth said, using the new term she'd learned from Griffin.

A hero was the one picture-perfect food that would wind up being the final shot. They all looked delicious, but only three made the cut.

"Is that enough?" Beth asked. "I can bake more."

"No, this will be fine."

"I had Mark help me move the kitchen table," Beth said. The vintage red Formica table her family had used for years had been moved aside for this shoot, and a small white oak one that she'd found at Stacy Thomas's shop, Timeless Treasures, was now placed in front of the window. The light was ideal.

"I think for this shot we won't use the tablecloth or the cake stand," Griffin said.

"What about the apples?" Beth asked.

Griffin didn't want to offend Beth. After all, it was her cookbook. Still… "I'm a little worried they'll distract from the perfection of the scone."

Beth shrugged, unoffended. "No problem. I'm sure I can find something to do with them."

Griffin smiled. Beth was so easy to work with, so easy to please. "Did you say you had some cloth dinner napkins?"

"Oh, you're going to put them right on the napkins?"

"It'll look really pretty," Griffin said. "And what if we took a bite out of one?"

Beth smiled. "Fun! You want to do the honors?"

Beth was always tempting her with fabulous goodies, and it was hard to stay strong. Sugar and carbs were like crack to her. "How about if you do it?"

Beth shook her head. "Has anyone told you recently that you'd blow away in a stiff wind?"

"I don't think there's any danger of that."

"You need fattening up."

She'd been there, done that. "If I have even one bite, I'll eat the whole batch, and then we won't get our picture," Griffin said with a smile.

"Okay. For now I'll let you off the hook, but you need to let me send a couple of these home with you."

No doubt about it. Beth was a food pusher. Griffin would take one back to the house just to placate her.

Back to the house. Interesting language. Beth had said *home* and Griffin had thought *house.* Hmm.

She tried to ignore that random thought and got busy choosing from among the assortment of napkins Beth produced.

Food photography styles were ever changing. They shifted from an overhead perspective to mimic the way a person usually saw her food to being shot with romantic lighting and props to extremely simple, clean and natural with few props, and even going messy, allowing crumbs or dribbles to sneak into a shot. There would be no crumbs allowed today, but Griffin did like the idea of having one scone with a bite missing, as if someone had been unable to resist it.

An hour later they had their picture, the scones cuddled together on top of a red plaid cloth napkin.

"I love it," Beth said. Which was what she'd said about everything Griffin had done so far. It was hugely gratifying.

"Now, why don't I put on some water for tea and we'll have a bite of one that didn't make the cut."

Just a bite, Griffin decided, and helped Beth move her regular kitchen table back in place. Five minutes later they were seated with mugs of steaming tea and little plates, each bearing an apple scone.

Griffin sampled hers and was sure she'd died and gone to carb heaven. "This is amazing."

Beth smiled. "My mom was amazing."

"So are you," Griffin told her. "I don't know how you do it, but your house has this great vibe. I feel so at home here."

"Good. That's the goal, to make people feel at home when they come over. Oh, before I forget…" She left the room to return a moment later with a small box wrapped in pink paper and tied with a satiny white ribbon. "Your present."

"But I'm not—"

"You can use this no matter what," Beth said, nudging it forward.

Feeling guilty but knowing Beth wouldn't let her refuse, Griffin opened it. Inside, nestled in pink tissue paper, were two china cups and saucers; one set was gold trimmed and decorated with pink roses, while the other had lilies of the valley on the cup and a pale green saucer.

"They're lovely," Griffin said.

"My mother always said things taste so much better when they're served in something pretty."

"They were your mother's? Then I can't…" Surely Mia Wright, Beth's niece by marriage, would want them.

"No. I found these at Timeless Treasures when I bought the table. I know most of us are more casual these days, but sometimes it's fun to enjoy a little elegance. And even though there's only one of you right now, you can still have a girlfriend over and use them."

"Thank you so much. I will," Griffin said.

In addition to the cups and saucers, Beth did, indeed, send her home with scones. When she got back to the house, she tossed the fat bombs before she could be tempted to inhale them. Then she gave the teacups a special place in the kitchen cupboard, which was full of cheap dishes and bits and pieces her mom had given her.

"I promise I'll feature you in a picture somehow," she murmured as she shut the cupboard door.

She put on a thick sweater, made herself a cup of tea in her favorite mug, then wandered out onto her back porch and plopped down on the steps. Steve had been promising to fix that broken one since last August.

Rain clouds were gathering and now they started spitting on her. A good day to edit some pictures on her computer. With a sigh she went back inside.

She spent the rest of the day working on her pictures, then decided to write something for the blog.

She needed a new photo, but it wouldn't be right to use any of the ones she'd taken at Beth's. Although Beth had said she didn't mind, Griffin felt those pictures should be kept top secret until the cookbook came out. So, what visual could she use?

Her new cups and saucers called to her from the cupboard. Of course! She pulled out the lace tablecloth her grandmother had given her and draped it over her coffee table. Hmm. Just cups and saucers wouldn't work. She made an emergency run to Bailey Black's tea shop and purchased some of Bailey's lavender cookies.

"I didn't think you were big on sweets," Bailey said in surprise as she loaded up the perfect cookies Griffin had selected.

"I'm not, but I want to feature these in a picture. I'll say I got them at Tea Time."

"Really? That's so cool. And in that case, the cookies are free."

"It's only for my blog," Griffin said.

"It's great advertising," Bailey said. "And for the cost of some cookies? Anytime."

In addition to the cookies, Bailey threw in a couple of Sweet Dreams truffles and some petits fours. Delighted, Griffin thanked her and hurried back home. It took her forty minutes to get everything set up but she was happy with the way her picture turned out. She posted it with the blog, which she'd titled "New Friends and Old Treasures."

Then she put all the goodies in a plastic container and braved the rain once more to drop them off at Stef's. With her house a mess, Stef could use some cheering up. No one was home yet, so Griffin left them on the porch and texted her friend.

Left goodies for you.

Yeah?

From Tea Time.

All right! Thanx.

Better your thighs than mine, Griffin thought. Not that Stef would gain so much as an ounce.

Her work done for the day, she put together a salad, which she ate sitting on the couch while surfing from one social media site to another. Her old college friend Joelle had just gotten engaged and flashed her bling on Instagram.

Griffin looked down at her own ring. What was she going to do with it now? Sell it, she supposed. She could use the money to live on.

She wasn't sure she wanted to stay here all by herself now that her future had changed. She liked Icicle Falls, loved the people, but somehow rattling around in this old Craftsman didn't feel right. It wasn't a huge house, but it felt too big for her now that she was on her own.

She hated being alone. She'd never in her whole life been alone, always living with someone—her family, her dorm roommate, Steve. Alone was…lonely.

If she fixed up the house she could sell it and probably make a small profit. Pay back her parents. Then what? Move to New York? Now that she was single, she had no reason not to go where the real business of food photography happened. This was the logical time for a change.

But she'd made good friends here. Did she really want to

leave them and go someplace where she didn't know anyone? She stared at her computer screen, contemplating. These days you could keep up with friends wherever you lived.

And she could make new friends in New York. It was the center of the universe, with lots of action and excitement and energy. She'd probably earn a lot more money in New York.

But New York was big and expensive. And the idea of moving there was a little scary.

Still, if she didn't at least go check it out, would she look back in ten years and regret it?

That brought her back to the question of the day—what was she going to do? She could stay in Icicle Falls and keep scraping by. She could move back home for a while. No, not an option.

A text came in from Steve. I'm at my parents' if you change your mind.

She wouldn't, and that made her feel a little guilty. Poor Steve. She'd really hurt him.

But she'd done the right thing—she was sure of it.

She spent the evening poking around online, researching, considering her options. She crunched numbers and gave herself several pep talks.

Finally, she left a message at Mountain Meadows Real Estate explaining that she'd like to know how much money she could sell her house for and asking one of the Realtors to call her. There. At least she'd made a decision.

CHAPTER FOUR

Grant Masters followed the path of flying bronze fish embedded in the terminal floor as he exited the Seattle-Tacoma International Airport on Monday evening. Fish. He'd seen enough fish to last him for a long time.

At first the idea of retiring early and living it up in Mexico fishing, drinking beer and flirting with pretty *señoritas* had sounded like paradise. He'd worked hard to build his construction company. Actually, he'd worked hard all his life. So after a year of coping with the loss of his wife and trying to run a company, he'd decided it was time not only to take life easier, but to take life easier someplace far from the memories. He'd turned Masters Construction over to his son who'd been managing most of the projects anyway, and took off.

But he finally got tired of catching marlin and trying to use his rusty Spanish. The damned sun never stopped beating down and the weather never changed. Just another day in paradise.

With no purpose and no sweet wife, the days were too long. He missed the mountains; he missed his kids. He even missed work. Not that he wanted to work as hard at sixty-two as he had at forty-two, but he wanted something to fill the days. Part-time would do it. He had skills. Might as well use them.

That had been his reasoning when one night he'd sat down with a Corona and a notebook and pencil and his new company, Honey Do, was born. Every woman had a honey-do list, and a lot of women these days were single with no honey to do it. By the end of the night, he had a business plan and a plane reservation for Seattle. Next stop, Icicle Falls, where his oldest son was living.

Now here he was, back in the States. At this time of night, traveler rush hour was past, so he didn't have to fight the usual crush of people. He was thankful for that, as he was now too tired to cope with women mistaking him for George Clooney and wanting his autograph. There'd been enough awkward moments on the plane.

He picked up his luggage, rented a car and then hit the freeway, heading to the north suburbs of Seattle. He'd spend a night in the city with his younger son, purchase a used truck the next day and then drive over the mountains to Icicle Falls. He already had a room reserved at Gerhardt's Gasthaus there, and that would do until he could buy a place he liked. Something modest, perhaps in need of some work.

But not too close to town. He hadn't spent much time in Icicle Falls, but he knew enough about the place to know it had become a big tourist attraction. He didn't need to encounter gawking strangers around every corner. Someplace in the woods or maybe on the river would suit him just fine—a place with easy access to mountain trails so he could hike in his spare time.

Hopefully, he wouldn't have too much spare time hanging heavily on his shoulders. He'd had business cards made up online, and he'd get busy posting them around town and see what happened. He was ready to start a new life.

Louise had been gone three years now, and he still missed her like crazy. What he'd had couldn't be replaced—he knew that.

But maybe he could find something to ease the constant low-grade ache in his heart. Being close to the boys would be good.

Yep, coming back had been the right decision. Lou would have approved.

He hit his son's house, a small place Matt and Lexie were renting, around ten.

"Hey, Dad, welcome home," Matt said, giving him a hug and a slap on the back. "You ready for a beer? I've got some Hale's Supergoose double IPA."

"Sounds great," Grant said and followed him into the kitchen.

The place looked a little bare, sparse on furniture and missing those feminine touches that proclaimed there was a woman in the house. No knickknacks, no flowers anywhere, and some of the pictures had left the wall. The kitchen was downright Spartan. No bowl of fruit on the counter, no figurines of French chefs. No canisters. Not a good sign. He knew his son had been having trouble in his marriage, but the impression he was getting here suggested they'd gone way beyond that.

"Where's Lexie?" he asked as he settled on a chair at the kitchen table.

Matt frowned at the bottle of beer he was opening. "She's gone." He handed it over and got busy with his own.

"Gone. As in forever?"

"Yeah. The divorce will be final end of May," Matt said and took a long drink of his beer.

Grant studied his second-born son. Dan had gotten Grant's darker coloring but Matt resembled his mom—less square jawline, light brown hair, freckles. He'd been a cute kid and he was a good-looking man. He and Lexie had made a fine-looking couple. Too bad they hadn't managed to make a fine marriage.

Grant wasn't surprised to hear it, though. He'd thought the girl was spoiled. And a whiner. Unlike his Lou, who'd been hardworking and always had a smile, this babe had been a leech

and a downer. Matt needed someone positive in his life, someone to encourage him. Grant wasn't sorry to hear she was gone.

He did feel bad for his son, though, and it saddened him that
Matt hadn't felt he could call and talk to him. Too embarrassed,
he was willing to bet, considering the fact that Grant had ques-
tioned whether he and Lexie were really a fit when Matt first
started getting serious.

"Want to talk about it?" Grant asked.

"Nope."

Then this wasn't the time to tell his son that everything would
be all right, that somehow his life would go on. He nodded.
"Okay. Got any pretzels to go with that beer?"

Matt dug out a bag, ripped it open and laid it on the table.
"You know what really gets me?"

Yep, didn't want to talk about it. "What?"

"She didn't even give me a hint that she wasn't happy."

"Are you sure, son?" Women left hints, verbal and nonverbal
cues that they laid out like a trail of breadcrumbs for a man to
follow. Only problem was, it seemed that most guys had a ten-
dency to step right over those breadcrumbs and not even see
them. He knew. He'd done his share of missing the clues when
he and Louise were first married.

Matt shrugged. Now he was blinking furiously, trying to
fight back unmanly tears.

Men ought to be allowed to cry, Grant thought, saving his
son's pride by pretending not to see.

"I could never please her. I mean, I was working my butt off
at the restaurant and then doing roofing jobs on my days off.
She was never happy, no matter what I did or how much extra
money I made. What more did she want?"

Who knew?

"Well, screw her," his son muttered.

That was how the kid had ended up here in the first place. If
you asked Grant, kids jumped into relationships way too quickly.

He kept his mouth shut on that topic and simply said, "I'm sorry, son."

Matt shrugged. "Shit happens, right? That's what you used to say. You hungry? I can make you a Philly steak sandwich."

"Oh, man. I haven't had one of those in ages."

It used to be his specialty. Lou had loved to bake, but she'd found the meat-and-potatoes stuff challenging. Grant had often pitched in and helped in the kitchen on weekends. He'd been the king of the grill and of Sunday-morning breakfast.

Matt had been his kitchen buddy, always happy to help out. The kid had wound up going to culinary school at Seattle Central, turning himself into a top-rate chef. He'd often talked about having his own place someday, but for the moment he was cooking at a high-end restaurant on the Seattle waterfront that specialized in seafood.

Matt nodded and began cutting sirloin into thin strips. He seasoned it with paprika, chili powder and a mess of other herbs, then cut up onions. He dragged out the old cast-iron skillet that had been his mom's, poured in olive oil and got to work. Half an hour later, they were both sitting at the kitchen bar, downing the best thing Grant had eaten in the last year. Oh, yeah, it was good to be in the States again.

"So, you're going back over the mountains, huh?" Matt said and chomped off another chunk of sandwich.

"I think so. Your brother tells me there's a real demand for handymen in Icicle Falls."

"There's a real demand for handymen everywhere," said Matt, who'd been lobbying for Grant to move to Seattle. "Way more action here than over there."

"At my age I don't need action," Grant informed him.

"Jeez, Dad, you're not dead."

There was an awkward moment as Matt realized he'd just brought the ghost of his mom into the room with that one word. "Shit," he muttered and stuffed more of his sandwich in his mouth.

Grant clapped him on the back. "It's all right, son. I know what you meant."

Now Matt really looked like he was going to cry. "I miss her, Dad."

It wasn't hard to figure out which "her" his son was referring to. "I know. I do, too."

Lou had been a stay-at-home mom and the heartbeat of their family. Death had come for her way too soon. So many times Grant had wished it had been him who'd had the heart attack and not her.

"I wish you were gonna stay here."

Poor Matt. People were leaving him right and left. "It's not that far over the mountains. We'll see a lot of each other, a lot more than we did when I was in Mexico."

Both his sons and their wives had come down to visit him at Christmas, and they'd all had a great time. Well, except for Lexie, who'd topped off a bad sunburn with a case of Montezuma's revenge. She'd been miserable and she'd done her best to make everyone else miserable, too. Yep, no loss there.

"I'm coming up on weekends during the winter," Matt threatened with a grin.

Skiing and snowboarding—both his boys loved their winter sports, just like he did. He'd see more of Matt now that he was back in the Pacific Northwest. And he'd sure see a lot more of Dan.

As he'd discovered, he wasn't cut out for the life of an old hermit crab.

Matt wanted him to stay a few days but had to work at the restaurant for the rest of the week, and Grant didn't want to sit around cooling his heels. He was anxious to get to Icicle Falls and get settled.

So a day later he had a truck and by late afternoon he'd arrived at his temporary new digs in one of Icicle Falls' favorite (and more affordable) B and Bs. "You'll get my Ingrid's incredible breakfasts every morning," Gerhardt bragged as he checked Grant in. "And my alpenhorn serenades."

Grant had heard about Gerhardt's famous alpenhorn serenades. One time he'd had too much of his German beer and serenaded himself right off the B and B's dining room balcony and broken his arm. The guy was a character.

Grant thanked him and towed his oversize suitcase to the room. It had everything he owned in the world—a couple of changes of good clothes, his favorite old work shirt and jeans, his tool belt, toiletries and his share of the photo albums his wife had so carefully kept over the years. Everything else from his life in America he'd given to the boys or sold before he went south, and what he'd accumulated in Mexico, he'd left behind. Except for his trophy marlin, which was being shipped up to him, care of Gerhardt. He'd hang that over the fireplace once he got a house.

After he was settled in, he walked to Zelda's Restaurant, which was owned and run by his daughter-in-law Charley. There was a bite in the air. The sun was still out but starting to cast shadows on the town before its evening slide behind the mountains. The shop owners had already welcomed spring, filling their window boxes with plants and putting up hanging flower baskets.

Icicle Falls was set up to look like a German village, with Bavarian-style architecture and murals painted on the buildings. The closest Grant had ever gotten to Germany was pictures he'd seen in magazines or glimpses of the country in movies. This place sure seemed like a dead ringer to him.

Charley's face lit up when he walked in. "Dad! You made it." She hurried over and hugged him and, darn, it felt good to be hugged, good to be back with family.

"How you doing, gorgeous?" he said and gave her a kiss on the cheek.

"Doing great," she said.

She looked like she was doing great. At least one son and his wife were enjoying married bliss. Charley practically glowed with happiness.

"Dan should be here in about ten minutes," she said. "We've got a table reserved for you."

He followed her to a booth toward the back of the restaurant. The retired set was already there, enjoying drinks and meals from the senior menu.

"Would you like a beer while you wait?" she asked.

"You know it," he said, and she went to put in an order for him.

A few minutes later, a cute little gal was setting an icy cold one in front of him. "On the house, Mr. Masters," she said with a grin. "I'm Melody and I'm new here."

"Thanks, Melody," he said. "And it's Grant. May as well get on a first-name basis, since I plan on being a regular."

"Grant," she repeated, smiling, and hurried off to deliver some kind of fancy drinks to two women seated at a table in the middle of the room. One of them, he noticed, was a real looker, with beautiful green eyes and chestnut curls. She glanced his way, blinked, blushed, then turned her head.

No, I'm not him. Thank God no one had come up to ask for his autograph so far. It often took a while to convince people that he wasn't George Clooney. Once he did, they were embarrassed, and so was he. He wouldn't mind if the redhead came over, though.

Charley was back now and saw him watching. "That's Muriel Sterling-Wittman, and yes, she's single."

He smiled and shook his head. "Just lookin'. Not in the market."

"You never know," Charley said. "I sure wasn't in the market when I met your son, who, by the way, is the best thing that ever happened to me."

Speaking of his son, there he was, obviously just out of the shower with his hair still damp, and wearing clean jeans and a shirt. "Dad, you made it," he said and hugged Grant. Then he slid into the booth, and Charley sat down and joined him. "How was Seattle?"

"Crowded."

"Matt's pissed you don't want to live there."

"Matt needs to move up here."

"That's what I keep telling him," Dan said. "He could come work for Charley." Charley seemed a little uncomfortable at that, so he added, "Well, if her chef ever quits."

"He's a good one," she told Grant. "And he's been with me for several years."

"Loyalty's important," Grant said diplomatically.

"But so is family," Dan said.

Grant shrugged. "Then why don't you guys open a second restaurant and let Matt run it?"

"Not a bad idea," Dan said, "but we're gonna be busy for a while."

"Oh?" The minute he saw Dan and his wife exchange smiles he knew, but he played dumb. "With what?"

"With a baby," Charley said, beaming.

"Well, now, that's terrific news," Grant said. "Congratulations, you two. When's the stork coming?"

"November," Charley replied.

That explained why his daughter-in-law looked so happy. There was something about a pregnant woman. She glowed like a candle in the dark.

As for his son, Grant sure recognized that goofy grin. If there was anything as exciting as learning you were going to have a kid, Grant didn't know what it was. "You got names picked out?"

"We're thinking Amanda Louise if it's a girl."

To honor both Charley's mom and Lou. Lou would have been out of her mind over all this. Damned heart attack. That should have happened to him, not her.

"And Ethan Grant if it's a boy," said Dan.

"A nod to Dan's neglected first name," Charley teased, nudging him.

"Sorry you get second billing, Dad."

"At least I'm on the bill. That's real nice of you. You two will be great parents."

"I hope so," Charley said. "I never thought I'd end up being a mom."

"It's happening, babe." Dan slipped an arm around his wife. "So, Dad, you're gonna be a grandpa."

"Works for me," Grant said.

And now he was really glad he'd decided to come back stateside. A new kid in the family and a new business. What else could a man want?

He caught a glimpse of the pretty woman at the other table and suddenly remembered what else.

Stef normally had Tuesdays and Thursdays off. Once upon a time, BD (Before Destruction), she'd enjoyed staying home on her days off, watching HGTV or puttering in the garden, doing craft projects or playing with Petey. These days, home wasn't exactly where the heart was, so on Thursday she was more than happy to take a latte break with Griffin at Gingerbread Haus.

"I'm going to poison Brad now and be done with it," she informed Griffin as they entered the bakery. "Then I'll replace him with a real carpenter."

"From what I hear, they aren't always very fast at getting work done, either," Griffin said. "Anyway, he'll get the living room finished eventually," she added, obviously trying to be encouraging.

Stef did not feel encouraged. "Eventually? Maybe. Right now, it's looking more like never." Stef shook her head. "I thought we were so perfectly compatible when we first got married, but I didn't know about…this." She sighed. "I do love the guy. What I don't love is the way he keeps starting projects and never finishing them. It's making me nuts. I just want to find someone to finish this so we can be done with it, but Brad keeps insisting he'll get to it."

Cass, who was ringing up some swan-shaped cream puffs for Muriel Sterling-Wittman, greeted them. "Still nowhere near done, huh?"

"He'll never be done."

Muriel took her purchase and smiled the all-knowing Mona Lisa smile she was famous for. "When we're in the middle of something challenging, it always seems like it'll last forever, but trust me, even the hard times come to a close."

"Thanks," Stef murmured, feeling like the queen of the wicked witches. Here Muriel Sterling had been widowed twice—talk about hard times—and she never complained. Stef's chaotic reno project, which had been feeling like a mountain, shrank to a molehill. Muriel gave her a reassuring pat on the arm and Stef sighed as the older woman left the shop. "I'm a bitch."

"No, you're not," Cass assured her. "I'd feel the same way if I was in your house. I feel the same way in *my* leaky house, only I don't have a husband to blame."

Another woman with no husband. Now Stef really felt guilty for complaining. Sometimes Brad did not bring out the best in her.

Oh, yeah. Blame it all on Brad. She needed therapy. "Give me two gingerbread boys and a large caramel latte," she said to Cass. "I'm going to smother my sorrows in sugar."

"Good idea." Cass looked at Griffin. "Are you going to walk on the wild side today and have a gingerbread boy?"

"I'll just have a cup of gingerbread tea. Beth's been stuffing me full of goodies the last three days."

Cass smiled. "Next to me, she's the best baker in town. Well, except for Janice Lind. I'm sure she'll win the Raise the Roof bake-off again this year."

"That was before you moved here," Stef told Griffin. "It was really fun, kind of like a county fair, but without the cows and pigs. At the end they auction everything off. They also have a silent auction. Last year I won a dinner for two at Der Spaniard and a huge basket of Sweet Dreams chocolates. You should come. I bet you'd get some great food pictures."

Griffin nodded thoughtfully. "I might have to."

As if on cue, Maddy Donaldson, one of the town's busiest volunteers, came into the shop, selling tickets to the event. "It's for a good cause," she reminded them.

"What does it raise money for?" Griffin asked.

"The proceeds go to maintaining our historical buildings in town. It's a big part of what keeps Icicle Falls beautiful, and the tickets are only ten dollars, a real bargain."

"I'm all for that," Stef said, digging her wallet out of her purse. "I'll take four," she told Maddy, then said to Griffin, "You can come with us."

"I can pay for my own," Griffin insisted.

"I know, but I want to." Griffin no longer had Steve to share expenses. Her budget had to have shrunk considerably.

"I'll take one, too," Cass said. "Give me a minute to get my money from the back room."

"I've got it," Stef said. "We can all go together." Was she being bossy or what? But it would be fun to have her two favorite Icicles with her.

"That's sweet of you," Cass said.

In light of the many times Cass hadn't let them pay for their treats, that was the least she could do.

"Raise the Roof is going to be great this year," Maddy said as she took their money. "We have so many wonderful things for the silent auction. The art gallery is donating a painting by Gray Wolf Dawson. And Sweet Dreams has come through again."

"I'm interested in that," Stef told her. "Now, if you could raffle off a temporary husband…"

"Funny you should say that. We have a new business in town—Honey Do—and he's going to be offering a whole day of work."

"It'll take more than a day to clean up my mess," Stef grumbled.

"You can always hire him for however long it takes after that."

"I hear he does roofs," Cass said, "so I'll be all over that."

"I'm sure he does. It's Dan Masters's dad. He's just moved here from Mexico. I talked to him on the phone yesterday and he's really nice. I hear he's gorgeous."

"He is," Cass said. "I met him when Charley and Dan got married."

"If that's the case, there's bound to be a bidding frenzy," Maddy said with a smile.

"I suspect there'll be a bidding frenzy anyway," Cass told her. "We've got two of us right here who'll bid on a handyman."

Maddy hung around for a while to chat, then went on her way, and Stef and Griffin settled at one of the bakery's bistro tables with their drinks and the gingerbread boys. Cass took a moment to join them.

"I sure would like to win that handyman for a day," Stef said. She could already see her new great room with its polished hardwood floors. All that space! Of course, what she needed would take more than a day. Maybe she'd hire him for…life. "If I could get the guy to finish some of Brad's other projects, I wouldn't have to murder my husband."

"You have to stop saying stuff like that in front of us," Cass teased her. "If anything happens to Brad, we'll get called into court to testify."

Stef sighed. "I know. It's just that he makes me so mad some-times. Why can't he finish *anything*?"

"He's a visionary," Cass suggested. "Lots of great ideas."

"Well, maybe he needs to envision sleeping on the couch for a while." The weekend was around the corner and had he saved any time to work on the house? No. Friday night he was sitting in for someone at Ed Fish's weekly poker game, Satur-day was T-ball for Petey, followed by a birthday party they'd all be going to, and Sunday he'd committed them to staying after church for a potluck. Generous of him to volunteer *her* to bring a casserole and dessert.

"That'll never happen," Griffin said. "You're too soft. He wouldn't be on that couch longer than a couple of hours."

"I'm done with being soft," Stef said. "I should've come down on him with the first unfinished project. I'm so bidding on that handyman."

"Me, too," Cass warned her. "I need a new roof."

"I may need someone, too," Griffin said. "I'm thinking of selling my house."

Stef nearly dropped her latte. "What?"

"With Steve gone, I'm not sure it's practical to stay there. I talked to a Realtor this morning, and she's coming later this afternoon to look at it and tell me what she thinks I can get."

They'd walked all the way down here and Griffin hadn't said a thing to her. Stef felt slightly hurt. Maybe Griffin had been afraid she'd try to talk her out of it. Maybe she would have.

"You'll probably get more for it than you paid," Cass said. "Real-estate values here are going up even on older homes. Where would you move?"

"I'm wondering if this might be a good time to go to New York and really pursue food photography."

"New York? Wow, that does sound glam," Stef said. "But do you have to go all the way to New York to do that? These days can't you do everything over the internet? Anyway, you're getting business right here." Yep, this was why Griffin hadn't said anything.

"I know. And part of me doesn't want to leave."

"Then don't," Stef urged. This was all Steve's fault. If he hadn't been such a loser…

"I think I could do better there. It's where all the big business is. And if I want to get noticed, I need to relocate, at least for a while. Now, when I'm on my own, might be the time to at least try, even though it kind of scares me."

"You know we'd all hate to see you leave," Cass said, "but I say go for your dreams."

"Cass is right," Stef said. "I hate the idea of you moving, though." She picked a cinnamon candy eye from her gingerbread boy and frowned at it.

"I haven't decided yet," Griffin said. "I need to see what I can get for the house first. And I need to finish up my project with Beth."

"I hope it takes a long time." Okay, totally selfish.

"Speaking of that, I've been sitting with you two for way too long. I have to get back to work," Cass said and left them to finish their treats. Well, Stef would finish hers, anyway.

She returned the conversation to the subject of Griffin's moving, and Griffin sighed.

"I doubt I can afford to stay here on what I'm making now, not living alone."

"New York won't be cheap, either." No hidden agenda in that remark.

"No, but if I actually wind up making good money it won't matter."

"True. Okay, I obviously need to be a noble friend and support you. But I'd rather find you a roommate. What about a really hot guy? Or somebody rich to support you while you work on your photography."

Griffin frowned and cocked an eyebrow. "A sugar daddy?"

"No. Someone who'll fall madly in love with you and believe in you enough to foot the bill while you're becoming a superstar on the internet, which is totally different from a sugar daddy." She wasn't sure how, but that was beside the point.

"I won't hold my breath on that one. Anyway, I'm not ready to jump into another relationship. Even if I don't like being by myself."

"Yeah, you're right," Stef admitted. "You don't want to rush into anything and end up with someone who drives you nuts." Gee, who could she have been thinking of when she said that?

When she got back to the house, seeing the drape hanging in the middle of her living room and knowing what was behind it didn't exactly improve her mood. She was glad she had to work the next day. At least she wouldn't have to be home to look at this. Brad had better pray she won that handyman in the Raise the Roof auction.

The fundraiser was the first weekend in May—not that far off. Still, living with this mess, it felt like it was a million years away. She hoped she could hang on that long.

CHAPTER FIVE

Nenita Einhausen from Mountain Meadows Real Estate arrived at Griffin's house promptly at three in the afternoon. She was short and slender and professionally put together in a black power suit and heels, her dark hair caught back in a ponytail to accentuate her delicate features.

Griffin, who hadn't bothered with makeup and wore jeans and a sweater, suddenly felt dumpy. Like her house. "Thanks for coming over," she said.

"I'm happy to," Nenita said cheerfully and walked into the room like a woman on a mission. "This place has so much potential. If I didn't already have a house of my own, I'd buy it in a minute."

That was encouraging. "So you don't think I'll have any trouble selling it?"

Nenita shook her head. "No, we'll find you a buyer. Hardwood floors, nice. Can I look at the kitchen?" Before Griffin could answer, she was on her way there. Griffin followed and watched as she assessed the dated appliances with a silent nod, then poked her nose out the back door. "Lovely little yard. The back porch needs some help."

"I know. My ex was going to get around to that," Griffin explained, then felt her cheeks burning. Why was she telling that to a perfect stranger?

Nenita gave her a sympathetic smile. "Been there, done that. As it turns out, it was the best thing that ever happened to me. It motivated me to get into real estate, which I love. What do you do?"

"I'm a photographer."

"Really? Can we see the upstairs?" Nenita asked and started power walking toward the stairs. "Do you do portraits?" she asked as Griffin trailed her up them. "Would I have seen your work for sale at any of our festivals?"

"No. I specialize in pictures of food."

"That sounds like fun."

"It is. I'm thinking of moving to New York, where I can get more work." *Or I could move back home and live with my parents forever. Which option should I choose?*

"Good idea," Nenita said. She looked in the first bedroom. "Nice size. So, are you in a hurry to sell?" she asked and moved to the next bedroom.

"Well..." Was she?

"The reason I ask," Nenita said, "is because you could get a lot more money for the place if you had time to fix it up a little. It needs some updating, a few repairs. New paint. Not that I couldn't sell it as is, but I assume you want to get top dollar."

"Of course," Griffin confirmed. "How much do you think I could get?"

"Fixed up?" Nenita told her and started dollar signs dancing in front of her eyes. "The market's on the upswing."

"Tell me what to do."

The list was daunting. In addition to fixing the broken back stair and painting the outside of the house, Nenita suggested painting most of the inside, as well—two bedrooms and the living room had been deemed in need of freshening.

"You should replace the stove and fridge and dishwasher if you can afford it," she finished. "Once you get all of that done and we stage the place, it'll sell pretty fast. Summer's the best time. People want to get moved and settled before the school year begins."

Okay, she could do this. It would be great to hire that new handyman everyone was talking about, but she could save money if she did most of the work herself. Painting wasn't all that hard. She'd tackle that first and then worry about the broken step and the appliances.

Highly motivated, she went straight to the hardware store with her credit card after Nenita left, and started looking at paint chips. So many different shades—it was almost overwhelming. She finally decided on a cream for the living room as well as one of the spare bedrooms and a light turquoise for her own room. It would pick up the colors in her bedspread and pillows, and that would help with staging. The cream would look attractive with the house's hardwood floors, which Nenita had suggested refinishing. Ugh.

Painting the outside of the house was going to be really spendy and would have to wait until she could work up the nerve to ask her dad for a loan. She selected her paint, brushes, roller and about a million other supplies, and took them to the cash register to be rung up. She swallowed hard when she saw the total but stoically handed over her credit card, reminding herself that you had to spend money to make money. She'd heard that somewhere. She hoped it was true.

She was pushing her cart full of paints out of the store when a man walked in past her. *Whoa.* "Oh, my gosh, oh, my gosh," she muttered and pulled out her cell phone.

Stef answered after several rings. "Did you see the Realtor?"

"Yeah, but never mind her. I just saw George Clooney!"

"What?"

"Seriously. I'm sure it was him. What's he doing in Icicle

Falls?" Was he making a movie here? And if he was, why hadn't it been splashed all over the papers? Why wasn't everyone talking about it?

"George Clooney in Icicle Falls? Okay, were you in that new cannabis store outside of town? Are you, like, hallucinating or something?"

"No. I swear it was him. I'm going back inside to check it out. I'll call you later."

Griffin loaded her supplies in her trunk and then hustled into the hardware store again. Okay, where was he?

"Did you forget anything?" asked Alan Donaldson, who owned the store.

"I was thinking I might need another paintbrush," Griffin improvised. She knew she was blushing, could feel the heat on her cheeks.

He gave her a sly grin. "You know where they are."

Yeah, but where was *he*? She hurried up and down the various aisles, passing everything from sandpaper to gardening supplies. Had she imagined him?

No. She turned a corner and ran right into the man. He dropped the tube of caulk he was carrying and she dropped her jaw. "Oh, my gosh. Mr. Clooney, I'm so sorry."

"No worries," he said, bending to pick it up. "And I'm afraid I'm not George Clooney."

"You're not?" He stood and she studied his face. Okay, maybe not. This man's nose was a bit different, and he had a few more wrinkles. But still, wow, you could've fooled her. Oh, yeah. He had. "I'm sorry. Of course you're not. What would George Clooney be doing in a hardware store in Icicle Falls? Except I thought someone was going to make a movie here or…something." Lame. Totally lame.

He smiled. "It's okay. It happens a lot."

"That must come in handy when you're traveling. Free drinks

on planes, stuff like that?" Okay, she sounded like a complete moron.

He didn't dignify that with an answer. Instead, he introduced himself.

"The Honey Do man! We were just talking about you. Both my friends want you." Hmm. Did that sound a little...sexual?

"That's good to hear."

"We're all going to be at the Raise the Roof fundraiser," she went on. What did he care? "I guess we'll see you then."

"I guess so. And your name is?"

Idiot Girl. "Griffin James."

"Nice to meet you, Griffin. I'm Grant Masters."

He had a friendly smile, and he wasn't looking at her as if she only had one brain cell. She didn't feel quite so stupid now and smiled back. "Nice to meet you, too. See you at the fundraiser."

"Or maybe in here again."

"I promise not to ask for your autograph."

"At least wait until I'm famous," he said, deadpan.

"Oh, sure," she said. Her cell phone rang and she excused herself and hurried out of the store, answering as she went.

"Did you find him?" asked Stef.

"Yeah, but it wasn't him."

"Doesn't matter. He's too old for you, anyway."

"This man really looks like him, though. And guess what? He's the new handyman and Mrs. Donaldson wasn't kidding. He's so nice."

"That's not surprising, considering how nice his son is. Dan's always sending Charley flowers. And he bailed Cass out when her roof was leaking."

Steve had gotten Griffin flowers. Once. For Valentine's Day. After she bugged him to. She thought of the broken back porch step and frowned. "Too bad somebody can't clone him." Dan, not Steve. One Steve was probably enough.

"I think he's got a brother. I hear he's single."

If the brother looked anything like Dan Masters or his dad… Woo-hoo. Oh, well. She was on her way to New York. She'd hold out for some slick metrosexual. Meanwhile, here in Icicle Falls, she had things to do.

She spent Friday morning working with Beth on another photo shoot—rhubarb-strawberry crisp—and then spent much of the afternoon editing. Come five o'clock, she tossed together cut-up sandwich meat and spinach and called it good (no one would ever take pictures of *her* cooking). Then she settled down on the couch to eat dinner.

All by herself. On a Friday night.

She'd complained to Steve about their life being boring, but at least they'd had one. Often on Friday nights they'd gone over to Brad and Stef's to play Mexican Train or watch a movie together or, when she insisted they had to get out, to Zelda's. She didn't want to go to Zelda's alone, and somehow it didn't feel right to go over to Stef's when it was only her. Friday night was couples' night. She wasn't part of a couple anymore. Now she was a third wheel.

Maybe she'd see if Cass wanted company.

She put in a call and got Cass's voice mail. "If it's after eight, sorry, I'm in bed. If you're calling on a Friday, sorry, I'm pooped. Leave a message, though, and tell me what I missed."

"You didn't miss anything," Griffin said at the sound of the beep. And how pathetic was that? Oh, never mind, she had a new Susan Wiggs book to read. She'd spend her evening with that. Then tomorrow it would be paint day. Oh, yeah. Look at the exciting new life she had now that she'd broken up with Steve.

It *was* going to be exciting, she promised herself. And it was going to be good to get her house fixed up. Who knew—maybe once it was all painted and pretty, she wouldn't want to move.

The next morning she donned her grubby jeans and an old sweatshirt and got busy. She decided to start with the living room, the first thing people would see when they walked in.

She laid out her drop cloth and opened her paint can. Then she went to the shed in the backyard and hauled in the ladder, a rickety old thing that had probably been around since the fifties. Just as well she didn't weigh a lot, otherwise it might not have held her.

She poured paint into her tray, set it on the ladder and went to work with her trusty new roller, starting from the top of the wall and working her way down. After she'd done a section, she stepped down to admire her work. Oh, yes. This place was going to look good enough for an HGTV show by the time she was done.

Back to the ladder, up to the top step. Paint, paint, paint, reach out just a little farther…lose balance, let out a screech, grab for the ladder and miss, tipping the roller tray and sending it—and her—flying. Land on right hand, right hip in roller tray. Experience pain. Big pain, super pain. Sit on the floor and wail. Yes, home improvement was such fun.

Her baking was finished for the day, and the kitchen was cleaned. Cass was ready to sneak away and leave Gingerbread Haus in the capable hands of Misty and Jet, her Saturday crew, and go home to shower and take a nap. Then, for the evening she had big plans—watch all her favorite TV shows that she'd recorded during the week. And make some popcorn. Popcorn and TV, real exciting. As Charley had said, she wasn't that old. Why was she living like it? Why did her life suck?

Your life doesn't totally suck, she reminded herself. She had three great kids, whom she'd raised single-handedly, thanks to her ex. He was finally back in the picture, along with his trophy wife and her ridiculous little dog and their trophy toddler. Ever since Dani's wedding, they'd made a habit of coming up and staying with her at Christmas, along with the kids, giving family holiday gatherings the feel of a cringe-humor movie. But, in spite of that, life in the family department was good. Her business was thriving and she was well respected by everyone in town and had great friends. Okay, her life didn't totally suck. It only semi-sucked.

But...she'd like to have sex again. Yes, sex would be nice. So would going out to dinner once in a while with someone who had a voice lower than hers.

Remember Mason.

Reminding herself how miserable and frustrated she'd been with her former husband was usually enough to convince her that she didn't want a man. Men were, for the most part, a selfish and inconsiderate breed. Yes, Charley's husband was great, and her other best friend, Samantha Sterling-Preston, had done okay. So had both of Sam's sisters. But Cass was still convinced that those were the exceptions, not the rule. At this point in her life, she didn't want to sort through the losers to find a winner. That would be like looking for a diamond in a gumball machine.

She'd just removed her apron when Misty raced into the kitchen. "OMG! You've got to come see who's here."

No, she didn't. She hadn't slept well the night before and she wasn't wearing any makeup to cover the dark circles under her eyes. Her hair was still in a hairnet and she was in her grubbies.

"I'll pass," she said.

"No, really!" Misty started towing her out of the kitchen, babbling as they went. "I don't know what he's doing in Icicle Falls. Maybe he has family here? Maybe he's hiding from the paparazzi."

"Hiding from the paparazzi in Icicle Falls?" Cass repeated with a snort. "Who are you talking about?"

They stepped out into the shop and she didn't have to ask. For a moment her heart forgot to beat.

"Hi, Cass," called Dan Masters. "You remember my dad, right?"

She'd have to have been brain-dead to have forgotten.

"I'm taking him around town to meet people. Thought we'd stop in for a cookie."

Why was she wearing this stupid hairnet? And why didn't she ever bother with makeup? Why hadn't she stuck to her diet? Why, why, why?

"How about it?" Dan prompted.

"Hmm?"

"Cookie?"

"Oh, yeah. A cookie, of course! I do owe you cookies for life." She'd give his daddy cookies for life, too. She'd give his daddy anything. "Jet, how about a couple of cookies for the gentlemen?" she said to her other gape-mouthed employee.

Jet nodded and produced the requested treats.

"No more leaks?" Dan asked Cass.

"So far, so good."

"Okay. But don't push your luck. You need to get that roof fixed."

Cass gave him a salute. "Yes, sir. Will do!" He chuckled.

"We're off to Zelda's for lunch. Wanna join us?" he offered.

Like she wanted to sit at a table with Dan and his gorgeous father for an hour so she could leave the man with an indelible impression of herself looking like this. "I'll pass, but thanks."

"Okay. We'll catch up with you later, then," Dan said and started for the door.

"Nice seeing you again," said his dad.

"Same here," Cass lied. *Nice* was hardly the word for it. *Torture* would be more appropriate.

"I thought for sure he was that actor," Misty said after they left. "He looks so much like him."

Yes, he did. Dan's father was the male equivalent of chocolate, cream puffs and key lime pie all rolled into one. He definitely made a lasting impression.

She didn't even want to try to imagine what he might have thought of her. Not that she was butt-ugly, but she wasn't going to win any beauty contests. A man like that wouldn't look twice at a woman like her. He probably hadn't even remembered her.

But since she wasn't in the market for a man, who cared, right? She took out the chocolate cake she had in the display case and cut off a large piece to take home. There. Who needed a man when you had popcorn, TV shows and chocolate cake?

CHAPTER SIX

Of course, Brad couldn't work on the house this weekend. Petey had his T-ball game that afternoon. "We got up too late," Brad pointed out.

Yeah, because they'd been busy in bed, working up an appetite for breakfast. "We have three hours until Petey's game," she said.

"I know but I'll just get going and it'll be time to stop. There's no sense starting something I can't finish."

Was he kidding? It was all she could do not to snatch away his plate of pancakes. Her husband didn't deserve pancakes. "You've started things all over the house that you haven't finished."

"I'm gonna get to them. Give me a break, Stef."

Stef, not Sweet Stuff. Okay, he was pissed. Well, so was she. She'd given him sex and pancakes, and this was the thanks she got? "All right, you had your chance," she growled.

"What's that supposed to mean?"

"It means you can be replaced."

His brows dipped down. "You shouldn't even joke about stuff like that."

"I meant as a carpenter. I've had it, Brad. I really have."

"Oh, come on, now. Don't be like that."

Yes, don't be so demanding. Be happy your house looks like a war zone.

"Is Mommy mad?" asked Petey, looking from one to the other.

"Not at you, sweetie." She leaned over and kissed the top of Petey's head. "So, guess what?"

"What?" he asked eagerly.

"You and Daddy get to hang out this morning and watch cartoons while Mommy goes out for a little while."

"Are you coming to my game?" Petey asked.

"Of course. I'll be back in plenty of time. We'll have lunch and then we'll all go together, and maybe Mommy can get in some batting practice with Daddy," she added, giving Brad the faux sweet smile that telegraphed *you're in deep kimchi, dude.*

That made Petey giggle. "Mommy, you don't play T-ball."

"I know. I won't have to worry about hitting the ball. I'll have a much bigger target." She drained the syrup out of her voice and said to her husband, "See you later."

"Where are you going?" he demanded.

"Someplace where I don't have to look at this," she said and grabbed her purse.

"Didn't your mother ever teach you that patience is a virtue?" he called after her.

"And didn't yours ever teach you to finish what you started?" she called back, then stormed out the door, slamming it after herself.

Honestly, he made her so mad. She needed a sympathetic ear, and that sympathetic ear was only a few houses down Blackberry Lane. The front room curtains at Griffin's house were open, and as Stef walked up the front walk, she could see signs of home improvement—a ladder, a drop cloth… She got closer and saw her friend sitting on the floor, holding what looked like a package of frozen vegetables on her wrist and rocking back and forth.

She banged on the door. "Griffin!" She anxiously turned the doorknob, found the door unlocked and rushed into the living room, where Griffin sat, tears racing down her cheeks. Her jeans were covered in paint and she was whimpering.

Stef knelt down beside her friend. "What happened?"

"I fell off the ladder," Griffin said through gritted teeth. "I think I broke my wrist." She moved aside the frozen peas to reveal a very swollen purple mess.

"Oh, not good," Stef said. "We need to take you to the emergency room."

"The paint spilled. Everything's a mess," Griffin wailed.

It was. There was paint all over the floor. "Don't worry about that. We'll clean it up. Let's get you taken care of first."

"I can't go to the hospital like this."

"Okay, I'll find you some new pants," Stef said.

"In my bedroom dresser. Ooh, this hurts."

Stef fetched a clean pair of jeans, and between the two of them, they changed Griffin out of her paint-covered ones and into the new pair. Then they got into Griffin's car and Stef drove her to the Mountain Regional Hospital emergency room.

Fortunately, not too many people were having emergencies on a Saturday morning, and Griffin was admitted right away. The doctor who examined her was an older man, a kindly father figure, who strongly suspected a radial fracture. "But we'll do an X-ray and a CT scan to be sure."

"If I've broken it, I'll never get my house painted," Griffin lamented.

Stef wasn't in a hurry for her friend to get her house fixed up and on the market, but she certainly didn't want her to have a broken wrist. "I'm sorry," she said.

The doctor's final prognosis was, indeed, a broken wrist. "I'll prescribe something for the pain, and we'll put it in a cast to make sure it stays immobile."

"A cast?" Griffin repeated weakly. "For how long?"

"Plan on six weeks."

"Six weeks," she groaned as they went to the pharmacy for her painkillers. "My house will never get painted at this rate."

"Not unless you hire someone," Stef said.

"Looks like I'm going to be bidding on that handyman, too," Griffin said with a sigh when they got back to her house.

That made three of them, Stef mused as she mopped the spilled paint off the floor for her friend.

"Just leave the rest," Griffin said. "Maybe I'll be able to at least paint the bottom half of the wall."

"Okay, but I'm thinking you'd better leave this for the handyman. I wonder how many people are going to be bidding on him."

"Probably a lot," Griffin said with a frown.

"This could get ugly."

Sure enough, on the night of the Raise the Roof fundraiser at Festival Hall, a day's work provided by Grant Masters, owner of Honey Do, was a popular item. In fact, it seemed there were more people mingling by the two long tables filled with silent-auction items than there were over at the table with all the cupcakes and cookies for sale. The majority of them were women, many of whom kept circling the table and checking the numbers on that sheet of paper beside the gift certificate with the graphic of the hammer.

"This place is a mob scene," Brad grumbled as Petey bounced between him and Stef, clamoring for a cookie.

"That's good, since it's a fundraiser."

He scowled at the paper where her name already appeared three times, each with a higher bid. "That's too much."

"Nothing's too much to get my house back," she retorted.

"Mommy, I want a cookie," Petey begged.

"All right, let's get you one," she said. She left her husband standing at the silent-auction table frowning and walked with her son over to where the goodies were being sold.

Next to that two more tables displayed the baked items that were competing for a first-place ribbon and a dinner for two at Schwangau. All these items would be going up for auction later. Janice Lind, the reigning queen of this competition, had entered a three-layer cake that made Stef's mouth water. She heard that Janice won every year, but some of the other entries looked good enough to give Mrs. Lind a run for her money. Cass had created an entire gingerbread town, a miniature of Icicle Falls, with colorful icing murals on the shops and a gazebo downtown. Maddy Donaldson had entered some kind of cream pie topped with coconut, and Bailey Black had entered a three-layer cake labeled as Chocolate Orange Delight that was decorated with chocolate-and-orange-tinted roses. Pies, cinnamon rolls and elaborately decorated cupcakes all cried out for attention. How did the judges manage to pick only one grand prize winner?

She bought Petey a snickerdoodle cookie and herself a brownie, then wandered back to see if anyone new had outbid her. Brad had drifted away and was talking with Blake Preston, manager of the local bank. His wife, Samantha, and her sister Cecily were both checking out a gift certificate for a day spa treatment at the Sleeping Lady Salon.

"Of course, we're driving up the price by bidding against each other," Samantha confessed, "but it's for a great cause."

"I think Cass and Griffin and I are doing that, too," Stef said, shaking her head. Both Cass and Griffin had bid on Grant Masters. And now here came yet another woman hovering over the coveted prize. She was dressed stylishly but her platinum blond hair didn't look quite as good as her clothes. Dry ends. Too much chemical torture.

"Who's that?" Stef asked.

"Priscilla Castro," Samantha said in a disgusted voice.

"Better known as Pissy," said her sister. "She works at city hall. And I wouldn't call her the most cooperative woman in town. She doesn't cooperate with us, anyway."

"Every year that woman manages to tie us up in red tape when it's time for the Chocolate Festival," Samantha said.

"She doesn't like Sam," Cecily confided, "ever since Sam beat her out as class valedictorian. She also lost the Miss Icicle Falls crown to Sam."

"And the scholarship money that went with it. Sore loser."

"So this town isn't perfect, after all," Stef joked.

Samantha smiled at that. "Hardly. We all have our flaws."

"What's yours?" Stef asked.

"Bossy," said Cecily, and Samantha stuck out her tongue.

"Oh, and here she comes," Cecily said under her breath. "Be nice."

"I'm always nice," Samantha said. She smiled at the newcomer. "Pissy, er, Prissy, how are things at city hall?"

Priscilla glared at her. "Fine. I see you're bidding on the spa day at Sleeping Lady."

Samantha shrugged. "Just for fun."

"I think I'll bid on it, too," Priscilla said. She stepped in front of Stef and wrote down her bid, jumping the bidding up by thirty dollars. "I really want this," she said and smirked at Samantha.

"She really needs it," Samantha muttered as the other woman walked away.

"So maybe we should let her have that day at Sleeping Lady," Cecily said.

Samantha considered for a moment. "You know what? No," she said with a grin and wrote in a fresh bid.

Meanwhile, three more women had gathered at the Honey Do offering, including Griffin. Stef hurried over to see what the bidding was up to.

"The competition is fierce," Griffin greeted her. "Who knew this would turn out to be such a hot-ticket item?"

"I did," said one woman. "I mean, look at him."

They did. He stood over in a corner of the room with his son Dan Masters and three women who were all doing their best to outflirt each other. Stef watched as a middle-aged woman in tight jeans flipped her scraggly fake red hair. Another woman, this one probably pushing sixty, gave his arm a friendly caress.

"They're like buzzards," Stef muttered.

"I can't blame them," said the stranger. "He's gorgeous. I know for a fact that Sally's gone at least a hundred dollars over what she planned to spend tonight."

"I bet they don't even need him to do any work," Griffin said.

"Who cares about need?" the stranger said with a shrug. "We all just want him."

Stef pulled Griffin away. "Okay, at the rate things are going, we'll never be able to compete."

Griffin frowned. "I can only spend so much."

"Me, too," said Stef. "I have to pay for materials as well as labor. We got our income tax refund, but that'll only go so far."

They both stared glumly over at Grant Masters and the handyman groupies.

There had to be something they could do. "I know! Let's pool our money. We can share him," Stef said excitedly.

"Who are you two sharing?" asked Cass, who'd come up behind them with a brownie in one hand and a cup of coffee in the other.

"The handyman," Stef explained. "We figure if we pool our money, we can outbid the competition. Want to go in with us?"

"But we all need him for more than a day," Cass pointed out.

"True, but maybe he'll give us a group discount," Stef said brightly. It was worth a try, anyway. Cass hesitated. "Come on," Stef urged. "Come in with us. Let's ace the competition."

"All right," Cass said. "Why not? I definitely need that man." Her cheeks turned pink and she quickly added, "To fix my roof."

"Oh, sure," Stef teased.

"Okay, then, here's the plan," Cass said. "The bidding closes in five minutes. We need to settle on how much we're willing to pay."

"Money divided in equal thirds," said Stef.

Griffin gulped but nodded.

"How high are we prepared to go?" Cass asked. "You two need to decide. I know what I'm willing to pay."

A quick powwow and they had their number.

"I can't go over that," Griffin said.

"If it goes over, I'll cover you," Cass promised.

"Don't worry. We won't have to," Stef told Griffin. "Uh-oh, here comes that Pissy person again."

Cass grinned. "Priscilla Castro? Sam and Cecily must have filled you in on her."

"She wants him," Stef said. "I saw her name on the bidding sheet."

"She seems pretty formidable," said Griffin.

"I'll distract her," Stef volunteered.

"Good idea," Cass said. "Do that, and one minute before the bidding closes, I'll write in our winning bid."

"Oh, no, here comes someone else," Griffin said, nodding in the direction of the fake redhead.

"Don't let her get here," Stef commanded.

"How am I supposed to do that?"

"Think of something. Meanwhile, I'll sidetrack Pissy."

Griffin hurried off and Stef moved to head off the newcomer. "Hi. We didn't get a chance to meet a few minutes ago. I'm Stefanie Stahl." Inspired, she added, "You're a friend of Samantha Preston's, right?"

Priscilla's mouth turned down. "I know Samantha, but we're not exactly friends."

"Oh? I'm still kind of new in town and I don't know every-one all that well. She seems nice."

"Looks can be deceiving," Priscilla said, her tone scathing. "Not that I'd say anything, of course."

"No, of course." Stef nodded. "I understand you work at city hall. You must know a lot about what goes on around here."

"You bet I do." And she proceeded to tell Stef, going into great detail on how the almighty Sterling family had once almost lost their chocolate company. Meanwhile, the mayor was taking up his microphone onstage to announce the end of the bidding—and Cass was writing in their final bid. Out of the corner of her eye, Stef could see Griffin talking with the other woman, standing in front of her and blocking her path to the table.

Finally, the woman shoved Griffin aside and marched to the table, just as the mayor said, "All right, my fellow Icicles, the silent auction is now at an end. So if you'll all find your seats, we'll announce the winner of our Raise the Roof bake-off competition this year. Then we'll start bidding on all those mouth-watering treats. And after that, we'll get to the winners of our silent auction."

Priscilla scowled. "I wanted to put in another bid on that handyman."

"Maybe you won him," Stef said innocently.

Priscilla moved past her, only to find Cass standing next to the Honey Do certificate, arms crossed and a grin on her face.

"Maybe you won one of your other bids," Cass said sweetly.

Priscilla stuck her nose in the air and marched off.

Now Griffin had returned. "Did we do it?"

"Yes," Cass told her, "and for less than we thought we'd have to."

"Yay!"

All three women hugged and congratulated each other on their cleverness.

"How did you stall that other woman?" Stef asked Griffin as they went to join Brad and Petey, who were sitting down with Samantha and Cecily and their husbands.

"I introduced myself and started babbling about my life. She now knows everything about me except what I weigh, and I'm sure she thinks I'm crazy. Totally embarrassing."

"But successful," Stef said with a smile.

Griffin smiled back. "Anyway, I'll never see her again, so I guess it doesn't really matter."

The reminder that her friend was planning to leave took the zip out of Stef's good mood. Sometimes it was hard to want the best for your friends when it meant the worst for you.

"Did you win your man?" Samantha asked as they seated themselves at the table.

"We did," Cass said.

"Now we just have to figure out how we're going to divide him up," said Stef, and her husband frowned.

"That sounds vaguely cannibalistic," Samantha observed.

"And not so easy to do," added Cecily.

Yes, how *were* they going to share this man? They'd each have to kick in more money, but how would they divide his time? "We'll make it work," said Cass, who probably needed him the most. "I'm not worried."

"I am," Griffin whispered. "What if we end up fighting over him?"

"We won't," Stef assured both herself and Griffin. "We're all friends."

"I know you've all been waiting to hear who won first place in our bake-off this year," said the mayor.

"Mrs. Lind, of course," Cass muttered, resigned to losing.

"Will Cass Wilkes please come up and get her blue ribbon?"

Cass's mouth dropped. "Seriously?"

"Get up there," Samantha commanded.

Blushing and smiling, Cass made her way to the stage, while

Millie Jacobs, the head librarian, pounded out some dramatic chords on the old upright piano in the corner.

"Congratulations," the mayor said, handing over a blue ribbon and a gift certificate promising dinner for two at Schwangau, the town's ritziest restaurant. Meanwhile, Priscilla Castro, looking self-important, strutted up to the stage, bearing the tray with Cass's creation, and everyone applauded.

A picture was taken for the paper—Cass and the mayor shaking hands and Priscilla holding up the gingerbread masterpiece—and then Cass was allowed to sit down.

"Way to go," Samantha's husband, Blake, commended her.

"You did it!" Samantha gave her a hug and Cecily beamed at her from across the table, saying she'd known all along that Cass would win.

Second-and third-place ribbons were handed out to Janice Lind and Beth Mallow. They, too, got their pictures taken for the paper and were each awarded a twenty-dollar gift card from Bavarian Brews.

"Now, are you all ready to start the bidding?" the mayor asked.

"Yes," everyone chorused.

"We've got some real treasures here, so don't be shy."

"That's sweet," Griffin said.

"Oh, yeah, Del's good with the BS," Samantha told her. "It's why he keeps getting reelected. That and the fact that he knows how to get Icicle Falls noticed. Tourism is our lifeblood."

"That and chocolate," Cass said, giving her a nudge.

"There is that," Samantha said modestly.

"All right, then. First we've got our grand-prize-winning gingerbread village. Who'll start the bidding?"

"I will," called Luke Goodman. "Ten dollars."

"Ten dollars," the mayor said. "Well, that's a beginning. But I bet Cass spent more than that on ingredients. Who'll give me twenty?"

"Twenty!" hollered a skinny guy in jeans, a Western shirt and boots, who was leaning against the far wall.

"Who's that?" asked Griffin.

"Yeah, he's kind of cute," said Stef.

"That's Billy Williams. Everyone just calls him Bill Will," Cecily said. "He's a lovely guy."

"But a doof," added Samantha. "He's not for you," she told Griffin.

"I'm not looking," Griffin said emphatically.

"Now we're making progress," the mayor continued. "I have twenty. Who'll give me twenty-five?"

"Twenty-five," Cecily's husband, Luke, called out.

"Thirty!" another man hollered.

"Bubba Swank. He owns Big Brats," said Cass.

"The sausage place?" Stef had eaten there. They served up great bratwurst.

"Yep. And he's single, too," Cass informed Griffin. "Really nice guy...if you were in the market."

Cecily shook her head. "He wouldn't be right for her."

"Cecily has a knack for knowing things like that," Samantha explained. "She used to be a professional matchmaker in LA."

The bidding went on and soon Cass's gingerbread town was up to fifty dollars. Now the bidding inched up a dollar at a time. Finally it looked like it was going to go to Bubba Swank when a voice called out, "Seventy."

"Too rich for my blood," said Luke.

"Whoa," Cass muttered, and Stef turned to see who'd jumped the bidding up so high.

"It's the handyman," said Griffin. "Wow."

"Wow is right," Cass said, smiling. "Who knew I was worth so much."

"You're worth a million times that," Samantha told her.

"Seventy dollars. Going once, going twice." Everyone stayed quiet and the mayor said, "Sold to the gentleman over there with

Dan Masters. Our newest resident, Grant Masters. Thank you, sir, for supporting the cause. I know you'll love this. And I bet Dan will be happy to help you eat it."

After that the baked-goods auction resumed as each baker was called up in turn to display her wares, Vanna White–style, to the audience. The bidding was good-natured and most of the cakes and pies went for a tidy sum, but none commanded the high bid that Cass's had.

"You're the queen of the day," Stef said to her.

"That's me, the queen of gingerbread," Cass joked.

With the baked items raffled off, it was time to announce the winners of the silent auction. Samantha and Cecily won the Sleeping Lady spa day, and Pissy, who was still up onstage helping, scowled. Dot Morrison won the Sweet Dreams package and did a little jig on her way up to collect her prize. There'd been much fighting over Bailey Black's gift basket, and the woman who got it whooped as if she'd won the lottery.

"That'll make Bailey feel better," Cecily said. Sadly, their sister hadn't been feeling well. Having a new baby and running a business was wearing her out, even though her husband helped her a lot.

Finally, the mayor announced, "And the services of Honey Do for a day goes to our gingerbread artist, Cass Wilkes."

"Yes!" Cass crowed, and she and Stef and Griffin high-fived each other.

"That concludes the auction portion of our evening," the mayor said. "Will our winners please pay the cashier? And the rest of you folks feel free to visit and enjoy yourselves."

"We are definitely going to enjoy the evening now," said Stef.

Grant smiled at the sight of the baker and her friends all celebrating. He remembered meeting her when the family went to Vegas for Dan and Charley's wedding. Most of his attention had been for his son and new daughter-in-law, but he'd liked Cass, with her wisecracks and friendly smile.

She looked damn cute tonight in those tight jeans and that soft blue sweater. She was wearing some makeup, too. He was a sucker for lipstick.

Don't piss in your own pool, he advised himself. It would be a bad idea to get involved with any woman who lived here. Small towns were hotbeds of gossip, and gossip was bad for both business and peace of mind.

On the other hand, a man might just find the right woman practically under his nose. He looked over at Muriel Sterling-Wittman, the woman he'd seen in the restaurant. She was sitting with a group of older women and she was just as pretty as the first time he'd seen her—and she fell into the right age group.

He couldn't say the same for Cass Wilkes. She might be unmarried, but she was way too young.

He walked to where she stood at the cashier table, handing over her credit card. "Hi. I guess you own me for a day."

She grinned. "I guess I do. Actually, how do you feel about being part of a foursome?"

He blinked. "A what?"

"We're going to share you," said one of the women standing next to her, an attractive blonde around his son Dan's age.

"Share me?" What the heck?

"The bidding was getting too high and we couldn't afford to keep outbidding each other, so we decided to go in together," explained the blonde.

He hadn't bargained for this, but if they only needed something small done... "What did you ladies have in mind?"

"Well, your son might've mentioned that my ceiling fell in," Cass said.

He had, but surely she didn't think...

"I need a new roof."

In a day. Yeah, right. Not even if he had a whole crew.

The third woman in the trio, a cute little redhead, held up her right hand, which was in a cast. "I fell off a ladder. I need my house painted."

"Your whole house?" Did these women think he had super-powers?

"Okay, one room?"

"That's probably doable." He turned to the blonde. "How about you?"

"My living room and dining room are completely torn up," she said. "My husband is… Well, he has a problem finishing things."

Oh, boy. Grant knew the type, the guy who thought car-pentry and home remodeling was easy—until he got in over his head.

"My house is a disaster," the blonde continued. "I wanted a great room and instead I have a curtain hanging between what used to be the dining and living rooms. My master bathroom is missing a tub and I'm losing my mind. You'll be saving my marriage."

"Ladies, I can't do all that in one day." Surely he was stating the obvious.

"We know," said the blonde. "We were hoping we could work something out with you, maybe get a group discount? We're desperate," she added.

No kidding. He looked over at Cass. Her situation seemed the most urgent.

"I do need a roof," she said. "I'm hoping you could at least fix the parts that are in the worst shape."

That was no way to do a job right and Grant said as much.

Her hopeful smile fell away like a loose shingle.

"But let me take a look at it."

The smile came back. The lady had a nice smile. Nice curves, too. He liked a woman with a little bit of flesh on her. Lou had been curvy.

The thought of his wife made it difficult to smile.

Suddenly anxious to escape the social squeeze and hide in his room at Gerhardt's Gasthaus with a beer and a movie on demand, he cleared his throat and got down to business. "I'll tell you what. Write down your phone numbers and I'll make an appointment to meet with each of you. I can't promise anything, but I'll give you an estimate."

Cass beamed and both of the younger women breathed a thank-you. They were all looking at him as if he was a god, and he could already see the writing on the wall. Someone was going to come out of this a real winner. Three someones, in fact, and he would not be one of them.

CHAPTER SEVEN

At the Raise the Roof fundraiser Grant had been swarmed by women all wanting his services. Some, he suspected, were hoping for services that fell outside the handyman range. The woman who called herself Priscilla had eyed him like he was steak on a platter, and he wasn't anxious to follow up with her. A few women, though, genuinely needed help, several of them widowed or old with husbands who weren't able to swing a hammer anymore. It looked like he was going to have plenty of business in Icicle Falls.

But the first order of business was to help the three women who'd bid on him. He'd arranged to meet Griffin James around one in the afternoon, as she'd said she had to work in the morning.

Pulling up in front of the old Craftsman, he saw a lot of potential in the place. The outside of the house was thirsty for paint but the bones were good. The yard had been mowed and Shasta daisies were starting to make their appearance in the flower beds. A lilac bush stood guard over one corner of the house and made Grant think of his grandmother's farmhouse. A tired-looking old Honda Civic was parked in the driveway.

You couldn't always tell a person's financial health by the age of his or her car, but judging from Griffin's age, Grant could safely deduce that she wasn't a millionaire hiding her wealth behind a worn set of wheels.

She answered the door wearing jeans, a green top and the cast on her arm. She was cute, with freckles and that long strawberry blond hair, and she had a girl-next-door kind of smile that said *Yes, you guessed it, I really am nice.* Too bad his son hadn't met someone like her instead of Miss Wrong.

"Thank you so much for coming over today," she said as she let him in.

"No need to thank me. It was your money that went for a good cause."

"Um, about the money. I know we only got you for a day but…"

"We're going to see what we can work out," he assured her. They walked into the living room and he saw the half-painted walls, plus the drop cloth, paint can and ladder camping at one end.

"Hardly anything would need to be done if I hadn't fallen off the ladder and broken my wrist." She frowned at the ladder as if it had deliberately bucked her off. Then she sighed. "I was hoping to get everything painted right away so I could put the house up for sale, but I have to admit, I'm a little afraid to get back on that ladder again."

"Maybe not such a good idea. So, you're moving?"

"I think so."

Interesting answer. "Where are you going?"

She took a deep breath. "I'm hoping to move to New York."

He nodded as he tried to picture this woman in the big city, striding purposefully down the street. Somehow she seemed more suited to a small-town setting. It was easier to imagine her sitting on the front porch, sipping lemonade, or teaching a class of second graders.

"What's in New York?"

"Big magazines and ad accounts. I'm a food photographer."

"Ah. So those pictures of hamburgers I see on billboards?"

"Were made by a food photographer. Not me, though. Not yet."

"Every time I drive by one of those billboards, I want a burger," he confessed.

"The food in those pictures is nothing you'd want to eat," she said. "Often the hamburgers get colored with a mixture of gravy color and clear liquid dish soap to make them look better."

"Now, that's disillusioning."

"I guess it's no different than Photoshopping models to make *them* look better. When we take pictures of food we try to make it look as appetizing as possible so people will want to eat it."

Wanting to eat food had never been a problem for him. "Well, you learn something new every day," he said. "You still able to take pictures with that hand?"

"It's a little awkward," she admitted. "But I'm managing. I'm sure glad I didn't break both hands, though."

It was always nice to meet someone who could look on the bright side.

"So, how long do you think this will take?"

"I can do your living room pretty fast."

"That would be great," she said eagerly. Then, not quite so eagerly, "What about the rest of the house?"

Griffin James was frantically counting costs. He could almost feel the anxiety coming off her. "What do you need done most?"

"Everything," she said with a frown. "The outside for sure, and I have two bedrooms." She chewed on her lip.

"Okay. Anything else?"

"I have a step on the back porch that needs to be fixed. My fiancé—" She stopped herself. "It didn't get fixed."

"Your fiancé isn't a handyman?"

Her fair skin went from cream to tomato in a blink. "Um, my fiancé isn't. Period. We broke up."

That would explain the move. Leaving the scene of the crime and going off someplace new to start over. Grant acknowledged this with a nod and then said, "Let's go check out that broken step."

She led him to the back of the house and through the kitchen. Not bad, but it could use a remodel. The porch was swaybacked and one stair was hanging like a loose tooth needing to be pulled. There was a tidy little backyard, though. It was already a nice place; some sprucing up would make it shine.

"A lot of potential here," Grant observed.

"My real-estate agent thinks it'll sell pretty quickly if I can get it in shape." She looked at him hopefully. "Can you help me, Mr. Masters?"

"Grant," he corrected her. "Yeah, I can. But I'm not sure how fast I can get all of this done. Did you have a time frame in mind?"

"The agent did say summer's the best time to put a house on the market, so I was hoping to do that in June."

They were already into May. "I can't make any promises, but I'll see what I can do."

Now she was looking anxious again. "How much will all this cost?"

The kid had just broken up with her fiancé. She was obviously trying to find her footing. He quoted her an insanely lowball price.

Even at that she gulped but nodded gamely.

"If you can't afford it, we can let it go at fixing the back porch step and painting the living room and the bedrooms."

"No, no. I need to do the outside, too. My parents will lend me the money."

Okay, she had parents. She had help. But he still felt…guilty. "Tell you what. We'll work something out."

She smiled gratefully at him. "Thank you so much."

"No problem," he said. He had money in the bank. He could afford to be generous. Anyway, he wasn't doing this to get rich. He was doing it for something to do. He didn't need to make a lot.

You won't make anything if you turn every customer into a charity case, he warned himself.

He'd get tougher. He was, after all, a businessman. He set up a loose schedule with Griffin, then went to Cass Wilkes's house later that day.

Cass had just gotten off work and was wearing jeans and a faded T-shirt, which informed him that bakers do it in the kitchen. Doing it anywhere sounded pretty darned good to him. It had been way too long. She wasn't wearing a hairnet, but her hair looked like she'd recently taken one off. Brown hair, no highlights. Unlike the other night, she was in her natural state, and she still had a smudge of flour on one cheek.

That cheek was rather rosy at the moment. "I must be running late," she said.

"I'm a little early. Sorry."

"I'm a mess." She raised a hand to her hair and fluffed it. Chin length, pretty. "But hey, I match my house."

There was something refreshing about a woman who could get messy. Lou had always been perfectly put together, and between manicures and pedicures, clothes and whatever they did at hair salons, she'd spent a small fortune. He'd thought she was pretty no matter what, and it had seemed like a waste to him. He really hadn't cared if her hair had highlights or if her toenails were pink. But he'd always complimented her anyway. It made her happy. And making her happy had made him happy.

"No worries," he said to Cass. "I think you look fine."

She smiled and shook her head at him. "With flattery like that, you're really going to be in demand." She paused. "So I imagine you need to go up on my roof?"

"I'm sure my son did a great patch job, but, yes, I want to check it out."

"I've got a ladder in the garage."

As she walked past him to lead the way, he caught a whiff of vanilla. It brought back memories of his mom baking his birthday cake every year. Of Lou in the kitchen, whipping up a batch of chocolate-chip cookies for the boys.

The thought of cookies was quickly replaced by other thoughts as he followed Cass into the garage. She had a nice ass. Being single, a man lost out on a lot of benefits.

She's not for you, he reminded himself. He didn't need to be taking up with someone who was almost young enough to be his daughter. He pulled his gaze away from her well-rounded bottom.

She was ready to help him carry out the ladder, but he assured her he could handle it. She nodded and let him do his thing on the roof. It didn't take more than a cursory check to see that, yes, indeed, the woman needed a new roof, just as his son had said.

He came back down and entered the house to find her missing. "Uh, Cass?" he called.

She appeared at the head of the stairs. Still wearing the same clothes but she'd put on some lipstick and brushed her hair. And the flour was missing from her cheek. "You might have told me I had flour on my face," she said with another smile. Yep, he remembered that smile. She had a little extra weight around the middle, but when you were a baker that probably went with the territory. Lou had gotten a little round herself, starting in her midforties. He hadn't minded. *It shows you're enjoying life*, he used to tell her.

With her ready smile, Cass Wilkes looked as if she enjoyed life, too. "So, what's the verdict?" she asked, reminding him why he was there. "As if I don't know."

"Dan was right. You need a whole new roof. Metal would be best."

"So I hear, but way too expensive."

"Okay, then composite. They have some good stuff out there now."

"Obviously you can't do this in one day."

"Afraid not, but if I get Dan to help me, we can do it fairly quickly."

"I guess you'd better give me a quote. Hopefully, it'll be less than thirty thousand."

"I can get under that. Dan mentioned you also have a deck in need of repair."

"I'm not sure I can afford to replace both my deck and my roof," she said. The smile was disappearing fast. "Kids in college."

She had kids. That meant she had an ex. Was she footing the bill alone?

Was it any of his business? "Let's go look at the deck anyway," he suggested.

With all that rotting wood, the deck was termite heaven, and not really safe to use. "I think you'd better replace this as of yesterday."

Now she was frowning.

"I'll give you a twofer," he said impulsively.

She looked hopeful, then guilty. "I can't do that to you. This is your business. You need to make a profit."

Yes, you do, agreed the businessman in him. "I'll make a profit," he said. If he did it would be a miracle, but this woman needed help.

Her relieved expression made him feel like a hero. *That feeling is priceless*, he told his hard-nosed self.

He threw out a lowball estimate and she happily caught it. "Are you sure this shouldn't be costing me more?" she asked.

"Remember you did win me for a day."

"I won you for a third of a day."

"We'll make it all work," he promised her.

"I might wind up owing you cookies for life," she said.

"I like the sound of that." Could he put in a request for chocolate chip?

"I'll put you on the same plan as your son."

"All right. Meanwhile, I'll order your roofing materials."

"Thanks. It really will be good to have this done," she said. "I don't want my ceiling crashing in again. And I'm more than willing to pay fair market price. I don't want to take advantage of you."

His baser self could think of all kinds of ways for her to take advantage of him. He told himself to quit being a letch. "No worries."

He started for the door and she walked with him. Part of him was inclined to stay a little longer, visit some more. But to what purpose?

You don't need a trophy wife and you sure don't need to be seducing younger women. Don't piss in your own pool.

That again. He sighed inwardly, said goodbye to Cass and headed for Stefanie Stahl's place.

Cass watched from the window as Grant Masters walked down the street to Stef's. *I don't want to take advantage of you.* Who was she kidding when she'd said that? She'd take advantage of him in a heartbeat. The man was too gorgeous for her own good. And what was it about a man in jeans and work boots? He'd had on a shirt, but it was unbuttoned, worn over a plain gray T-shirt that lovingly hugged his pecs…something she was sure she'd have no trouble doing.

"Oh, stop," she scolded herself. As if a hot man like Grant Masters would ever be interested in a chunky baker. She needed to get a grip on reality and quit thinking about getting a grip on Grant Masters.

If only she'd had time to shower and change into a nicer outfit. Okay, she didn't exactly have a closetful of power suits or drawers full of sexy camisoles, but she could at least have changed out of her baking grubbies and into clean jeans and a pretty top. She'd done a quick toothbrushing while he was on the roof and put on some lipstick, dragged a brush through her hair. But that was all she'd had time for.

Anyway, would more makeup and a cute top have made that much difference? Of course not, she scoffed, not with a man who looked like a movie star—literally—and could have any woman he wanted.

Still, she was sure that at one point he'd been checking out her boobs.

No, idiot. He was probably reading your stupid T-shirt.

Ugh, why had she worn that today?

She took a shower and slipped into her favorite sweats and yet another T-shirt. This one said Bakers Have Nice Buns. (There was a clear case of false advertising!) Good Lord, she had to tell Dot to stop giving her these goofy T-shirts every Christmas.

She studied her reflection in the bathroom mirror. Was it her imagination or was this shirt fitting a little more tightly? She couldn't use the old it-shrank-in-the-wash excuse, because the thing had been washed multiple times. Obviously, she didn't have a shrinkage problem. Quite the opposite.

Her cell phone rang, Dot calling to see if she wanted to pop over to Zelda's for dinner.

"Sure," she said. She'd order a salad.

Good idea. Salad for dinner…for the rest of her life.

Would it help?

CHAPTER EIGHT

Grant's final appointment was with Stefanie Stahl. He got to her house as she was pulling her car into the driveway, her little boy in the backseat. She waved, lowered the window and called out that she'd be right with him, then drove into the garage, the door shutting after her. He stood on the walkway for a moment, taking in the house. It was an old Victorian that had recently been painted. A small bicycle leaned precariously against the front porch and a softball lay in the yard, which was ready for a mowing. In short, the Stahl house seemed to be a typical young family's home. Looking at it from the outside, you'd never suspect it wouldn't look as good on the inside.

Once Stefanie Stahl let him in and drew back the oddly placed curtain, he knew precisely why she was not a happy camper. She'd warned him—but it was even worse than he'd guessed.

"Mama, I'm hungry," said the little boy, who was hovering beside her.

"Okay, let's get you some graham crackers and milk," she said to him. "First, can you say hello to Mr. Masters?"

"Hello, Mr. Masters. I'm Petey." The child put out his hand.

Well-trained kid. Grant leaned down and shook it. "Hello there, Petey. I saw a softball outside. Are you a baseball player?"

Petey nodded eagerly. "I'm playing T-ball. My daddy's the coach."

"Cool." Coaching his kid's T-ball game, trying to do home improvement projects—even if he wasn't very good at them—the woman's husband sounded like an all-around decent guy.

Petey had just enough time to give Grant a smile, then returned his attention to his mother. "Mommy, can I have graham crackers now?"

"*May* I have graham crackers?" his mother corrected him. "Yes, you may. I'll be back in a minute," she told Grant. "Feel free to look around."

She disappeared into the kitchen and Grant took a better look at what lay behind the curtain. It sure as hell wasn't the Wizard of Oz. What a mess. Stahl had randomly chopped away at the wall, then, tired of that, had moved on to making something, God only knew what. Boards lay scattered around the floor in what had once been the dining room, and there sat a table saw, awaiting the chance to help create more chaos. No wonder the woman was pissed. And, good Lord, the wall her husband had half demolished looked like a load-bearing one.

This guy had obviously jumped in with a lot of enthusiasm, then gotten in over his head. Grant suspected he'd gone into procrastination mode, hoping he'd be able to figure out the mess on his own.

Grant doubted he would—or could. Best to stop him before he brought the house down around their ears.

He crossed the room and, turning to the right, saw the arch that led from dining room to kitchen. At least that wall was still intact. The kitchen was in relatively good shape. The counters were quartz and the cabinets had been painted white. The appliances looked new. A previous owner must have updated the kitchen, since the current owner didn't have a clue what he was doing.

The little boy was sitting at the kitchen table, digging into his treat, and his mother was setting a glass of milk in front of him. Grant couldn't help flashing back to when his own boys were that age. They were always bugging him to play catch with them. Of course he did, even when he was dog-tired, but he remembered times when the hard work and the crazy zoo at home—with the boys and all their friends constantly whooping it up—had him longing for some peace and quiet.

Peace and quiet was overrated.

Stefanie glanced at him hopefully. "Can you help us?"

"I think so."

She left her son snarfing down his cookies and joined Grant in the disaster room. "This is just the tip of the iceberg, Mr. Masters."

"Call me Grant." Considering how much time they'd be spending together, they'd soon be on a first-name basis anyway. Besides, hearing himself called Mr. Masters made him feel old.

"Call me Stef," she said, smiling. The smile didn't last long. "Our master bathroom is torn apart. No tub, no tiles. And out back he started to build a patio." She frowned. "My husband…" She bit off the sentence.

Is in deep shit. "Let's take this one project at a time," Grant suggested. "I assume you want your dining room fixed first."

She nodded. "I thought it would be good to take down the wall between that and the living room and turn it into a great room. But I didn't mean for Brad to do it."

"Well, you have a smart idea, but you can't go off half-cocked on this kind of project. That wall between the two rooms is a load-bearing wall. You can't just take it down."

Her expression fell. "Oh."

"You need to put up a special load-bearing beam."

"But it can be done, bringing the two rooms together?"

"Yes, it can. And I'm happy to work with your husband—"

"No! Don't let him… I mean, he's busy working."

Grant nodded diplomatically. "If he does bring up the subject, you might mention about the wall to him." *Don't let him near it.*

She got the unspoken message. "I will," she said, a martial light in her eyes.

The poor guy was going to get an earful when he got home.

"So, um, I guess we should talk about cost."

"Obviously, I can't put this place to rights in one day."

"Can we just apply the amount from the auction to your labor?"

"Of course."

"And how much will that cost?"

Was it his imagination or was she holding her breath? Oh, boy. Here he went again, for the third time.

He certainly couldn't walk off and leave this woman with Mr. Fix-It. That half-demolished wall gave him the heebie-jeebies. "What can you afford?"

"We did get an income tax return and I have a little money saved."

"Some of that will need to go toward materials."

"How much do you think those will cost?" He estimated the amount and she nodded and bit her lip. "Okay. And your labor?"

"After the cost of materials, how much will you have left?" She told him. Of course, it was about a third short of what he'd normally charge. "All right. That's what you can pay me."

"Really?"

He was such a sucker. "Yeah, really."

"Oh, my gosh. You're wonderful!" she cried and hugged him. "Thank you so much."

"No problem." At this rate, Honey Do wasn't going to be a business. It was going to be an expensive hobby. Maybe he needed to turn it into a nonprofit.

It already is a nonprofit, fool, said his hard-nosed business side.

Still, what could he do? These women all needed help. And in Stefanie Stahl's case, he suspected he'd not only be helping her, he'd be saving her husband's skin.

"When can you start?" she asked excitedly.

"Well, I'm going to be doing some painting for your friend tomorrow, and I have a couple of other small jobs I need to do. How about I come over Thursday and get started here?" He'd have to get some help putting up that beam.

"Perfect."

For her. Not so much for him. He was halfway back in the construction business, something he didn't particularly want to do. He hoped Dan would lend him one of his guys for the heavy lifting.

He walked back to where he'd left his truck, got in and sighed deeply. After this, he was going to be firm. Once he was done with these three, it would be only small handyman jobs.

And no more lowball estimates.

Yeah, that, too. If he didn't go completely broke and could still afford to be in business.

Stef was putting a frozen pizza in the oven for dinner when Cass called. "I'm on my way out to meet Dot but I figured I'd call and see how it went with Grant."

"Great. And thank God we hired him. Do you know that Brad was about to pull down a weight-bearing wall? The house could've fallen down on us!"

"Whoa," Cass said. "Home renovation doesn't seem to be Brad's gift."

"Ya think?" Stef looked out the kitchen window at her son, who was happily trying to scale the apple tree. Fortunately, he was clueless that Mommy had been on the verge of poisoning Daddy. "I swear, the man's just saved Brad's life. Or at least our marriage."

"That's good to hear."

"I'm so glad we bid on him. It'll be just like having Danny Ocean from *Ocean's Eleven* working for us," she added. The movie had been Cass's pick for the latest chick-flick night, and thoughts of Brad Pitt and George Clooney were still fresh in her mind. She wondered if meeting Grant Masters had inspired Cass to choose it.

She was about to tease Cass, since she'd been drooling over George Clooney all through the movie, when a sudden thump on the kitchen floor made her whirl around. There stood Brad, scowling, his briefcase at his feet.

"I'm home," he snapped.

"Oh, hey, Brad's home. I'd better go," she said and ended the call. Pretending not to see his thundercloud expression, she said a cheery hello, danced over and kissed him on the cheek. "I didn't hear you come in."

"Obviously. Just like Danny from *Ocean's Eleven*?"

"We watched that at the last chick-flick night at Cass's house. I told you. Remember? Honestly, Brad. Sometimes you don't listen to anything I say."

"I listen. Why do you think I started on the great room?"

"Right before Griffin's shower? I have no idea."

Brad picked up his briefcase and marched off.

She followed him. "Come on, Brad. Don't pout. This is a good thing. We'll finally get it done."

"*I* was going to do it."

"Yeah, and bring the whole house crashing in on us. You know that wall you were about to tear down? Well, it *can't* come down. It's a weight-bearing wall."

"Load-bearing," he corrected her. "I figured that out. That's why I stopped."

"So what were you going to do?"

"I was going to do something. I was still thinking about it."

"So now you can stop thinking." He should be relieved. Grateful, even.

"Thanks," he said most ungratefully. He left his briefcase at the foot of the stairs and stomped off to the bedroom to change out of his suit.

More like pout, if you asked Stef, and she marched back to the kitchen to put together a salad to go with their pizza.

Dinner was a strained affair, with Brad saying very little and glaring at his pizza before every bite. "Honestly, Brad. You're making too big a deal out of this."

"Am I? How much is he charging?"

"It's very reasonable."

"I'll bet. It's gonna take our whole income tax return, isn't it?"

And then some. "It'll be the best money we've ever spent."

"Yeah?"

"Yeah."

Brad ripped off a bite of pizza like some kind of feral animal, managing to chew and glower at the same time.

"Are you mad, Daddy?" Petey asked in a small voice.

Brad wiped off the scowl, smiled at his son and ruffled his hair. "Not at you, big guy."

Petey looked relieved and he, too, ripped into his pizza slice, trying to mimic his father.

Stef picked at her salad. Why was Brad being like this?

After dinner, he took Petey off to play with his LEGO and Stef cleaned up, fuming. The way Brad was acting, you'd think he'd caught her having an affair. It was an easy cleanup, but still it left her feeling cranky. Usually Brad did part of it. Petey, too, who was in charge of helping Daddy clear the table. A small chore, but a nice little bit of family togetherness.

There was faux family togetherness after Petey's bath, when they both tucked him in and heard his prayers. The minute her son was snuggled under his blankets, Brad went downstairs to his man cave, leaving Stef alone upstairs. They usually cuddled on the couch and watched something on Netflix or Hulu when there was nothing going on. Not tonight. Brad was holed up down in the basement, and there wasn't even a ball game on TV.

Fine. She'd watch something *she* wanted to. She picked a romantic comedy and settled in. They sure weren't making very funny romantic comedies these days.

Or maybe she simply wasn't in the mood to laugh. She turned off the TV, grabbed her phone and started playing a game, resisting the temptation to go down to Brad Land and grovel, begging his forgiveness. Why should she? She hadn't done anything wrong. *She* wasn't the one who kept tearing up the house and leaving it looking like a war zone. She wasn't the one who promised to finish things and then somehow never got around to it. She hadn't tried to pull down a weight-bearing—load-bearing, whatever—wall. She had nothing to apologize for. Nothing! Brad should be up here groveling.

They usually went to bed at the same time. Together. Come bedtime, she climbed the stairs to their bedroom alone. Once there, she could hardly ignore the unfinished master bathroom. There was the bathtub, half-out, filled with a rubble of tile. How would he like it if she went downstairs and ripped out the toilet in the half bath off the man cave?

Probably wouldn't bother him at all. He'd just go off into the woods behind the backyard and find a tree to mark.

She went to the bathroom down the hall and took a bubble bath, telling herself it was relaxing her. She wasn't stalling going to bed alone. She finally got tired of adding more hot water to the cooling tub and climbed into their queen-size bed. Fine. If he wanted to be sleep deprived, let him.

She rolled over onto her side, shut her eyes and stayed awake until midnight, when he finally came to bed.

She turned on her bedside lamp and greeted him with "You should be glad we're getting this mess fixed."

"This mess that I made?" he said sarcastically.

He looked neither penitent nor reasonable. The scowl was still firmly in place, set in cement.

Okay, wrong approach. She tried diplomacy. "Admit it, Brad. We bit off more than we could chew."

"I was chewing just fine," he snapped.

"Well, I wasn't."

"I don't want to talk about this now," he said stiffly. Stiff, stiff as a board, stiff as the pile of boards out in the backyard.

She could feel her blood pressure rising. "We could've talked about it earlier if you hadn't been hiding in your man cave. Must be nice to have a place all your own that's finished."

"It's not my fault this place came with a finished basement," he growled.

"And it's not my fault that I can't stand living in an unfinished mess. Jeez, Brad."

"I've been doing the best I can. Sorry it hasn't been good enough for you." He grabbed his pillow and the afghan she kept at the end of the bed and started for the door.

"Where are you going?" she demanded.

"Someplace where I can sleep," he called over his shoulder and stalked out of the room. A moment later she heard the guest bedroom door shut.

The next morning he didn't look as though he'd gotten any more sleep than she had. "Remember what Pastor Lawrence said when he married us? You should never go to bed angry," she reminded him as he stood over the Keurig.

"Pastor Lawrence isn't married to my wife."

Okay, that was mean. "If that was supposed to be funny, it's not."

He lifted his cup and pointed it accusingly at her. "You bid a lot of money on that guy."

This again. "We agreed I could spend money at the auction."

"*Some* money. I didn't know you were going to spend our entire income tax return."

This wasn't a good start to the day. "Come on, Brad. Don't be like this."

"Like what? Pissed that you committed us to spending all that money? We always decide together what we're going to do with our income tax return."

Guilt gave her a sharp poke. "I'm sorry. I guess I got carried away."

"With a guy who looks like George Clooney."

Was he jealous? "The man's old."

"I heard you."

"I was teasing Cass. Honestly, Brad." She came up to him and put her arms around his neck. "You can't really be jealous of a man who's probably twenty-five years older than you!" He was still frowning. "Look," she went on, "I'm sorry I didn't check with you. It was just that I was so excited to get this…" *Don't say "mess."* "This…well, everything done and—" *Don't say "out of my hair"!* "—off your plate. I would think you'd be glad." There. That was pretty diplomatic.

He wasn't falling for it. "Yeah? Well, thanks for deciding what goes and stays on my plate. You just couldn't trust me to handle it, could you?"

"Maybe because you weren't handling it?" she retorted.

"Thanks for the vote of confidence." He took his mug of coffee and left the kitchen. "I'm late for work."

Late for work. Right. He was his own boss. He could come and go as he pleased.

And usually it pleased him to hang out another half hour and have breakfast with Petey. Not today. Very mature.

"If you're having that big a problem with it, I'll just spend my half of the return," she called after him.

No answer.

She grabbed a sponge and began to attack the sink. If that was the way he was going to be, fine. Let him go to the office and sit at his desk and pout. Let him be miserable for a day or two.

It would be nothing compared to the misery she'd been endur-ing for the last nine months.

Nine months. A woman could grow a baby in nine months. Why couldn't her husband finish a couple of home improve-ment projects in that time?

She got Petey up and off to school, and then, feeling irritable, she texted Griffin. Lattes?

Can't, Griffin texted back. Working with Beth today.

Poo. Well, Cass would be at the bakery. With luck, she'd be able to offer a listening ear. Stef made her way to Gingerbread Haus and found it unusually busy for a Tuesday morning. Cass was too occupied with waiting on customers to have time for a shrink session.

She did ask how things were going, but Stef merely said, "They'll go better with a latte."

"The usual?"

"Yes. And give me half a dozen gingerbread boys, too."

"That's not your usual order," Jet remarked as she rang it up.

"I feel like a splurge." She also felt a little like a rat. Although, really, she had no reason to.

"This looks like a peace offering," Cass said as she handed Stef the cookies.

"Let's just say my husband is in a sour mood. I'm thinking some gingerbread boys will sweeten him up."

"Good idea," Cass said. "And good luck."

Stef took her latte and sat at a bistro table in the shop, sipping and hoping that things would calm down and Cass would have time to talk. It didn't happen. One of the moms from school came in to pick up an order of cupcakes—regular, gluten-free and vegan—to take to school in honor of her son's birthday. Maddy Donaldson was having company for lunch and picked up half a dozen cream-puff swans. Pat York and Muriel Ster-ling-Wittman popped in for lattes and said a friendly hello to her, then settled at a nearby table to talk. People came and went and smiled and laughed.

There was simply too much contentment in this place. She took her box of cookies and left.

Brad was on the phone when she walked into the office. He didn't smile at her as she came in.

She set the box on his desk and headed back to the door.

"Let me know what you decide, Herb. Great talking to you," he said. Then he called out, "Stef, wait."

She turned back around and gave him a look that showed him he wasn't the only one who was unhappy.

"Thanks for the cookies," he said and managed a smile.

"I thought maybe they'd sweeten you up."

The smile hardened into a thin line. "Oh, so that's the problem, is it?"

"You're not being very reasonable. Or mature," she couldn't help adding. And she probably wasn't being very diplomatic, but this mess he'd made had called for more than diplomacy. It had called for action, and that was what she'd taken.

"Yeah, well, that's me, immature and unreasonable," he said and dumped the box in the garbage.

"Oh, yes, *that* was mature," she taunted.

"I have work to do, Stef."

"I have things to do, too," she said and steamed out of the office. The steam turned to tears as she walked back home. Why was he being like this? Why couldn't he simply admit he didn't know what he was doing and let her get the house finished? Why did he have to be so stubborn? Why, why, why? What was his problem? Her?

No way. She was not the problem here.

For a moment she was tempted to call her mother and complain, but only for a moment. Mom would side with Brad. She was a big believer that any problem in a marriage needed to be fixed by the wife. "Someone always has to make the first move," she liked to say, "and that's hard for men. When it comes to a happy marriage, we women are the glue that keeps it all together."

Mom wasn't living in rubble and Stef didn't want to be glue.

Back inside the house, she took one look at the disaster area and knew she'd done what needed to be done. Brad would have to live with it...just like she'd lived with his mess.

CHAPTER NINE

"Hi, sweetie. How are you doing? I've been thinking about you," said Mom. Translation: I've been worried.

"I'm fine," Griffin assured her mother.

"You're all by yourself up there."

Maybe she shouldn't have answered the phone. "Not exactly." Yes, she was all by herself in the house and she had to admit she still hated that. She still heard every creak and bump in the night, every twitter and howl that drifted in from the woods. But she wasn't without support.

"I've got friends here."

"Friends are not the same as family," her mother said.

Griffin poured hot water over her herbal tea bag and sat down at the kitchen table with her mug. The sun was shining, the flowers were blooming. Her mother was worrying.

"Are you eating?"

When she was fat, the big concern had been that she was eating too much. Now that she was skinny, the big concern was that she was hiding an eating disorder.

"Of course I'm eating." Griffin moved to the toaster and inserted a piece of sprouted wheat bread.

This was accompanied by a big sigh on the other end of the line. "Well, once you sell the house..."

"I'll come and visit before I move to New York." Emphasis on the word *visit*.

Another big sigh. "That's on the other side of the country, darling. And do you really want to be there all by yourself?"

"You lived there by yourself," Griffin reminded her. She'd seen pictures of her mom when she was young. She'd been gorgeous. She'd also been a lot more adventurous than she was now.

"Yes, and I was robbed twice. That's why I moved to the West Coast. It was the best decision I ever made. I met your father."

"Maybe I'll meet the man of my dreams in New York." The toast popped up and she spread on a small amount of almond butter and took a bite. Not as good as Beth Mallow's blackberry scones but a lot less deadly for her waist.

"Big cities are dangerous. Honestly, Griffin, you're doing so well right where you are. I simply don't understand why you have to move clear across the country."

Because she *wasn't* doing all that well right where she was, and it was now or never. She said as much.

"You know we want to be supportive."

Substitute *overprotective*.

"But we don't want to see anything happen to you."

Griffin was ready for something to happen to her. She was tired of being stalled out. And yet the more her mother talked about the dangers of moving so far away, the more she began to wonder if relocating was a wise idea. She liked living in Icicle Falls. She'd found a close friend in Stef, and she loved hanging out with Cass and the women she'd met in the book club. Was she crazy to want to leave all that?

Was she crazy to want to make more money?

"You're not being very realistic, dear. It's awfully risky. And what if you don't succeed?"

"Thanks for believing in me," Griffin muttered. Suddenly

she didn't have an appetite and dumped the unfinished toast in the garbage. Mom wouldn't approve of that. Wasteful.

People are starving all over the world. How many times had her mother used that line when she and her brother were kids? Mom mostly used it on Jeremy, who'd been a picky eater. Griffin had rarely needed to be coaxed to eat. And once the pounds sneaked on, food became her best friend. A shy little girl didn't have to worry about what to say to a cookie. Of course, the pudgier she got, the more the kids teased her and the more cookies she needed. It had been hard work shedding those pounds in high school, but she'd done it. And she'd kept the weight off ever since and liked it that way, so the toast could just stay in the garbage.

"Of course we believe in you," her mother insisted. "We just want you to be practical. We only have your best interests at heart."

"I know." Still, this wasn't exactly an inspiring conversation. "I have to get going, Mom. Can I call you later?"

"Oh, that's right. You have that cookbook job. See? You don't need to move so far away to get work."

Griffin didn't point out that the cookbook job would soon be ending. Then she'd be back to hoping her agent could sell some more stock photos.

She said goodbye to her mother, got dressed and brushed her teeth. She was ready to go to Beth's for another photo shoot when Grant Masters arrived to finish up her living room.

The ladder and paint were still where she'd left them, along with the paint pan and roller. The paint on it had now hardened to cement. She apologized for the sad state of her tools. "I should have washed it."

She hadn't bothered, since washing things was more of a challenge in a cast. Even doing dishes was a pain. Not that she did dishes much these days. Paper plates worked fine.

"No problem," he said. "I've got what I need."

"Can I get you something to drink? Some coffee? Bottled water?"

"Don't worry about me. Do whatever you'd normally do."

"Okay. I have to go to a photo shoot."

"I'll be right here," he said and started unpacking tape and rollers and small paint sponges.

"Okay," she said and left him to go to Beth Mallow's house for more food temptation.

Today's temptation was chicken curry sandwiches, the filling packed with not only chicken but also walnuts and apples and stuffed into Beth's crusty home-baked raisin bread.

"I made extra," Beth said after they'd finished, and began wrapping sandwiches in plastic wrap.

"I can't eat that much," Griffin protested. Actually, she could have, once upon a scale. A woman had to be ever vigilant.

"But don't you have our new resident handyman over at your place doing some work today? He'll be hungry."

Griffin didn't have much in her fridge to interest a man unless he liked spinach salad from Zelda's and take-out General Tso's from the Safeway deli. She'd like to be able to offer him something, especially since he was giving her a deal on his services. She took the sandwiches.

Back at her house, the front door was open and she could hear some kind of old rock and roll playing. Inside Grant was on a ladder, working the roller up and down the wall while his phone sat in a wireless speaker, serenading him. The living room was already three-quarters done.

"Wow," she said. "This looks great!"

"Glad you like it," he said, still working away.

"I, uh, brought you some lunch."

"That was nice of you. Not necessary, though."

"Beth Mallow sent it. We were taking pictures of sandwiches today. You might not have met her yet, but she's a wonderful cook."

Grant came down the ladder, picked up a rag and wiped his hands. "Is that one of the perks of taking pictures for people? They feed you?"

"They do if they're Beth. She's putting together a cookbook of family recipes. I gather her mom was an excellent cook, too."

"Okay, you talked me into it. I'll take a ten-minute break."

He went to the bathroom to wash up, and she went to the kitchen and put the sandwiches on a plate, then got out a napkin and a bottle of water. By the time he entered the kitchen, she had everything on the table.

"You going to join me?"

"Oh, not right now."

"Don't like chicken salad, huh?" He helped himself to one of the sandwich quarters and took a bite. Nodded. "This is good. Probably good for you, too. All that protein."

He nudged the plate in her direction and she picked up one of the quarters and took a bite.

"So, you were taking pictures of this today?"

She nodded. He was looking at her expectantly, so she fetched her camera and brought up the photos she'd produced. She thought they were charming. Beth had liked them. But Griffin always felt a little nervous when she first showed people her work.

She studied the picture again, trying to see it with fresh eyes. Two quarters of a sandwich sat on Beth's kitchen table on a white plate, one lying down, the other upright, leaning against it like a miniature pyramid, the filling nearly (but not quite) spilling from both, a perfect ruffle of lettuce poking out like an edible slip. A vintage ceramic rooster strutted in the background, unaware of the fate of some of his relatives.

Grant nodded in approval. "What else have you done for her?"

Encouraged, she brought up some more pictures—the apple scones, begging her to bake a batch and eat every one; a tureen of mulligatawny soup, promising warmth on a cold day; an apple pie with a scoop of faux ice cream.

"I'm eating and these still make me hungry," he said.

"That's the general idea."

"Have you talked to my daughter-in-law? She might want to do a cookbook featuring some of the restaurant's food."

"No, I haven't. After I finish this project, it'll be time to move to New York." *Clear across the country.* "My mom doesn't want me to go." Now, why had she shared that?

"Oh? How come?"

"She's worried about me moving so far away. This is already far away, in her opinion. My family lives in Oregon."

"Moms worry," he said.

"She thinks I'm taking a big risk."

"Well, maybe. But it's important to have a dream." He took another quarter of a sandwich and, once more, nudged the plate toward her. She shook her head. "Taking pictures of food only gives you half the experience," he said.

"I'm not a very big eater." He said nothing to that, at least not verbally.

She wanted to assure him that she wasn't anorexic or bulimic, just careful. Instead she asked if he'd ever had a dream.

"Oh, yeah. When I was framing houses in the dead of winter and freezing my ass off, I used to dream about getting away, going someplace where life was easy, the fish were always biting and the beer was cheap. The good life."

"I guess you found it. Somebody said you were in Mexico."

"Yeah, but in the end, it wasn't that good." He took one final quarter of a sandwich and got up. "I'd better get back to work. Thanks for showing me your pictures."

It wasn't that good. What did that mean? Grant's words left her feeling a little unsettled. She grabbed another quarter of a sandwich and took a bite. Protein. Good for you, right? She ate the rest.

Ugh, bad for you, white bread. What had she been thinking? That it tasted really good!

Grant had finished Griffin's living room and promised he'd be back as soon as possible.

"I understand you have to do stuff for Cass and Stef," she'd said. "And they need help more than I do."

"Understandable that you want to get this done," he'd said. Putting the house on the market as soon as possible and all that. He got it.

"But I'm not living like Stef is, and I don't need to worry about rain, like Cass."

"We'll get you taken care of," he'd assured her and wished he could clone himself.

Good grief, he was right back to his construction days, hopping from job to job, doing one thing at one house, then running to another when supplies came in, while at every site owners pressured him to hurry up and finish.

He'd planned for this to be easy and part-time. No pressure, just something to do. It was all snowballing, out of control.

Still, Griffin had been so delighted. "It looks so much better with a fresh coat of paint."

"Things usually do," he'd said.

His stomach rumbled as he walked to his truck. The sandwich he'd had at Griffin's had been great, but he'd worked that off in no time. Charley had insisted he drop in at the restaurant later, but he needed something to tide him over, so he swung by the store for corn chips and a six-pack of beer.

Once he was there, he decided some fruit would be in order and wandered over to the produce section. Apples or oranges, which did he want?

He suddenly caught a whiff of strong perfume. It danced up his nose and tickled him, making him sneeze.

"Well, if it isn't our newest resident," cooed a female voice behind him.

He turned to see Priscilla something-or-other, one of the women he'd met at the fundraiser.

"We met at Raise the Roof," she said. "I'm Priscilla Castro. I'm the office manager at city hall."

He nodded. "Of course. Good to see you." Sort of. Not really. She'd come on strong at the fundraiser and he wasn't particularly fond of predatory females.

"I'm glad I ran into you," she said. "I've got a problem and I really need a man." She reached out and started fondling a banana.

Oh, boy. How to get out of this? "Well, uh, I'm completely booked these days."

"I bet you are. All those women wanting you for silly little jobs. Are you free right now? This probably wouldn't take long." She took a step closer.

Boundaries, lady. He inched away.

She inched along with him. "I'll make it worth your while."

He wasn't the only one here who was hungry. Her hormones were growling so loudly he was surprised people all over the store couldn't hear them.

She had him up against the bin and there was no place farther to go, although he still tried. The apples shifted behind him and suddenly he'd started an avalanche. Apples began bouncing every which way and rolling along the floor. He bent to pick one up and she bent over, too, showing off her cleavage. *Don't look!*

He grabbed a couple of apples and returned them to the pile. She held an apple in each hand and ran her tongue along her mouth. Oh, man, he was getting turned…off, big-time.

"I've got an Icicle Ridge cabernet at my place just waiting to be opened."

"What's your problem?" He meant that on so many levels.

"My sink is clogged," she said mournfully.

"That's an easy fix."

"Great."

"A plumber can take care of it in a few minutes."

She frowned. "A plumber?"

He plucked an apple out of her hand. "That's your best bet, since you're in a hurry. Nice seeing you," he lied and took the apple and scrammed. He dashed down the beer-and-chips aisle, half fearing she'd come chasing after him, then went through the self-checkout line. Got back in his truck and let out his breath. That was a close one.

His cell phone rang and he jumped. It was an unfamiliar number. He hoped it wasn't Priscilla Castro coming up with a new urgent home repair. He said a cautious hello.

A wavering voice on the other end of the call asked, "Is this Grant Masters?"

Only if you're not related to Priscilla Castro. "Yes."

"Mr. Masters, my name is Lucille Schoemaker. Your daughter-in-law thought perhaps you could help me and gave me your number."

Charley was the best. "How can I help you?"

"It's a little delicate," she said and cleared her throat. "I need some bars installed in my bathroom. By the toilet."

One of the many joys of aging. The knees didn't work the same as they used to. He remembered when his own mother had reached that point. "I can take care of that for you."

"If you could, it would be wonderful!"

"Not a problem." He'd fit her in somehow.

He missed two more calls when he was showering in his room at Gerhardt's. Good Lord. His part-time job was swiftly morphing into overtime. He was going to have to hire help. How happy was Matt over there in Seattle?

It was a fleeting thought. Matt wanted to be in the restaurant business. Grant couldn't drag his son away from that to spend his life fixing broken porches and painting houses. Still, maybe

Matt would be open to coming to Icicle Falls on his next days off, just to help his old man get caught up.

His call went to voice mail, of course. Matt would be working at the restaurant by now. "Hey, son. Wondering if you're interested in coming up here for a couple of days and helping me out with a project or two." Matt had done some roofing and he could handle tearing up shingles. He could also spray paint a house. "I need some help painting a place." If he could at least delegate that to Matt, he could get busy over at Stef's while he was waiting for the roofing materials for Cass's house. "Give me a call if you're interested in making a few bucks. I'll throw in a six-pack of beer."

He doubted he'd have to pay his son much once Matt saw the cute woman who lived in the house. She seemed genuinely sweet. If he could have, Grant would've picked someone like her for a daughter-in-law. Too bad she and Matt were on different paths. It might have been a good match.

Not that Grant did that kind of thing. Dangerous business playing around with people's lives. Better to let relationships happen naturally.

Of course, *happening naturally* hadn't worked so well for Matt. Hopefully, down the road he'd find someone, settle down, maybe even move over the mountains and start a restaurant somewhere nearby.

After catching up on the nightly news, Grant wandered over to Zelda's, where his son was already digging into a plate of nachos. "Hey, Dad. I waited for ya, just like one pig waits for another."

"I can see that," Grant said, sliding into the booth across from him.

The same young server he'd met when he first hit town came up to the table. "Hi, Mr. Masters. I mean Grant."

"Hi there..."

"Melody," she reminded him.

"Melody. How about bringing me some of what my son's having. And a beer."

"IPA?"

"Sure."

"Right away," she said and hurried off.

"Nice kid," Grant observed.

"Yeah. Her family moved here from Seattle. She's working a couple of days a week for us, and Charley's kind of taken her under her wing. Gonna transfer to WSU this fall."

Sometimes Grant was a little jealous of young people. They had their whole lives ahead of them, lots of adventures waiting. *You're not in your grave*, he told himself. But sometimes he felt like he had one foot hovering over it. Why did life have to zip by so fast?

Melody returned with his nachos and beer, and he dug in. Corn chips buried under melted cheese, black olives, shredded beef, green onions, jalapeños and black beans, the whole thing topped with sour cream, guacamole and chopped cilantro. Oh, yeah. It paid to know food people.

Charley had been seating guests but she stopped by the table. "How are my men doing?"

"Great," Dan said. "I think Dad likes your nachos."

Grant had pretty much vacuumed them off the plate. "Best nachos I've had this side of Mexico."

She smiled. "Good. Wait until you try one of our steaks. Have it with a beer float," she advised and left to seat more early birds.

"Gross," Dan said under his breath.

It did sound like a terrible thing to do to beer, Grant had to admit.

"But that's nothing compared to some of the food combinations she's come up with lately at home. Peanut butter and yogurt? Pickles and pretzels? God help us."

"Your mother never had any weird cravings when she was pregnant. I always thought that stuff was a myth."

"Not at our house," Dan said and shoved a cheese-draped chip in his mouth.

Charley was on her way back now, passing them with two middle-aged women in tow. One of them happened to glance in Grant's direction. She stopped in her tracks and did a double take. "Oh, my gosh! Suzy, look."

Her friend Suzy turned around and her jaw fell open. She approached the table like a hungry puppy hoping for a scrap. "Oh, Mr. Clooney, I know you probably want to guard your privacy, but I've been a big fan of yours ever since *ER*. Could I trouble you for an autograph?"

"I'm afraid I'm not," Grant began.

He was drowned out by her friend. "Me, too! Where's a piece of paper when you need one?" She started rummaging in her purse.

Meanwhile, Suzy had snatched the napkin from Dan's lap and shoved it in front of Grant. "Here. Could you sign this? No one back in Sequim is going to believe this."

She had that right. "I'm not Clooney."

The two women gaped at him as if he'd told them the world would be ending at midnight.

Then Suzy gave a knowing nod. "Of course," she said with a wink. She lowered her voice. "Don't worry, Mr. Clooney. We won't tell a soul."

"Really, I'm not him," Grant insisted.

"But would you sign this anyway?" Suzy begged, waving the napkin at him.

Doing this always made him feel twitchy. Anyone could look online and find the real celebrity's signature. But sometimes giving in was the only way to make the hounding stop.

Ignoring his son's snickers, he signed the napkin.

"I can't find anything," moaned the other woman. "Here." She stuck her arm in front of him. "Sign my arm. Maybe I can get it tattooed on permanently."

A permanent fake signature. Great. "I wouldn't do that," Grant cautioned. "The ink might get infected."

"I'll risk it. Just sign anyway."

He obliged, feeling like a fool the whole time. *Don't sue me, Clooney. I had this face first.*

"Thank you," the woman breathed. "I'll never wash this arm again."

"I'll never wash this arm again," his son mimicked in a high falsetto after the women had moved on.

"Very funny," Grant snapped. "You could have said something, you know."

"What would be the point? No one listens. Anyway, what can it hurt… George?"

Grant pointed a finger at him. "You gonna post bail if I get arrested for impersonating a celebrity?"

The women were seated now, but still ogling him. This was probably how animals in zoos felt. "You know what—I think I'll head on back to Gerhardt's," he said, pulling a couple of bills out of his pocket.

"Yeah, it's a tough life," Dan teased. "You'd think you'd be used to it by now."

"Yeah, you'd think." But he wasn't. He hated all the fawning and fussing. As if a guy had any control over how he looked.

Charley was with them now. "Sorry about that, Dad. They're from out of town and I couldn't bring myself to burst their bubble."

"I know," Grant said. He stood and kissed Charley on the cheek and two besotted sighs escaped the tourists' table. "I'm going to take off. There's something on ESPN." He hoped.

Dan smirked. "Still can't handle being George Clooney."

"It's your cross to bear," Charley said, straight-faced.

"Ha-ha." Everyone was a comic.

Oh, well. He was ready to kick back and relax anyway. He strolled past Gingerbread Haus on his way to the inn and found himself wondering what Cass Wilkes did on her days off. *Forget the ladies and focus on the job.* Or the sports channel.

Working and sports, both good. But not enough. Life without a woman was like a half-built house. Empty.

Aw, Lou, why'd you have to leave me?

CHAPTER TEN

Grant had made a good start on painting Griffin's house, and he'd ordered the necessary materials for Cass Wilkes's roof and taken time to help with a few "honey do" emergencies in town, including Lucille Schoemaker's. The next order of business was to get over to the Stahl residence and start fixing that mess, so Thursday found him at Stef's place, shoring up the wall so he could get the all-important beam installed. He had help coming later for that—one of Dan's guys was going to swing by after the job they were doing up on Mountain View and bring along a lift. Meanwhile, Grant had plenty to do here.

It was one of Stef's days off, and he'd sent her to his supplier in Wenatchee to pick out flooring, then gotten to work. He'd done as much as he could on his own, shoring up the wall some more and cutting joists. Then he switched to pulling up flooring in the dining room. He was working up a fine sweat when Stef's husband, Brad, walked in.

He was an average-looking guy, probably about five-ten and maybe weighed a hundred and fifty if he was lucky. Not a lot of muscle power under that shirt. He checked out Grant's progress with a frown.

"Your wife's not here," Grant said, getting his crowbar under one end of the old wood and prying it up.

"Oh. Well, I just came home for lunch. Where is she?"

"I sent her to pick out the wood for your new floors."

Stahl nodded. "I thought we were gonna do that together."

Grant decided it would be best not to comment and kept prying up boards.

Stahl strolled over to him. "I was working on this. Did she tell you?"

"She said you were having trouble getting it done." That could be taken the wrong way. "Too busy," Grant improvised.

"I am," Stahl said, almost defensively. "My business is growing."

"Good to have a growing business." Grant pulled up a plank of wood and started on the next one.

"I was going to get this finished."

And clearly the guy wasn't happy about his wife bringing in someone to mop up after him. "Women get impatient," Grant said diplomatically. "My wife always wanted things done as of yesterday."

"How'd you deal with that?"

"I got stuff done as of yesterday."

"Sounds like she has you whipped," Stahl teased. He was smiling, but Grant knew a barb when he heard one.

He didn't rise to the bait. "She did."

"Did? You're not together anymore?"

"Afraid not. She died three years ago."

Stahl's gloat vanished. "Oh, man. I'm sorry."

"It happens." Grant gave the wood a vicious tug. Very philosophical. But the reality of it still hurt. Maybe some wounds never closed. He'd give anything to have Lou back, busy coming up with projects for him. This kid didn't know how lucky he was. He needed to. "I have to admit, there were times when she drove me nuts with all the things she found for me to do around the house, but I loved her and I miss her like hell. Life's short, sometimes shorter than you think it's going to be. So yeah, all that crazy-making? I'd take it back in a heartbeat."

Stahl nodded, still looking uncomfortable, then retreated to the kitchen. Grant hoped he'd given the guy something to think about.

Five minutes later his wife was back. "I found the most gorgeous wood," she gushed to Grant. "Brazilian cherry. The man said it's one of the toughest woods and I'm figuring with Petey we'd better go for tough."

Her husband appeared in the kitchen doorway. "You picked out the flooring? I thought we were going to do that together."

"Well, one of *we* has not been available."

Brad Stahl's frown was back. He disappeared into the kitchen once more and his wife followed him. Grant turned up his music, determined not to hear whatever got said in there.

He didn't need to hear to guess that it wasn't a lovey-dovey conversation. Within minutes, Stahl was headed for the door, jaws clenched tighter than a U-clamp.

Then Stef herself was back, offering Grant something to drink.

"I'm fine, thanks," he said and kept working, hoping she'd take the hint and leave. He strongly suspected her husband wouldn't appreciate the fact that Stef was airing her grievances to a stranger. Anyway, he was a handyman, not a marriage counselor.

She didn't seem to know the difference. "Brad doesn't get it. He has no idea what it feels like to live with everything turned upside down."

Grant pointed out that her husband was living under the same conditions.

"He couldn't care less," she scoffed. "As long as he's got his man cave, he's happy."

Grant wasn't about to take sides. "This'll be done soon and then you can both be happy."

Judging from the expression on her face, that wasn't what she wanted to hear. "I'll be at Griffin's if you need me for anything."

Yep, pissed at the husband. All her girlfriends would know it before the day was over. He understood the woman's frustration, but he couldn't help feeling sorry for Stahl. The guy had tried. He ought to get some credit for that.

But that was how it went sometimes. When it came to women, a man was damned if he did and damned if he didn't.

He'd had a few times like that himself. Still, those occasions when he got it right… The smile on his wife's face, the enthusiastic hug. Oh, yeah. Those were the moments a man savored. He hoped that once this place was all put together, Stef would give her man one of those smiles and enthusiastic hugs, and all would be well.

By Friday, she'd certainly started smiling more as he began making progress on the great room. "It's going to be fabulous," she said when she came home from work. The glulam was installed, all the old flooring had been taken up, and the moisture barrier was in place. The new flooring had been delivered, and all that remained was to lay it down. He'd come back and do that after he'd finished Cass's roof. Then his work here would be done. He knew she wanted that bathroom fixed, but some other sucker would have to deal with that. He'd had enough. The tension in the Stahl house was so thick you could cut it with a skill saw.

He said goodbye to Stef, got in his truck and headed for his temporary home. He had just turned onto Cedar when he saw a car parked by the side of the road, its trunk open. The attractive woman with the chestnut curls was standing there, holding a car jack and staring at it as if she'd never seen one before.

Woman in trouble. Hero needed. He pulled up behind her and got out of his truck. "Could you use a hand?"

"That would be wonderful! Thank you. I'm afraid I never mastered the art of changing a tire."

"You don't want to," he said, relieving her of the jack. "It's dirty work."

"I must confess, I don't like getting dirty."

He suspected she had plenty of men willing to get dirty on her behalf. Probably plenty who'd like to get dirty with her, too.

"I don't think we've met," she told him.

"I saw you the other day at Zelda's."

"I understand you're Dan's father."

So she'd been doing some checking on him. He smiled as he pulled off the hubcap. "I am. Grant Masters."

"I'm Muriel Wittman. I don't know if you've met my daughter Samantha yet, but she's one of Charley's best friends."

"I think I have." Had she been at the wedding? Probably.

"I have two other daughters, Cecily and Bailey. You may not have met them."

"Don't think so," he said. He loosened a lug nut and tossed it in the upended hubcap.

"Cecily works at our chocolate company, and Bailey owns Tea Time, a tearoom here in town. Her husband owns the Man Cave. Maybe you've been there?"

"Not yet." He heard they had pool tables. "I'll have to check it out."

"I'm sure you're still busy settling in."

"Slowly."

"It's a friendly town, lots of good people."

"I can see that. I think I've just met one of them," he added.

That made her smile. Man, she had a great smile. She had to have some guy waiting in the wings.

"So, Muriel, I'm curious. Is there a man in your life who's going to wonder why you didn't call him to change your flat?"

Her cheeks turned pink as a rose. "No. I'm alone."

All right. His lucky day. "I find that hard to believe," he said and yanked off the tire.

"I'm a widow."

Charley hadn't mentioned that. He stopped in his tracks, the tire in his hand. "I'm sorry. I lost my wife, so I know how you feel."

Her eyes filled with tears. "I'm sorry to hear that. It's not easy, is it?"

There was an understatement. He dumped the old tire in the trunk and got busy putting on the spare.

"Actually, I've lost two husbands."

"Two." Hard enough to lose one spouse. "I'm surprised you can still smile."

"You can always find something to smile about," she said. "Like having someone show up just in time to change your tire."

"Happy to do it." He screwed the last lug nut in place and popped the hubcap back on, then started letting the car back down.

"Thank you again so much. I'd love to give you something to show my appreciation. If you like chocolate…"

Not particularly. But he did like Muriel. "I'll pass on the chocolate. But how about having dinner with me? If you don't have any other plans, that is."

"I'd love to."

"Great." He was still in his work clothes and his hands were dirty from changing her tire. "Let me clean up first. Then I can pick you up."

"No need to go to that trouble. Would you like to meet at Zelda's? Say six o'clock?"

He'd rather have picked her up. But maybe she liked to play it cautious. Maybe she didn't want some guy driving her home and expecting a good-night kiss. Or more.

"Sure," he said. "That'll be fine."

Dinner out with a beautiful woman was fine, no matter how they arranged the details.

So much for the *don't piss in your own pool* rule. It wasn't practical anyway, he decided. Not when the pool was filled with attractive women.

★ ★ ★

Cass arrived home from work to find the surprise she'd ordered for Charley. She and Samantha had already informed her that they were throwing a baby shower when it got closer to her due date, but this was something Charley could enjoy right away. Cass had gotten the idea when she'd seen the wedding keepsake book Stacy gave Griffin at her bridal shower and figured there had to be something similar for expectant moms. Sure enough, there was. Charley would love this. She'd been so sure she'd never get pregnant and now here she was, expecting a baby. She and Dan were both excited and all their friends were excited on their behalf.

So after Cass had showered and fixed herself a bite to eat, she ran over to Johnson's Drugs and picked up a gift bag and some tissue paper. Then, with her gift properly dressed, she made her way to the restaurant.

Six o'clock was rush hour at Zelda's, but Charley still found time to greet her friend and, of course, open her present. "I love it!" she cried and hugged Cass. "You're the best."

"Aw, you're only saying that 'cause it's true."

"Did you eat?"

It was a wonder Charley ever made a profit with all the free drinks and meals she handed out to her friends. "Yes, and you have to stop letting us all freeload off you."

"Hey, I write it off," Charley quipped. "How about a drink?"

Cass was about to say yes when she spotted Grant Masters seated at a corner table with Muriel Sterling-Wittman. Good thing she'd already eaten because there went her appetite.

Seriously, though, did she think she'd have a chance to grab his attention when a beautiful woman like Muriel was around? In addition to being beautiful, Muriel was also smart, kind and, yes, sweet. Who could compete with that?

Still, seeing them together was...well, disheartening. And she sure didn't want to sit at a table and watch that for an hour.

Charley caught her looking and her easy smile was replaced by friendly concern. "Oh."

"Don't go ohing," Cass said. "I'm not in the market for a man." True enough. She didn't need to go down that bumpy road again.

"They just met," Charley explained.

It was bound to happen.

"She had a flat tire and he changed it. I don't think it's anything serious."

It would be. How could it not? Two gorgeous people together. When it came to love, like called to like. Which meant Cass needed to keep her eyes peeled for a pudgy couch potato.

"Oh, stop! I wasn't interested," Cass lied. "Just drooling."

"Then how about that drink?"

Sitting and watching pretty, perfect Muriel Sterling add another fan to her club would probably not be good for the old self-esteem. "I'll pass. I've got an errand to run." What that errand was would come to her once she was in her car.

Charley let her off the hook. "Okay. See you Sunday."

Sunday was chick-flick night at Cass's house. Yep, see? She had a social life. It just didn't take place on Fridays.

Friday night, and she was on her own. But so what? It had been a long week, and she was too tired for a social life anyway. She had to work in the morning.

She was going home to an empty house.

The place hadn't felt so empty back when she had her dog for company. No dogs, she told herself firmly. She already got little enough sleep. She didn't want to have to house-train a puppy. Still, the animal shelter seemed to be drawing her like a magnet. It was open until seven and there was no harm in going in and seeing what they had.

Chita Wolfe was volunteering there, along with her husband, who was the local vet. Dr. Wolfe had taken care of Tiny when he was alive, helped Cass deal with the Saint Bernard's death, even sent her a sympathy card afterward. He greeted her warmly as she came in, and Chita gave her a hug.

"We haven't seen you in ages," Chita said.

"I know. I've been busy." Not to mention too upset over losing Tiny to consider another dog.

"I understand," said the good doctor. "You're interested in adopting a pet?"

"Well, maybe. I don't want a puppy, though. Too much work." She shook her head. "Actually, so is a dog." Walking the dog, feeding the dog, cleaning up after the dog. What was she thinking, anyway?

"How about a cat?" Chita suggested.

"A cat." Cass's family had a cat when she was growing up. Tiger hadn't been very friendly. In fact, Tiger had scratched Cass on more than one occasion simply for petting her when she wasn't in the mood. Kitty PMS probably. "I don't know. Cats are such snobs."

"Not necessarily. Wait here." Chita went through the door that led to the area where the animals available for adoption were kept. She returned a moment later, holding a gray cat with white paws. The animal was looking around as if to say, *Why am I here? I deserve better.*

Chita put the cat in Cass's arms and it nuzzled against her neck and started purring. It was love at first sight. "Oh, my, you are darling," Cass cooed. Then to Chita, "Why is she here?"

"Her owner died suddenly. The daughter is allergic to cats and couldn't take her." Chita frowned. "At least that's what she said."

"You're an orphan. Poor kitty."

"I doubt she'll stay an orphan for very long. In fact, I'm half thinking of adopting her myself."

"Then you should," Cass said, but she couldn't bring herself to give the cat back.

"We already have a menagerie. Anyway, she'd rather be an only child."

"Would you?" Cass whispered to the cat.

The purr got louder.

"Does she have a name?"

"Lady Gray. She's five, so she's got plenty of good years left in her."

It would be nice to have company, and a cat would be a lot less work than a dog. Or a man. Right? "So, Lady Gray, want to come home with me?"

"Of course she does," Chita said. "Let's have you fill out the paperwork. She's been spayed, needless to say, and she's all caught up on her shots, so you can take her home now. No home visit needed. We already know you've got a good home for her."

Cass completed the paperwork, whipped out her handy-dandy credit card, and twenty minutes later she had a new roommate. Chita loaded Lady Gray into a temporary cat carrier, and Cass set out for home by way of Safeway, where she spent a small fortune on everything from cat food to a flea collar.

"Don't feel guilty," she told the cat as they drove off. "You're still a heck of a lot cheaper than Tiny was. I spent that much on dog food in one week."

Once they got home, Cass let her new furry friend loose and watched as the cat prowled the house, inspecting furniture, looking in corners. "You probably smell Tiny. Don't worry, though. No dogs here anymore. Just us girls."

She put away the cat paraphernalia, set out some food for Lady Gray and watched with satisfaction as the cat hunkered down and enjoyed her first meal in her new home. She set up the litter box in the downstairs bathroom and later that evening the cat used it like a pro.

Cass finally sat down to watch the latest episode of *Game of Thrones*, which she'd recorded, and the cat kept her distance. But partway through the program, she cautiously made her way across the couch and then onto Cass's lap, where she kneaded

Cass's thighs, then settled down. Obviously, this animal had been well loved.

"So, you were brought up to believe the world revolves around you, huh? Of course it does. You're a cat."

Lady Gray head-butted her hand, demanding Cass put that hand to good use and pet her, and Cass obliged. Later, after Cass turned in for the night, something jumped onto the bed. A furry face sniffed at her and a loud purr announced, *I'm here.*

Cass smiled. It was good to have company. Who needed a man, anyway?

Had Grant Masters kissed Muriel good-night?

CHAPTER ELEVEN

The weatherman was predicting unseasonably warm weather and several days without rain, so Saturday found Grant up on Cass's roof, Dan helping him pull off the old shingles. He'd hated to bug his son, since Saturday was normally Dan's day off, and he and Charley usually spent time together, but Dan had volunteered.

"Cass is a good friend. I don't mind helping. Anyway, you need me there to make sure you don't fall off the roof and break your neck," Dan had teased. "Besides, Charley's pooped and is planning to lie on the couch all day and watch the Food Network, so you might as well use me."

What the hell. He liked working with his son, always had. Dan had enjoyed building things ever since he got a toy hammer at the age of five. Both he and Matt had helped Grant with projects around the house when they were growing up and both had worked summers for him, learning the trade as they went. Until Matt decided he preferred the heat of the kitchen to the heat of the great outdoors. That worked for both Grant and Dan, as they'd often benefited from Matt's passion for cooking.

"I hear you had a hot date last night," Dan said as he tossed a handful of shingles into the rented Dumpster.

"Just dinner."

That about summed it up. Muriel Sterling was a beautiful woman and a beautiful soul. But the sparks hadn't exactly flown. She was sweet. Too sweet. So sweet she made his fillings hurt.

Talking with her had felt like reading some cheesy self-help book. When the subject of the loss of their spouses came up, she'd smiled—sweetly, of course—and said, "But isn't it comforting to know they're in a better place?"

No, actually, it wasn't.

"I think without the hard things in life, we never find out what we're made of."

He didn't want to know what he was made of.

"It's hard being alone, but I'm thankful I have my daughters and so many good friends. People talk about seeing the glass as half-full. When I look at my life, I see that glass as overflowing."

Gack.

Okay, it was good to have a positive attitude, but if he had to listen to that on a regular basis he'd probably climb Sleeping Lady Mountain and jump.

"Just dinner, huh?" Dan prodded.

"She's a nice woman. Not really my type. Anyway, it's best not to get involved with the local women." Back out of the pool.

"Yeah, you might decide you want to end up with one of them, like I did."

"Charley's one of a kind."

"She's got friends. Like Cass."

Grant shook his head. "Too young."

"Well, then, maybe it's time you came into the same century as the rest of us and tried some online dating."

Grant frowned. "Did your wife put you up to this?" Women couldn't stand to see a man single. What was that about, anyway?

"No. Well, we were talking."

"Find somebody for the old guy and get him out of your hair?" Grant joked.

"No. Hell, no. We just… Well, you know, Dad, it's been a while since…" He clamped his lips shut and threw some more shingles off the roof.

"I know."

"Mom would want you to be happy."

"I'm happy," Grant insisted. As long as he kept busy and didn't think about Lou and the life he'd lost when she died.

"Nobody's saying you have to run out and get married to-morrow, but you could at least have some fun."

"What? We're not having fun up here?"

"Oh, yeah. I like sweating on a hot roof," Dan said with a teasing grin. He sobered. "You should check it out. There's a whole bunch of sites out there for people your age."

"Old guys," Grant translated.

Dan ignored him. "Charley found a couple of them. One's called Mature Mates."

"Oh, yeah. That appeals to me." Not.

"Time to Connect?"

"Time to talk about something else." Mature Mates? Ugh.

Cass came home from the bakery to find Grant and Dan Masters up on her roof. Both men had their shirts off and were sweating. It had to be hot up there.

It was hot down here on the ground. Just looking at Grant Masters's broad shoulders and washboard abs got Cass feeling warm and toasty in all the right places. She didn't even want to guess what he thought of her. She'd ditched the hairnet as soon as she was done with work (not that it helped—sweating in a hot kitchen didn't do much for your hair's body and bounce) and she'd put on some lip gloss before leaving. But the grubby cut-offs and ratty T-shirt with a picture of a rolling pin on it weren't exactly high fashion. Neither was the caption on the shirt. This

Is How I Roll. Well, it was. She didn't have a high-fashion job and she wasn't a high-fashion dresser.

"Hey there, you two," she called. "How's it going?"

"Great," Dan called.

"You look like you could use a drink. How about some iced tea?"

"Oh, yeah. I'm ready for a break," Dan said and started down the ladder.

Cass hurried inside the house with the box of treats she'd brought home from work. Grant had told her he'd be over, so she'd come home, if not gorgeous, at least prepared.

As if gingerbread boys could compete with a beautiful woman. Still, she couldn't not feed someone who was sweating in the blazing sun on her behalf. She laid her offerings on a plate, then filled two glasses with ice and lavender iced tea, put everything on a tray and carried it out to where the two men now sat on the front steps.

"All right! Cookies," Dan said and scooped up one.

Grant took a long drink of his iced tea. "This is good."

"It's got lavender in it."

"A girl drink," Dan teased, but he downed most of his in one gulp.

"Yeah, I can see how much you hate that girl drink."

"Hey, I'm being polite. And I'm thirsty. How about some more?"

"You got it," she said and went to fetch the pitcher. By the time she returned, both Dan and Grant had drained their glasses.

"You gonna join us?" Dan asked as she poured refills.

"Maybe for a minute." She dropped into an Adirondack chair, all the while wishing she'd had a chance to pretty up. Why was it that when men got all sweaty and grubby, they looked sexier, while women just looked wilted?

A whiff of musky man drifted her way and sent her hormones

into a screaming fit. *Settle down, ladies. There's nothing happening here.* Darn.

"These are really good," Grant said and helped himself to another cookie.

"Everything Cass bakes is really good," Dan said, wolfing down the last of his second one. He took a third and started for the ladder.

"There's still one left," Cass said, just being polite, of course. No sneaky ploy to keep Mr. Masters on the step, talking longer. Oh, no.

He picked up the last cookie and took a bite. "You always liked to bake?"

"Oh, yeah."

"What made you decide to do it for a living?"

"I was a single mom. I had to do something and I was good at this."

"You still like doing it?"

"I do. People love what I bake and that boosts the old self-esteem. Heck, *I* like what I bake. Carbs and sugar, there's nothing better in the whole world. Well, except..." Sex. Sex, sex, sex! She censored herself before she could go further. Judging by the smile on his face, he'd known what she was about to say. Her cheeks suddenly felt as if she'd been leaning over a hot oven. "I spend way too much time with my girlfriends. I forget how to behave in polite company."

"Nobody's ever called me that before," he said.

"You seem polite."

"I can be good."

She suspected he could be bad, too. Sigh. Here she was at her sexual peak, and she had nobody to peak with.

He was regarding her curiously. *Interesting specimen, Cass Wilkes.* "You're still a young woman. Ever think about getting out there and dating?"

"In Icicle Falls? This isn't exactly Singles Central. What about you? You're single." *And I saw you having dinner with Muriel last night.*

He shrugged.

"Chicken."

"That's me. And on that note, I guess I'd better fly back up to the roof."

And maybe she'd fly up to the shower, change clothes, put on some perfume. Silly. He'd already seen her looking like Miss Frump of Icicle Falls. Still, she hated this current mess to be the last thing he saw.

And that matters because?

Because Dan had snagged his cookie and gone back to work but Grant had lingered. That had to be a sign of something.

Yeah. Politeness.

She needed a shower, anyway. So there.

And she felt much better after she'd gotten cleaned up. She dragged out a white blouse she'd had hanging in the closet since forever and pulled on a pair of stretchy jeans. They were supposed to be skinny jeans, but with thirty extra pounds, they were more like I-wish-I-was-skinny jeans. She blow-dried her hair and put on foundation, blush, eyeliner and mascara. Then she regarded herself in the mirror.

Wow. What a transformation. From pudgy, middle-aged, grubby woman to pudgy, middle-aged woman in clean clothes. She frowned. The woman in the mirror frowned back as if to say, "Don't blame me for your carb addiction."

"I'm not middle-aged," she told her reflection. "That doesn't come until fifty." Which meant old didn't come until about eighty. She could go with that.

Her new housemate sat on the bed, watching the transformation. "What do you think, Lady Gray? Add some jewelry?"

The cat blinked, hopped down and rubbed against her legs.

"So, you think I look good? I don't want to look like I'm trying too hard. Which I'm not, really. I just needed to get cleaned up." And she needed perfume.

Lady Gray kept twining around her legs and she picked the cat up. "I seriously doubt all this affection is without a hidden agenda. Want some food?"

The cat purred.

"Yeah, I don't blame you. I like to eat, too. But I'm not going to give you too much. Trust me, once you put it on, it's really hard to peel off."

She set the cat down and Lady Gray darted across the room in front of her, then led the way downstairs to the kitchen. Cass spooned some canned cat food into her dish, then took a couple of chicken breasts out of the freezer to thaw. That way she'd have something for tomorrow. Or maybe Grant would like a home-cooked meal. The least she could do was offer to feed him.

Except once he and Dan came down from the roof, she didn't. "I'll be back tomorrow," Grant promised, and it was on the tip of her tongue to ask him what he was doing for dinner.

But what was the point? He'd almost certainly be seeing Muriel Sterling.

"Come on, Dad. Admit you're interested," Dan had teased once they were back on the roof.

"No, I'm not," Grant had insisted. "Anyway, she's too young for me." Guys his age who took up with younger women were pathetic. What were they doing, trying to recapture their youth, prove their virility? He didn't have to prove anything.

"Nobody cares about that stuff these days," Dan had said.

"Well, they should," Grant had informed him, closing the subject.

That didn't keep thoughts of Cass Wilkes out of his mind, though.

She'd looked pretty cute in that stupid T-shirt. She'd looked even cuter once she'd cleaned up, and she'd smelled like a garden after a summer rain, all ripe and luscious and…

Okay, it had obviously been way too long since he'd been with a woman. He returned to his room at Gerhardt's, pulled out his laptop and went to the Mature Mates (*ugh*) site. There on the home page was a collage of faces, both male and female. All mature, yes, but all nice-looking, too. What the heck. It was worth a try.

The happy matchmakers of Mature Mates had made it easy for him. Right there on the home page was a box with a dropdown where he could state his sexual orientation and what he was looking for. He chose *man seeking a woman*, then entered the Icicle Falls zip code.

But he wasn't done. The site wanted his email address so the mature matchmakers could contact him if necessary. He hated getting spam.

No spam, the page assured him, and his email wouldn't be shared with anyone. That was good to know, since he already got more than enough emails offering him Viagra at a bargain price.

Anyway, the stupid site wasn't going to allow him in any further unless he gave it what it wanted. He entered his Hotmail account and the gate opened, letting him into the wonderful world of online dating. Well, almost. First he had to buy a Lover's Leap package. *An investment in your future.*

Okay, he could go month by month. That seemed like a fairly small investment to make.

Welcome to Mature Mates, the site told him. *We take your love life seriously.*

This was followed by a list of warnings and suggestions for how to proceed. First contact would be done through the site, and no one would see his email address. He was to share it only when he felt comfortable. Once things progressed he was cautioned to meet a potential mature mate in a safe, public place. In addition, he was cautioned not to give money to anyone who asked and to report such behavior immediately. Times had sure changed since the days when he was dating.

His internet matchmaker wanted to know what age range he was interested in.

Old enough to have listened to the Beatles' *White Album.* Young enough to want to take a mountain hike on a Sunday afternoon. He typed in *55–60.* No, make that sixty-two.

What was he looking for in a woman? He thought of Lou. Someone who was kind. And who liked to laugh. Wasn't that one of the most important things in life? Okay, and someone who enjoyed the outdoors. Maybe someone who'd like to keep him company at the river while he fished. Yeah, that would be good. Religious preferences? Well, he didn't want a druid. Someone who believed in God, yeah, but not someone who'd whack him over the head with her Bible if he got mad and swore. *Church okay,* he typed, *but not every Sunday.* That probably made *him* sound like a druid.

Now he had to put up his profile—his age, interests, general area where he lived. That was easy, except he sounded boring. *Semiretired, like to fish.* Was that all he could think to say about himself? He added that he liked Mexican food and sixties rock— and then gave up.

Next he needed to post a picture of himself. He didn't have a lot of pictures that weren't of him with Lou or the kids. He found one Dan had snapped of him in Mexico when the kids visited him last winter. He was seated in a restaurant, holding a beer. That would do.

He posted it, then hit Save.

Now what? Wait for someone to contact him? Go looking?

What the hell. He went looking. One woman seemed like a good candidate. Blond hair—going by the wrinkles, he could guess what color the roots were, and they weren't blond. But she had a nice smile, was slender and well dressed. She'd obviously been at some kind of party and was raising a wineglass in salute. *Here's looking at you, kid.*

He did the necessary follow-through and within a few minutes actually had a notification. *Someone wants to talk with you!*

The message was from the slender faux blonde. Hey, this was kind of fun. He opened it and read.

Someone wanted to talk, all right. *You've got a lot of nerve putting up a fake picture!*

What? "Fake picture, my ass," he growled and responded, *That's really me.*

A reply came back pronto. *Nice try, creep. George Clooney doesn't have a brother.*

George Clooney again! Why couldn't the guy have done something else for a living? Accountant, teacher, gigolo. Why did he have to pick actor and make that face so famous?

Grant typed back. *Trust me, that's really what I look like.*

No reply.

Now he had another notification. Someone new was interested. She'd sent an icon with a waving hand and had attached a message, as well. He stared at the profile picture. This woman had to be pushing eighty. He'd asked to get matched with women in their fifties and early sixties.

Mr. Clooney, I didn't know you were in the market. When did you get divorced? I'd love to help you heal your broken heart.

Oh, boy. He told the poor disillusioned woman that he'd made a mistake and was getting back together with his wife. Was this what online dating was going to be like?

Apparently, since he heard from women either promising not to reveal his true identity or threatening to report him for impersonating a celebrity. *And a married one at that,* scolded one woman. *You should be ashamed!*

Next thing he knew, his profile was taken down. The reason listed was fraud. *Applicants may not post fake pictures.*

He could almost hear Lou laughing as he slammed his laptop shut.

"Go ahead, laugh," he grumbled. "You're not stuck down here by yourself."

Maybe he needed to try a more personal approach. One of Lou's horseback-riding buddies came to mind. Last he'd heard, Kathy was divorced. She'd always been a lot of fun and she'd been extremely sympathetic at the celebration-of-life ceremony.

He searched out her number and gave her a call.

"Grant, it's good to hear from you. How are you doing?"

"Okay." He was still here, still functioning.

"I heard you went to Mexico."

"I did, but now I'm back."

"In Wenatchee?"

"Nearby. I'm in Icicle Falls."

"Practically in my backyard," she said cheerfully.

That sounded encouraging, so he plunged on. "I was wondering if you'd like to meet for a drink, talk about old times. If you're not busy." *If you're not remarried.*

"Sure. I just got in from a ride, though, and I need to clean up. How about meeting around seven?"

"Seven's good," he said, and they picked a restaurant. It had been one of Lou's favorites. "Hope you don't mind, babe," he said after he'd ended the call.

Mom would want you to be happy.

He hadn't been really happy since Lou died. He'd been okay. When he was with the boys, he was almost happy. But true happiness? He wasn't convinced he'd ever find that again. Still, he'd like to try. This hanging around at the edge of life was not very satisfying.

He showered and changed, then got in his truck and made the twenty-mile drive from Icicle Falls to Wenatchee. The place they were meeting was an alehouse with a relaxing atmosphere and great barbecue. He grabbed a table on the patio. If drinks went well, they could move on to dinner.

He'd already settled at the table with his beer when Kathy made her appearance. She looked as good as she always had—light brown hair about the color of Cass Wilkes's, stylish clothes showing off a trim figure. Muscular thighs, shaped by hours of gripping a saddle... "Grant, wonderful to see you!" She came up to him in a delicate cloud of perfume, arms outstretched, gave him a big hug. Not one of those modest hugs people used when they wanted to avoid full-body contact. Oh, now this was up close and personal, and it felt good.

"You look great," she told him.

"So do you. You haven't aged a day." He'd aged ten years the night Lou died.

She shook her head. "It gets harder and more expensive the older I get, let me tell you."

She slid into her seat and the waiter appeared instantly. "Dirty martini," she told him. "Extra olives." She pointed to Grant's glass. "Still only drinking beer. Boring," she teased.

"What can I say?"

"That's all right. We love you anyway."

Yes, and a couple of women in their circle of friends had flirted pretty heavily with him in an effort to prove it. Kathy had been another story. "Everyone wants you," she'd told him once at a party. "They can't help it, Grant. Women love gorgeous men. But we also love Lou and nobody would do anything to hurt her."

Yes, she'd been a good friend to both of them. Loyal and kind. She'd helped Grant plan the memorial and had hosted everyone at her house afterward.

"Tell me. What are you doing in Icicle Falls? Are you back to stay?"

"Yeah. Mexico was nice but it's not home."

"There's no place like home," she agreed. "Now, what are you up to?"

He told her about his new business and she listened as raptly as if he was imparting insider trading information.

"Sounds like a great idea," she said. "God knows there've been enough times after Hank and I split that I wished I had a handyman. There still are, as a matter of fact."

"So, there's nobody in your life?"

She shrugged. The waiter returned with her drink and she took a sip and sighed. "A great martini, best thing after a long ride."

Save a horse, ride a cowboy.

Grant told himself to cool it and drank some of his beer.

"The kids, of course," she said, getting back to the conversation. "Naturally they're busy with their own lives. Julie had a baby, so I'm a grandma now and I watch the baby a couple of times a week. And, to tell you the truth, that's about as exciting as my life gets these days. I miss Lou."

His throat suddenly felt tight. He nodded and took another pull from his beer.

The waiter was back now. "Would you folks like to order?"

Grant turned to Kathy. "How about it? Want some dinner?"

"Sure. Why not?"

Dinner was enjoyable. Kathy had another martini, Grant had another beer. They split a piece of carrot cake for dessert, and he remembered doing the same thing with Lou when she was alive. "All I want is a bite," Kathy said, and then, just like Lou always did, she ate half the cake.

"Look at me. What a pig. You should've taken the plate away," she scolded when they were done.

"I wouldn't dream of separating a woman from her cake."

She shook her head at him and smiled. "Anyway, I'm absolutely stuffed now. Thank you."

"My pleasure."

He paid the bill and they left the restaurant. Then they were in the parking lot next to her car, and all of a sudden, he was unsure what to do.

"I'm glad we did this, Grant," she said.

"Me, too." Now what? Should he hug her again? Kiss her? Ask her if she wanted to go out with him next week?

A kiss, he decided. A friendly let's-see-where-this-goes kind of kiss. He caught her hand, drew her a little closer—hmm, was she balking or was it his imagination?—and kissed her on the cheek.

She pulled back. He wasn't imagining that frown. "Grant, what was this about?"

I'm lonely? Horny? Pathetic? "Um."

"You're not thinking of dating, are you?"

"Well, the thought did cross my mind."

The frown turned to a full-fledged scowl. "Grant. Your wife is barely cold in her grave."

It had been three years. How cold did she have to get?

"You need to go back to Icicle Falls and think about what you're doing," she said sternly. Then she got in her SUV and gunned the engine.

Grant jumped back as she roared out of the parking slot, fearing for the safety of his feet. Then he stood there and watched her drive off, feeling both rejected and guilty.

"I don't know what I'm doing, Lou. Maybe it *is* too soon. Or maybe it's too late. I miss you. I miss our old life."

A couple of guys walked by and looked at him as if he was crazy.

Well, he was standing alone in a parking lot, talking to himself.

He got in his truck and drove back to Icicle Falls.

CHAPTER TWELVE

Matt called on Sunday morning, saving Grant from a horrible dream. He'd been out for dinner with a beautiful woman he'd met on Mature Mates, and all had been going well until he took her home.

Home was a white stucco mini-palace by a river with peacocks strutting on the vast lawn. There was a limo parked in the circular driveway and Tom Cruise, wearing a chauffeur's uniform, was waxing it.

"Want to come in for a nightcap?" asked Grant's date.

"Sure," he said and followed her down a long hallway to a huge room dominated by a rustic stone fireplace exactly the kind Grant wanted to have when he got around to buying a new place. Oil paintings hanging on the wall, a champagne bottle in an ice bucket by the couch. A silver tray on the coffee table with silver goblets. Of course, there was a fire crackling in that fireplace. It was the perfect setting for a man about to get lucky. And he was all primed to do just that.

Until the woman turned around and pulled off a rubber mask like the ones they always wore in those *Mission: Impossible* movies. Suddenly there stood someone else who looked even more like George Clooney than Grant, determined to pull off Grant's mask. The next thing Grant knew, he was fighting to keep his face attached to his skull.

"Aaah!"

Thank God the phone woke him before the woman could lop off his head. He grabbed it like a lifeline, pushed the receive button and croaked, "Hello."

"Hey, Dad. Did I wake you?"

"That's okay." It was more than okay.

"Just wanted to let you know I'm coming up to help you."

"Great."

"Dan and Charley and me are doing a house swap. They're gonna stay in my place for a couple of days and I'll stay in theirs and eat all their food. I should be up there around noon."

"Okay. I've got plenty for you to do."

"Sounds like it."

Grant gave his son Cass's address to put in his GPS, then said goodbye and got up. No way was he going back to sleep and giving his attacker another shot at him. It was time to get moving anyway.

An hour later, he was at her place, hoping to get a lot done before it was too hot.

It got hot pretty quickly when she came outside to weed, wearing shorts and a top that showed off cleavage whenever she bent over. An excellent view from the roof.

You're a letch, Grant scolded himself and turned his back so he couldn't see. Considering the last twenty-four hours, it was no wonder he had women on his mind. Weren't there supposed to be more women than men after a certain age? Where were they?

"Hey up there, you thirsty?"

He looked down to where she stood, holding a glass filled with ice and what appeared to be lemonade.

Yeah, he was thirsty. Hungry, too, for something he had no

business taking from a woman who was probably at least fifteen years younger than him.

Maybe she was older than she looked.

Right. And maybe pigs really did fly.

He came down the ladder and took the glass.

"I feel bad about you having to be up there in the heat," she said.

He was in heat down here, too. The sun had put a blush on her cheeks and her skin was glistening with a fine film of sweat from working in the yard. She had a few gray hairs hidden in among the brown ones. Nothing fake about Cass Wilkes. A natural woman. A too-young natural woman.

"So how's it going?" she asked.

"I should have all the old shingles off by the end of the day. Then I'll get your ice and water barrier and the asphalt felt down and start putting on the new shingles next week. Looks like the weather's going to hold for us."

"I can't tell you what a relief it is to get this done."

"Definitely needed it. You had some serious rotting in your sheath."

"Nothing worse than a rotting sheath, I always say."

He liked this woman's sense of humor. "Me, too." He drank the last of the lemonade and handed her back the glass. "Thanks."

"You're welcome. I've got to keep you hydrated. I can't have my roofer getting sunstroke and falling off. I'm not sure I could catch you."

A sudden vision of landing on top of Cass Wilkes invaded his brain. *Don't go there. Get back up on the roof.*

Yeah, the view's better up there, especially when she bends over.

Okay, he was out of control. He needed to rein himself in. He hurried up the ladder and got back to work, instructing himself not to look down. Hard to avoid it, though. She'd moved to the edge of the lawn and was bending over, pulling weeds from under a rhododendron bush. That was one well-rounded butt.

"Hey, Dad!"

Grant gave a start. Matt's Jeep was parked out on the street and he was walking across the lawn. When had he pulled up?

"About time you got here," Grant called and climbed down the ladder.

Cass walked over and they all converged at the side of the house.

"Cass, this is my son Matt. He's going to be helping me on his days off."

"I think we met in Vegas at Dan and Charley's wedding," said Cass. "Nice to see you again."

Of course. Duh.

"Same here," Matt said. "Sorry I'm late," he told Grant. "My neighbor was having car problems."

That was Matt, always ready to give anyone a hand. "That's okay. There's still plenty left to do," Grant said. "I need you to take on some painting tomorrow, but first you can help me get the last of this old roof off."

"It's way past lunchtime. You're probably getting hungry," Cass said. "Want a sandwich before you go back up there?"

No, he wanted to stay away from temptation.

"That'd be great," Matt said. "I haven't eaten since nine."

"A lifetime," Grant joked.

"Hey, it is when you have a fast metabolism," Matt shot back.

"I wouldn't know about that, darn it all," Cass quipped, then went inside the house.

"Come on," Grant said, walking toward the ladder.

"But she's gonna feed us."

"You can work while you're waiting."

"I forgot what a slave driver you are," Matt teased, but followed him back up the ladder.

"So, you seeing her or something?" he asked once they were up on the roof.

"No. Why?"

"Just wondering. The way you two were looking at each other, I thought maybe you had something going."

"Nothing going. Not interested."

"You seemed pretty interested in her ass when I drove up."

"You need to mind your own business," Grant informed him and he laughed.

Ten minutes later, Cass had ham sandwiches for them, as well as potato salad, chips and more lemonade.

"This hits the spot. Thanks," Matt said. "Good potato salad," he added, talking around a mouthful.

"One of my specialties," she told him. "I like to cook."

"Yeah? Me, too. Dad here got me started. Breakfasts on Sundays, right, Dad?"

"Yep," Grant said. "We were the waffle kings." Sunday mornings had been special, unhurried. Family time. On Easter, Lou dragged them all to church and they went out for brunch afterward, but the kids had liked breakfast at home the best. So had he.

"What do you do now?" Cass asked Matt.

"Head chef at Salmon Run in Seattle. Someday I want to follow in Charley's footsteps and have my own place, maybe something with a Northwest-Asian fusion."

"Sounds good. I'll be your first customer." Cass smiled and he saluted her with his glass.

"She's sure nice, Dad," Matt said after they got back to work.

"Yeah, she is."

"You oughta ask her out."

"Have you, by any chance, been talking to your brother?"

"No."

Grant knew when he was lying. "You two need to quit pushing. I'm not in the market for a woman."

Last night's fiasco with Kathy had been strike three. He was out of the game. He'd never find anything like what he'd had with Lou anyway.

Matt shrugged. "Okay, but this one seems pretty cool."

She was, but Grant wasn't going there, no matter what his libido wanted.

"Just sayin', Dad."

"Yeah, well, you've said enough."

Matt dropped the subject, and they worked in silence for another hour. But then Griffin came up the street, dressed for a warm spring day in a pair of shorts and a flowery top, and his assistant suddenly forgot about replacing rotten wood.

"Who's that?"

"One of the women I'm helping."

"Please tell me she's got the house I need to paint."

"She does."

"Sweet."

"She just broke up with her fiancé."

"Was he brain-dead or something?"

"I don't know the details, but I do know she's not planning on staying here. And is your divorce final yet?"

"Almost."

"Well, you might want to wait before you go rushing into anything. You'd both be on the rebound."

Matt had apparently gone deaf and was already moving toward the ladder.

If the timing had been different, Griffin and his son would have been perfect for each other, but right now this was just what neither of them needed. Rebound romances never worked. And who was the idiot who'd thought it was a good idea to bring Matt up here?

"Somebody kick me," Grant muttered.

Griffin took one look at the man walking toward her and forgot why she'd come over to Cass's.

"I'll go get that book for you," Cass said with a wink.

"Book?" *What book?* "Oh, yes. Thanks."

Cass grinned and disappeared inside the house.

Before she came over, Griffin had been feeling a little lonely, actually missing Steve. This newcomer was enough to wipe all thoughts of Steve from her hard drive. Unlike her ex, who had gotten sloppy and out of shape, this man was fit and beautiful. He smelled spicy, and his smile... Well, that in itself was enough to turn her all soft and melty.

"Hi, I'm Matt," he said. "I'm up here to help my dad."

"Mr. Masters is your dad?" They didn't really look much alike. Same square chin and big eyes, but while his father was dark and swarthy, Matt's coloring leaned more toward fair, and his hair was light brown.

"Yeah, I was adopted."

She blinked. What to say to that?

"Just kidding," he said. "I like to mess with people 'cause I don't look much like him. I look more like my mom."

"Your mom must've been beautiful." Oh, no. Did she say that out loud? Judging from his amused expression, she had. Her face felt instantly sunburned.

"If we're gonna talk beautiful, you've got the market cornered."

Now her face was truly flaming.

"I could use some help up here," Grant called.

"Guess I'd better get back to work," Matt said. "But I'll see you tomorrow. Dad's sending me over to paint your place."

"That'll be great." On so many levels.

"What time can I come over?"

Anytime. "Um, does nine work?"

"Sure." He gave her one last smile and then went back to join his dad.

Griffin stood for a moment, watching him. He sure knew how to make jeans and a T-shirt look sexy. Was he with anyone?

She hurried into the house, anxious to pump Cass for information. She found her friend in the kitchen, making iced coffee.

"So, what do you think of Matt?" Cass said casually. "As if I have to ask."

"He seems really nice."

"Pretty cute, too," Cass offered. She handed Griffin a glass.

"Yeah, he is. What do you know about him?"

"Nothing, other than that he's Grant's son. I'm afraid you'll have to pump him for info yourself. Such a hard job." Cass winked. "One thing I'd be willing to bet—he's a step up from your ex."

Griffin took the drink and settled at Cass's kitchen table. "I was thinking about Steve this morning, wondering if I made the right decision."

Cass joined her there, her expression serious now. "Are you having doubts, chickadee?"

Griffin shook her head. "Not really. I think I miss the idea of Steve more than I miss him. Is that terrible?"

"Not at all. It means you did make the right decision."

"Sometimes I feel lonely in that house all by myself."

"I get that," Cass said. "But it won't go on forever. You'll be moving soon and making new friends, filling your life with new adventures. And I don't see you going through life without a man. You want to make sure you're with the right one, though."

Griffin nodded. "Whoever I wind up with, I want it to last. And you know, I really don't think it would have with Steve. I need more than what we had. And he needs... Well, I'm not sure what he needs."

Actually, she did know. He needed a gamer, someone who'd happily get sucked into that other world with him. She preferred the world of words and art and imagination. He loved the one of reflex and visual stimulation. Pictures and loud sound effects versus words and quiet. Side-by-side interaction versus face-to-face. Toward the end, it had become increasingly challenging to make those two worlds meet.

A gray cat wandered into the kitchen and rubbed against Cass's legs.

Here was a new addition. Griffin noticed the divided dish on the floor with water and a few crumbs of cat food. "You got a cat!"

"Yes, I did." Cass picked up the kitty and it began to purr. "This is Lady Gray, my new housemate."

Griffin reached across the table and petted the cat, who leaned her head into Griffin's hand. "She's beautiful."

"Yes, she is. And she's good company. Much easier to deal with than a man," Cass joked.

"I think I'd still like to have one, though. A man, I mean."

"Of course you would. And you'll find your match. You're young and talented and beautiful. Once you get to New York they'll be lining up. In fact, it looks like the line might be starting in Icicle Falls."

She and Matt had been vibing, that was for sure. But vibes alone didn't mean anything. Way back when she and Steve first got together, there'd been vibes aplenty. She wanted more. She wanted friendship. She wanted... Mr. Darcy, Rhett Butler, Edward from *Twilight*. No, even more than that, she wanted a best friend, a soul mate. Catherine in *Wuthering Heights* had said it all. "Whatever our souls are made of, his and mine are the same." Sigh. Okay, so theirs hadn't been the healthiest relationship in literature, but still...

"Meanwhile, this book might help you," Cass said, sliding Muriel Sterling's book across the table. "I know for a fact it helped Bailey sort things out when she came back here, and let me tell you, she had a lot to sort out."

Griffin had been planning to buy this book. She picked it up and studied it. *New Beginnings*, the gold embossed title promised. The cover was simple and elegant—a single red rose stood out against a blurred black-and-white garden.

"Thank you." Griffin reached into her shorts pocket for money.

"Don't even think about it," Cass said. "I told you, this is a gift."

"That's really kind of you."

"I thought so. Seriously, I hope it makes a difference. One thing I know for sure—I wish I'd had something like it when I was suddenly single. I found my way, but it was hard at first. Life would've been easier if I'd had a plan to begin with."

"I'm going to start reading it this afternoon." Griffin polished off her drink. Then she stood up and gave the purring cat in Cass's arms a final pet. "See you later, Lady Gray."

"Happy reading," Cass said.

Yes, happy reading, indeed. She was about to carve out a whole new life for herself.

In a big city, where her mother was sure she'd get mugged.

Of course, Mom would've said the same thing about any city in America. She hadn't been happy when Griffin and Steve had moved to Seattle. As far as her mother was concerned, there was no place like home.

Maybe not, but Icicle Falls came close.

Griffin shaded her eyes and looked up to where Matt and his father were working on the roof. He caught her looking, smiled and waved. "See you tomorrow!"

Tomorrow, yes. She went back to her house, feeling not quite so lonely. True, it was quiet and seemed too big for only her. But it was also quiet enough to read, listen to music, do whatever she wanted, and that was a good thing.

She walked past the couch. Nobody sitting there now. The TV was silent. No booms and crashing, yelling avatars. Steve was surely on another couch at this very moment, shooting virtual machine guns and driving virtual tanks.

Her cell phone pinged with a text from him. Her heart

sank. He was still hoping they'd get back together. He needed to move on. She read the text.

What I said earlier about getting together...

Oh, no. Poor Steve.

Never mind. I met someone.

Guilt and pity turned into irritation. He sure hadn't waited very long for her to change her mind. What kind of true love was that?

Already? she texted back. Okay, that was mature. And more than a little selfish.

Yeah. Guess you were right to break up.

Guess she was. She told herself that at least she didn't have to feel guilty over hurting him anymore. Still, she couldn't help feeling a little...rejected, which wasn't exactly rational.

She shook her head in disgust, texted Steve that she was happy for him, then took her book out onto the back porch and sat down to read.

The first chapter was titled "Death of a Dream." That sounded depressing. She had to force herself to read on. The subtitle was better.

"Death in Winter, Growth in Spring."

Okay, that sounded more encouraging.

A garden is God's constant reminder to us that we live in a world of change, a world of birth, death and rebirth. What happens to us is often exactly like what happens in our gardens. Winter comes and the garden dies.

Hopefully she was past the dead-garden stage.

It's the same with our lives. We plan for certain things and hope for positive outcomes, dream big dreams, only to see our plans crumble and our dreams die.

Yikes! That was depressing!

You may be mourning the death of a dream, but you don't have to mourn without hope. Like a flower in winter experiencing a period of dormancy, use this time to heal and gather strength for spring, when a new dream will crop up.

That was better. She kept reading as Muriel gave examples of women who had rebuilt their lives after disappointment. Surprisingly, one of them was Cass.

When Cass Wilkes came to my town, she was newly divorced with three small children and no idea what the rest of her life would look like.

Griffin read on as Muriel detailed how Cass had found her way, starting out with little but eventually buying her own business. It was inspiring. So were the other stories Muriel shared. Some of the women, like Dot Morrison, Griffin knew; others she didn't. All the stories had one thing in common. Each woman had created a vision for her life and gone for it.

Griffin reached the next chapter. "What Now?"

"What do you really want?" Muriel asked. "What would most fill you with joy? To move forward, you need to know the answer to these two questions."

What did she want? Success?

Not necessarily. What Griffin wanted went deeper than that.

She wanted a meaningful life. She wanted to do something and do it well. Perhaps success was the proof of that?

One thing she knew for sure—she needed to get out there and really experience life, not always pick what was safe. And if that meant going to New York, then that was what she'd do.

She thought of the hunky man up on Cass's roof. Where did he fit into the picture?

He didn't, of course. She couldn't let herself be distracted by a man with big muscles and a big smile.

CHAPTER THIRTEEN

It looked as if a truce had been called in the Stahl renovation war. Brad was still a little sulky, but that hadn't kept him from accepting the offer of Saturday-night sex. Of course, it helped that they'd had a nice day. Petey'd had an afternoon ball game and afterward all the parents had taken their hyped-up little ballplayers to Italian Alps, the number one pizza destination in Icicle Falls. The team hadn't won, but the boys had been distracted from their loss by the promise of food.

It was easy to distract boys of all ages, Stef thought as the family made their way to church the next morning. Cinnamon rolls from a package (okay, baking wasn't her thing), eggs and a cup of strong coffee started the day off right, and that—coupled with the knowledge that her house was getting pulled together—put Stef in a good mood.

But after church someone asked her how things were coming with the house and she made a tactical misstep.

"Great," she said. "The wall's knocked out and the old floor's all ripped up. My new flooring gets laid this week. Something's finally getting done."

"Something's *finally* getting done?" Brad challenged as they returned to the car. "Something was already getting done before Masters came along."

"Well, now it's getting done right." She realized she'd stepped on a land mine practically the second the words were out of her mouth. "You know what I mean."

"Yeah, I do."

They got in the car and Brad slammed the door. He started the engine and threw the car into gear. "Do you have any idea how that makes me feel?"

"Do you have any idea how I've felt with you tearing everything apart and leaving it like that?"

"I was going to get it done." Brad's jaw was clenched so tightly it was a wonder he managed to get the words out.

This would be the time to say something consoling, defuse the situation. But why should she be the one to do it? He'd created the problem. "Then why didn't you?" she demanded.

"I was doing research."

"Research in how to procrastinate," she muttered.

"Daddy, are you mad at Mommy?" Petey asked in a small voice.

This was not exactly setting a good example for their son. And it was hardly following the advice the minister had shared in his sermon. *Remember, a soft answer turns away wrath. God commands us to be kind to one another. Now, you may not always feel kindly toward each other, but you still need to act kindly.*

"Daddy's fine," she lied. "And Mommy's sorry." Well, not really, but she hoped this counted as acting kindly.

Now Brad was the one muttering. "Mommy should be."

Wait a minute. How did she become the villain in this story? "So should Daddy," she said, turning her voice to syrup and giving him a sour smile. Maybe they should've stayed home from church. The sermon had been wasted on them.

Once inside the house, she sent Petey off to wash his hands for lunch and started for the kitchen, Brad following behind. As they walked through the great room in progress, he observed that her handyman hadn't been around for the last couple of days. Underlying message—See? He's not doing any better than I was.

Right. The wall was down and that all-important beam was up to keep the house from caving in, and the old flooring was completely gone. Soon the new one would be in.

"He's been at Cass's, doing her roof," said Stef. "Anyway, the great room is still getting done faster than it would be if we were doing it ourselves." *We*, as in they were both in this together, nothing accusatory. Just a statement of fact.

"I could've finished it and we'd actually have had an income tax return to spend on a vacation this year."

"I'd rather have my house back." Stef pulled out her panini maker. "Anyway, we can have a staycation this year. There's plenty to do in Icicle Falls."

Petey was back now, so they dropped the subject and her two men got busy setting the table while she made lunch. The meal wasn't exactly filled with warmth and conversation, unless it was Brad talking with Petey. After lunch cleanup, he took their son outside to play catch. Then he washed the car with his little shadow helping him. Then he went down to his man cave to watch a ball game and stuff himself and his son with chips and peanuts and pop. Definitely a male-bonding Sunday, which would've been fine except for the fact that Daddy hadn't said one word to Mommy all afternoon. Mid-May temperatures might've been warming in Icicle Falls, but here in the Stahl house, the atmosphere was definitely experiencing a cooling trend.

She fed the boys pizza and a tossed salad for dinner, then left for the chick-flick gathering at Cass's. "'Bye, Mommy!" Petey sang happily as Brad put in a Pixar movie for him.

Brad said nothing.

She fumed her way down the street to Cass's house. Brad was being a jerk; that was all there was to it. He should've been relieved that she'd let him off the hook for finishing up this latest renovation disaster. It would get done, and he'd have more time to enjoy life. Men were always joking about how illogical women were. Well, they weren't the only ones. Here was a fine example of a complete lack of logic.

She arrived at Cass's to find the rest of the guests already there. Samantha Preston and her sisters, Cecily and Bailey, were all present, and Bailey had brought along the usual batch of lavender cookies, her specialty. The Sterling family supplied chocolate for every party and event, but not on movie nights. On these nights, the fare was typical movie treats—Junior Mints, Milk Duds and Good & Plenty—and Cass had already set them out on the coffee table in festive Fiestaware bowls, together with her ever-popular Parmesan popcorn. Charley Masters was there, along with her new server Melody, and both were curled up in easy chairs and had already had their bowls filled.

"Good, the root beer has arrived," Cass said, taking the bottle Stef handed over. "Now we can make our floats."

"Yay! I love floats," Melody enthused.

"Add some chocolate syrup to mine," Charley requested.

"Gross," said Bailey. "That's so wrong."

"Hey, I'm pregnant. My taste buds are expanding," Charley retorted. Then added, "Right along with my waist."

"Enjoy it," Samantha told her. "It's the one time you can eat like a pig with no guilt."

"I do that anyway," Bailey gloated and grabbed one of her cookies.

"So, how's the reno going?" Charley asked Stef.

"We're really making progress now," Stef said. She was about to add that Brad wasn't appreciating it, but Charley made a comment about how good her father-in-law was, which put the conversation on a new track, with a discussion about how well his business was doing and how popular he was.

"There's a real need for someone like that," Cecily observed.

"I bet home repairs aren't the first need the women who call him are thinking about," Samantha said.

"Probably not," Cecily agreed. "He isn't with anybody, is he?" she asked Charley.

Cass was back now, bearing a tray of glasses filled with ice cream and foamy root beer. One was drizzled with chocolate.

"Oh, that does look good," Bailey said, eyeing it.

"Mine," Charley joked as she took her glass.

"I'll get the syrup," Cass said.

"So, *does* he have someone?" Cecily asked, returning them to the subject at hand.

"No. He's been widowed for three years now, and Dan's been after him to start dating."

Cass was back in the room, and Cecily looked at her speculatively. And what was this? Cass was blushing. Was there some interest on her part?

"Do you picture him with anyone here in town?" Charley asked her.

Cecily had a reputation as a matchmaker. She'd done it for a living before she moved back to Icicle Falls. Everyone followed her gaze to Cass, whose cheeks were even redder now.

"Don't look at me. I've got a cat," she said and picked up her new pet. "We don't need a man, do we, Lady Gray?"

"Grant's a great guy," Charley persisted.

"It's a shame he's so ugly, though," Samantha said, straight-faced, and the others giggled.

Cass shrugged. "I think he's interested in your mom."

"Mom? She's still got a shrine to Waldo in her bedroom," Samantha scoffed.

"Anyway, I don't see them together," Cecily said.

"You may not, but I did," Cass muttered.

"Where?" Samantha wanted to know.

"They had dinner at the restaurant on Friday," Charley said.

"I'd be surprised if anything comes of it," said Cecily.

"How about we watch the movie," Cass suggested. "I found a real classic, in honor of Stef," she added with a grin.

The Money Pit with Tom Hanks and Shelley Long was an old romantic comedy chronicling the adventures of a couple fixing up a home in desperate need of some TLC. Stef would've laughed a lot more if she hadn't been so upset with her husband.

"So, could you identify?" Cass asked her as the credits rolled.

"Oh, yeah," she said and left it at that.

Petey was in bed when she got home and Brad was in his man cave, where all was in order. No renovations needed down there in Man Land. She didn't see him again that night.

Matt showed up at Griffin's house on Monday morning, wearing torn jeans and a faded brown T-shirt. His grubby painting clothes somehow made her think of Steve and the slobby outfits he'd favored. Except Steve hadn't looked this good. Yes, he'd been thin when they first met, but he'd never been sculpted with pecs and biceps that promised he'd be able to carry her to bed. She never would have asked him. That would've ended with him dropping her or spraining something. Matt Masters looked like he could pick her up with one arm and not even break a sweat.

"Hey there," he greeted her. "How's it going?"

Great now.

"Dad says he left the stuff for masking off the windows on the back porch."

"He did," she said and led him through the house.

"Nice place," he said. He took in the broken step. "That could use some help."

"I think your dad was going to get to it."

"I can take care of it for you."

He could probably take care of a lot of things for her, things that had nothing to do with the house. She flashed on an image of him scooping her up in his arms and carrying her upstairs. Just like Rhett did with Scarlett.

She banished the image from her head by reminding herself that he was only there to paint. Maybe it was a good thing Beth had asked her to take more pictures that morning. The less she was around this man, the better.

He motioned to her hand. "What'd you do?"

"I broke my wrist."

"Doing what?"

She grimaced. "I fell off the ladder when I was trying to paint my living room. I know—it was stupid," she hurried on.

"Not as stupid as falling off a skateboard," he said. "Did that when I was sixteen. My brother was towing me behind his car."

She could feel her eyes getting big.

"It was on a back road and he wasn't going that fast. Dad grounded us anyway." Matt smiled at the memory. "Threatened to keep us grounded until our frontal lobes grew together. You do dumb shit when you're young."

Like getting engaged to the wrong man.

"So, how long do you have to wear the cast?"

"Until next month. I can hardly wait to get it off. It's so clunky." But at least she could still take pictures. And Beth continued to be pleased with her work.

Beth! She needed to get going. "I have to leave."

"Work?" he guessed.

She nodded. "I'm a photographer."

"Yeah? What kind?"

He seemed genuinely interested. Unlike Steve, who'd never quite understood her fascination, especially if she cooked something that turned out well and wanted to get a shot. "Quit screwing around and let's eat," he'd say. Her best shots were always taken at someone else's house.

"I'm a food photographer," she said.

"Seriously?"

Was he about to mock her? "Seriously."

"Sweet."

That comment made her smile. "One of the women here in town has done a cookbook, and she wants pictures of some of her dishes."

"Yeah?" Now he really seemed interested. "What's on the menu today?"

"Something called apple stir-fry."

"Sounds interesting. I want to hear all about it when you get back."

And she didn't think he was saying that just to be polite. She promised full details, then loaded her camera and lenses and her valise of food-styling tools and left for Beth's house.

"I thought I should wait until you got here to make it," Beth said as she let Griffin in. "I picked up the canned frosting like you asked. And I have a ton of powdered sugar."

Those would be combined to simulate ice cream—no worries about it melting like the real stuff would.

Griffin got busy putting together the faux ice cream, while Beth worked on the dessert. Apple stir-fry consisted of apples sautéed in butter and cinnamon, along with chopped walnuts and raisins.

"It's like apple pie, only faster since you don't have to deal with the crust," Beth said as she poured in a little water. Next came some cornstarch for thickening. "There we go. We're ready."

"Almost," Griffin said and added some food coloring to the mixture.

For this shot Griffin selected a thick soda fountain–style sundae dish from Beth's seemingly endless supply of dishes. She artfully scattered apples (sprayed with oil for extra shine) around it.

"It looks great," Beth said approvingly.

It did, and Griffin got some good shots. There was still something missing, though. "We need a person in this shot."

"Don't point that camera at me," Beth said, horrified.

"At some stage we'll want to take a picture of you. For your author photo."

Beth frowned. "I never thought of that."

"Most celebrity cookbooks have a picture of the chef on the cover," Griffin pointed out.

"I'm no celebrity."

"You will be around here," Griffin said, making Beth roll her eyes.

"Well, we can deal with that later. Meanwhile, I guess my apple stir-fry will have to be the lone star of the shot. Too bad your friend Stef's little boy is in school. He'd be ideal."

Griffin thought for a moment. There was no little boy handy, but she knew a big one who'd probably be willing to help them out. "I think I have someone who'd be almost as good." She'd bet her camera that he was photogenic. Hopefully, he wouldn't upstage the dessert. "I'll be right back," she said and hurried home.

Matt was busy covering her windows with heavy plastic sheets when she arrived. "That was quick," he said.

"Actually, I'm not done. I need you for a minute."

He cocked an eyebrow. "Only a minute?"

The double entendre sent heat racing up her neck. "Well, maybe a little longer. Would you be open to being in a picture?"

"Eating food?"

"You won't want to eat this, although it *looks* yummy. Anyway, this shouldn't take too long."

"It's your dime," he said and climbed down the ladder.

Minutes later they were back at Beth's. "Here's our model," Griffin said and introduced him.

"Perfect," Beth said with an approving nod. "Apples and an all-American male. That'll make a great photo."

"I'm not exactly dressed up," he said, indicating his faded shirt.

"All the better," Griffin said. "It'll look more natural."

Adding Matt to the picture made all the difference. They positioned him behind the dessert and he needed no coaxing to act as if he was ready to dig in.

"Oh, yes, I love it," Beth said as Griffin showed her the pictures on the camera's screen. "Thanks for being willing to help us out," she said to Matt.

"Anything to do with food, I'm on it," he said.

"How about some of this with real ice cream?" Beth offered.

"Oh, yeah. Twist my arm," he said, rubbing his hands together.

"And you, Griffin? Can I tempt you with just a little?"

"How about a cup of tea instead," Griffin suggested.

"I'll eat her share," Matt said with a grin.

And he did. "I don't know how you could eat all that and not get sick," Griffin said when they finally walked back to her car.

"I don't know how you could not eat any of it."

She shrugged. "I'm not a big eater."

"You seem more like a not-at-all eater. Man, I couldn't live like that. I love food."

"Do you like to cook?"

"I'd better. It's what I do for a living."

"Really?"

"Yeah. I work at Salmon Run. It's a restaurant in Seattle. Ever hear of it?"

She shook her head. "Is it expensive?"

"Depends on what you call 'expensive.'"

"Anything that's not fast food. I'm on a budget."

"Your budget probably wouldn't take you too far at my restaurant. But good food well done, that's worth the price."

She smiled. "That almost sounds like a slogan."

"Maybe someday, when I have my own place, it will be."

"You must be pretty good in the kitchen to be talking about having your own place," she said.

"I am. I'm pretty good in other parts of the house, too," he added. Her cheeks flushed and he chuckled.

Where had this man been all her life?

What did it matter? She wasn't going to be around. He lived

in Seattle and soon she'd be living in New York. It would be dumb to start something at this point.

In spite of her advice to herself, when he offered to hang around and show her what a good cook he was, she wound up taking him up on it. "Kind of hard to cook for yourself one-handed, isn't it?" he asked.

It wasn't as though she was crippled, but, yes, it *was* awkward. So of course it made sense for him to stay and help her with all that cutting and chopping.

"If you're not too tired." Even though he'd used a paint gun and a compressor to spray paint the house, it had been a long day.

"I'm never too tired for food," he assured her.

Well, okay, then. "Maybe I'll blog about it," she said.

"People still do that?" he teased.

"They do if they're hoping to build a following and promote their photos."

He pulled his cell phone from his back pocket. "What's your website?"

"Food and Fun."

"That's something I need to bookmark." He brought it up and she looked over his shoulder as he navigated the site. Standing that close, she could catch the faintest hint of what was left of his aftershave. It mixed with the musky scent of sweat and suddenly she was thinking about sex.

Stop it, she scolded and forced herself to concentrate on the images in front of her. He was now on the recipe page, where she occasionally shared some of her mom's favorites, along with entries about interesting kinds of food she'd read about and then prepared. "'What is syllabub?'" he read, checking out one of her older entries. "Yeah. What the heck *is* syllabub?"

"It's an old English dessert made with whipped cream, sherry and sugar, often infused with lemon. Most people have never heard of it. You see it mentioned a lot in Regency romances."

"I guess that would explain why I've never heard of it. Sounds good, though. Looks good, too," he said, pointing to the picture. "You took that, of course."

She nodded. "I had some friends over for dinner and made it." Stef and Brad had enjoyed it, but Steve had sneered at it, pronouncing it too girlie.

Matt moved on to the section she'd titled "People and Parties." Here she'd posted shots of friends enjoying food at various gatherings—fried chicken, chocolate cake, cherry pie. There was a picture of slices of watermelon piled on a plate with little Serena Goodman eyeing it eagerly. Another shot had been taken at one of her book-club meetings, and she'd taken a picture of an open book lying next to a cup of eggnog residing in one of Stacy's vintage Christmas cups. One of the things she loved about pictures, she thought, was that they kept special moments with you forever.

"These are good," Matt said. "Really good."

Compliments about her work were as satisfying as the richest piece of chocolate. This one was doubly satisfying coming from a chef. She smiled and thanked him.

"Time for a new blog post," she said. "Maybe I'll do a piece about being a one-handed cook and take some pictures of the help." It would be no hardship taking pictures of Matt, that was for sure.

They went to the store together, and it was fun strolling through the various departments, picking out the makings for a perfect spring meal.

"Beer or wine?" he asked.

"Wine," she decided, and he picked out one that was moderately priced but much more than she would've spent.

"Don't worry," he said as if reading her mind. "I'm paying."

"That wouldn't be right."

"Sure it would. I'm the one who invited myself for dinner."

Back home again, they got to work, starting with a spinach salad, to which they added finely sliced pears, sunflower seeds and cherry tomatoes along with fresh cilantro. She took several shots of him working, smiling over his shoulder at her. A smile like that could drop a woman's panties at twenty paces. She took more pictures of him. She also captured their salad up close and personal.

He fired up the ancient barbecue she'd bought at a garage sale when she first moved to town and they barbecued chicken. He made an Asian glaze for it with soy sauce, sesame oil, fresh ginger and red pepper flakes. A baguette instead of brown rice (which he claimed was boring without saffron) and the white wine they'd picked up completed the feast. They settled on her back porch, and she captured that moment, too.

"Nice," he said when she showed him the pictures. "Here, let me take one."

She handed him the camera and he snapped a shot of her sitting there with her plate balanced on her lap, a forkful of salad raised in salute. He caught a piece of spinach in midfall and showed her, and she grinned. "You're pretty good at this yourself."

"It's easy when you've got a great subject," he said, making her cheeks sizzle. "You're cute when you blush," he added, and of course that made her cheeks flame all the more. The curse of fair skin. He gave her a break and changed the subject. "Next time I come up, I'm gonna fix that step for you before I get started on the trim."

"Thank you! My ex was always going to fix it and never got around to it."

"So things didn't work out, huh?"

"No, they didn't."

"How come?"

"We grew apart. It was nobody's fault, really. I think we were just too young when we got together." She sighed and tossed the piece of bread he'd torn off for her back on her plate. "Have you ever been with somebody who you thought was...well, right, and then that person turned out not to be?"

"My divorce is final at the end of this month, so I guess the answer would have to be yeah."

"I'm sorry."

"It's been hard. I wanted what my folks had, thought she'd be the one to have it with. You think you know someone, and that you're going to have such a great life together, and then somewhere along the way it's not so great anymore, and you realize you didn't know as much as you thought you did."

It sounded like her life with Steve.

"It about killed me when she left."

"Sometimes it isn't working," Griffin said and realized that she wasn't defending Matt's former wife as much as herself.

"Yeah, I guess. You can't keep trying to build a house on a bad foundation. When it came down to it, we wanted different things." He shook his head. "I don't know why I couldn't see it before. Maybe because when we first got together we had a lot of fun. It felt...right. This probably sounds hokey but I thought we were soul mates."

Griffin understood that. "Same with Steve and me," she said sadly. "We seemed to have so much in common at first. We did all kinds of stuff together. But then I looked up one day and realized we were facing different directions."

Matt polished off the last of his wine. "My dad said I was rushing things. I guess he was right."

What about this cozy dinner? Did it put them at the starting gate for a fresh race into a new relationship? Of course it did. Here she'd just broken up with her fiancé and Matt's divorce wasn't even final yet. She could only imagine what Grant Masters would have to say about this. Suddenly she didn't have much appetite. She moved her plate away.

He began to freshen her wine, but she shook her head and covered the glass. "I think I'm done."

"Oh." He blinked in surprise. "Okay."

She got up and went into the kitchen, put her plate in the sink.

He followed her in. "Did something go wrong out there?"

"No, it's, well… Maybe we shouldn't start something we can't finish."

"You saying it's too soon?"

"More like it's too late. I'm getting the house ready to sell. I'm moving."

"Where?" He still looked hopeful.

"New York."

Not so hopeful now. "New York, huh?"

"I want to see if I can get something going there."

"As a food photographer?"

She nodded.

"You can do that anywhere, can't you?"

"That's what my mother says. She'd prefer it if I moved back home. But everyone has a website, everyone has stock photos. If I'm going to succeed, I need to go to where the business is. All the big food stylists are there, all the big food commercial directors, the big magazines and publishers. I don't know if it'll work out but I have to try." And how did Matt fit into that picture? Not at all.

He nodded solemnly. "Yeah, you do. I get that. But hey, you haven't moved yet." He stepped just a little closer.

Whoo, boy. She felt like a cube of butter on a hot day. The way he was looking at her, for a moment there she thought he was going to kiss her. She swallowed. "You don't want to rush into anything." Except rushing sounded like a pretty good idea just now…

He took a deep breath and let it out. "You're right. But I'm not going to let one screwup keep me from being open to whatever comes next. Wherever it leads."

Wherever it leads. What did that mean? She was about to ask him when he gave her nose a playful tap and said, "I'll be up again next Sunday. See you then."

He ambled out of the room and she stayed there, braced against the counter. They'd cooked together, shared their stories. He'd almost kissed her and she'd wanted him to.

New York suddenly seemed far away and out of focus. Right now, here in Icicle Falls, the picture was looking good.

CHAPTER FOURTEEN

"You were smart to break up with Steve," Stef said to Griffin as they walked to Gingerbread Haus on Tuesday for a morning latte. "Men are nothing but a headache." More people should give aspirin as a wedding present.

"I thought everything was going okay now," Griffin said.

"It was, but then Brad got ticked off because I actually had the nerve to be happy that we're making progress on the house. He should be glad, but instead he's being a jerk."

"I'm sorry things aren't going well."

There was an understatement. "That makes two of us."

The bakery was busy as usual. They passed two older women leaving as they went in, both carrying pink bakery boxes. Inside, Cass's helper Misty was ringing up a sale, and Cass was just putting out a freshly created gingerbread house.

She greeted Stef and Griffin with a smile and a wave. "How's everything, you two?"

"Great," Griffin said.

"I need carbs," Stef announced. "A double serving."

"Uh-oh," said Cass. "What's the problem?"

"Don't ask," Griffin cautioned.

"I don't need to. It's got to have something to do with the house. I thought Grant was getting a lot done over there."

"Grant's not the problem. Mocha, double shot, please," Stef told Misty.

"Just a tea," Griffin said.

"The way you eat, it's like diet prison camp," Stef said in disgust. "I don't know how you stand it."

Now Griffin wasn't smiling anymore. "I'm fine with tea."

Okay, her sour mood didn't mean she had to pour lemon juice on everyone else's day. "Sorry, I'm so bitchy."

"Just a little," Griffin said.

"More like just a lot, but thanks for being diplomatic." Stef took her latte to a table, sat down and frowned at it. She'd been so happy to see progress being made. Why couldn't Brad let her enjoy it? She said as much to Cass when she joined them. "I make one comment about being glad something's finally getting done, and he goes ballistic on me."

"Maybe you hurt his pride," Cass suggested. "Remember, he wasn't happy about you hiring Grant in the first place."

"There's pride and there's practical," Stef insisted. "I mean, was I supposed to live in chaos forever? It's not like he hasn't had months to finish these projects. You know I still don't have a working bathtub in the master bathroom?"

"I wouldn't want to live like that," said Griffin.

No woman would. She wasn't being unreasonable. *She* wasn't the problem here. "I wish there was a way to make him see how I feel."

"I guess you'll have to mess up his man cave," Cass joked.

Wow! Cass was positively inspired. "That's genius!" How would Brad like it if the chaos came closer to home, to his favorite retreat? She was willing to bet he wouldn't be so happy. He'd probably do anything to fix it. Just like she'd done with their main floor.

Cass looked horrified. "I was only kidding."

"Well, I'm serious. I'm going to give him a taste of his own medicine. Let him see what it feels like to live in a disaster area. Then he'll finally get it."

"Or he'll get really mad," said Griffin. "I don't know about this, Stef."

"Trust me, it's not a good idea," Cass said.

"I wouldn't do anything permanent. I'd mess it up a little, maybe take out some furniture." Maybe take out all the furniture. Heh, heh.

"I still don't think it's a good idea," Cass repeated.

"Well, I have to do something."

"Bake him cookies and have sex," Cass said.

"I'm not much of a baker."

"So just have sex. But don't mess with the man cave. I know it sounds kind of fun, but don't do it. Real life doesn't play out like an episode of *I Love Lucy*."

Stef had never seen an episode of *I Love Lucy*. "It'll be fine. Thanks for the inspiration."

"You're not welcome," Cass said. "I wish I'd kept my big mouth shut."

"Maybe Cass is right," Griffin said as they walked back home. "Brad's already not happy. Why make things worse?"

"Because *he's* making things worse for me. He's pouting and cranky and resentful, and he's acting like a six-year-old. Oh, wait, I take that back. Petey's much better behaved. In fact, if Petey acted the way Brad's acting, he'd be sent to his room."

"Send Brad to his room and leave it at that," Griffin suggested.

"Oh, I'm going to send him to his room, all right. And when he gets there he's going to get a big surprise." She chortled. Oh, this was going to be fun.

That afternoon, she made a couple of phone calls and lined up some teenage labor. Then, on Friday, coincidentally around the time high school let out, she went home sick from work. Not really a lie, she told herself. She had cramps.

She left her son at his after-school day care, where he went on the days she worked. Petey would just get underfoot. Plus, he'd be bound to spill the beans to Daddy and ruin the element of surprise, and Stef didn't want that. In fact, she didn't want Brad to see his basement retreat until after Petey was in bed.

Cass's warning came back to her. Maybe this wasn't such a good idea. Something else was nagging at her. What was it?

Her workers were here now. She shoved aside her doubts and moved forward with the plan. "I need everything cleared out," she said to the boys.

And there was plenty to clear out—Brad's beat-up old recliner, a huge black fake leather sofa that his parents had given them, the mini-fridge where he kept an extra supply of pop and beer, an old pinball machine that one of her happy helpers was drooling over. She was half-tempted to give it to him but decided against it. Brad would be furious if she got rid of that. She did decide to lose the old card table and chairs. They were in bad shape and needed to be replaced anyway. By the time her workers were done, the only things left were the TV and the DVD player, which were on the wall. She'd have taken those, too, but, in the end, felt that messing with Brad's technology would be a mistake.

She paid her helpers and they left, taking the old card table and chairs with them. Then she went online and checked out game tables. She found a nice one, not terribly expensive, that she put on her credit card. She'd get it for Brad as an early anniversary present. She placed her order and printed out the picture. Once he'd seen the error of his ways and they'd kissed and made up, she'd show it to him. He'd be the envy of all his poker buddies.

Poker! Now, after all the furniture had been relocated to the garage and the card table and chairs had been hauled off and her workers were gone, she realized what had been nagging at the back of her mind. Brad was hosting a Friday-night poker game.

Oh, no! Oh, no! Oh, no! With a poker game looming, he

would have zero sense of humor about this. Never mind that
it was no more than he deserved, no different from what he'd
done to her. She had to get the boys back, and that was all there
was to it. There was no point in providing her husband with a
teachable moment if he wasn't in the mood to be taught.

Her cell phone rang. *Don't let it be Brad.*

It was Mrs. Biddle, who ran Mountain Tikes Day Care.
"Stefanie, can you come pick up Petey? He's complaining that
his tummy hurts. He doesn't have a fever, but I think you should
come get him anyway."

"Of course." The mess at home would have to wait.

Stef rushed to the day care and collected her son. "I don't feel
good, Mommy," he whimpered. "I want to go home."

Petey always enjoyed his afternoons at Mrs. Biddle's house
with its big backyard and swing set and collection of local kids to
play with. Wanting to go home was proof indeed that he didn't
feel well. There'd been a twenty-four-hour bug going around
at school. It looked like he'd caught it.

"I'm so sorry, baby. Let's get you home and in bed."

She thanked Mrs. Biddle, told the woman she hoped no one
else got sick, then put her son into the car. They'd barely made
it home and to the bathroom when he threw up. She put him
in his pj's and tucked him in bed. Then she hurried downstairs
to get some ginger ale.

She was just opening the can when she heard Brad call, "I'm
home."

Speaking of opening cans... Here was a can of worms she
wished she'd never opened. Nothing for it now but to brave it
out. Brad would get the point and she'd hire the boys to come
back and return all the furniture. The guys could play poker at
the kitchen table tonight. It would all work out.

He was in the kitchen now. "Where's Petey?"

"He's in bed," she said, pouring ginger ale into a glass. It made a good excuse not to look at her husband. "He came home with an upset stomach."

"Poor kid. I'll go see him."

"Take this," she said, handing Brad the glass. "Don't let him have more than a sip. He threw up a few minutes ago."

Brad disappeared upstairs and Stef made a phone call, hoping she could get the boys to come back now. She only needed everything out of the room long enough to make her point. Why hadn't she asked them to hang around?

And why had she gotten rid of the card table? Maybe they could get it back from the donation center.

"Sorry, Stef, Randy went to Herman's with Buck and James," said her teenage mover's mom. "Did you need them for anything else?"

Boy, did she ever. Could she drive to the hamburger joint and home before Brad came downstairs?

Now Brad was back in the kitchen. "Thanks. Um, I'll get hold of him later," she said.

"Who were you talking to?" he asked as she ended the call.

"Oh, no one." Okay, how could she start this conversation? *Brad, before dinner we need to move some furniture. Guess what? I have a surprise for you.* That would do it. Everything would be all right once he learned about the new game table. "I have a surprise for you."

"Yeah?" He was smiling. It was almost as if the miserable week they'd been having had never happened. His cell rang. "Hold that thought." He took the call. "Yeah, we're still on for tonight. No, I've got beer. The game? Oh, man, I forgot to set it to record." He started walking away, down the hall, toward the basement steps.

"Brad, don't go down there!"

"Be back in a minute," he called over his shoulder.

That was what she was afraid of.

He was back in less than a minute. He wasn't on the phone

anymore and he wasn't smiling. In fact... What was that old saying about if looks could kill?

"What happened to my room?"

This was not the moment to ask how it felt to have everything upside down right before a party.

"You did this on purpose, didn't you? Some kind of sick joke?"

"I only wanted you to know how I felt when you tore up everything right before Griffin's shower." *You weren't going to say that. Remember?* But it was out. The point had been made.

Why didn't she feel good about it?

His eyes narrowed. "Cute, Stef. Real cute. There's just one difference. I was trying to do something nice for you. This..."

Was vindictive. And that was why she felt like crying instead of snickering. Her self-righteous anger died, like a strong wind that had blown itself out. "I forgot about the poker game."

"Yeah, right."

He marched upstairs and she followed him. "I really did, Brad. I'm sorry."

"Where is everything, Stef? At the dump?"

"No, it's out in the garage. Well, all except the card table."

"Where's that?"

"Um, I donated it."

"What!" They were in the upstairs hall now and he whirled around and gaped at her. "You gave away my card table?"

"It was old and ratty. I've got something better coming."

"There's always something better, isn't there? It was mine, Stef. You gave it away without even asking. But then, what's new about that? You've been doing a lot of stuff without talking to me first." He marched into the bedroom and pulled a duffel bag from the closet.

"What are you doing?"

"You moved out all my stuff. Obviously, I'm next." He threw the duffel on the bed, strode to the dresser and yanked open a drawer.

"Brad, don't be like this."

He ignored her, throwing jeans and socks and underwear into the bag every which way.

"Brad!"

"Daddy?"

She turned to see her son standing in the doorway rubbing his eyes, his hair mussed, cheeks flushed. Great.

"Where are you going, Daddy?" he asked.

Brad grabbed his duffel. He walked over to where his son stood and knelt in front of him. "Daddy's going to go visit a friend for a while."

"Can I come, too?"

"Not this time, big guy." Brad took his hand and led him back to his bedroom, and Stef trailed miserably after. She watched as Brad tucked him in. "You need to stay here with Mommy. She's in charge." He didn't smile at Mommy when he said it.

"Brad. Please."

He ignored her. "Don't worry," he told Petey. "If you feel better tomorrow, I'll come get you and take you to your game."

Petey nodded, reassured that all was well. "Okay, Daddy."

Brad kissed him good-night, then ruffled his hair. "I'll check on you tomorrow." He picked up his duffel and started to leave, walking past Stef without looking at her.

"You forgot to kiss Mommy," Petey called.

Brad took a step back and gave her a frosty kiss on the cheek that stung like a slap, then left the room.

"Mommy will be right back," she told her son, then chased Brad down the stairs. She caught him at the door. "I'm sorry, Brad, but I just wanted you to see how it felt."

"Yeah? Well, maybe you need to see how it feels not to be appreciated." With that parting shot, he threw open the door and marched off down the front walk.

Charley was hosting a party on the back patio of Zelda's to celebrate the restaurant's sixth anniversary. "If you can make it past five years, chances are good that you'll be around for another ten. And that's worth celebrating."

Indeed, it was. Charley had survived a lot, everything from a husband cheating with one of their employees to a fire that closed her down while she rebuilt. But she'd come back stronger than ever and had ended up with a much better second husband. All her friends were more than happy to help her celebrate.

The mountains provided a beautiful backdrop and a tired sun still managed to warm people's shoulders as they milled about, drinking cocktails and eating appetizers.

Cass had been put in charge of the anniversary cake and had made a gigantic chocolate one with raspberry cream filling, decorated with the profile of a flapper to fit the restaurant's art deco image. She'd sampled both the filling and the frosting, and they were delicious, if she did say so herself.

Speaking of delicious, here came Grant Masters strolling up to her. He was dressed casually, in jeans and a shirt with a soft brown sweater that complemented those dark eyes. She told her hormones to behave themselves and took a drink of her Chocolate Kiss.

"If it isn't my favorite roofer," she greeted him.

"My favorite baker," he responded.

"How are you enjoying Icicle Falls?" she asked. "Do you feel you're settling in?"

He nodded. "Oh, yeah."

"Met any interesting people?" *Like Muriel Sterling-Wittman.* Yes, she was fishing.

The fish didn't take the bait. "A few," he said vaguely.

She tried again. "I assume you've met our local celebrity by now."

"Celebrity?"

"Muriel Sterling-Wittman. She's had several books published."

"Oh, yeah. Nice lady."

"Not to mention beautiful." And wise and kind. Impossible

to compete with. Cass consoled herself with another sip of her chocolate drink. Oh, yeah, crème de cacao, chocolate syrup, booze—if a woman couldn't be beautiful she could at least drink Chocolate Kisses.

"Yeah, she is."

"She's available." Why was she reminding him?

"She's not really my type."

Hmm, now, that was interesting. There was hardly a man in Icicle Falls—including younger men—who didn't drool over Muriel. "Don't tell me you've got something against beautiful women."

A waiter came up with a platter of hot wings and Grant took one, checked it out, took a bite.

Quit keeping me in suspense. "I heard you guys went out." Okay, now she sounded like a fourteen-year-old girl, trying to squeeze info out of her crush. She needed to stop fixating on Grant Masters. But darn, how *could* she stop when he was so darned sexy?

He shrugged. "We did. Like I said, she's nice."

"Whoa, damning with faint praise."

"I like my women a little...cheekier."

"*Cheeky.* There's a word you don't hear very often."

"Not these days. Are you old enough to know what it means?"

"Of course I am!"

He studied her. "How old are you, anyway?"

"Didn't your mother ever tell you it's rude to ask a lady her age?"

"Are you even fifty?"

"Hey, don't rush me."

"That's what I thought."

"Don't tell me you're prejudiced against younger women. Not that I'm young enough to qualify for that."

Her phone summoned her. Someone had a very bad sense of timing. Who was it? Most of her friends were here. It had to be one of the kids.

"Go ahead, answer it," Grant told her. "I've learned that no woman can resist a ringing phone."

"I can," she said, but he grinned and walked away. Darn. Probably using the phone as an excuse to leave. At least she now knew she didn't have to compete with Muriel. And Grant almost seemed interested.

Except why was he asking about her age? Surely there wasn't that big an age difference between them. Anyway, who cared? They were both adults.

The call was from Stef and, remembering their conversation at the bakery, Cass suddenly had a bad feeling. She took the call.

"Brad's left," Stef wailed. "I should have listened to you! I hate this house and I hate my life."

"I'll be right over."

CHAPTER FIFTEEN

Cass gave Charley a congratulatory hug, explained that Stef was having a crisis and then raced home to Blackberry Lane. Stef was a mess when Cass got to her place. She'd already used almost a whole box of tissues. All that was left of her makeup was a faint brown track down one cheek, and her eyes were puffy and bloodshot.

"He's gone. We're through," she wailed. Loud enough to wake the dead.

"Where's Petey?" The last thing her son needed was to see his mommy like this.

"He's in bed. He's not feeling well."

"So he has no idea what's going on?"

"He saw us fighting. Brad told him he was going to visit a friend. Oh, Cass, what if he doesn't come back?"

"Did he take his golf clubs?"

"No."

"Then he'll be back."

"That's not funny," Stef informed her and started sobbing again. "We should never have left Seattle. We had a nice little rental in Skyway. We were happy."

"You'll be happy again," Cass reassured her, rubbing her shoulder. At least she hoped they would. "Every couple fights."

"We don't. Not like this!" The wailing began again.

"You need a drink," Cass said.

"Easing my sorrow with alcohol, that can't be good. I'll turn into an alcoholic." Louder wailing.

"Chamomile tea, not booze. Do you have any?"

"I think so. Tea won't help. Nothing's going to help."

Cass gave her shoulder another pat and then went to the kitchen to heat water. She also called in reinforcements. "We've got trouble over here at Stef's. You'd better come over."

"I'll be right there!"

Griffin showed up minutes later, and soon the three women were sitting at the kitchen table, mugs of tea in front of them and a fresh box of tissues next to Stef. Petey had been checked on and was soundly and cluelessly asleep.

"You guys told me not to do it," Stef said, her voice wobbling. "Why didn't I listen?"

Good question. "Because you were angry," Cass said. She'd been there, done that, let the anger build until it reached the inevitable point of explosion. In her case, there'd been too many explosions. Finally there'd been nothing left.

Except three great kids. Because of them, she could never completely regret marrying Mason.

"I thought somehow he'd laugh it off," Stef said miserably.

Griffin gaped at her. "Seriously?"

Stef crumpled up a tissue and added it to the growing pile. "I don't know why I thought that."

"Well, he is normally pretty easygoing," Griffin conceded.

"It was stupid. He was having friends over for poker tonight."

"Oh, no," Griffin said as the story got worse.

"Oh, yes. I forgot. I really did. I tried to explain that to him." Here came more tears. Stef yanked another tissue out of the box. "Now look what's happened."

"It'll be okay," Griffin said earnestly.

"What can I do?"

"First of all, put his room back together," Cass advised. "And come up with a good peace offering. And you have to pull yourself together for Petey's sake. You can't drag him into your drama."

Stef nodded and blew her nose.

The little cuckoo popped out of Stef's kitchen cuckoo clock and began to chime the hour. Eight o'clock already. "I've got to get home and get to bed," Cass said. When you were a baker it was early to bed and early to rise. "Can you stay?" she asked Griffin.

"Of course," Griffin said.

Cass told Stef one more time that everything would work out, then made her way down the street to her own house. After the craziness at Stef's, the quiet in her place offered a spa-like calm.

Lady Gray trotted up to greet her, and she picked up the cat. "So much drama," she murmured. "Be glad you're a cat."

Lady Gray leaped out of her arms and trotted off down the hall toward the kitchen.

"Very subtle," Cass called after her. "But I'm not feeding you again."

Hmm. Speaking of food, she hadn't had a chance to eat at the party. But it wasn't healthy to eat right before bed.

She followed the cat to the kitchen and poured herself a glass of milk. Then she got her stash of Oreos from the cupboard. A baker eating store-bought cookies—what would her customers say? Well, woman did not live by gingerbread alone.

She limited herself to two cookies, then went upstairs, brushed her teeth and went to bed, where she lay a long time thinking about Stef and her troubles and then marriage in general, which of course led her to think about her own marriage.

Really, she and Mason were better off apart. And her life as a single mom hadn't turned out badly. It still wasn't. Except, darn, the problem with being on your own was…well, you were on your own.

Lady Gray jumped onto the bed, then started walking up her middle. She stomped on a boob a couple of times before settling down, giving Cass's chin a head butt and purring.

"I have you, don't I?" she said, petting the cat. "And you'll do just fine. *We'll* do just fine."

Sure.

It was a long night, the longest night ever. Griffin sat up with Stef until around one, before Stef took a step outside her own misery and realized she was being selfish and talking her poor friend into a stupor. How many hours could you spend listening to a woman's reminiscences about everything from when she first met her husband (Starbucks on lower Queen Anne) to their first kiss (under the mistletoe at her parents' house) to where he proposed (in front of the troll under the Aurora Bridge). She talked about the first time she'd tried to make lasagna and what a mess she'd made. "But it turned out great. And I can't say that for our marriage," she'd concluded and started crying again.

Poor Griffin. She hadn't signed on to be a shrink when they became friends.

Nonetheless, she'd told Stef to call her in the morning if she needed her for anything. Stef had finally dozed off sometime in the wee hours. She was far from ready to wake up when Petey came into her room around seven thirty. "I'm all better."

"Good," she said, reaching up and pushing his hair back from his forehead. He was such a cute little boy. He had Brad's friendly face and reddish hair. Brad's disposition. Which was just as well. She certainly didn't want him to take after her.

"Can I go to my game?"

"Let's see if your breakfast stays down first."

"It will," he said. "Will you tell Daddy?"

"Yes." If she could find him. "First, though, you need to get dressed and have some breakfast."

"Okay!" Petey bounded out of the room and Stef dragged herself out of bed and into the shower. Nothing like a shower in the morning to make a girl feel...no better at all.

She went downstairs to the kitchen to make pancakes, Petey's favorite. Brad's, too. The tears started. She didn't even know where Brad was. She set aside the pancake mix and grabbed her phone, searching through the Icicle Falls online directory for the list of lodgings in town. After writing them down, she began calling.

She struck out on the first two, and her call went to voice mail at Gerhardt's Gasthaus, which meant the lines were all busy.

"No, he's not here," said Mrs. Clauson, who ran the Icicle Creek Lodge. She sounded puzzled as to why her happily married young insurance man would be at her lodge instead of home but was polite enough not to ask.

Stef hung up and tried Gerhardt's again. It was the logical choice, nice but not too expensive.

"We do have a Bradley Stahl here," said the woman at the desk. "Would you like me to put you through?"

"Please."

The phone rang. And rang. And rang. And rang.

He was probably hiding in there, unwilling to take her call. Her best bet was to go over and talk to him one-on-one. She put in an SOS to Griffin, who sounded groggy. Obviously still trying to sleep.

"I woke you up, didn't I?" Look in Wikipedia under "World's Most High-Maintenance Friend" and there would be Stef's picture. "I'm sorry."

"No, that's okay. Did Brad come home?"

Tears prickled her eyes. "No."

"He will."

"He's staying at Gerhardt's. I need to get over there and talk to him. Can you stay with Petey for a while?"

"Sure. Let me just brush my teeth."

"God bless you. I owe you big-time for this."

"No, you don't. This is what friends are for."

That did send the tears spilling. "Thank you. So much."

Petey came into the kitchen. "Is that Daddy?"

"No, sweetie. That's Griffin. She's going to come over and make you pancakes while I go talk to Daddy."

Petey frowned. "Daddy needs to know I'm all well."

"I'll tell him." *If I can get him to talk to me.*

Griffin arrived and took over pancake duty, and Stef went to Gerhardt's. By way of the bakery, which, fortunately, was already open. Cass was behind the counter and she looked questioningly at Stef.

"He didn't come home. I need two of your cream-puff swans."

Cass nodded and boxed them up. When Stef pulled out her wallet, she shook her head. "On the house. Good luck."

Stef nodded gratefully, took the bribe and went to Gerhardt's, praying that neither Gerhardt Geissel nor his wife would be handling reception. They were valued customers at the bank and she saw them both often. She sure didn't want to see them today, though. This was hard enough without adding the humiliation of asking what room her husband was in when the room he *should've* been in was their bedroom at home.

"He's in number six," said the woman at the front desk. Someone Stef didn't know. *Thank you, God.*

Brad's car was nowhere in sight and no one answered when she knocked on the door of his room. Her heart sank. Where was he?

Maybe at the office. She drove over there. Sure enough, he was inside, seated at his desk, working on his laptop. The door was locked but she had a key and let herself in.

He looked up but didn't smile at the sight of her. He used to look up from whatever he was doing and smile at her as if the sun had just come out.

She held up the bakery box. "I brought a peace offering. Cream puffs."

"No, thanks."

"Pancakes for breakfast at home," she offered.

"I'm not hungry."

She chewed her lip. "Petey's feeling better."

"Good. I'll pick him up for the game."

It was like Antarctica in here. "Are you going to stay mad at me forever?"

He shrugged.

"I said I was sorry."

He shut down his computer and walked over to her. "Prove it."

"I will. I'll put everything back." Well, everything she hadn't given away.

"That won't prove anything." He opened the door, put the key in it, indicated they were leaving now.

She stepped outside with him. "What do you want?" Sheesh.

"Get rid of the tool man."

"What? But, Brad, he's not done!"

"He's done the hard stuff. I can finish the floor."

But would he?

She hesitated too long. "Forget it. I have to pick up Petey. The game starts at ten and we need to warm up." He moved toward his car.

"Brad, wait!"

He didn't. He drove off and left her and the cream-puff swans behind.

Petey was just finishing his pancakes (Mickey Mouse–shaped, like Griffin's mom used to make for her) when Brad showed up. Alone.

"Where's Stef?" she asked.

"Back at the office." The words sounded curt. No smile for his wife's friend. He did put a smile on for his son. "Hey, buddy, you feeling better?"

Petey nodded eagerly. "I'm all well."

"Don't feel like those pancakes are gonna come back up?"

Petey shook his head vehemently.

"Okay, then, brush your teeth and we'll go."

"Yay!" Petey cried and raced from the room, leaving Mickey's ears uneaten.

"Thanks for watching him," Brad said. Still no smile. Then, without another word, he walked out of the kitchen. Griffin followed, unsure what to say.

Petey bounded back down the stairs and then was out the door, calling, "'Bye, Aunt Griffin!"

She shut the door, which he'd left wide open, and watched from the window as Brad loaded a big canvas bag full of baseball equipment into the trunk of his car. Then, with Petey buckled in the back, he drove off.

She returned to the kitchen and cleaned up the breakfast mess, then sat at the table, expecting Stef to walk in any minute.

But the minutes dragged on and there was still no sign of her friend. Worried, she pulled out her phone and texted. Where are you?

At the office eating cream puffs. My life sucks.

He'll come around.

Only if I fire Grant. Know anyone who wants a half-remodeled house?

Want me to come over there?

No. Going to Petey's game. Thanks for being such a good friend.

Griffin wished she knew how to be a better friend, wished she knew how to help Stef fix her problem. But when it came to love, you were on your own.

Stef and Brad would patch up their marriage. They had to. What they had was solid.

Unlike what she'd had with Steve. It was a little scary that she had so easily gotten over breaking up with the man she'd planned to marry and that he'd moved on so quickly. Obviously it had been a bad plan.

Well, that was what came of rushing into things when you were young. They'd barely been going out six months when they'd moved in together. Her grandmother had been horrified. "You're too young to know what you're doing," she'd scolded.

Gram was right. She *had* been too young to know what she was doing. She still wasn't sure she knew what she was doing.

Back home again, she put in a load of laundry and then settled down at her computer to work on her blog. Using her handy dictation app—much easier than trying to type wearing a cast—she started a new entry—"Cooking with One Hand." Hmm. Kind of boring. She changed it to "Cooking with Three Hands," smiled and then wrote about her evening making dinner with Matt while she had one hand in a cast. The pictures were both fun and attractive. She had one of him posing with a bunch of cilantro stuffed sideways in his mouth and labeled it Cilantro Tango. Another shot of their finished salad was, if not magazine-worthy, at least attractive. So was the selfie they'd taken.

They looked happy. More than that, they looked like they belonged together. She reminded herself that she'd thought the same thing about Steve.

Muriel Sterling's book was sitting on the coffee table, silently commanding her. *Read me.*

She picked it up and turned to the next chapter. "It's natural to have doubts when you're about to embark on a new adventure," Muriel told her. "Sometimes we even look for excuses to stay home and not go."

Was Matt an excuse? An excuse to avoid moving to New York?

"But stay true to your dream. In the end, you'll be glad you did."

Yes, she would. She'd stalled out with Steve. This was her chance to hit Restart. She had to take it.

She just wished she could take it and take Matt, too.

CHAPTER SIXTEEN

Stef went to her son's baseball game and sat in the bleachers with the other moms and dads, pretending that nothing was wrong. It was a little hard to pretend when, after the game, Brad came over and said, "I'm going to take him out for ice cream. I'll bring him home afterward."

How many of the moms had heard that? She glanced over her shoulder to see one of them looking in her direction with raised eyebrows. She lowered her voice. "I don't know if ice cream's a good idea, considering he had an upset stomach yesterday."

"He's fine. Anyway, you gave him pancakes for breakfast."

Pancakes for breakfast. So now she was not only a terrible wife, she was a terrible mother, as well. She frowned at Brad. "Make him eat a sandwich first."

Brad nodded curtly, then strolled off, calling to Petey.

The same mom who'd overheard Brad was at her side now. Anna Nettles. More like Anna Meddles. "I couldn't help over-hearing," she said.

Yes, she could have.

"Is everything okay with you and Brad?"

"Fine," Stef lied. "We just came in separate cars."

Anna nodded, but her expression said, *You're not fooling me, you poor, pathetic loser.*

How many people already knew that Brad was staying at Gerhardt's Gasthaus? How many people would soon know that Brad wasn't coming home after T-ball games, that he was only dropping off his son and then leaving?

She stopped at Sweet Dreams Chocolate Company and bought herself a consolation box of chocolates. Brad and Petey were out having ice cream, but she had chocolate. So there.

He dropped Petey off an hour later, and Petey wasn't looking at all happy when he walked in the door. "How long does Daddy have to stay at his friend's house?"

"Not much longer," Stef said and hoped she was right.

That afternoon, Petey went to a neighbor's house to play, and Stef weeded her flower beds and felt sorry for herself. For dinner she made an easy meal of tuna casserole. Not gourmet fare, but Petey enjoyed it. She played three games of Cootie with him and two games of Sorry before popping him in the tub.

By the time her son went to bed, she was ready for bed, too. Pretending you were happy when you were miserable was exhausting. She fell asleep on the couch watching *House Hunters International.*

The next morning, it was still only her and her son. Rather than show up at church alone and set tongues wagging, she played hooky.

At one in the afternoon, she got a call from Velma Tuttle, one of the church deaconesses. "We missed you at church today, Stefanie."

"Oh. Well, I wasn't feeling up to it." No lie. Let Velma draw her own conclusions.

"That's what Bradley said."

So Brad, who hadn't been home since Friday, was now at church pretending to be Mr. Spiritual? She could feel her jaw start to clench.

"I hope it's nothing serious," Velma persisted.

It was getting more serious all the time. "No, no," Stef said airily. "Petey had a little bug." It was true. He had. "I might have caught it."

"I'm glad to hear it's nothing more. But still, Bradley should have stayed home and taken care of you. And I told him so."

Good old Velma, always about the Lord's business. And everyone else's.

"Thanks for checking on me," Stef said. She hung up, cutting Velma off in midplatitude, and texted Brad. You hypocrite.

He texted back within minutes. What?

You know what. Telling people I wasn't up to coming to church. You are such a jerk!

She got no reply. Big surprise.

Petey had another play-date invite from a friend two streets over, and after dropping him off, Stef found herself with nothing to do except be angry. She decided to go over to Griffin's and see if she wanted company.

But as she approached Griffin's house, she saw that her friend already had company, and good-looking company at that. So this was Grant Masters's son. Griffin had told her that Grant had delegated painting her place to him. She hadn't told Stef the guy had the body of a cover model. Of course, that should've come as no surprise considering how fit both his dad and his brother were.

Griffin's house was now a lovely shade of robin's-egg blue and he was in the process of painting the trim on the windows white. She was standing next to him, a brush in her left hand. He said something and she laughed. She obviously did not need company.

Stef kept walking. She'd just stop by Cass's place and see how

the roof was coming along. And then find out when Grant
would be back at her place.

Get rid of the tool man, Brad had said. She would…as soon as
he'd put in one more day.

Grant was up on her roof, sweating in the hot sun. Cass decided the least she could do was make him lunch. A BLT on
some of the sourdough bread she'd brought home from the bakery. And maybe a strawberry shortcake.

Since Grant had started working on her roof, it seemed she'd
been getting a lot of urges to whip things up in the kitchen. The
kitchen wasn't the only place where things were getting stirred
up. She slid the biscuits in the oven and then took some whipping cream out of the fridge. Suddenly she was envisioning herself in here with Grant, putting the kitchen table to good use.
And they sure weren't eating strawberry shortcake.

"Get a grip," she told herself. But she didn't listen to her own
advice, just kept right on fantasizing about Grant Masters.

She whipped the cream and sliced the strawberries. Then she
got busy on the sandwich. By the time she'd finished, the biscuits were out of the oven and the kitchen was getting warm.

So was she. She poured him a glass of lemonade, then took
that and the sandwich outside and called him down from the
roof.

"You don't have to feed me, you know," he said as he settled
on the porch step with the plate.

"What the heck. I have to eat anyway. It's no harder to make
something for two instead of one."

"Where's yours?"

"I'm saving myself for strawberry shortcake."

"You made shortcake?"

"I'm a baker. We love to bake."

"I haven't had shortcake since…" His sentence trailed off.

Oh, no. From treat to torture. "Did your wife make it a lot?"

He nodded and took a sudden interest in the profile of the mountains that surrounded the town.

Cass felt guilty for even thinking about getting romantically involved with this man. He wasn't ready. Maybe he never would be.

"I'm sorry about your wife," she said. "I can't imagine what it would be like to lose someone you love."

He took in a breath, let it out. "Sometimes I wonder why it wasn't me instead of her. I thought I'd be the one to have a heart attack." He put the sandwich he'd been eating back on the plate.

Cass didn't know what to say, so she sat there and kept her mouth shut. Grant and his wife had been married a long time. She had been beautiful. She'd certainly been loved.

Cass couldn't help feeling inadequate. Most of all, though, she felt sympathy. When it came to covering grief, sympathy made a sadly thin blanket.

He gave her an apologetic look. "It's always a downer listening to people talk about the person they lost."

"That doesn't mean they shouldn't," she said. "It's got to be hard to move on."

"It is, but I'm working on it."

"This town is a good place to do that. Lots of kind people."

"So I've discovered." He managed a smile. "I do like strawberry shortcake."

She got the message and went back in the house to dish some up.

Everyone loved Cass's shortcake. She made her biscuits with butter and sweetened them with a quarter cup of sugar. She sweetened the berries, too, and mashed them just enough to extract some juice. She never sweetened her whipped cream, though. Vanilla needed no competition. Still, when she came back out and handed him a bowl of biscuits stuffed with juicy berries and smothered in whipped cream, she felt self-conscious, as if she were in some sort of competition.

He took a bite, nodded and smiled. "That's good," he said after he'd swallowed.

She wondered if it was as good as what his wife used to make. She certainly wasn't going to ask and shadow a moment of pleasure with sadness from the past, especially when he was trying to move on.

Was Grant Masters ready to move on? Really?

He finished off the shortcake, then said, "I'd better get back to work."

"Yes, it's important to keep your favorite baker dry in the winter," she cracked.

"Absolutely. Can't have you catching cold and sneezing all over those gingerbread boys," he said, and his smile returned. When he stood up he towered over her. Nice to meet a man who could do that. She was no petite bunny.

But as he walked off, she could almost see the ghost of his wife hovering over her. *Hey, I had someone before, too*, she informed the first Mrs. Masters. *But I don't now and neither does he.* And there was something addictive about the man. The more she saw of him, the more she wanted.

Darn it all, she was tired of being by herself. She wanted someone to laugh with, someone to cuddle next to in bed. *Sorry, Lady Gray.* Someone to share the ups and downs of life. And the calories.

Speaking of calories, she had to get serious about shedding some pounds. Willie's college graduation was right around the corner and she wanted to look her best, especially for the bash Mason was throwing after the ceremony. Now it was crunch time.

"You should've stuck to your diet," she scolded herself.

As if it mattered. Willie saw her only as Mom and didn't care what she looked like. And no matter how many pounds she lost, people would still compare her to Babette, the trophy wife. She wouldn't come out ahead.

Her musing was interrupted by Stef, who strolled up and joined her on the lawn. "I thought I'd see how the roof is coming along," she said. "It looks great."

Cass nodded. "It's a relief to have it taken care of. After this all we'll have left is the deck."

"How long will that take?"

"I don't know, but I'm sure he'll get back to you before he starts on it."

"I really need him to."

Cass didn't miss the anxious expression that flitted across her friend's face. "Brad still hasn't come home?"

Stef scowled. "He's being stubborn."

"Maybe if you—"

Stef didn't let her finish. "I apologized. I said I'd put everything back. I even ordered him a fancy game table for our anniversary. Of course, I never got a chance to tell him. He won't listen. And he's paying a fortune staying at Gerhardt's. Here he was, getting on me for what I'm spending on putting our house back together, and look what *he's* spending staying over there and pouting. He's being completely unreasonable," she added, her voice quavering.

"People often are when they're hurt," Cass said gently.

"Well, I'm hurt, too. He just walked out, Cass."

"He'll walk back in, I'm sure. Brad's a good man and he loves you."

"He doesn't love me enough to let me get our house put back together after *he* left it in a mess. He says he's not coming home until Grant's gone."

"Stef, maybe it's more important to put your lives back together."

Stef looked at her as if Cass had just suggested she cut off an ear. "I thought you'd be on my side."

"I am. That's why I'm trying to give you some advice. Fire Grant and bring Brad home."

"I will. As soon as the floor is finished."

Cass shook her head. "I hope that turns out to be a good decision."

"If I don't get that mess cleaned up, I'll be checking into Gerhardt's, too," Stef said. "Brad will never finish it."

"Okay." She pointed in the direction of the roof. "Feel free to go on up there and talk to Grant."

Stef looked warily at the ladder. "I'm afraid of heights."

"Call him down," Cass said. She wasn't going to. She wasn't going to have any part in helping Stef keep Grant and keep her husband away.

Stef walked over to the ladder and hollered up at Grant. "Can I speak to you?"

"Sure," he called back. A moment later he'd joined Stef on the lawn.

Cass remained on the porch, determined not to participate in the conversation, but she could easily hear every word.

"I know Cass needs her roof finished, but do you think you could come and work at my place tomorrow? I really need to get the great room done," Stef told him.

"I'm almost done here," he told her.

"Can you take a break and come to my place? It's not supposed to rain this week."

"I'll see what I can do," he said. "I might be able to get over there tomorrow afternoon."

She smiled. "Thank you! I'll leave the back door unlocked."

Cass shook her head again as she watched Stef leave. Her friend was practically skipping. As if she'd somehow solved her problem.

"What was that all about?" Grant asked.

"She and her husband aren't remotely on the same page about their home improvement project."

"I gathered that."

"Did you know he moved out?"

Grant frowned. "No. That's news to me."

"He's staying at Gerhardt's. Stef seems to think that once everything's done, he'll have to accept it. But getting that room done isn't the problem now. I think she wounded his pride when she brought you in, and she keeps doing things to make it worse. I've tried to talk to her, but she's not listening."

"Like my dad used to say, you can't put an old head on young shoulders."

"Hey, watch it with the 'old' remarks," she joked. "But I do know what you mean. If I were in her shoes, I'd fire you. Stef has no idea how easy it is to lose your footing in a marriage. Once you start sliding down that slippery slope, it can be hard to climb back up."

He regarded her, head cocked to one side.

"Yes, I know that from personal experience," she admitted. "It was for the best that we split. We're actually friends now, but we were never really a match. Brad and Stef, though, they're happy together. At least they were before he started tearing up the house."

"Home improvement isn't for the faint of heart."

"Neither is marriage, I guess."

"But worth it if you can make it work."

Obviously, Grant had. "Lucky you that you could," Cass said. How could marriage to such a good man *not* work?

Back home Stef tried not to look at the mess her house had become or think of the mess her life was. She checked in with her sister, talked to her mom, lied to both, telling them everything was fine. "We love it up here." At least she had when they'd first arrived and bought the house. They'd gotten it for a bargain. The people who'd owned it were divorcing.

Maybe the house was cursed.

"Don't be stupid," she told herself. She finished the family catch-up calls, then cleaned the kitchen and did a load of laundry. Went upstairs, sat on the bed and cried. Wished Brad would come home. Polished her nails and told herself Brad was a jerk. Picked up Petey from his friend's house and did the drive-through at Herman's, trying not to think about the fact that normally Brad would've been with them.

"When's Daddy coming home?" Petey asked as he unwrapped his hamburger.

"I don't know, honey."

"Is he still with his friend?"

"Yes." His friend Gerhardt. Gerhardt Geissel was an older man. He should be counseling Brad to go home.

"He likes his friend better than us," Petey said, his lower lip jutting out.

"Now, you know that's not true. Daddy was with you at your game yesterday."

"I want him to come home."

"So do I. And he will, soon." He had to return to his senses at some point. The way he was behaving was ridiculous. And immature. And lose the tool man? Really? Then what? The fix-it fairies would show up at night and finish the house?

The more she thought about the whole situation, the angrier she got. Why should she be the one to cave? She shouldn't. Their disaster area had needed cleaning up, and she'd only done what needed to be done to make that happen. If Brad wasn't being such an oversize brat he'd see that.

After Petey was in bed, she loaded up on ice cream and found a movie on Netflix. Neither proved satisfying.

CHAPTER SEVENTEEN

Griffin had enjoyed helping Matt with the trim on the windows, but once the afternoon got hotter, he shooed her inside. "I can take it from here. Anyway, you're not that good at painting with your left hand," he'd teased.

So she'd gone in and cleaned up, then wondered if he'd like to stay for dinner again. He was at the back of the house now, up on the ladder and painting the trim on one of the bedroom windows.

"Are you interested in staying for some pizza?"

"Sure," he called down. "Give me another couple of hours to finish and go to my bro's to wash up."

"You can wash up here," she said. *In my shower. Need someone to scrub your back?*

What was she thinking? In fact, what was she doing? Hadn't she only a week ago told him she didn't want to start something? She was leaving. She wished she hadn't opened her big mouth and invited him to stay for dinner.

Too late. She'd offered.

She'd stuff him with pizza, then send him on his way. Yes, good plan. That was what she'd do.

When he came back to the house all cleaned up and carrying a Safeway grocery bag with ice cream, hot fudge sauce, maraschino cherries and whipping cream, she knew she wasn't going to be simply shoving pizza at him and sending him on his way. And part of her—the part completely devoid of common sense—was perfectly happy with that.

"Bring on the pizza," he said as he walked toward the kitchen, already at home in her house.

The pizza was from Bavarian Alps, and they ate it lounging on her back porch. He took one bite and pronounced it the best pizza he'd ever had. "And I've had some good ones."

She smiled and took a bite of hers.

She ate it all except the crust.

"Don't like the crust, huh?" he asked as he helped himself to another piece.

"No, I do," she said and took a bite to prove it.

"You sure don't eat much," he observed.

"I eat."

"I think you spend more time taking pictures of your food than you do eating it."

"I don't want to get fat."

"At the rate you're going, no worries there." His brows furrowed. "You don't... You're not— Never mind," he said and took another bite of his pizza.

"I don't have an eating disorder, if that's what you're getting at," she said, mildly irritated.

"Hey, sorry. It's just that you don't seem to enjoy your food very much."

"You know the saying. Some people eat to live, others live to eat." She'd lived to eat once upon a time. But in the end, she hadn't really been living, at least not happily.

"Can't you do both?" he countered. He picked an olive off his slice, regarded it and then popped it in his mouth. "Food is like sex. It's a gift. You should enjoy it."

Sex. Sex with Matt Masters. Mmm.

Don't go there, she told herself.

"Do you enjoy what you eat?"

"Of course I do! Well, I guess I don't *always* get a chance to enjoy eating it. I'm too busy taking pictures of it."

"That's sick and wrong," he said.

"What about you? You spend your nights cooking for other people. How often are you able to enjoy your food?"

"Every chance I get. I'm enjoying it right now. Good food, good company, that's the best. But I think you need some help." He stood up from the couch and held out a hand. "Come on."

"Where are we going?"

"Back to the kitchen. Time for Food Appreciation 101."

She let him take her hand and lead her to the kitchen, where he sat her down at the kitchen table. "Watch and learn from the wise one."

She watched as he whipped the cream, directing him where to find the beater and the sugar and vanilla. He'd purchased a high-end chocolate bar and grated that into a small mixing bowl. "It's all in the wrist, you know." He opened the jar of cherries and smiled at her over his shoulder. "Are you drooling yet?"

"Yes," she admitted.

"Bet the food looks pretty good, too," he joked. "Okay, now we need a bowl."

She pointed to the cupboard where she kept the dishes.

He passed up the smaller dessert bowls and took out a serving bowl.

"I can't eat that much," she protested.

"Don't worry. I'm gonna help you," he said, then got busy building a mountain of a sundae. When he was done, it was a work of art. Chocolate-chip mint ice cream overflowing with chocolate sauce, shaved chocolate and bits of cherries, capped with whipped cream and the traditional cherry on top.

"I should get a picture before it melts," she said.

"No, no pictures. You'll get all sidetracked with angles and focus. Just sit there a minute and take it in."

She did, eyeing the chocolate sauce, the whipped cream. She loved chocolate-chip mint ice cream. Her mouth began to water.

He sat down next to her, crossed his arms on the table and leaned his chin on them. "Edible art."

"You do excellent work," she said.

"Yes, I do. Now. Close your eyes."

She complied.

"Open your mouth."

She opened her mouth and he spooned in the sundae.

"Okay, this is the sundae equivalent of a wine tasting. Let it sit in your mouth. What flavors are you tasting?"

All of them! The ice cream swirled with the chocolate, melting on her tongue, rushing the intense flavor of mint over her taste buds. And there was the lighter sweetness of the cherries. And whipped cream. She'd always loved whipped cream. She hadn't had whipped cream in ages. She was going to have an ice cream orgasm right here.

His voice was soft in her ear. "So tell me."

She swallowed. "Everything," she said on a sigh.

"Want more?"

She licked her lips. "Yes, please."

In went another spoonful, just as delicious as the first.

"Are you enjoying yourself?"

She smiled. "Yes."

"Good. Now, open your eyes. Here's your spoon. You're on your own."

She opened her eyes and watched as he dug into the sundae. He put it in his mouth, closed his eyes and nodded. Swallowed. She watched the muscles in his throat work. Ice cream and sex for dessert. That would be…delicious.

He opened his eyes and looked at her, and his gaze dropped to her mouth. Was he a mind reader?

But he didn't kiss her. Instead, he took a second bite of ice cream. "Go ahead. Have another one. I promise it won't kill you."

"Too much will. It'll clog your arteries."

"Maybe. In another twenty years. If I do nothing but eat ice cream. I'm not that worried. You shouldn't worry when you eat. It's bad for your digestion."

"I'll remember that."

"Will you?" he countered. "I know it's none of my business. But seriously, what's with the barely eating? Seems kind of funny for someone who takes pictures of food."

"There's more than one way to enjoy food. Taking pictures of it is a feast for the eyes."

"True. But it's kind of a waste not to follow through and eat it."

"I'm not starving. I just..."

"Don't want to get fat," he finished with her. "Were you?"

She found it embarrassing to meet his gaze. "When I was a kid. The other kids made fun of me. But that was a long time ago," she said to prove she had no baggage. No fear of people saying *What a shame. She'd be so pretty if she could lose some weight.*

Not that kids were ever that kind. From her peers she'd received lovely nicknames like Lard Butt and Hefty Bag. Of course, not everyone called her names. Some people simply looked at her with judgmental faces or tsked when they saw her eating a cookie. Which was why she'd found it was best to eat cookies in her room.

Then came the day she overheard her parents out on the back patio, talking. Mom was, as usual, insisting Griffin was simply large-boned.

"That's not bone hanging over her pants, Danielle. She's too young to be so overweight," Dad had continued, and even from her position of eavesdropping behind the sliding screen door, she could hear the disgust in his voice. "We need to do something.

She starts high school next year and I don't want her being the
fat girl. The kids already tease her—you know they do."

"Children are cruel," Mom had said.

Yes, they were.

"Who's going to want her if she keeps ballooning like this?
It scares me to look at her."

Scared him to look at her? Griffin had covered her ears and
run to her room, but her father's words followed her.

She'd learned her lesson. No one will love you if you're fat.

That summer, her parents sent her away to camp. Not just any
camp, but a camp where kids with weight issues got whipped
into shape.

Her father hugged her when she came home. "See how beautiful you are," he'd said. "I'm proud of you."

He was finally proud of her now that she wasn't the fat girl.
This was what it took to earn people's approval. You had to
control yourself. Stay away from food you loved. Food was the
enemy.

Her parents pulled strings to get her enrolled in a better high
school where she made new friends. Nobody knew her past and
nobody called her Lard Butt. And in spite of still being shy, she
began to develop a social life. And some confidence. She started
dating, joined the photography club. Looked longingly at the
milk shakes when she went out with her friends and ordered diet
pop. But she stuck with it, and pretty soon she didn't miss the
cookies, was just as happy with a bite of cake as the whole piece.

"I can't imagine you ever being fat," Matt said, bringing her
back to the present. "You probably got teased a lot."

She nodded. Needless to say, she hadn't kept in touch with
any of the gang from the old neighborhood.

"I was scrawny," Matt said. "My friends called me Weenie
Wiener."

"Nice friends."

He shrugged. "We all called each other names. My best

friend's nickname was Banana Nose. It's what kids do. You grow out of it. Anyway, you're not a kid anymore and you look great."

"That's because I work at it."

"You'd look great even with another fifty pounds," he assured her. "Some men like a babe with some back. My dad did."

His father was ridiculously handsome. Griffin found it hard to imagine him with any woman who wasn't gorgeous, and said as much.

"Yeah, my mom was really pretty. But she got kind of pudgy when she got older. She was so much fun, though, you didn't notice."

"It's better for your health not to carry around extra pounds." Oh, wait. Did that sound judgmental? "No offense to your mom," she quickly added. "How did she die?"

His smile fell away. "Heart attack, not long after Dan and Charley got married. Totally unexpected. She and Dad were in Fiji for their anniversary. They'd saved for that trip for a year."

Horrible. "I'm so sorry."

He shrugged. "Shitty timing, huh? We all still miss her. But we've got a ton of memories. She was the best. She knew how to enjoy life."

Was that a subtle dig? "I enjoy life," Griffin insisted. "I just want to make sure I stay healthy." *And never get looked at with disgust again.*

"There's healthy and there's paranoid."

"I'm not paranoid."

"Prove it. Take one more bite." He dredged up a spoonful of ice cream and waved it in front of her.

Images of herself as a child swam before her eyes. She was never going to repeat that experience. But she easily could. This was how you fell off Slim Mountain and landed in Lard Lake, one mouthful at a time. "No judging, but are you positive you don't have an eating disorder?"

She grabbed the spoon from him and stuffed the ice cream

in her mouth. It still tasted good, but it didn't make her feel good. She stuck the spoon back in the bowl and shoved it at him. "You're an enabler."

He smiled, unoffended, then scooped up a big mouthful of ice cream and downed it. "Goin' to diet hell with a smile on my face."

Now he was making fun of her. She frowned.

"Sorry. Seriously, I'd never encourage anybody to overeat, but I don't think you should be afraid to enjoy your food."

"I do," she said. Not like Matt, though. He seemed to have a gift for enjoying not only his food but every facet of life.

"Well, I know you like taking pictures of it," he said.

"And you like cooking it," she retorted.

"So that makes us a pretty good team." He smiled. "Hey, we've still got a lot of daylight left. Let's go for a drive. I'll take you to one of my favorite places."

Before she could remind herself that she was leaving, she said, "Okay," and next thing she knew, she was in his Jeep and they were headed away from town and up Sleeping Lady Mountain. Occasionally a cabin would peek out at them from behind the fir, pine and hemlock trees. She saw a few sprawling homes, too, granddaddies to her small Craftsman. Mostly, though, it was trees and rocks, salal and ferns, wild huckleberry bushes and an occasional deer bounding through bracken. He pulled off the main road onto an old logging road and they bumped along, climbing farther and farther away from civilization.

At last he stopped the Jeep. They got out and he led her to a rocky outcrop that offered a view of the town below and the surrounding orchards and farms, which looked like green quilt squares with the brown lines of the roads running between. The Wenatchee River was a thick ribbon making its way down the valley. And, of course, the mountains reigned in stately glory, craggy and almost bare, having thrown off their coat of snow in preparation for summer. She could hear a bird singing in the distance, and little wildflowers peeked out at her from between the crevices in the rock.

"It's beautiful," she said.

"I love it on this side of the mountains," he told her. "I grew up in Wenatchee. Spent summers working for my dad. In fall I picked apples after school and on weekends."

"How did you end up in Seattle?" she asked.

"Found a job as a sous chef. Then I met Lexie, my ex. Well, about-to-be ex."

"I'm sorry things didn't work out," Griffin said.

Matt shrugged. "I tried and that's all you can do." He shook his head. "I didn't get it right the first time around, but I'm moving on with my life."

"Me, too. That's why I'm going to New York. To start over."

"Do you really want to go to New York?" He slipped his arms around her, turned her to face him. One hand went to her cheek and he brushed her lips with his thumb.

He was going to kiss her. She shouldn't let him.

But she did. And she let herself enjoy it. She could still taste the chocolate from the sundae they'd shared.

What was she thinking?

Maybe that there were all kinds of ways to start over.

Grant had enjoyed dinner at Dan and Charley's place. They had a charming three-bedroom fixer-upper that Dan had slowly been working on. "He got the kitchen done, and that's all I care about," Charley had said.

It was a kick-ass kitchen, with concrete countertops and a slick glass backsplash in earth tones, a pantry, a subzero fridge, plus a high-end stove and a kitchen island. Here his daughter-in-law cooked meals to rival what she offered in her restaurant.

Tonight they'd sat out on the deck and enjoyed salmon cooked in a puff pastry, twice-baked potatoes loaded with cheese, and broccoli salad that tasted just like the one Lou used to make.

"That's because it's Mom's recipe," Dan said.

"I'm really enjoying making everything in her recipe box," Charley told Grant. "It was sweet of Matt to give it to me."

"He doesn't need a flowery recipe box. Anyway, he's got them all in his computer," Dan said.

Lou had gotten the recipe box as a wedding shower present from her mother, who'd shared recipes for some of their family favorites—meatballs, salmon loaf with creamed peas (never his favorite), snickerdoodles, chocolate cake. She'd added to it over the years, including recipes for enchiladas, cinnamon rolls, and the broccoli salad they were eating now. He hadn't been able to look at the damned thing after she died. He'd given it to Matt, figuring he'd want it. Turned out he'd had just as hard a time looking at it and had passed it on to Charley when she and Dan got married. Charley treasured it, and that would have made Lou happy.

"Well, thanks for making the salad," Grant said.

The topic of the recipe box had led them to a conversational dead end, and for a moment all that could be heard was the evening song of a robin.

Dan put them on a new road. "How are things going at Cass's?"

"The roof's pretty much done. I'll fix her deck next."

"That means more cookies," Dan teased.

"She made shortcake today," Grant said.

"Cass is good in the kitchen," Charley said. "She's a good woman, period."

Grant nodded but said nothing.

"Why don't you ask her out?" Charley persisted.

Hadn't he just had this conversation with his son up on Cass's roof? Were they tag-teaming him?

More to the point, how did you politely tell your daughter-in-law to mind her own business? "Oh, I don't think so," Grant said, taking another bite of salad. *See, Lou? I'm eating my vegetables.* She'd always been after him to eat well, and then she was the one who died. What kind of sick cosmic joke was that?

"You can't be a monk the rest of your life," Dan said.

At the rate Grant was going, that was where he was headed, but the last thing he needed was his son pointing it out. "Worrying about your old man's sex life is kind of kinky, don'tcha think?"

"What if I'm worrying about my old man being alone?"

Okay, this was getting out of hand. "Last I looked, I could manage to take a shower without falling."

"You know what I mean," Dan said with a frown.

"I know," Grant said. "And I appreciate your concern."

"Cass is awfully nice," put in Charley.

"A little too young for me." Actually, a lot too young for him.

"Come on, Dad. You're not that old. You can still take a shower without falling down," he added, making Grant smile. "Anyway, plenty of guys marry younger women."

"Got me married off already?" Grant joked. "You want a stepmom to come in and steal your inheritance?"

"I'll risk it," Dan said. "Anyway, I'm not saying you have to run off and get married. But you guys could hang out, have some fun."

All the more reason not to start something. It could get awkward down the road.

"You should think about it anyway," Charley said and yawned. "Sorry. Being pregnant makes me tired."

"I should get going anyway," Grant said. Being on a roof on a hot spring day had made him pretty tired, too.

"You going over to Cass's again tomorrow?" Charley wanted to know.

Women, they never gave up.

"No."

"Back to the mess at the Stahls'?" Dan asked.

Only to give a certain woman some unrequested advice. "I'll probably be somewhere else tomorrow."

He thanked the kids for dinner and returned to Gerhardt's. Thoughts of Cass Wilkes accompanied him. He gave them a mental boot, told them to climb into some other guy's truck.

Thoughts were a lot like dogs once they were off the leash. They didn't mind very well.

CHAPTER EIGHTEEN

Stef assumed Grant would be at her house hard at work by the time she got home. But after she picked up Petey from Mountain Tikes, she arrived to find his truck parked in front of Griffin's. Had Griffin stolen him right out from under her nose?

Angry, she steamed over to Griffin's house, Petey in tow. Before Griffin could get out a hello she snapped, "Grant was supposed to be working for me today."

Griffin's eyes got big. "I didn't know that. He didn't say anything to me."

What was going on here? "He told me yesterday he'd be over."

"Maybe he's planning on coming to your house next. He's almost done here. He painted my bedroom today."

Good for him. "I need to talk to him."

"Uh, okay."

At that moment Grant himself came down the stairs, wiping his hands on a rag. "Hi, Mr. Masters!" Petey greeted him. "Can I help you today?"

"We'll see," Grant said. Very noncommittal. Very irritating.

"I thought you were going to work at *my* house," Stef accused.

Sheesh. First her husband, now her handyman. You couldn't depend on anyone.

"I was, but we need to talk. Griffin, mind if we use your front porch?"

Griffin looked curiously from Stef to Grant but said, "Sure. Hey, Petey, you want to help me make some lemonade?"

"Okay," Petey said cheerfully and skipped off to the kitchen beside her.

With Petey occupied, Grant settled Stef on one of the plastic Adirondack chairs on Griffin's porch. "I hear your husband's not at home right now."

Stef's cheeks burned. Who had told him, Griffin or Cass? Probably Cass, since they'd been all chummy at her place the day before. What a tattletale.

"That's why I need you to hurry up and finish," she said. "So he can come home."

"Is that what he wants, for me to finish?"

It was what *she* wanted. Didn't that count for anything?

He waited a moment, then obviously gave up on getting an answer. "Look. I'm happy to help you two once you're back together, but right now working for you is not a good idea."

"What are you saying?" Please let it not be what she thought he was saying.

"I'm quitting."

No, no, no! No. This was bad. Bad, bad, bad. "But you can't quit and leave everything like it is! The whole floor still has to be done."

"Your husband can handle that. I've already put down the moisture barrier. I'll lend him the tools he needs and leave him instructions."

Stef slumped against her chair. "He'll never finish it."

"I think he will. If he needs help, he can call me."

"This is not right," she said bitterly.

Grant leaned forward and took her hand in his big work-calloused one. "You can always buy another house. It's not so easy to replace a good husband and father."

That made the tears prickle her eyes. "I don't want to replace him."

"I know you don't. Take some advice from a guy who's been around awhile. Put your marriage first. Show your man you've got some faith in him."

Petey was back on the porch now. "We made lemonade, but not from a can. Griffin let me squeeze the lemons and she took my picture. Come see." He grabbed Stef's hand and towed her inside the house and into the kitchen, where Griffin had several glasses out as well as a pitcher filled with lemonade and ice. She poured Petey a glass and he sat down at the table and began gulping it down.

"What's going on?" she asked.

Stef scowled. "My husband's left me and now my handyman's quit. And—"

"Daddy's visiting a friend, Mommy," Petey interrupted. "You said."

"Yes, I did say that, didn't I?" Covering for Brad, who didn't deserve it. Okay, yes, she'd started this mess, but she'd said she was sorry. Why was this all her fault? Grant's advice stung.

"What are you going to do?" Griffin asked.

"Drink lemonade," she said and poured herself a glass.

"When's Daddy coming home?" Petey wanted to know.

At the rate they were going, never. Something had to be done.

"You know, I think I'll take some lemonade out to Grant," Griffin said and beat a hasty retreat, leaving Stef to spin out a fairy tale for her son.

"Mommy," Petey nudged.

Daddy needed to come home now. His son missed him.

So did his wife. But the house...

"Soon, honey," she said. Surely Brad would change his mind. "Come on. Let's go home."

★ ★ ★

Grant had showered and was leaving Gerhardt's to go to Dan's when he encountered Stahl coming down the flower-lined walk from the opposite direction, obviously making his way to his own room.

He hesitated at the sight of Grant, then set his chin and began speed walking, nodding as he got close.

He would have sped right past if Grant hadn't moved and blocked him. "Got a minute?" Grant asked.

Stahl frowned. "I'm kind of in a hurry."

"To get to that room you're in by yourself?"

The frown turned into a glare. "Not sure that's any of your business."

"You know, it's not," Grant agreed. "And you can tell me to go to hell. It's no skin off my nose."

"Okay. Go to hell," Stahl said and tried to walk away.

Grant blocked him again. "I get that you're pissed. It makes a man mad when his wife disrespects him."

Now he had the guy's attention. "Yeah, it does."

"You had the best of intentions."

Now Stahl was looking at him as if he were an oracle. "I did."

"And she screwed up."

Stahl nodded his agreement, his jaw tight.

"But wives do that sometimes. So do husbands. You still love her, right?"

Grant knew the emotions behind that expression. Every man felt them at some point in his marriage—pride and regret duking it out.

"I do." Stahl said it as if it was his cross to bear.

"You made your point. Go home to your wife, son. In the end, you'll be sorry if you don't."

With that parting remark, Grant stepped away and continued down the path. He hoped the kid had gotten the message. But who knew?

★ ★ ★

The house was not only a mess, it felt…empty. Stef sighed. Brad shouldn't have stomped off. He should've gotten the point she was trying to make. Most of all, he should've accepted her apology. He was the one who was in the wrong, not her.

But did she want to be right or did she want to be happy? She'd spent a lot of time complaining what a mess her house was, but apparently the house wasn't the only thing on Blackberry Lane that needed renovation. She had a wall of her own that needed to get torn down, a thick wall of pride that she kept building higher and higher.

"Would you like to help me with something special?" she asked her son after she'd fed him dinner.

He practically quivered with eagerness. "What?"

"Let's bake some cookies for Daddy. How does that sound?" Maybe she wasn't the world's best baker, but she could handle chocolate-chip cookies. She could also handle giving up the battle.

"Okay!"

"Chocolate-chip cookies are Daddy's favorite," she told Petey as she pulled out the ingredients.

"I like chocolate-chip cookies, too."

"I think we can spare one for you."

Petey got a cookie from the first batch, still warm, along with a glass of milk. "This is good, Mommy. Daddy's gonna like these."

She hoped so. He'd had no interest in the cream-puff swans. But then, those had been more a bribe than an apology. This offering was coming along with a big change of heart.

An hour later, they were at Gerhardt's Gasthaus with a plate of cookies and an envelope containing a note that said "He's gone and I'm sorry. Please come home." She signed it "Love, Stef." She did love him. She could only trust that this would prove it.

She was too chicken to try his room, so she went to the reception desk.

"Is Daddy here?" Petey asked as they crossed the lobby.

"Yes."

"Are we going to see him?"

"No. We're going to leave our surprise and then go home."

Petey's lower lip jutted out. "But I want to see him."

"You will soon. I promise." At least she hoped he would. She gave the cookies to the desk clerk and asked her to deliver them to Brad's room. "I want to surprise him," she explained. *I'm also too nervous to do this in person.*

"I'll make sure he gets them," the woman promised.

Back home again, Stef called her neighborhood helpers and spent another twenty bucks getting the boys to move the furniture back from the garage to the man cave, instructing Petey to stay out from underfoot. After they left, she laid out the picture of the new game table in the middle of the room. There, all set. Now only Brad was missing.

He continued to remain missing and by seven o'clock he still wasn't home. Maybe he'd had a meeting with a prospective client? Or maybe the reception desk hadn't gotten the cookies and her note to him yet. Yes, that was it. It had to be.

Meanwhile, though, Petey was not happy. "You *said* Daddy was coming home." He looked at her accusingly.

"He is, honey. Meanwhile, time for your bath."

"I don't want a bath. I want to see Daddy!"

"Honey, you'll see him when he gets here."

"I want him here *now!*" Petey's face was starting to take on an angry flush and his eyes were filling with tears.

"Well, Daddy won't want to see you all dirty and smelly."

"I'm not smelly!"

"Come on," she coaxed, taking his hand. "Let's get you cleaned up for Daddy."

Petey balked. "I want to see Daddy now!"

"Petey," she said sternly. "I'm not a magician. I can't wave a magic wand and bring him here."

"He likes his friend better than us," Petey cried.

Obviously Daddy liked his imaginary friend better than one of them. Stef picked up her angry son. He was getting too big to carry, but she managed to struggle up the stairs with him, Petey crying all the way.

"I want Daddy," he howled as she ran the bathwater.

"Hey, big guy, what's all the crying about?"

Stef turned and there stood Brad in the doorway, his duffel bag at his feet.

"Daddy!" Petey leaped into his arms. "Are you done staying with your friend?"

Brad looked at Stef. "Yes, I am."

It took a while to settle Petey down. After his bath, he had to tell his father how he'd helped Mommy bake cookies.

"They were very good," Brad said and smiled at Stef.

Petey dragged the conversation out as long as possible, then insisted Daddy read him a bedtime story. Stef left them alone for some father-son time and went downstairs. To the unfinished mess.

She sat on the sofa, which was still covered in a sheet to protect it from construction dust. It would probably be covered by that sheet forever. She sighed, not for the first time that day.

Twenty minutes later, Brad came downstairs. She patted the couch. "Want to join me?"

"So, he's really gone?"

Stef nodded and Brad sat next to her.

"I didn't mean for things to get so out of hand," she said.

He looked at the disaster area surrounding them. "Me neither."

"Grant thinks you should be able to finish up on your own."

"How about you, Stef? What do *you* think?"

She decided not to share what she really thought. "You're more important to me than this house."

He studied her for a moment, then edged closer and put an arm around her, pulling her against him. "I was beginning to wonder."

"Oh, Brad. Just because I got mad…"

"It wasn't that you got mad—it was that you lost faith in me. You complained about everything. I couldn't do anything right. I only wanted to please you."

"I know," she said, feeling about two inches tall.

"Yeah, I got in over my head a couple of times," he admitted.

A couple? How about every time he started a new project?

"But I was going to figure it out. When you hired Masters, it was like a knife in the back."

"I was only trying to help."

"Well, it felt like you were taking over."

Okay, she had. And who could blame her? "Grant did know about the weight-bearing wall," she said in her own defense.

"Load-bearing. I'd figured it out, too," he reminded her.

They sat in silence for a moment. Then she asked, "Will you finish the floor?"

"Yes. I think I can handle that."

"I think you can, too," she said.

"So, listen, I was an ass hat."

"I was poop."

"No, I was wrong. I'm sorry, Sweet Stuff."

Sweet Stuff. She'd been anything but sweet. She felt the tears start to rise.

"Can we start over?" he asked, wiping away the first drops with his hand.

She smiled at him. "I want to."

They sealed the bargain with a kiss. And, just to be sure it was sealed, another kiss. And then another. And then, well, if you were going to seal a bargain, you should really make it worth your while. They did.

Later, after they'd showered together and were back in their clothes, she said, "About your man cave."

He groaned. "I had it coming. Can we leave it at that?"

"No. I have something to show you."

"Oh, boy," he said warily.

"No, it's all good. Well, at least I hope it is."

She led him down to the basement and opened the door to his manly-man retreat. Everything was back in place except, of course, for the card table.

"Looks good," he said.

"Look again," she told him, pointing to the paper in the middle of the room.

"What's this?" He walked over and picked it up, stared at it.

"Happy anniversary—a little early," she said. "It's being delivered next week."|

She hadn't seen him that gleeful since the day they bought their first new car. "Really?"

She nodded. "Really. I owe you."

He came over and put his arms around her. "You don't owe me anything, Stef. I'm the one who owes you. I've made you crazy trying to do all this stuff when I had no idea what I was doing. But I wanted to please you."

"I know. But you don't have to be an HGTV star to please me. Anyway, it's the thought that counts." *But, Lord, please let him get beyond the thought phase and actually finish the room.*

That was the plan for Tuesday. Brad took the day off and began working on the floor. She gave him a hearty breakfast, then tried not to hover as he got started. It didn't sound promising.

"This wood is harder than cement," he grumbled. He must have seen the *oh, no* expression on her face because he hastily added, "Don't worry. I'll get it done."

She'd thought maybe she should hang around and help him, but with the floor project getting off to such a bumpy start, she decided it would be better to scram and let him get the hang of things on his own.

She called Griffin. "Brad's fighting with the flooring. I need a latte."

"At least he's working on it," Griffin said as they made their way to the bakery.

"So far. I did mention that Grant said he'd come help him if he needed it. That didn't exactly go over well." A wifely tactical error. Add it to the list. Sigh.

At the bakery she updated Cass, finishing with "I'm just glad to have him home again. Grant was right. Marriage improvement is more important than home improvement."

"I'm happy for you," Cass said.

"Meanwhile, we have a birthday to celebrate," said Stef. "I got my e-vite from Charley this morning."

Cass frowned. "I'm getting so old."

"We'll console you with chocolate and presents," Stef promised her.

"Anyway, you look thirty," Griffin said.

Stef wasn't sure she'd go that far. But Cass did look good for a woman in her forties. "Are your kids coming up?"

Cass beamed. "They'll all be here, including Dani and Mike and the baby. That's the advantage of having a birthday on Memorial Day weekend. Everyone's already got time off for the holiday."

"Who all will be there?" Griffin asked.

"Oh, the usual gang. The Sterling family, Stacy Thomas and her husband, Dot and Tilda and Devon, you guys. Grant and Dan's brother."

"Dan's brother? Hmm," Stef said and gave Griffin a sly look.

Griffin's cheeks turned pink.

"You two seem to be getting along pretty well," Stef observed. "I saw you out there on Sunday helping him paint. You seemed to be having fun."

"We were. But his divorce isn't even final until the end of the month and I just broke up with Steve. Anyway, it would be crazy to start something right before I leave."

"You don't need to rush into anything," Cass said.

Griffin nodded. "He's really sweet, though. If I was staying…"

Her friend leaving, there was a depressing thought.

"The house should be ready to put on the market in June," Griffin continued.

June. By the end of summer her buddy would be gone. "I hate that you're leaving."

"I need to," Griffin said. "I've played it safe a lot. It's time to take a risk."

"You can always come back if things don't work out," Cass told her. "But I think you're right to go for it."

"So do I," Stef said, determined to be noble. "How's it going with Beth's cookbook?"

"Almost done. She wants three more pictures."

"That cookbook is going to be a hot seller for Pat at the bookstore," Cass predicted.

"Once the book's printed they're going to have a booksigning party. I hope I'm still here for it."

"If not, we'll all chip in and fly you back," Stef said. "And maybe I'll have to take a trip out there once you're settled. I've always wanted to see Times Square."

"I'd like that," Griffin said. For a moment she looked a little wistful. "I'm going to miss everyone here so much."

"Just because you're moving doesn't mean you're leaving." Cass smiled. "Don't forget. Once an Icicle, always an Icicle."

Cass's words wrapped around Griffin's heart. Yes, she'd be moving away, but she'd still have the friends she'd made here. Stef would visit her in New York. Her parents certainly would.

What about Matt?

The afternoon they'd shared had been more satisfying than a six-course meal. And that kiss had been the best dessert ever. What would happen with him if she stayed?

She knew exactly what would happen if she left. Nothing.

Back home, she picked up Muriel Sterling's book and turned to the page she'd bookmarked.

It's easy to get derailed from your dreams. The best way to prevent that is to set goals. Make checklists and set dates. Moving forward will be so much easier.

That was what she needed to do—set goals, set dates. She pulled up the calendar app on her phone and began to do exactly that. The house would go on the market in June. With luck, it would sell quickly. She wasn't a real-estate expert, but she knew it took a while for deals to close. Still, maybe by the end of July, she could leave? Yes, the end of July.

End of July. May was almost over. That meant in two months she'd be gone.

The thought both excited and depressed her. She was doing the right thing, though; she was sure of it.

And where did that leave Matt? Nowhere on the list of dates and goals. He'd be coming up this weekend, going to Cass's birthday party. He'd even mentioned inner tubing down the river. It was going to be a fun weekend. She decided not to think beyond that.

Stef had returned home to find that Brad hadn't made much progress beyond miscutting several pieces of wood. "I'll get the hang of it," he assured her, and she kissed him and told him she knew he would. What a lie. This was still a disaster.

The afternoon and the progress on the floor slogged on. Petey came home from school and wanted to help. Stef thought it would be best if he didn't after he reported that Daddy was saying bad words.

By dinner Brad was sweaty and cranky. If only he'd call Grant, this could be done in a few hours. At the rate Brad was going, it would be more like a few years. She bit her tongue.

She put Petey to bed and heard his prayers while Brad stayed downstairs, sawing, banging and swearing. She kept a safe distance, hanging out in the bedroom and watching a movie on her laptop.

He finally came up at ten. "We should've bought a condo," he grumbled.

"You don't have to be good at everything," she said gently after he'd showered and come to bed. Maybe now he'd be open to bringing in help. "Why don't you just—"

"Don't say it."

"Okay, not saying a word." She kissed him, rolled over and turned out the light on the nightstand.

She was almost drifting off when he said, "Call the tool man."

She snuggled next to him and smiled. Within minutes she was asleep and happily dreaming of her beautiful completed great room.

CHAPTER NINETEEN

Grant found himself back at Stef's house on Wednesday afternoon. Her husband had taken the day off and they got busy with the boards and nail guns. Cutting the boards for the cantilevered bump-out in what had originally been the dining room took some time and patience. Stahl felt frustration when nails bent or split the board, until Grant assured him that he had to expect that.

"Comes with the territory," he said. "This is a really hard wood, so it can be a challenge."

Once the guy knew that some of his difficulties were the fault of the wood and not due to his incompetence, he began to take a more laid-back view of the project. He was beaming like a new father when his wife came home from work and went into ecstasies when she saw the floor was more than half-done.

"It's gorgeous!" she raved. "Thank you," she said to Grant, making her husband's smile slide off.

"Don't thank me. I was just the grunt. Your husband did the heavy lifting."

She threw her arms around Brad's neck and kissed him. "Thank you, babe. I love it."

That brought the smile back. "It's going to look good when it's done."

"And it's getting done. Yay!"

Grant promised to come back the next day and left the two of them happily celebrating—and their son begging to help Daddy.

"Next project," Brad said.

Oh, boy, he'd created a monster.

Grant was back in his truck when his phone rang. Another woman in need of a handyman. Priscilla Castro, the stalker from the store.

"The plumber didn't fix my sink. It's worse. In fact, it's flooded. Please, can you stop by? I'm desperate."

She'd better be, Grant thought as he put her address in his GPS.

Priscilla Castro lived in a three-bedroom rambler on a quiet cul-de-sac. The lovely treed lot next to her place was for sale. Nice lot, bad location.

She opened the door before he even got a chance to knock and her perfume was the first thing to greet him. Subtle was not this woman's middle name. The perfume made him sneeze. Or maybe it was her. Maybe he was allergic to Priscilla Castro.

"Thank you for coming," she said. "You've saved me."

A little overdramatic, but he simply nodded and asked her to show him the problem sink.

"When you're a woman alone, dealing with these things can be such a challenge," she said as she led him through the house. "Did I mention I'm divorced?"

Only within the first five minutes of meeting him. "Yes, you did."

Now they'd reached the master bedroom. The curtains were drawn and a bedside lamp was on, illuminating a sheer black nightgown draped across the bed.

He caught her looking at him, gauging his reaction. He

brushed past her toward the master bath, keeping his toolbox between them as a barrier, and went into the bathroom.

There was indeed water on the floor.

"Oh, let me mop that up." She grabbed a towel off the rack and bent over to mop it up, using the old show-the-cleavage ploy. Ugh.

He took out his flashlight, then opened the cabinet door and checked under the sink. Water there, too, naturally. It only took a moment to see what the problem was. The slip nut on the P-trap was loose.

"Any plumber could fix this," he told her. For that matter, anyone with a wrench could loosen it. He wouldn't put it past this woman.

"Mine couldn't," she said.

"Who's your plumber?"

She shrugged. "I can't remember."

Yeah, and he couldn't remember the name of his doctor. "You need to change plumbers."

"Or keep you on speed dial?" she suggested and giggled. Gag. She knelt down next to him. "I really appreciate you coming over."

"Not a problem." He sneezed again.

"Bless you," she said. "You must be coming down with something."

Yeah, a severe case of disgust. For sure he was allergic to Priscilla Castro.

"No, I'm fine," he said as he tightened the slip nut.

There, done. He backed out from under the sink and almost knocked her over. "Sorry," he said, hurrying to put away his wrench.

"So, it's all fixed? Already?"

"Good to go." He snapped his toolbox shut and stood.

"Well, that was fast. Let me get my checkbook."

He didn't want to stay in this over-perfumed spiderweb any longer than he had to. "That's okay. This one's on the house."

"Oh, that's so sweet of you," she cooed.

"No problem," he said and began to make for the front door and freedom.

She was fast, though, and managed to get ahead of him, slowing down his escape. There was no getting away, short of pushing her aside and bolting.

"How are you getting along?" she asked.

"Fine."

"I'd be lonely all by myself in a new town."

"I'm not exactly alone. My son lives here." They were at the door now. He clutched the doorknob.

She put a hand on his arm. "Yes, but he has his own life. Are you sure I can't pay you? Some way?"

She was closing in for the kill. "Uh, Priscilla, I'm not in the market for, uh, anything."

She stared at him, disbelieving.

"Try a different plumber next time," he added, then opened the door and made his bid for freedom.

He heard the door slam after him and smiled in relief. That was one predatory female he probably wouldn't have to worry about again.

He was rolling into Gerhardt's and thinking he really needed to start looking for someplace of his own when Dan called. "Don't make any plans for Saturday night, Dad. Charley's having a party."

He'd wanted to hike up in the mountains and camp overnight.

"Command performance," Dan added. "It's a birthday party for Cass."

"What is she, all of forty?"

"Older than that," Dan said. "I forget. Forty-six or something."

Still, way too young. "I had plans."

"Come on, Dad. Charley will be pissed at me if you don't show up."

"Okay, I'll be there," Grant said. He had to admit, he liked the idea of seeing Cass Wilkes again. He liked the idea of Cass Wilkes, period. If only they were closer in age.

Maybe he *should* go camping. Far away from temptation.

Her kids Amber and Willie came in for the Memorial Day weekend festivities on Friday night, and Cass was ready for them with lasagna and French bread along with the requisite Caesar salad and chocolate cake for dessert, all family favorites. Dani and her little family would arrive later the next day, in time for the birthday party.

The very sight of her children was tonic for a mother's soul. Willie had shot up to six feet now and was still as skinny as ever. He was majoring in environmental science and resource management and would, hopefully, land a good job once he graduated. Amber, who'd been the designated gray-hair-giver of the family, had grown into a responsible young woman. With a nose ring and a tattoo. But it was a cupcake tattoo and Cass took that as a compliment. She just didn't like the fact that said tattoo resided on her daughter's lower back, which qualified it for tramp-stamp status. But oh, well. Artistic expression and all that.

Amber fell instantly in love with the newest member of the family. "Oh, look at this sweetie," she said, picking up the cat. Lady Gray draped herself over Amber's shoulder and began purring. "What's her name?"

"Useless," said Willie in disgust.

"That's mean," Amber scolded.

"Her name's Lady Gray," Cass said. "Don't listen to my rude son," she told her kitty, petting the cat's soft head.

"Get a dog, Mom," Willie told her. "Something big, like a German shepherd, to protect you."

"As if I need protecting in Icicle Falls. From what, some kid playing mailbox baseball?"

"Hey, the town's growing."

Yeah, criminals were moving in right and left.

"Well, I think Lady Gray is really sweet," Amber said, rubbing her cheek against the cat.

"She's good company," Cass said, "and I need someone in the house besides me now that you ingrates have all abandoned me."

Willie snorted but Amber looked concerned.

After dinner, her son went out with some of his old buddies from the football team, but Amber opted to stay home with Cass. "Do you get lonely, Mom?" she asked as Cass popped corn to go with the movie they'd picked up at Redbox.

"Now, why would you think that?" Oh, yeah. "I was joking earlier."

"But you're all by yourself. You could date, you know. I mean, Daddy remarried."

"If I find a cute boy toy, maybe I'll consider it. Come on. Let's go watch our movie."

She and her daughter settled on the couch to watch Matt Damon in action. It was so good having her daughter home. Until, halfway through the movie, one of Amber's friends called. Cass knew once the credits rolled, her baby would be rolling out the door to hang with her friends.

And why not? Most of them were home for the weekend. Of course they'd all want to see each other.

Still, she hated to share. Did the other parents feel the same way? Theoretically, kids came home to see their parents. In reality, Mom and Dad often took a backseat.

"Do you mind if I go out for a while after the movie?" Amber asked.

Yes, darn it. I want you all to myself. "Of course not," Cass lied. That was how it went with grown kids. You shared. If you got them to yourself for even a short amount of time, you felt lucky.

Amber made her plans and Cass put Matt back in action. Once the action was over she, like Willie, was gone, and the house was quiet. "You'll have them all tomorrow," Cass consoled herself. She sat up awhile longer and read her latest issue of *Bon Appétit*. Then she and Lady Gray went to bed.

"Our life is good," she informed the cat. So what if she was alone a lot of the time? She didn't need a man.

Her subconscious thought differently, and in her dreams it sent her to a giant toy store filled with—oh, good grief—giant Ken dolls. (Did they even make Ken dolls anymore?) And toy soldiers. And...what was this? Anatomically realistic inflatable men.

"We hear you're lonely," called one of the inflatables, bouncing down from the shelf to sling an arm around her.

Now a giant Ken doll was on her other side. "You need a boy toy?"

"No, no. I have a cat."

"Your daughter thinks you need a man," said Mr. Inflatable.

"*We* think you need a man," said Ken, raising her hand to his plastic lips. "How about it, baby?"

"I'm fine. And really," she said, "should you be cheating on Barbie like this?"

Here came a toy soldier. "Hey, I've got a friend."

He turned stiffly and gestured with a metal arm and she looked to see Grant Masters approaching. He was wearing jeans and a tool belt. No shirt. Sigh.

"You know, I think what you need is a mature man," he said to her.

"Me, too," she agreed.

He smiled, drew her up against him and licked her face. Gosh, his tongue was as rough as sandpaper. He licked her again and meowed.

Meowing? Wait a minute.

Cass opened her eyes to find Lady Gray making her presence known. "Really? Just when things were getting good."

It was almost 6:00 a.m. She'd slept late. She cleaned up and went downstairs to bake cinnamon rolls. She thought about her dream as she made dough. Maybe it was a sign.

Yeah, of a sick mind. Inflatable men. Eew.

While the rolls were rising, she got busy putting together an egg casserole. She'd gotten the recipe from Olivia Claussen, and it had quickly become a family favorite. Cinnamon rolls, egg casserole, sausage and cut-up melons. The kids would be happy with this breakfast. Of course, by the time they got up to eat, it would be closer to lunchtime.

Once breakfast was assembled, she puttered around in the kitchen some more, making ginger cookies for her son and a batch of brownies for the girls. Dani, who was also a baker, would most likely bring along her specialty, oatmeal-M&M cookies. There was never a lack of food when her family got together. The kids ate like locusts. And all stayed skinny. Lucky for them they took after their father rather than their mother, who could put on a pound simply by looking at a cookie.

"No cookies for you," she told herself.

She'd been trying to behave. She'd sent the rest of the short-cake home with Grant and had been eating nothing but salads and disgusting egg-white omelets. The torture was starting to pay off, though, and she'd actually lost a couple of pounds. She'd hardly be svelte when she went to Willie's graduation, but she'd still feel better about herself.

With all the weekend festivities, she was in danger of gaining back what she lost. After all, she'd have to eat cake at her party tonight. Sunday they'd be picnicking at the park, along with half the town, and that would mean fried chicken and po-tato salad. Beth Mallow would bring cherry pie, Janice Lind her prizewinning cake. Cass would have to sew her lips shut before leaving the house.

"Cinnamon rolls," Willie said happily when he came down for breakfast. "All right!"

"And egg casserole and sausage," Cass said as he kissed her cheek. "I'll heat you up some."

"Man, I love coming home," he said, making his old mom glow inside. She was going to be sorry when he moved out for good.

It was what kids did, though. You raised them to be strong and independent, and they left and started their own lives. And that was how it should be. Meanwhile, she'd enjoy them while they were here.

There were more to enjoy by midmorning when Dani and her husband, Mike, arrived with Cass's two-year-old granddaughter, Emma.

"Maw-Maw," cried little Emma, running to her, arms outstretched, dark curls bouncing.

Cass swept the toddler up in her arms. "Hello there, my darling. Have you missed your maw-maw?"

The child nodded and hugged Cass's neck. "My maw-maw."

"I sure am," Cass told her. "Do you want a cookie?"

"Cookie!" Emma crowed.

"Brownies?" asked Dani.

"Of course," Cass said. "And ginger cookies. You guys get settled and Miss Emma and I will go have a cookie and some milk." Well, Emma would have a cookie.

She ate it in record time. "More, Maw-Maw."

"How about some milk instead?"

Emma rocked eagerly in her chair. "Milk, please."

"Aren't you polite?"

"Cookie, Maw-Maw," she added.

Her mother was in the kitchen now. "You had one cookie. That's enough," she said, and Emma turned into a tiny thundercloud.

"I want cookie," she whined.

"I know. Later. There'll be lots of cookies at Grandma's party."

"I want cookie." The statement became more insistent.

"One is never enough," Cass said. And that, of course, was part of her problem.

"It is when it's nap time. I thought she'd sleep in the car on the way over, but she didn't."

Now, because obviously no one was getting the message, the statement was accompanied by tears.

"Okay, one more," Dani said. "But only if you stop crying."

The crying hiccuped to a halt.

"Give her half, Mom. Then we're going to take a nap so we can enjoy the party," she informed her daughter. "Okay?"

"Okay, Mama."

"That's my girl," Dani said as Cass handed over a final bite.

The bite was gone and the milk was gone, so Dani took her daughter up to settle her in the crib Cass kept in the guest room. She passed Mike, her husband, on the way out.

"Do I have another taker for some brownies?" Cass asked. "Also, I've got egg casserole left."

"Sounds good. Thanks, Mom," Mike said and settled at the table.

Will joined him and, a moment later, Amber was there, too. Cass brought over plates and the whole pan of brownies, knowing they'd be gone within minutes. By the time she'd fed Mike, Dani was at the table and hungry for some casserole.

"You sure you want that last brownie?" Willie teased her as she reached for it. "Looks like you're getting fat."

"Yes," she retorted. "And I'm not getting fat. I'm working on Mom's birthday present."

"Birthday present?" Cass echoed.

"Baby number two," Mike said proudly. "Happy birthday, Mom."

"Congratulations, you two!" Cass cried and hurried to hug them both.

"You having a boy this time?" Willie asked Mike.

"We don't know yet."

"Make it a boy, sis. The men in this family are getting out-numbered."

"I'll see what I can do about that," she said and bit into her brownie.

With the food consumed, the guys went outside to play some one-on-one basketball, leaving Cass and her daughters to visit.

"When's the baby due?" Cass asked.

"December."

"A baby for Christmas." Cass could hardly wait.

"I wouldn't want to have my birthday at Christmas," said Amber.

"Why not?" her sister demanded.

"Because everybody gives you one present and tells you it's your Christmas and birthday combined."

"And you know this how?"

"Don't you remember Shelby Digler? Her birthday was December fifteenth and her family was always doing that to her."

"Well, our baby's due at the beginning of the month, so that won't happen."

"We don't care when the baby comes," Cass said. "Just so long as he or she is healthy."

"You should've waited to get pregnant later," said Amber.

"Okay, that's enough," Cass said sternly. "When it's your turn, you can show us how it's done."

"I'm not going to have kids," Amber said. "I want to have fun and travel."

"You'll change your mind once you're married," Dani told her.

"Kids are great," Cass said. "Look how much fun I have with you guys when you're here."

"Yeah, but we're not here that much now," Amber said. And that led her back to the subject of the night before. "Don't you think Mom should start dating?" she asked her sister. "She's lonely."

"I am not lonely," Cass insisted.

"You should, Mom," Dani said. "We're all moved out now, so why not?"

Cass flashed on an image of a giant Ken doll.

Yeah, why not?

Would Grant be at the party tonight?

CHAPTER TWENTY

It turned out that Cass didn't have to wait until the party to see Grant. Along with every other person in town, he was at the Saturday-afternoon parade, which always kicked off the weekend festivities. It was the same every year, featuring the Icicle Falls High School marching band, as well as bands from Wenatchee and Yakima. The local VFW was represented, its members driving vintage jeeps. The police and fire departments showed up with lights flashing and sirens blaring, and the sheriff's department made its presence known, too. The local rodeo queens added glamour, dressed in fancy Western attire and riding their mounts, leaving all the little horse-crazy girls with something to aspire to. They could also enjoy the show of horseflesh when members of the equestrian club rode past. Spectators could always count on two floats, one with Miss Icicle Falls and her court, and the one bearing the current Lady of the Autumn Leaves (a woman honored every year for her community service). These were followed by the mayor, perched in the back of a convertible and throwing candy to the children. (You could never start courting voters early enough.) Members of the local gymnastics club cartwheeled their way down Center Street, followed by the German Club, dressed in their lederhosen and stopping occasionally to play their alpenhorns. Like some of the other clubs and floats, they had little to do with the purpose of the holiday, but when you were putting together a small-town parade, you took whoever was willing to participate.

People lined the street to wave flags and cheer for friends, which was what Cass was doing when she spotted Grant on the other side of the street, standing next to Charley and his two sons. Griffin was there, too, smiling up at Grant's younger son. They were spending as much time talking to each other and laughing as they were watching the parade.

As for Grant, he looked bored. She couldn't blame him. It wasn't the most exciting parade on the planet. But, like everything the people of Icicle Falls did, it was heartfelt.

Come Monday, the little cemetery would be filled with people, and the laughter would have subsided to reverence as family members laid flowers on the graves of those they'd lost to war.

For today and tomorrow, though, it was patriotism and celebration. After the parade, people would visit the various arts-and-crafts booths set up in the park. They'd hit the street where the food vendors were and buy soda and hot dogs, deep-fried Twinkies, Belgian waffles and, of course, chocolate concoctions from Sweet Dreams. They'd visit with friends, gossip and generally enjoy themselves, along with the strangers who came to town to soak up the German flavor, shop and hike the mountain trails.

Cass envisioned herself and Grant strolling past the vendors' booths, checking out the work of the local artisans. He'd probably really enjoy seeing what the chainsaw wood-carvers had to offer.

His gaze was starting to roam the crowd. It settled on Cass and he smiled.

She smiled back and gave him a small wave.

Dani nudged her. "Mom, who's that man over there?"

"He's the guy who put on my new roof."

"You never told me he looked like a movie star."

Cass shrugged. "You never asked."

"Is he single?"

"Widowed. He's Dan Masters's dad."

"He's got a lot of gray hair. I wonder how old he is," Dani mused, then studied her mother speculatively.

Cass could feel her face growing warm. "Look what's coming," she said in an effort to distract her daughter.

"Oh, they're sweet," Dani said wistfully.

The Saint Bernard Club was walking past now. People had decked out their big dogs in red, white and blue ribbons. Some pulled wagons with kids in them, all waving flags. Cass had walked Tiny in the parade in years past. She sighed. Poor old guy. She still missed him.

The Saint Bernards were followed by the crew that cleaned up after the horses, wheeling their trash cans, brooms slung over their shoulders like rifles. Their appearance signaled the end of the parade.

The crowd began to disperse, and Charley and gang crossed the street to greet Cass's kids. "Hey, guys, glad to see you all made it."

"We wouldn't miss Mom's birthday," Amber said.

"We wouldn't dare," Willie added, draping an arm over Cass's shoulder.

Charley introduced Grant, and as they all stood chatting, a middle-aged woman with a hairstyle that had escaped from the eighties shyly approached. She hovered at the edge of their group for a moment, then tapped Grant on the arm.

"I'm your biggest fan, Mr. Clooney," she gushed. "I see you're busy, but could I get your autograph?"

"I'm sorry. I'm not George."

She blinked in surprise. "You're not?"

Cass tried not to snicker.

"No," he said. "Sorry."

"Me, too," the woman said with a sigh.

"Another disappointed fan," Cass teased as the woman walked away, looking like she'd just lost the winning lottery ticket.

He frowned at her.

"Hey, guys, we're going to go check out the booths," Charley said.

"Great." Dani started toward the park.

"I'll catch up with you later," Grant said.

Cass couldn't resist teasing him one more time. "What? You afraid of your fans?"

"Anyone ever tell you you've got a smart mouth?"

"Oh, maybe once in a while," she said agreeably. "But hey, when you're old you're allowed to say all kinds of obnoxious stuff."

"So you're old now, is that it?"

"That's why your daughter-in-law's throwing a party tonight, to console me. Are you coming?"

"You bet. I want to see how you old people celebrate."

Stef and Brad had spotted them now and came up to say hi. "My floor looks great," she crowed to Cass. "You have to come over and see it." She linked an arm through her husband's. "Brad did an incredible job."

"Thanks to the good coaching I had," Brad admitted as he shook hands with Grant.

"I will," Cass promised. "Are you guys coming tonight?"

"Of course. We wouldn't miss it." She turned to Grant. "Are you coming?"

"I am."

"He wouldn't miss it, either," Cass joked. "I'm going to teach him how to age gracefully."

"I'll be sure to take notes. See you later," he said and walked off.

Cass wished he would have hung around. Sometimes she

could almost imagine that he was interested in her. Of course, those were the times when she was being delusional.

Maybe it wasn't too late to request a Ken doll for her birthday.

If Cass thought she was old, what did she think of him? Grant wondered. She was friendly enough but she never really came on to him. Still, she'd checked to make sure he'd be at her party. Was she interested? It was hard to tell.

Not that it mattered. She was too young. He didn't need to be fishing in those waters.

Fishing. Yes, it was time to head for the river. In May, Icicle Creek was a good place to catch early-season salmon, which could range from eight to sixteen pounds.

He went to a spot one of the locals had told him about. It wasn't that far from town but it was a world away. The only thing you heard was birdsong. A man could stand in the shade of giant fir and pine trees, take in the beauty of nature and ponder life. But not think about a certain curvy little baker with hazel eyes and a great smile.

Charley's backyard was packed with partiers. All of Cass's family was present, and little Emma was chasing the other children around the yard. The entire Sterling family was there, too, with their offspring. So was all of Dan's family. Including Grant.

"Your fans were disappointed they couldn't find you," Cass told him.

He rolled his eyes. "Sorry I missed it."

"It must be hard to be so gorgeous."

"I don't know. Is it?"

She practically choked on her wine.

"Don't tell me—let me guess. You don't think you're beautiful."

"Beautiful is Muriel Sterling, Cecily, Griffin."

"I don't understand why you women always do that."

"What?"

"Compare yourselves to each other."

"Oh, and men don't? I wonder where that saying 'size matters' came from?"

"Not from me."

Dani joined them. "Mom, have you seen your cake? Charley told me it's lavender with buttercream frosting."

Cake, Cass's biggest weakness. And Bailey Black's lavender cake was her favorite. She let her daughter lead her over to the refreshment table.

Charley had decided to rib her friend, draping the food table with a black tablecloth and setting out a cake with a tombstone that said Rest In Peace, Cass's Youth.

"Ha-ha," Cass said sourly. "Thanks for reminding me."

"Don't blame me," Charley told her. "Bailey did it."

Cass turned to Bailey Black, the town's other resident baker, who was standing next to her. "See if I ever come to *your* tearoom again."

"She made me," Bailey said.

"Not even fifty yet and look what you're doing to me," Cass muttered good-naturedly.

"Well, the way you've been complaining, anyone would've thought you were turning eighty," Charley said.

Dot Morrison, Cass's friend and mentor, joined them. "Don't worry, kiddo. I laid my youth to rest years ago and I'm doing great."

She was in her usual attire—jeans with an elastic waistband and a sweatshirt. Dot's sweatshirts always made a statement. The one she was wearing tonight proclaimed, Inside This Hoodie Is a Sexy Woman Trying to Get Out.

"I like your sweatshirt," Bailey said to her.

"I think I need one of those," Cass said. Oh, no. She shouldn't encourage Dot.

"Glad you said that 'cause guess what you're getting for

your birthday." Dot held up a large gift bag stuffed with black tissue paper.

Cass dug in and pulled out a replica of Dot's sweatshirt.

"Ha! I love it," said Charley. "Put it on."

Why not? She was only wearing a T-shirt. It would get nippy once the sun went down.

"That's you, Mom," called Amber after she'd donned it.

"We all think you're sexy," Cass's best buddy, Samantha, said with a grin. "Maybe not in that sweatshirt, though."

"I don't know. I think it's me," Cass said and struck a pinup-girl pose.

She looked across the sea of heads and saw Grant watching her. Suddenly she felt silly and self-conscious. He saluted her with his wineglass and she braved out her embarrassment by blowing him a kiss.

People began to move toward the refreshment table, but both Samantha and Charley stayed next to her. "Okay," Samantha said. "Is it my imagination or is he checking you out?"

"It's your imagination," Cass replied.

"Right. The party's barely started and you two are already shooting enough sparks to light the flames in the fire pit," said Charley.

"Well, you'd have to be dead not to be attracted to your father-in-law. But he hasn't made a move. I think his libido's stuck in Park."

"He thinks he's too old for you," Charley informed her.

"How old is he?"

"Sixty-two."

"Seriously?" He looked more like fifty-two.

Cass did the math. Sixteen years. Yes, there was an age difference between them. But so what? There'd been a big age difference between Celine Dion and her husband, and look how happy they'd been. Until he died.

But everyone died. Grant's wife had, and she couldn't have

been that old. So really, what did it matter what age you were? It was your attitude toward life that counted, right? Anyway, Cass liked older men. And she liked one older man in particular.

"That is kind of old," Samantha said.

"Yeah," said Cass. "It would be such a drain to wake up every morning and look at George Clooney the Second."

"Yeah, if you can't have Matt Damon, you may as well take George." Charley grinned. "I say go for it. He's a nice man and he's more fit than most forty-year-olds."

"You don't have to convince me," Cass said.

Obviously, the person who needed convincing was Grant.

With the appetizers consumed, it was now time for dinner, which consisted of a pizza buffet, with every imaginable variation of Cass's favorite food laid out. In addition to that, people had brought various kinds of salads, as well as desserts. Glutton heaven. There would be no dieting tonight.

After dinner, Charley insisted that Cass open her presents. It was a haul, everything from bath salts and lotions to bottles of wine and, of course, Sweet Dreams chocolates from the Sterling family.

"Thanks, everyone. You sure are making this aging thing less painful," Cass said with a smile.

"It's only a number," Dot said.

"Okay, time for cake and champagne," Charley announced. "And sparkling cider," she added. "For those of us who are underage. Or pregnant."

"Or both," Dot cracked.

"Don't look at me," Amber said in mock horror.

There were plenty of toasts. From Dot, "You're only as old as you act. So keep acting like you're thirty, kiddo." From Dan, "Live long and prosper." From Muriel, "The best years are still to come."

"Hear, hear," said Dot. "Just remember. Every year is a gift. Take it and live it to the max."

"We love you, Mom," said Dani.

Cass teared up as everyone raised their glasses. She had great kids, great friends and a good life. She was truly blessed.

Dan got a bonfire going in the fire pit, and Charley brought out a karaoke machine. Dot was convinced to go first and rendered a terrifying version of "You Make Me Feel Like a Natural Woman" that left her daughter, Tilda, the cop, threatening to arrest her for ear torture in the first degree. Dan and his brother rapped out "Baby Got Back," followed by an encore performance of "YMCA." Samantha and Cecily sang "Honey, I'm Good," and what they lacked in musical talent, they made up for in cuteness. The performances went on, with the partiers slaughtering songs by Dolly Parton, Adele and Bruno Mars.

Cass managed to avoid making a fool of herself until Charley insisted the birthday girl do a number.

"No way," she said.

"Oh, yes. Way." Charley grabbed her hand and dragged her up. "How about a duet?"

"I'll sing with you, too," Cecily said and joined them.

After much consulting, they decided on "Girls Just Want to Have Fun." It was almost as bad as Dot's performance. No one cared. The others roared their approval.

"Encore, encore," shouted Dan.

"Oh, here's one," Charley said, looking through the list of songs. Next thing Cass knew, she was singing "I Want to Dance with Somebody," and Charley had pulled Grant up and stuck him between them. Very subtle. But she braved it out, crooning to him while Charley hammed it up on his other side.

"Speaking of dancing," said Charley. "Let's do some before I run out of energy."

Cass was a year older now. She didn't have time to waste being coy. Charley had started playing Maroon 5's "Animals," and Cass took Grant by the hand. "Come on—I want to dance with somebody." *Somebody who loves me.* Tonight she'd settle for *like.*

He reluctantly joined her on the patio and made a halfhearted attempt while she danced around him. The music slowed as Cass played a Jake O'Brien song, "Here for You," and he tried to escape.

She caught his arm, saying, "I don't think so. You barely danced on that last song."

"What do you want to be dancing with an old guy for, anyway?"

"Where? I don't see one."

"How old are you now?"

"Old enough to know what I want."

"What do you want?"

Maybe it was time she let him know. *Go big or go home.* She pressed closer. "I bet you can guess."

He put some distance between them. "Behave yourself, young lady."

"I'm not a lady, and I don't qualify for the young club anymore."

"I think they'll still let you in."

"You're not so old yourself."

"Almost old enough to be your father."

"I'm not looking for a father."

He sobered. "What are you looking for, Cass?"

The song ended and "I'm a Believer" by the Monkees began to play.

"I love this song," she said and started to sing along as they left the improvised dance floor.

"I bet you weren't even born when those guys were making records. You do know what a record is, don't you?"

"Ha-ha. Vinyl is back."

They wandered over to a couple of camp chairs placed near the fire pit and settled in to watch little Serena Goodman and Petey roasting marshmallows under Muriel's careful supervision. Interesting (and encouraging) that Grant and Muriel weren't all over each other. By all rights they should've been. Two beautiful people... Maybe Grant was jaded when it came to beautiful women and was ready for someone...interesting.

Cass wasn't sure she'd qualify as interesting, but she *was* sure she felt something zipping between them, a sort of sexual force field. *May the force be with you.*

Griffin was taking pictures of the kids now, Matt by her side, and Matt was studying his dad thoughtfully. Grant actually squirmed in his chair.

"I don't want a lot," Cass said softly. "Someone to hang out with, fill the empty nest with some conversation."

"That's all?"

No, she wanted the whole dream. She wanted to get married and live happily ever after. Have someone in bed with her who had two legs instead of four and a five-o'clock shadow on his chin. She wanted someone to sit on the couch beside her and watch movies, someone to take a hike up Lost Bride Trail. She wanted to see the legendary ghost of the Lost Bride, every woman's lucky love charm.

Spilling all that would probably be the equivalent of saying "By the way, I have a social disease." Except she hadn't been social enough all these years to catch anything. Did the equipment even work anymore?

"I'm not propositioning you, Grant." Actually, she was. "I like you and I think maybe you like me and, well..." *Darn it all, man up and say something. Don't make me do all the work here.*

"You need a man who can go the distance."

She raised an eyebrow. "You can't manage that?"

His cheeks flushed. "I mean in life."

"Okay, how about we do the friend thing? We are becoming friends, right?"

"I'd like to think so."

"How about becoming friends with benefits? I always wanted to kiss George Clooney," she cracked. "But I'd settle for you."

She leaned forward but he didn't meet her halfway. "Not a good idea. I'm working for you."

"Okay, then. You're fired."

"Nice try. I'm not leaving until I finish your back deck."

"Hurry up and finish. I'm not getting any younger."

Wrong thing to say. The age joke made him frown. "Me neither."

Todd Black, Bailey's husband, came up to them. "Come on, Cass—salsa with me. Let's heat it up for your birthday."

She wanted to heat it up. With Grant. Obviously, that was one birthday present she wouldn't be getting. He'd given her a box of chocolates and the card had been signed simply, "Your handyman." She wished he really was hers.

When it came to dancing, there was no one better than Todd. Well, except Jonathan Templar, who had married and moved away and now only came to town for holidays and summer vacations. What the heck. She probably wasn't going to get another dance out of Grant, and things had definitely cooled off here by the fire.

She went with Todd and did her best to keep up. It was fun. The whole party was fun. It would've been even more fun if someone would get over his age bias.

"You've taken enough pictures of everyone else," Matt said to Griffin, snatching the camera out of her hand. "Make a s'more and I'll take yours."

He was turning her into a total pig. She'd already had pizza and half a piece of cake.

But the s'mores did look good. And she hadn't roasted a marshmallow since the last time her family vacationed at the beach. She'd been twelve. Maybe she should revisit her childhood, rewrite history. Instead of four s'mores she'd have one.

"Roast me a marshmallow, too," Matt said, sliding another one onto her fork.

So she did, holding them over the coals at the edge of the fire until they were golden brown. He helped her assemble their treats, then snapped a shot of her taking her first bite. Oh, wow, that tasted as good as it looked.

"We need a s'mores selfie," he said and took out his phone. "Smile."

The sun had dipped behind the mountains, and the only lighting they had came from the twinkle lights Charley had hung over the patio and the glow from the fire, but his phone camera caught the smiles on their faces just fine.

Caption this: Where's the Guilt? There was none. She was enjoying herself.

"Okay, now let's go dance off whatever pounds you think you just gained," he said.

Todd was teaching a line dance, and they joined several of the others who'd formed two lines on the lawn. A fast country song started, and Griffin found herself racing through a series of grapevine steps, kicks and twirls. And laughing. And realizing that she was no longer a spectator, taking pictures from the sidelines. She was part of the picture, and she felt...happy.

Matt walked her home from the party, entertaining her with stories about his life growing up and all the crazy things he did, everything from climbing the water tower to setting a trap for Santa with a bucket of water he and his brother had rigged over the bedroom door. "That was the last time Santa hung our stockings on our bedposts."

Griffin chuckled. "I can imagine. Your poor dad."

"He was a good sport," Matt said. "I loved hanging out with him. Dad worked a lot, but when he was around he always made time for us."

"Sounds like you had a great life growing up."

"I did. Everything a kid could want, really. Camping and fishing, and he and Mom sent us to summer camp every year. I learned how to water ski up at Malibu. At one camp, we made the world's largest ice cream sundae. How about you? Did you ever go to camp?"

"Oh, yeah," she said casually. Fat-kid camp, where you ate nutritious food and there wasn't even a hint of ice cream, let alone the world's largest sundae.

"Hanging out up here with friends, it kind of makes me feel like I'm at camp. I think someday I'll get a cabin around here. Snowboarding in the winter, fishing in the summer..."

It sounded idyllic. "You can buy this place," she joked as they walked up the front porch steps.

That wiped away the smile. "I wish you weren't leaving." He closed the distance between them and pressed her up against the front door. "You know I'm falling for you in a big way, don't you?"

She nodded, and that was all the encouragement he needed to kiss her.

She was falling for him, too. This was a bad idea. She could feel her resolve to go to New York melting like that marshmallow over the hot coals. Bad idea or not, it didn't stop her from asking, "Do you want to come in?"

He nodded and they barely made it to the couch before he was kissing her again, tipping her against the sofa cushions, his hand running up her thigh. *Oooh, more please.*

CHAPTER TWENTY-ONE

In spite of a certain romance-shy handyman, Cass had a great birthday weekend. The kids hung out with her on Sunday. They all gorged themselves on burgers and garlic fries and shakes at Herman's Hamburgers. Then they put out the ancient croquet set in the backyard and played a highly competitive game, Emma doing her part to make it a challenge by picking up everyone's balls and throwing them, then crowing, "Did it!" That night they played cards and watched a movie. Family togetherness and plenty of laughter—the best birthday presents imaginable.

Come Monday, though, the party was over and the kids all went back to their lives.

Dani and her family left first. "Mom, you should move to Spokane. We could add on to the house and you could live with us."

"Because I had a birthday?"

"No, it's not that. It's just that you're all by yourself up here."

With a community full of friends. "I'm hardly alone."

"Yeah. We're still here," said Amber. "Where am I supposed to go when school's out for the summer?"

"Okay, after Amber's done with school. Think about it—you

could spend as much time as you wanted with your grandchildren."

There was that.

"She'd make you babysit 24/7," Willie cracked.

"You two are really funny," Dani said, insulted. "At least someone's thinking about Mom."

"Mom doesn't need anyone thinking about her," Cass informed her daughter. At least not that way. "I'm not even fifty yet. That hardly qualifies me for a nursing home."

"You did say you were lonely," Amber reminded her.

"No, I didn't. I said... Well, I don't remember what I said, but it wasn't that. Now scram, Danielle. You guys have a long drive ahead of you."

"Okay." Dani hugged her. "The offer stands anytime you want to take advantage of it. Spokane's a great city."

"If you move to Spokane, then I get the house here," Amber said, and her sister told her she was spoiled.

"What do you expect? She's the baby," said Willie, and Amber stuck her tongue out at him.

It was hugs all around and promises to return for Willie's graduation ceremony in June, and then Dani was off. Willie left an hour later, and then Amber, too, was gone. And the house was awfully quiet.

"Maybe we *should* move to Spokane," she said to Lady Gray.

The cat voiced no opinion. Instead, she began to groom herself.

"Yeah, I don't want to move, either."

It was sweet of her daughter to want her nearby, but Cass didn't think she'd be happy somewhere else. Icicle Falls had been her home for too many years. She loved the people, loved the beautiful mountain setting, loved working in her bakery. Yes, there was something missing, but she probably wasn't going to find it in Spokane.

Grant Masters, that was what she wanted. The irritating man

had gotten her all revved up the moment he walked into her bakery. He was interested—God alone knew why, but she was sure of it. Why couldn't he get past his stupid fixation with their age difference?

Because he was a big coward.

He confirmed her assessment of his cowardly character by staying away all week. Finally on Thursday she left a message on his voice mail. "Cluck, cluck, you big chicken. Get over here and fix my deck."

Friday she came home from the bakery to discover him out there working. It was a hot afternoon and he was shirtless, showing off those well-tended muscles. He was a tease.

She opened the sliding glass door and poked her head out. "I knew you couldn't resist me."

"Just don't want this collapsing out from under you."

"I appreciate that."

And to show him how much she appreciated it, she got busy and baked a chocolate zucchini cake dense with chocolate chips. He had just finished and was packing up his tools when she took it out to him still warm and topped with a scoop of ice cream drizzled with caramel sauce.

"You need sustenance," she told him.

"Where's yours?" he asked.

"I'm trying to be good."

"Being good is highly overrated when it comes to cake."

Being good was highly overrated when it came to a lot of things, she thought, ogling him as he took a bite.

He nodded as he chewed. "You sure can bake," he said once he'd swallowed.

"I should hope so. Actually, it's only one of my many talents." She was moving closer, ready to demonstrate, when her cell phone rang.

"Saved by the bell," she grumbled and stepped back into the kitchen to grab it off the counter.

It was Charley and she was nearly hysterical.

"Melody got hurt on the river."

"Oh, no!" The river was a source of both beauty and fun for the residents of Icicle Falls, but it could also be dangerous.

"She's in the hospital. Her dad just called me. I'm on my way over right now and I don't have any idea what to say to her parents," Charley finished on a sob.

Charley had become very attached to her newest employee, almost viewing the girl as a little sister. She'd taken Melody under her wing and the family had been to Charley's house on more than one occasion.

"I'll meet you there," Cass said and ended the call.

Grant stepped into the kitchen. "What's wrong?"

"Charley's new server's been in an accident. She's in the hospital. Charley's really upset." Cass grabbed her purse and started for the door.

Grant followed her. "I'll come with you."

They climbed into his truck and zoomed their way to the hospital. They found Charley with the girl's parents and younger sister waiting in the lobby of the emergency room, along with another girl, probably a friend. All four women were crying. The father was hugging both his wife and daughter and was barely holding it together himself.

Grant dropped onto a seat next to Charley and put his arm around her, and Cass knelt in front of her. "What happened?" she asked.

"She was with some kids on the river, over by the trail to the Indian petroglyphs. She dived in."

Charley didn't need to say more than that. You never risked diving, even in parts of the river that looked deep enough, which that part did. The result was bound to be a spinal cord injury and possibly death.

"I should have told her," fretted the girl's friend. "I know we're not supposed to climb on those rocks."

They sure weren't. There was a sign posted right there warning people. It was easy to slip and fall in.

"She wanted me to take her picture on that big boulder, and next thing I knew, she was diving in."

"It's not your fault," Charley assured the girl, taking her hand.

The doctor was out now and Cass could tell from his expression that this was the beginning of a very long, hard road for this family. She thought of the famous artist Joni Eareckson Tada, who'd wound up a paraplegic after a similar event. The woman was an inspiration to many. Maybe, at some point, that would be worth sharing.

The news was even worse, though. The girl was dead.

"No!" her mother wailed and collapsed against her husband. Both the sister and the friend started sobbing in earnest. Charley hugged the sister and Cass moved to comfort the friend.

"I can't believe this," the girl kept saying over and over.

It was surreal. And hard to accept. To die so young with her whole life ahead of her. Cass immediately thought of her own children, at the beginning of their life's adventures. The idea of having to face what these poor parents were facing left her feeling ill and brought the tears racing to her eyes. Dear God, was there anything worse in the whole world than losing a child?

The family followed in the doctor's wake to see their daughter and begin dealing with the horrible business of death.

"She was going to be a vet," her friend said and started sobbing again.

"This is awful," Charley said miserably.

Indeed, it was. The news spread quickly, leaving the entire town in shock. The funeral was held at Festival Hall because none of the churches in town was large enough to hold the crowd. It wasn't that the girl had known so many people, since the family was relatively new. It was that in a small town, one family's loss was everyone's loss.

The citizens of Icicle Falls closed in around the grieving parents, pouring out love and condolences. A memorial was set up at the river—a stone plaque in her memory. The hall itself became a garden of flowers with wreaths and overflowing vases everywhere. The entire high school turned out to support the younger sister, teenagers crying and horrified by the stark reality. A volunteer choir formed to sing "You'll Never Walk Alone." Mothers organized to make sure the family had dinner provided for the next month.

Cass closed her bakery for the day, and she and Bailey Black catered the reception after the funeral. Sometimes, if the person who died had been older, there were smiles and occasional laughter during this portion of the affair as people shared fond memories and funny stories. There was no laughter this time, no smiles. This was a tragedy and there was no way to lighten it.

Cass couldn't help asking herself how it was that some people died so young, while others got such long lives. One error in judgment and a young life was snuffed out. She thought back to some of the dumb things she'd done at that age. Drag racing on the highway, hitchhiking one night when her car broke down. She could've been picked up by a serial killer. Instead, an old man had given her a lift, as well as a lecture about the danger of hitching rides from strangers.

The one thing she heard people murmur over and over as she set out platters of cold cuts and cheese—"You never know. Life is short."

In some cases, unfairly short.

"It's awful," Griffin said as she and Stef sat at their usual corner bistro table in the bakery with Cass. The girl had only waited on Stef and Brad once and Griffin had never met her. Still, it was horrible to even think about.

"She was a sweet kid," Cass said. "It always seems so wrong when someone dies that young."

"My cousin died of a drug overdose when he was nineteen,"

Griffin said in a small voice. "I was only thirteen, but it sure made a lasting impression. Made me afraid to even try marijuana."

"You know, you read in the news about people getting shot or killed in car accidents, and it sort of doesn't make your radar," said Stef. "Something like this…" She bit her lip.

"Well, ladies," said Cass, "this drives home a very important truth. None of us knows how long we have on this earth, so we need to live life to the fullest." She shook her head. "It always sounds so trite when you say that, but it's true."

Griffin had read a similar message in Muriel Sterling's book earlier. *Pursue those dreams now*, Muriel had written. "Don't put off till tomorrow what you need to do today to make them come true. If you wait for too many tomorrows all you'll have is a pile of yesterdays, and you'll be no closer to reaching your goals."

Or maybe you'd never live to reach them. She'd heard that the girl who died had wanted to be a vet. She never got the chance.

Griffin had a chance to do something; she needed to take it. Icicle Falls was a wonderful place to live, but in her case it was also a wonderful place to hide. She'd come here with Steve and settled into a safe little routine. Now she had an opportunity to take her own road and it was wide open. She needed to do it.

Except what about Matt? If she left Icicle Falls, she'd probably be leaving behind what they'd started. It was one thing to come from Seattle to visit her here in the mountains. Quite another to go clear across the country.

Relationships were fragile. Look how easily what she'd had with Steve had broken. Of course, that had been slowly cracking over the last few months. Surely, if you really had something it wouldn't break so easily.

She needed to stick with her plan, put the house up for sale and move forward. Maybe, if she was lucky, if Matt really cared, he'd move forward with her.

Either way it was time. She got her cast taken off the following day and that felt somehow symbolic. The house painting was finished, and Matt had replaced the broken step on the back porch when he was up for Memorial Day weekend. All that remained was to upgrade her appliances.

She went home from the doctor's office and ordered a new stove and fridge from the Home Depot website. Then she called Nenita Einhausen and told her she was ready to list her place.

When Matt came up to visit on Sunday, the for-sale sign was already in the front yard.

"Jeez. You didn't waste any time." He didn't sound particularly happy about it.

She wasn't particularly happy herself.

"It's normal to be a little fearful before you take a leap," Muriel's book had explained. "I was nervous about getting married again after having lost my first husband. But in the end, I was glad I moved forward."

Griffin would be glad she'd moved forward, too. Or so she hoped.

"So you're really leaving," Matt said.

"I am, as soon as the house sells."

He nodded, taking that in. "You're good at what you do. You can probably go a lot further in New York than if you stay here. But damn, I hate to see you leave."

Then ask me to stay. Or, better yet, say you'll come with me.

He didn't. And of course, why would he? It was way too early for him to take that kind of leap. Instead, he said, "I'll come visit you."

People always said stuff like that. Maybe he would. Once. They'd text, talk on the phone. Then, gradually, the texts would taper off, the phone calls disappear.

"You'll be back for Christmas."

Christmas was a long ways away. *You could come to New York with me. Say it!* She didn't.

She couldn't even work up the nerve to tell him how she felt.

If she couldn't do that, how was she going to make it in the competitive big-city market?

By hard work. She had confidence in her talent.

Relationships were a different animal, one in which she had little confidence. Anyway, maybe her judgment was clouded. They were both rebounding. Maybe what they had wouldn't last.

Okay, she'd take what they had right now and be grateful for that.

CHAPTER TWENTY-TWO

Willie's graduation ceremony was slated for the second Saturday in June at the University of Washington's Husky Stadium. He'd gotten tickets for all the family members and an extra one for Cass in case she wanted to bring Dot.

But Dot had called her early Saturday morning and said in a croaky voice, "I'm going to have to bail on you, kiddo. I feel like shit."

"You sound like shit." And that meant...

"Sorry. I know you didn't want to go stag."

She sure hadn't. It was hard enough to host her ex and his trophy wife and their stupid little dog and perfect little daughter at Christmas (the fact that this had become a tradition proved that God had a sense of humor), but, somehow, going alone to her son's graduation ceremony felt like the ultimate in loserhood. *Yep, there's the mom. Still by herself. Dad remarried but nobody wanted her.* Ugh.

Well, she'd have to brave it alone. Drive to the big city on her own, figure out parking. The kids were staying at Mason's house. He'd invited her, too—he and she had finally signed a peace treaty when Dani got married—but she'd turned down the offer. Being stuck with them every year at Christmas was more than enough.

And she'd been fine with getting up early and driving over the mountains, been looking forward to spending time with Dot, seeing her boy graduate.

She was still looking forward to seeing Willie graduate. Going solo to the party at Mason's afterward, not so much. She'd actually lost eight pounds for the occasion, taking such extreme measures as eating nothing but cabbage soup for three days in a row, tossing the last of the chocolate zucchini cake she'd made for Grant (not that she'd had any appetite for it after the tragedy on the river), and staying out of the ice cream in her freezer. She'd even squeezed in a couple of brisk walks during the wee hours before going to work. She was looking pretty darned good, if she did say so herself. And all for nothing. No matter how much poundage she lost, she'd still be alone. Mom the love failure. If only she had a date.

A certain George Clooney look-alike sprang to mind. If she showed up with Grant, it would be like armor for her pride. And heaven knew Mason had dealt that a blow when he married Babette the trophy wife.

Except Grant was avoiding her.

Still, nothing ventured, nothing gained. She called his cell and got a sleepy hello. "I need a really big favor."

"What's wrong?"

"Nothing's wrong at the house, but Willie's graduation ceremony is today. In Seattle. Dot Morrison was going to go with me, but she's sick."

"You need an escort."

Although he didn't exactly sound excited, she pressed on. "I need to not look like a discard. I know that sounds stupid to a gorgeous hunk like you, but it's different for women. If a man's alone, everyone figures it's because he wants to be. If a woman is, people figure it's because she has to be. My husband's remarried. His wife is gorgeous. Their kid is gorgeous." Okay, this did sound stupid and immature. "I know it's ridiculous and I shouldn't feel like this," she admitted. How old was she, anyway? Sixteen? She should never have called him. "You know what? This was dumb. Forget I called and go back to sleep."

"I'll go. What time do we need to leave?"

"No, seriously. I should never have called you. I was having a midlife crisis or something. Reverting to being a teenager." What had she been thinking? This was ten times more humiliating than it would've been to go the graduation alone. She should have sucked it up. It wasn't like her family didn't know she had nobody, so what was the big deal, anyway?

The answer to that was easy. The party after. Friends, neighbors, people she hadn't met. Having Dot along would've helped her cope with that.

"Like I said, what time do I need to pick you up?"

Okay, he was willing. She was saved. She let go of her guilt and embarrassment. "You're my hero. We need to leave by ten."

"I'll be there."

"Thank you," she said humbly.

"I owe you for this," she said to him later when she climbed into his truck.

"No, you don't."

"I'm being stupid, really. It's not like me being single is a big surprise to anyone."

"It is to me," Grant said. "How come you never remarried?"

"At first? Too bitter, too busy." She looked out the window as they whizzed by forest and river. It felt as if the years had gone by that fast. "Then I got in the habit of being on my own. I suppose if I'd wanted to avoid this, I could've stayed married."

"Why didn't you?"

"I got tired of being ignored. Mason was in the navy, gone more than he was home. Then, after he got out, he was busy getting a degree. Everything seemed to take precedence over us. He was already an absent husband and father. I simply made it legal. We actually talked everything out a few years ago, and we get along now. They come up for Christmas and we all spend the holiday together."

"You have Christmas with your ex."

"Does that sound like something out of a bad movie?"

"Kind of."

"What can I say? The kids are there, too, and I do it for them. To give him credit, he's become a much better father to them now than he was when they were little. So we're all one big, happy, dysfunctional family."

"Not quite happy enough for you to want to show up at something alone."

Cass shrugged. "Maybe because this is in Seattle. His turf, not mine. I don't know. All I know is I'm grateful you're coming with me."

He smiled at her. "My pleasure."

Pleasure. The word coupled with that killer smile was enough to make her go weak in the knees. Good thing she was already sitting down.

She reminded herself that he was only doing her a favor. This wasn't a date. Nothing was happening here.

Darn.

They got to Husky Stadium in plenty of time and, thanks to Cass's cell phone, were able to find the rest of the family in the multitude. Her daughters were standing with Mason. Dani was holding Emma, and Amber had Mason's three-year-old, Julia. Mason's wife, Babette, looked svelte and put together in a beautiful sundress, a coral sweater and heels. She was carrying a Kate Spade purse. Cass suddenly felt frumpy in her white pants and butt-covering navy top. And flats. Why had she worn flats?

Because she didn't do heels.

She should have done heels.

"I should've dressed up more," she muttered.

"You look fine." Grant put a hand on the small of her back as they moved forward. Whether for moral support or to help with her illusion that she could do as well in the love department as her ex, she didn't know. But she appreciated it.

"Cass, you look lovely," Babette greeted her as she gawked at Grant.

"Thanks. Stunning dress," Cass said as they hugged. "And look how Julia's growing." She was a beautiful child with big eyes and lashes a yard long. She was going to grow up to be just as lovely as her mother.

More hugs and hellos followed, along with introductions.

"At first I thought you were—" Babette stopped midsentence and blushed.

"Don't worry—I'm not," Grant said.

"He gets that a lot," Cass said. She noticed that Mason wasn't smiling and she took perverse delight in it. *See. I'm fine without you.* Of course, like it had with Cinderella, the spell would end, and at Christmas she'd be welcoming them alone. Oh, well. For now she'd enjoy the magic.

As they joined the throng searching for seats, Grant got plenty of curious stares, but no one accosted him and they finally got settled. They were some distance up. Cass hoped she'd be able to zoom in and get a good picture of Willie as he walked up to receive his diploma.

"I knew we should have gotten here earlier," Mason said irritably.

"I guess I should've had you save us seats," Cass said.

"That would have been a lot of seats to save."

Two? She frowned at him and he frowned back. "What is your problem?" she hissed.

"This is supposed to be for family."

"I am family, in case you forgot."

"Well, he's not," Mason hissed back.

Grant sat on the other side of her, pretending deafness.

"Not yet," she said and hoped she wasn't taking her little deception too far. "Just deal with it, Mason."

Mason practically growled, but Babette put Julia on his lap and the distraction worked. She winked at Cass, and Cass couldn't help smiling. Sometimes she thought that if they'd met under different circumstances, she and Babette could actually have become close friends.

The day was warm and the ceremony was long, lasting for three hours. Hardly surprising, since there were eighteen hundred graduates. Families cheered and applauded their graduate, and the afternoon had the same air of excitement as a Huskies football game.

Afterward there were pictures to be taken with Willie in his cap and gown, and then it was on to Mason's big, fancy house for the party. Cass had offered to help, but Babette had assured her she had it covered.

She did, indeed. White-coated caterers made their way through the crowd, passing out everything from canapés to champagne. Platters of shrimp, barbecued chicken wings, sliders, bruschetta, skewered fruit, chips, dip. And that was just for openers. Tables had been set out on the lawn for dinner, which featured prime rib and salmon, roasted potatoes with rosemary and salads. Babette had ordered a cake for dessert—a gigantic sheet cake frosted in the university's colors of gold and purple, with *Congratulations, Willie* scrawled across it.

Presents abounded, and Willie received everything from gift cards to fancy pen sets. Cass had gotten him a set of binoculars and a compass, figuring he could use them tramping around in the forest, and he was delighted with them.

"Thanks, Mom," he said, hugging her. "This is great."

She was feeling very pleased with herself until Willie opened the little box from Mason and Babette. Car keys to a shiny new Mustang. "Wow! Sweet. Thanks, Dad."

Yeah. Thanks, Dad. Where had he been when his son was sick during the night or having a bad dream? Could material things make up for all those years he'd been an absent father?

Cass found it difficult to smile until she reminded herself that past mistakes were water under the bridge, and this day was not about her. It was a wonderful gift for her son, and he deserved it. Anyway, wasn't it a good thing that Mason was finally getting it right as a father?

Her smile got bigger and, more important, became genuine.

"That was some party," Grant said when they started back over the mountains that evening.

"Yes, it was. Thanks again for coming with me."

"My pleasure."

There was that word again. Sigh. "I doubt it was all that pleasurable."

"I had a good time. Talked to some guy about fishing in Mexico. I think he was a neighbor."

"Probably." Everyone in Mason's neighborhood could easily afford fishing trips to Mexico.

"And I enjoyed talking with your kids. You've got great kids, Cass. You did a good job raising them."

She had. It was something to be proud of.

"Your son liked what you gave him. Perfect choice for a graduation gift."

"It's hardly a car."

"Yeah, getting a car for graduation is a sweet deal. In the end, I don't think it really gives you that many bonus points, though."

"It doesn't matter," she said. "I'm happy to see Mason stepping up to the plate."

"Your son's very proud of you. He informed me that you're the best mom on the planet. He also happened to mention that he wouldn't want to see you hurt."

"Oh, Lord," she groaned. "He really said that?"

"Yes, he did."

"What did you tell him?"

"That we're friends."

Bleh. The f-word.

"And that I have no intention of hurting you."

He might as well have added "Or getting involved with you."

She nodded. "I know." Well, that settled that.

When they pulled up in front of her place, she didn't bother to ask him in. She did thank him one more time, though. "I really do owe you for this."

"You don't owe me anything."

"Yeah, I do. It's not easy to boost the old self-esteem, but today did." She smiled at him. "You're a good man, Grant Masters. Your wife was a lucky woman." Then, before he could stop her, she leaned across the seat and gave him a quick kiss on the cheek. Poor impulse control, but who could blame her? She quickly scooted out the door. "Good night."

There was no "Wow, what was that?" No "Come back here." No nothing. Instead he simply said, "Good night," and rumbled off in his big truck.

She sighed and went inside the house. Her cat came running to greet her. "Yes, it was a lovely day," she said. And darn, she'd have liked it to continue. If only Grant had grabbed her and kissed her. Then she'd have invited him in. Clean sheets on the bed. She was ready.

She frowned. "I think I'm in heat," she told her cat. "And I let him get away."

Lady Gray meowed her sympathy.

Grant drove back to Gerhardt's on autopilot, his mind obsessed with that simple little kiss on the cheek. Cass had left him feeling as horny as a teenager. If she'd lingered so much as one more minute in that truck, he'd have lost it and had his hands all over her. And that would've been a very bad idea. Her ex might have been comfortable with marrying a woman half his age, but Grant thought that was pathetic. It wasn't hard to see that the guy was trying to hang on to his youth.

Well, and what was so wrong with that?

Grant frowned and reminded himself that he had no intention of doing the same thing. It wasn't fair to the woman.

Too bad, though. He'd enjoyed himself with both Cass and her family. He hadn't been shining her on when he said she had good kids. She did. They were personable and friendly. And loyal.

He shook his head and smiled over the son's protective attitude toward his mom, a sure sign that she'd raised him right. The daughters were as good-natured and clever as their mother, and the youngest had shown no qualms about matching up her mom, subtly trying to find out what Grant thought of her.

He thought a lot of her. Thought *about* her, too. A lot. She was laid-back and fun to be around. And she was nice-looking. Okay, maybe not stunning like her ex's second wife, but still very pretty with a great smile. Hard to imagine the guy taking her for granted.

He hoped she'd find someone. She deserved to be happy.

He could almost hear Lou saying, "So do you."

Yeah, but not with Cass. It wouldn't work, not with the age difference between them. Maybe nothing was ever going to work.

Damn it all, he wished he'd never moved to Icicle Falls.

Nenita had an open house scheduled for Griffin's place on Sunday, and Griffin was under orders to make herself scarce.

"Come to Seattle and hang out with me," Matt had suggested. "I'll put you up in the extra bedroom like a true gentleman."

She'd be leaving soon. What was the point?

The point was that she'd get to spend more time with Matt. "Okay."

So while her Realtor worked on selling her house, she went

to the city to play. She and Matt went to the EMP Museum and experienced music. They rode the monorail, ate lunch at P.F. Chang's in Westlake and explored the waterfront. There they took selfies with Sylvester, the famous mummy in Ye Olde Curiosity Shop.

You're here and you didn't let me know? texted one of her old college friends.

Next time, she promised.

Yeah, I can see you're busy. Hope this one's a keeper.

So did Griffin. Although how she was going to keep him when he was here and she was in New York, she had no idea.

She pushed aside the negative thought and focused on seeing Puget Sound from the dizzying height of the waterfront Ferris wheel.

"That was fun," she said later as he drove them up the freeway back toward his place.

"It was. You're fun," he added, smiling at her. "It's nice to have someone to do things with."

"It's nice to be with someone who wants to do things," she said, thinking of Steve the couch spud.

"Lexie and I used to do stuff together." He shook his head. "Everything unraveled after we were married and had to live on a budget."

Hmm. How did you spell shallow? L-e-x-i-e.

"She lost her job," he went on. "That didn't help. I used to think that if our life had been a little easier she would have stayed."

"Or maybe you weren't meant to be together," said Griffin.

"That, too. Anyway, things have a way of working out," he added with another smile. "So I'm not complaining."

Neither was she. She especially wasn't complaining later that night when they sat out on his back deck, bundled in blankets, watching the stars. This was what she'd wanted with Steve.

Come to New York and stargaze with me.

She kept the words tethered to the tip of her tongue. It wasn't fair to ask him to leave his job and his life and follow her clear across the country. What if things didn't work out? His ex-wife had already hurt him enough. She didn't need to add to that.

"Hey, there's a shooting star," he said, pointing. "Make a wish."

She did. You never knew. Maybe it would come true. Maybe things would, somehow, work out for them.

And maybe that whole shooting-star thing was totally bogus.

CHAPTER TWENTY-THREE

Cass, Charley and Samantha often met for coffee on a Monday. It was a day off for Charley and Cass, and Samantha could always manage to get away for lunch or a latte.

This Monday they'd gathered at Bailey's tearoom, which was closed, to give their opinions on the chicken-curry-salad croissant sandwiches Bailey was thinking of adding to her menu.

"Thumbs up," Cass told her.

"I think you've got a winner," Charley agreed, making Bailey beam with pleasure.

She looked to her big sister. "What do you think, Sammy?"

"You already got the experts' opinions, but I agree."

That clinched it. "I'm going to definitely include it," Bailey said. "It's actually Beth's recipe. It's in her new cookbook."

"I can hardly wait for that to come out," Charley said. "You should do one," she said to Bailey. "I'd pay the price simply for your lavender sugar cookie recipe." Her sunny expression clouded over. "Melody loved those."

Cass laid a comforting hand on her arm.

"What happened to her sucks," Bailey said with a shake of her head.

"How are her parents doing?" Samantha asked.

"They're struggling," said Charley. "Talking about moving. I can't say I blame them. I'd want to get away, too." She broke off a piece of croissant and crumbled it. "I wish there was something I could do."

"Short of bringing back their child, there isn't anything," Samantha said. "Other than to let them talk about her. Probably the worst thing is feeling like people have forgotten that person you lost. I know Mom felt that way after Dad died. Everyone turns out for the funeral, but then people get on with their lives."

"Well, and people are afraid to talk about the person who died for fear of upsetting the family," Cass added. "But then I think the family themselves start to feel forgotten."

"I don't want her parents to feel that way," Charley said.

"How about some gesture to let them know you're still there for them?" Cass suggested. "Like flowers."

"Oh, yes," Bailey agreed. "Say it with flowers."

"That sounds like an ad," her sister said.

"It sounds like a good idea," said Charley.

So after lunch she and Cass left Bailey working on her menu and sent Samantha back to Sweet Dreams to keep the town supplied with chocolate while they made their way to Lupine Floral.

Heinrich Blum, the owner, was putting a summer arrangement in the cooler when they walked in. His partner, Kevin, was ringing up a sale for Brad.

"Oh, look! Beauty times two," called Kevin.

"You're so full of it," Cass told him, then said to Brad, "Roses, huh? You going for the good-husband award?"

Brad's cheeks turned almost as red as the roses, and she instantly regretted her cheeky comment. She hadn't meant anything by it, but he probably thought she was alluding to his naughty behavior during the great remodel war.

"You're a good husband," she added, hoping he'd get the

message that she'd never taken sides. Brad hadn't been the only one misbehaving.

"Thanks," he said, his cheeks still red.

"Stef will love them," Cass assured him.

"I hope so. Well, better get going," he said and hustled out of the shop.

"And what did he do, I wonder," Kevin said and looked hopefully at Cass.

"Honestly, Kevin, just because a man buys flowers for his wife it doesn't mean he's in trouble," Charley said.

"Nine times out of ten it does," Kevin insisted. "I'm sure he's done something."

Cass wasn't about to feed Kevin's curiosity. "Never mind him. Charley's looking for a nice arrangement for Melody's parents."

Kevin immediately sobered. "That's sweet of you. Those poor people. I can't even begin to imagine what they're going through."

"Me, either," Charley said, slipping a hand to her belly.

Heinrich came over with the arrangement he'd put in the cooler. "How about this? I just made it."

"That will do the trick," said Charley. "It's beautiful and you are a true artiste."

"Don't tell anyone, but he's a retiring artiste," said Kevin.

"What? You're too young to retire," Cass protested.

"Dear girl, I'm fifty-eight. I'm ready for a change."

"We're off to San Francisco," Kevin said and began to croon the famous song about leaving his heart there.

"Why would you want to leave Icicle Falls?" Charley wondered.

"How about for a nightlife?" countered Kevin.

Charley frowned. "We have a nightlife at Zelda's."

"You know we love you all," said Heinrich, "but this crazy thing wants to get back to a big city. So what could I say?"

"Oh, you could have said any number of things," Kevin quipped. "But lucky for you, you didn't."

"What about the flower shop?" Charley asked.

"Sold it," Heinrich said. "To a nice woman from Seattle. She was here this last weekend looking at houses. I think she looked at one over on your street," he told Cass.

"Griffin's house?"

"Maybe. Anyway, she's planning on making an offer."

"That'll make Griffin happy." And it would make Stef sad.

Charley turned over her charge card and Kevin promised to deliver the arrangement that afternoon.

He turned to Cass. "And how about you, Miz Gingerbread? What would you like?"

For Grant Masters to show up on her doorstep with or without flowers. The chances of that happening were about as high as a blizzard in Hawaii.

She pointed to a big bouquet of stargazer lilies in the cooler. "I'll take that." A little extravagant but she was worth it. She, too, handed over her charge card.

Once home with her flowers, she set them on the kitchen counter and admired them. Flowers truly were good for the soul.

Lady Gray hopped up on the counter to investigate, and Cass put her back on the floor. "Nice try, but you don't get to be up there. I paid too much for these for you to be knocking them over. And no rude comments about having to buy my own flowers," she added as the cat meowed. "I don't need a man to send me flowers. I don't need a man, period," she muttered for what felt like the millionth time. "I've gotten along on my own all these years."

And it looked like she was going to be getting along on her own for a lot more. Darn that chicken Grant Masters.

Griffin's house sold to the new owner of Lupine Floral, and now it was time to organize for her big move. Stef and Cass came over to help her get started on her packing.

She was keeping very little. Her high school yearbook, her

Jane Austen novels, the teacups Beth had given her...those and her linens and extra clothes she'd take to Oregon for her parents to store until she got settled. As soon as the house closed she'd send Steve a check for his share of the profits, pay her dad back and have a little left over to live on in New York.

Very little. She'd have to be frugal. But that was a skill she'd already honed. *You'll be fine*, she kept telling herself. Alone and scared, but fine.

"Take your spices with you," Cass advised. "They won't take up that much room in your suitcase, and spices can be expensive to replace."

Speaking of replacing, she'd never be able to replace these two women, who had been such good friends to her. "I'm so going to miss you guys."

Stef's eyes filled with tears. "It's not going to be the same without you. But we'll have a place to stay when we come to New York," she added with forced joviality.

"Absolutely," said Griffin.

"You've got to be getting excited now that the house has sold," Cass said.

"I am. I'm a little nervous, too, though."

"You'll be fine," Cass assured her.

"And if you don't like it you can always come back. Once an Icicle, always an Icicle, right, Cass?"

"Absolutely," Cass said.

Once an Icicle, always an Icicle. There was a lot of truth in that. This town felt like home. Would she ever feel at home in New York?

Between working and keeping up with her friends as well as helping Griffin get ready to move, Cass had kept busy. But in spite of her full schedule, in spite of the pep talks she kept giving herself, she was aware of the empty space in her life that could have been filled so well by a certain handyman.

Other than running into Grant a couple of times at Zelda's, Cass saw little of him. He was always friendly. She tried to tease him the way she had when he'd been working at her place, encouraged him to stop by Gingerbread Haus for cookies.

"I owe you. Remember?"

He'd smile and say he did, indeed, remember, but he never took her up on her offer. And she became increasingly cranky. She actually snapped at Jet for forgetting to lock the door of the shop. And she'd complained when the gang wanted to watch a romantic comedy on one of their chick-flick nights. "I'm sick of romances."

Charley had pointed a finger at her. "You are in serious need of sex."

"Well, that's not happening. Let's watch something grisly."

"That won't be good for the baby," Charley had said, patting her growing baby bump.

Cass had been outvoted and pouted her way through the entire movie. Romantic comedy, bleh. There was nothing funny about romance.

Griffin's approaching departure put Stef in a bad mood, as well, and she spent more than one evening over at Cass's house, mourning the upcoming loss of her friend. "Maybe we need to rename our street," Cass said one evening as they sat on Stef's front porch watching Brad and Petey play catch in the front yard. "Instead of Blackberry Lane we should call it Grumpy Gulch."

"Why are you grumpy?" Stef asked. "Your roof and deck are done."

That was the problem. No more reason for Grant to come over. "I don't know," she lied.

Nobody knew how fixated she was on Grant except her cat. She meant to keep it that way. As far as Stef was concerned, she and Mr. Fix-It were only friends.

But friends saw each other more than she and Grant did. The big coward.

June melted into July, and Cass's house came back to life with two of her kids back home for the summer. Willie was job-hunting—sending out résumés and vanishing every few days for job interviews. Amber was working part-time at the nearby dude ranch while she waited for fall quarter to roll around. When she wasn't working, she often had friends over, and Cass found her evenings busy as she baked cookies and sometimes even let herself be persuaded to play board games or cards. She enjoyed her kids' friends, and having the house full of youth and laughter distracted her from the fact that a certain man was no longer around.

More distraction came when Dani and her family came home for the Fourth of July celebrations. And there would be plenty. On the Fourth, the town would have a parade, which would pretty much be a repeat of the Memorial Day parade. The food booths and arts-and-crafts displays would return, too. There'd be picnicking in the afternoon and fireworks on the river at night. And, of course, everyone would turn out for the annual street dance on the third.

Dancing. Bah. But her kids insisted she go.

"You can't sit home alone, Mom," Dani declared, and just in case her daughter started talking about moving her old mom to Spokane again, she donned a denim skirt and red top and her favorite flats and went to the street dance.

"How come you're not going with Mr. Masters?" Amber asked as they walked into town.

Because Mr. Masters is a big chicken. "We're just friends, honey." And not even friends with benefits. What a rotten deal.

"He's really nice," Dani said.

"Don't be matching Mom up, guys," Willie scolded.

"Why?" Dani retorted. "You don't want her to be alone all her life, do you?"

Dani turned to her mother. "Has he kissed you?"

Amber took it further. "Have you guys done it?"

"Aw, jeez. Don't go there," Willie said in disgust. "My mom having sex, that's an image I don't need stuck in my head."

"And just how do you think you got here?" Cass teased.

"That's different. You were young then."

"Mom's not that old now," Dani pointed out.

"Yeah," said Cass. "And watch it with the insults or you're out of the will."

"Ha-ha, we're the new favorites," Amber gloated.

Happily, after that the subject was dropped. The last thing she needed was her children poking their noses into her love life. Or rather, her nonexistent love life.

She supposed it was only natural that they'd think she had something going with Grant. She'd brought him to Willie's graduation. Probably not the wisest move. Still, it had felt good to show Mason that she hadn't ruined her life forever by divorcing him. That she, too, could actually move on, find someone who'd love her.

Too bad that wasn't true. She was now forty-six and still alone.

And whose fault was that? It wasn't as if she'd been actively looking all these years.

But when had she had time? She'd been busy raising her children and running a business.

She had time now, though, and it was extremely irritating that the man she wanted was not cooperating. She'd enjoyed that trip over to Seattle. Grant had fit in so perfectly at the party. They'd felt like a couple. At least they had to her.

She had to let go of her fixation with Grant. Trying to nudge him into taking friendship to the next level was like trying to get a fallen soufflé to stand up again. You couldn't.

Would he be at the street dance?

Center Street was the place to be, with people of all ages milling around and many already dancing to a popular local band called Good Times. An appropriate name considering the fact that everyone was having a good time. Grown-ups stood chatting, while their kids created sidewalk art with chalk supplied by local merchants. Food booths lined the sides of the street, offering Fourth of July favorites like strawberry shortcake, ribs, hamburgers and corn on the cob.

Griffin had come with the Stahls.

"Where's Matt?" Cass asked as Brad and Stef joined the dancers, little Petey jumping along behind them.

"He can't come up. He's working tonight, and his restaurant has a booth all day for the Fourth of July in Seattle. We need to start cooling things anyway."

She didn't lack for men to dance with. Billy Williams, the local doofus affectionately known as Bill Will, came up, convinced her she was in for a treat and hauled her into the growing crowd.

Oh, yeah. It was going to be a great evening standing here watching everyone else, Cass thought irritably. Willie had already found a couple of friends and wandered off. Danielle and Mike were dancing with Emma, and one of the cowboys from the local guest ranch had taken Amber to a food booth for corn dogs.

Well, it was fun to people watch, anyway. Brad and Stef were having a terrific time. Ever since they'd patched things up, they'd been acting like newlyweds, and Stef had reported that this last anniversary was the best yet. Brad had loved his new game table and she had loved their trip to Victoria.

Tilda Morrison was in her cop uniform, watching the dancers with a vigilant eye. Her husband came up beside her and offered her a bottle of water, and her stony don't-mess-with-me expression softened into the smile of a woman in love.

Farther down the street, Muriel strolled along with Dot. An old guy came up next to them and, even from where Cass stood, it wasn't hard to tell he was hitting on Muriel.

Everyone here was coupled up, it seemed. Oh, yeah, Cass was having fun now.

Then she caught sight of Grant, a few bodies down to her left. He'd been cornered by a sixtysomething pudgy woman wearing shorts and a sleeveless red top. She'd accessorized with cat's eye sunglasses, a floppy red hat and red flip-flops with poufy fake red flowers on them.

Grant looked miserable. Cass to the rescue.

She strolled up to the pair and tapped him on the shoulder. "Did you forget where we were meeting?"

"Uh, yeah. I did."

"Oh, you're with someone?" The woman lowered her glasses and frowned at Cass.

"Um," Grant said.

"He's with me," Cass said and gave his arm a tug.

He followed like a reluctant pony. But he had the grace to thank her for rescuing him.

"It's more than you deserve. Some friend you turned out to be, always dodging me."

"I've been busy."

"Busy hiding from me." The band started a slow song, and she looked longingly at the dancers and heaved a sigh.

"That was subtle," he said.

"I thought so."

He shook his head, took her hand and led her to the edge of the crowd. "Why don't you find someone your own age to play with?" he complained as they began swaying to the music.

"I like older men. More mature. Anyway, you know I've got a crush on George Clooney and you're as close as I can come."

"Funny," he said sarcastically.

"Listen, Grant. I know you're bothered by the age difference between us. But what does it matter, really?"

"How did you feel when your husband got together with his trophy wife?"

"That was different."

"How?"

Because Babette is an airhead.

That would hardly be either kind or appropriate to say. "We're both adults. I'm not twenty. I'm old enough to know my own mind."

"Easy for you to say that now. But what if we got serious?"

"Works for me."

"Will you be saying the same thing when I'm hobbling around in a walker and you want to go dancing?"

"So you'd stand there and look cute and I'd dance around you."

"Don't joke."

"Okay. No joking. Yes, there's an age difference. So what? Do you think Babette cares? I can assure you Mason doesn't."

"Ask them how well it's working in twenty years."

"Maybe they're happy right now. And you know what? Twenty years is a nice, long time to be happy."

"Well, I may not have twenty years," he said, sounding as grumpy as she'd been feeling for the last few weeks.

"No, you may not. But who knows how long I have? I could get cancer or have a heart attack." He paled. "I'm sorry," she said gently. "You've been down that road, and it had to be terrible. But doesn't that show you what a crapshoot life is? Think of that poor girl who died last month."

"You're really cheering me up here."

"I'm trying to make a point. All we have is now. You're here. So am I. All our body parts are working. Let's use them while we can."

It was a tempting offer. Here was Cass, in his arms, soft and lovely, ready to give him anything he wanted. And he was feeling more and more like taking it. But that would be selfish.

He looked away, trying to form some sort of rational argument that would get through to her. It was hard, because in a way what she said made sense. And he did want to spend more time with her. He was tired of being on his own.

Then he happened to see Muriel on the other side of the street. She was visiting with a couple of other women, one of them Cass's friend Dot, who owned Pancake Haus. They were both widows. Muriel had lost two husbands. Now here she was, alone again.

If he and Cass got together, she'd wind up alone, too. That was how the odds were stacked.

Muriel saw him looking, smiled and waved. He nodded a hello and said to Cass, "Is that how you want to end up, alone like Muriel?"

"In case you haven't noticed, I'm already alone." She glanced over in time to see a man leading Muriel to the edge of the dancers. "Boy, she's really suffering."

"Maybe not at the moment. But she'll go home alone."

"So will we. Is that what you want?"

No, he didn't. But he wasn't going to be selfish. Not getting involved with Cass was for her own good. The dance ended and he said, "Have fun," and turned and walked off.

"How am I supposed to do that when you keep running away?" she called after him.

Online dating. Maybe it would work out better for her than it had for him.

Cass watched Grant leave and ground her teeth. The man was infuriating. And hopeless. She was through wasting time on him. There were other fish in the sea, other cookies in the oven, other pigs in the pen.

Pigs in the pen? Whatever. She was done.

CHAPTER TWENTY-FOUR

The sale on Griffin's house had closed and she had to be out by the end of the month; come the thirty-first she'd be leaving for New York. She wanted to spend more time with Matt. She knew it was a bad idea, though, so instead she went home to visit her family and drop off the things she needed stored.

That didn't turn out to be a particularly good idea, either. While she was there, her father returned the check she gave him to repay him for the deposit on the house, along with instructions on how to manage her money.

"If you find yourself in a pinch, you call us," he said.

"I'll be fine," she told him, but he looked doubtful, and that was hardly encouraging.

"I think you could do just fine staying here," Mom said. "There's too much competition in New York."

Such a vote of confidence. Griffin found herself longing for a hot fudge sundae.

And Matt. Perversely, now that she'd run away to Oregon, she wished she'd hear from him. He didn't text or call and she'd resisted the urge to text him, not wanting to look pathetic.

A week with her family was all she could take. Even though

she now allowed herself to enjoy her mother's cooking (thank you, Matt, for that lesson!), she still stopped eating when she was full and left food on her plate, which prompted Mom to worry that she had an eating disorder and bemoan the fact that they'd sent her away to that awful camp. This, of course, made her father look like a thundercloud with legs. Her brother reverted to their childhood roles, teasing her and hurling good-natured insults in her direction. And Dad reminded her constantly that if she failed (why did he think she would fail?) they were there for her.

She loved her family but she decided it was best to love them from a distance.

She was glad to return to Icicle Falls, where people didn't know her past, didn't see her as the fat girl. Or the timid girl who was bound to mess up. Here she was loved and appreciated. Beth Mallow had been delighted with the job she'd done, and it seemed that everywhere she went, people stopped her to tell her they could hardly wait to see the cookbook.

"That's why I can't stay longer," she'd told her mother when Mom was urging her to visit for another week. "I have to get back for the book-signing party."

"Just think, our daughter's pictures are in a cookbook," Mom had said. "You need to get me one."

The last thing her mother needed was another cookbook. She already had twenty. But Griffin promised.

Now here she was at Mountain Escape Books on a Sunday afternoon, seated next to Beth at a little table and signing her name on the inside title page. The store was packed and everyone was raving over how beautifully the book had turned out. Beth had published it herself, sparing no expense, and it was, indeed, beautiful. When Beth had given her a copy as a present, Griffin had spent a good hour simply going from page to page, staring at the pictures. She'd done these. She really had.

She'd take this to New York with her. In fact, she'd get several copies to hand out. If this didn't sell her talent, nothing would.

"You did an incredible job," Cass told her. "Maybe someday I'll write a cookbook and get you to do the photos. If you're not too busy and important by then."

"I'd love to be busy and important, but I never want to be too busy for my friends," Griffin said. Would she ever get back here? Would she ever see them again? Of course she would, she told herself firmly.

Muriel came to the table to get her copy signed and give Beth a hug. "Your mother would be so proud," she said to Beth, making her tear up.

"I can't thank Griffin enough for the fabulous job she did," Beth said, taking Griffin's hand and squeezing it.

"The pictures are charming." Muriel smiled at Griffin. "They make my mouth water."

"Then I've done my job right," Griffin said.

"You'll be a huge success in New York," Muriel predicted.

"I hope so. Your book inspired me to go."

Muriel nodded her approval. "Good for you. I'm sure you won't regret it."

There. Muriel Sterling-Wittman, the resident wise woman of Icicle Falls, said she wouldn't regret it. Still, when she went to her going-away party at Cass's house the following Sunday, she went with mixed feelings—fear, excitement, regret, happiness and, when she saw Matt there, doubt. What was she doing?

What she needed to do, of course. Since she'd told him she was going to Oregon to visit her parents, it was as if she'd said she was going to the edge of the world where there was no cell phone reception. And he'd only called once after she got back to tell her that he couldn't come up for the book signing. His work schedule had changed.

Yeah, right. She knew what he'd really been saying. She was

leaving and he was cooling it. She told herself once more that it was just as well. The timing had never been right for them.

But now here he was, looking casually gorgeous in a shirt hanging loose over jeans, and some flip-flops. And, speaking of flip-flops, there went her heart.

He was by her side in a minute. "It feels like forever since I've seen you."

"It feels like forever since we talked. You never called while I was at my parents'." Boy, did that sound accusatory. As if they were boyfriend and girlfriend instead of two people who'd been rebounding from failed relationships.

"I didn't want to bug you when you were with your family."

A man in love wouldn't care. She shrugged. "Oh, well. It doesn't matter."

His brows furrowed. "It doesn't, huh?"

Her cheeks heated. "I mean, you didn't have to. I just thought maybe you would."

"I guess I should have."

Yeah, you should.

"When are you leaving?"

"Tomorrow."

"I can take you to the airport. I've got tomorrow off."

"I thought your schedule had changed."

"That was only temporary."

Rather like their relationship. "Stef's taking me. She took the day off so she could."

He nodded, taking that in. "Maybe it's better that way. It's hard to say goodbye. We'll stay in touch, though. You'll send me food pics on Instagram," he added with a smile.

"Facebook, Skype," she reminded him.

"There are some things you can't do on Skype," he said, suddenly morose, and she thought of his kisses.

Their conversation ended when Stef came over and told her it was time to open her presents.

Presents again, just like at the bridal shower for the wedding that never happened. But this time she was really going through with her plans.

The presents were mostly gift cards and money. "Being a starving artist isn't all that cool," Cass joked as Griffin gasped over the hundred-dollar bill that fell out of her card.

She had so many good friends here. "Thank you, everyone," she said, smiling at them all. "You're making it very hard to leave."

"Then don't," Matt said later when it was just the two of them sitting on her back porch with iced tea and a bag of pistachios.

"I have to. I have to at least try."

He nodded slowly. "Yeah. I get that. In a way I'm kind of jealous. You're going to get out there and make something happen. I'm still all talk, no action."

"What are you waiting for?" Okay, *that* sounded rude. "I don't mean what's your problem. I mean, do you have a plan? Are you saving up?"

"I was. Since the divorce, I feel like I'm back at square one."

"I'm sorry," she said softly.

"Oh, well," he said with a fatalistic shrug. "I'll get there eventually. Probably not as fast as you." He smiled at her. Funny. She'd often read about characters smiling sadly. She'd never been able to imagine how they could do that. Now, looking at Matt, she understood. The lips went up halfheartedly, and his eyes… He almost seemed to be in pain. Maybe he was.

She put her hands on his cheeks and kissed him, and he pulled her against him and kissed her back. He didn't say it verbally but she could feel it in the passion behind his kiss. *Don't go.*

She did, though. The next day Stef drove her to the airport.

Stef parked the car and went in with her as far as the TSA line. She pulled out a fat card envelope. "One more gift before you go."

"Friends forever," the card read. She opened it to find a print-out of her flight schedule for December, from the twenty-third through New Year's Day. "I can't believe you did this!"

"I got hold of your mom," Stef said. "Your whole family's coming up for Christmas. They're going to stay at the Icicle Creek Lodge. And," she added, "you're staying with us."

Tears invaded Griffin's eyes. She'd been doing so well up until now. "I don't know what to say."

"Say you'll use it."

"Of course I will. Thank you!" Griffin hugged her and allowed those tears to fall. "You're the best friend I ever had."

"And don't you forget it. Just because you're moving doesn't mean you can't come back for visits."

"I will." Griffin said it as much for herself as her friend. Then she picked up her carry-on and moved into line, terrified but determined. She could do this.

But did she want to?

Too late now.

Stef returned home feeling down. But her spirits lifted when she found Brad and Grant busy installing the new tub in her master bathroom, with Petey a fascinated observer. "My tub!" she cried happily and hugged her husband. He was sweaty and dirty. And the best husband ever.

"I figured you'd want to de-stress with a bubble bath tonight," he said.

That tarnished her moment of happiness and she decided she needed to take a walk to Gingerbread Haus.

"Did you get her safely on her way?" Cass greeted Stef.

"I did. It was so hard to let her go."

"It's always hard to let friends go. At least you've still got the rest of us."

Yes, she still had her support system in Icicle Falls. Poor Griffin. She was all on her own.

★ ★ ★

Griffin had been in New York for two weeks, and they'd felt
like the longest two weeks of her life. The city was crowded and
expensive. And hot. She often longed for the fresh mountain
air of Icicle Falls. But it was exciting here, too, she told herself.
This was where the action was.

Not that she'd seen any action yet. She'd dropped off a lot of
portfolios, showed off a lot of cookbooks, but still hadn't gotten any work yet, and that scared her. She'd found a place to
stay through Airbnb and was currently renting a room from a
nice older couple in Harlem while she figured out where she
wanted to live and made the rounds of the various ad agencies
and magazines.

"Don't worry," Mr. Johnson, her temporary host, had told
her. "It takes time to settle in."

Too much time.

On a sunny Sunday afternoon she bought herself an iced coffee and took Muriel's book to the Shakespeare Garden in Central Park, settling on a bench to read and get inspired. Today
Muriel wasn't all that inspiring. Anyway, it was hot. Too hot.
She scowled up at Belvedere Castle.

Her cell phone rang. "Hey there," said a familiar male voice.

Matt! "Hey there." Hearing his voice did more for her than
reading an entire chapter of Muriel's book.

"How are ya?"

Should she be honest? No. "Okay."

"Just okay?"

"I'm still adjusting."

"Want to meet for a drink?"

"What?"

"I'm here."

There was a lot of noise in the background, voices, traffic.
Still, she wasn't sure she'd heard correctly. "Here? As in here?"

"Yep. So, got time to meet me for a drink or something?"

Did she ever! "Yes!"

"I'm under the Coke billboard in Times Square."

"I'm on my way."

She raced to the subway. Emerging from underground to see Times Square still left her blinking, trying to take it all in. The tall buildings, the flashing neon ads, the traffic, the noise, the people—it all swarmed her senses. She immediately spotted the gigantic interactive Coca-Cola billboard, then gaped in shock as she saw the names on two toasting Coke bottles, hers and Matt's. And there he was, standing amid a swirl of tourists, smiling at her.

She rushed up, threw her arms around his neck and kissed him. Yes, those lips were real. He was real, not some crazy heat-induced hallucination. "What are you doing here?"

"I'm following you. I quit my job in Seattle, listed the house, and boom, here I am. What the heck. New York is full of restaurants, right? Somebody's got to need an awesome chef."

"You followed me?" He'd cared enough to come after her.

He smiled at her. "You know how I said it was hard to say goodbye? I decided I'd rather say hello."

So would she!

CHAPTER TWENTY-FIVE

Grant had been concerned when his younger son announced his intention to pick up stakes and follow Griffin James to New York, but not surprised. Matt had found reasons to be with Griffin long after the painting was done. He definitely approved of Matt's choice but he'd been concerned about the timing of it all. He was still concerned. The last thing he wanted to see was either of those two rushing into something and then ending up hurt.

But he also was a little jealous of his son's boldness. "What can I say, Dad? She's the best thing that's ever happened to me and I'm crazy about her. I have to be with her."

And so off he'd gone.

Grant was crazy about Cass Wilkes, too. But he wasn't crazy. Or selfish. And that was what he'd be if he pursued her. She didn't think their age difference was a big deal. She was too young to get it. Another sign that they shouldn't be together. He knew he was right about this.

But his attitude of rightness was challenged when he went to the home of Andy and Lois Beckenworth to put in a wheelchair ramp. Andy was a sinewy, fit-looking guy probably not too much older than Grant. He greeted Grant with a hearty hand-shake and equally hearty thanks for fitting them in.

"When it comes to carpentry, I'm all thumbs," he confessed.

"Happy to help," Grant said. Andy had told him on the phone that his wife had had a stroke. She'd been in a nearby nursing home, recovering, but would be returning to their house soon. Walking was a distant possibility, so for the time being she'd be in a wheelchair.

"I don't know how many more years we have together, but we're going to make the most of what we have left," Andy told him. "This ramp will make it easier." He pulled his wallet from his pants back pocket and showed Grant a picture of them as a couple. It looked fairly recent. His wife wasn't aging as well as he was.

"Nice picture," Grant said diplomatically.

Andy smiled, glanced at it one more time before shutting his wallet and putting it back. "She's a great gal. She was a looker, too, let me tell you. Still is."

Love was blind.

"She was my prof back in college," Andy continued. "Had a crush on her even then. Of course, it took another ten years of me growing up before she'd even look at me. She kept telling me I was too young. And at twenty I was. But hey, by the time you're thirty, things have a way of evening out and a ten-year difference isn't that big a deal."

Except now it was.

"I finally won her over," Andy continued. His smile fell away. "I don't know how much longer I'll have her, but I'll be grateful for whatever time we get."

Those words ricocheted through Grant's mind as he worked, dogged him all the way back to his lonely room at Gerhardt's. The last few months flashed before him. Flirting with Cass, dancing with her at her birthday party, eating cake on her back deck, that trip to Seattle. Then came the memory of their last serious conversation at the street dance.

He needed a beer.

He swung by Safeway to pick up a six-pack of Hale's. Once inside he decided to get some chicken from the deli, as well.

Muriel Sterling-Wittman was standing at the nearby gourmet cheese display. Awkward. He'd pretty much tried to avoid her after their nondate, nodding at her from a distance at parties or community events. Maybe he didn't want chicken after all.

Too late. She'd seen him. She smiled and said, "Hello, Grant. How've you been?"

"Busy." *Yes, much too busy to call you again.*

"I'm glad things are going so well for you here. You've certainly filled a need. And it looks like you're getting plugged in, getting to know people."

He sensed the conversation heading for shaky ground and was about to tell her it was good seeing her and escape.

Before he could, she said, "I couldn't help noticing that you and Cass seem to be hitting it off."

Crap. Was she jealous? She hadn't seemed the type but you never knew. "We've become friends," he said cautiously.

"I saw you together at the street dance. You make a lovely couple."

Okay, not jealous. Nosy.

"We're just friends."

"Always the best way to start."

"We're not really starting anything."

Muriel cocked an eyebrow.

Oh, no. Not the cocked-eyebrow thing. Lou had been good at that, too. It invariably left Grant feeling foolish and fumbling for a defense, like a lawyer who suddenly had no idea how to win his case.

"There's nothing going on," he insisted.

She looked disappointed. "Oh."

"There shouldn't be."

Now she looked puzzled. "Why is that?"

Muriel Sterling was a busybody. He frowned.

Maybe he should have cocked his eyebrow, too, because she wasn't intimidated. "I know it's none of my business," she said.

He wanted to say, "That's right—it's not. So butt out." But Muriel had this air of sweetness about her that made it challenging to be stern. She was a cross between Mother Teresa and Dr. Phil. How did a man stand up to that combination? Anyway, his mother had raised him to be polite to ladies.

"Muriel," he began, hoping the rest of the words he needed to gently put her in her place would magically materialize.

She laid a hand on his arm. "I know it can be difficult to start over."

"It's not that," he said. Good Lord. Didn't the woman have eyes? Couldn't she see the problem?

"Then what?" she asked, genuinely perplexed. "You two seem to enjoy each other, and Cass is a lovely woman."

Lovely. Yes, lovely couple, lovely woman, lovely life. Did Muriel know any other word? Did Muriel know anything, period?

"She deserves a man who can go the distance," Grant said bluntly. "There's a huge age difference between us, in case you hadn't noticed."

She shrugged. "I noticed. I'm sure she's aware of that, too. Perhaps it's not a concern for her."

"It should be."

"Maybe," Muriel said. "I have to admit it's hard being the one left alone."

Ha! There. I rest my case.

"But I wouldn't trade the time I had with either of my husbands for anything. Love is a treasure. Why not grab it and hold on to it for as long as you can?"

"It would be selfish."

Muriel shook her head at him. "Maybe you should let Cass

have a say instead of deciding for her." She gave his arm a pat. "It's just a suggestion, Grant. You're a good man. You deserve to be happy. I think your wife would want you to be happy." Now she smiled a beatific smile. "And I suspect you could make Cass very happy. Think about it." She gave him a final pat, dropped a wedge of Brie cheese in her shopping basket and strolled off, leaving him feeling like a character in the old *Lone Ranger* TV series he'd watched as a kid. *Who was that masked man?*

That was Muriel Sterling-Wittman, the Lone Ranger in drag.

He got his chicken and his beer and went back to his stinkin' room and ate his stinkin' chicken and glared at the stinkin' TV. What was he doing, anyway? Being all noble and for what? Cass wasn't bothered by their age difference. His family wasn't bothered by their age difference. Her family...well, her ex had opened the door to the trophy-wife store. Now he even had townspeople telling him to go for it. So maybe he needed to do just that.

Stef and Amber had gone blackberry picking, then talked Cass into making blackberry scones. They were in her living room with Petey, sampling the treats, when Cass's doorbell rang.

She answered it and her mind stalled. Okay, she was seeing things. This had to be a sugar-induced hallucination. "Grant?"

"Are you busy?"

"Uh, no. Come on in. Stef and Petey are over, and we're all eating scones."

"Oh." He looked uncertain. "I can come back."

He was here. And she wasn't letting him slip away. "No, come on. We've got plenty."

He followed her into the room and Stef glanced up in surprise. "Oh, Grant. Are you doing some more work for Cass?"

"No, I just stopped in to say hi."

Just stopped in to say hi. Grant Masters had never just stopped in to say hi.

"Mr. Masters," Amber greeted him. "It's about time you came to see my mom."

Stef caught on quickly. "Well, you know what, I need to… do something. Come on, Petey. We need to go home."

"But I want another scone," he protested.

She grabbed one. "We'll take one with us. Nice to see you, Grant," she said and towed her son away.

Amber followed suit, but not before she gave Grant a hug and told him it was good to see him.

Cass suddenly felt as twitchy as a girl on her first date. "What are you doing here?" she asked.

"I'm visiting you. Why don't you put on some music and let's dance?"

"That's a switch," she joked, but she put her phone in her wireless speaker and brought up her playlist. Sting began to croon "When We Dance." "You know this song, right, old man?" she teased.

"I've heard of it."

Okay, enough joking around. "Seriously, what are you doing here, Grant?"

"What does it look like I'm doing?"

"It looks like you're leading me on."

"Well, I'm not." He drew her closer.

Okay, this was good. But he'd been so adamant about their age difference. "I'm a little mystified. In fact, I'm a lot mystified. We're still the same age we were when you ran away from me at the street dance. Nothing's changed."

"Something's changed. Me."

She liked the sound of that. She slipped her arms around his neck. "Yeah? Tell me more."

"I'm better at showing than telling," he said and kissed her. Every nerve ending in her body felt the jolt. Thrills and chills, folks.

And there was more where that came from. Plenty.

He stayed the whole evening. They sent out for pizza and talked. Talked about their marriages, their kids, their hobbies, their pasts and their present.

Grant told her about the couple he'd worked for. "I guess talking with Andy was a tipping point. Well, that and a talk with Muriel."

"Muriel!"

He shook his head. "I don't know how that woman gets away with being such a busybody."

"Me neither. I think I'll send her flowers," Cass added with a grin.

"Listen, though, if you change your mind at any time..."

"Not on your life," she said and pushed him down on the couch.

"Would your wife approve of me?" she finally asked. Why was she even bringing that up? Did she want to jinx this? She waited for his answer, holding her breath, wishing she could take back her dumb question.

"Yeah, I think she would. If she was still alive, you two would be friends."

"I hope she's happy up in heaven to see you moving on."

"I hope she's got better things to do up there than spy on me," he said and ended the conversation, replacing it with more physical communication.

It was late when Amber came back in and they were still on the couch, wrapped together.

"Don't mind me," she said as they sprang apart. She went upstairs, calling, "I'll put clean sheets on the bed," making her poor old mom blush furiously.

"You have to work in the morning," he said. "I need to let you get some sleep."

Sleep? She was too happy to sleep.

But she did, and her dreams sent her back to that toy store she'd visited earlier in the summer. This time she was with

Grant. The giant Ken dolls all pouted and the inflatable man told her, "You sure know how to deflate a guy's ego." But this time there was also a good crowd of Barbie dolls, and they all applauded her.

"Way to work it," said one. "You two are going to be very happy."

Yes, they were. She woke up with a smile on her face.

One evening at the end of August they were relaxing on her couch, with him giving her a foot rub as the credits rolled on one of her favorite movies, *Murphy's Romance*, when he said, "I'm tired of staying at Gerhardt's. I think it's time I started looking for a house."

"I know a place you can stay while you look," Cass said with a coy smile.

"Yeah?"

"It's in good shape, has a new roof and a deck."

"Sounds perfect," he said, and by the next day he was moved in.

The days skipped happily along, and summer turned to fall. The leaves burned orange and red, and the weather cooled. But Cass's love life stayed white-hot.

She'd come home from work, take a nap, then get up and get creative in the kitchen. And Grant was there to appreciate every morsel. On Sunday afternoons they'd go hiking.

They even hiked Lost Bride Trail once. Cass had hoped to see the famous ghost of the lost bride, who'd mysteriously disappeared during the town's gold-rush years. Seeing the ghost flitting behind the falls was supposed to be a sure sign of an impending marriage proposal.

She never saw the bride, but oh, well. She was happy with what she and Grant had. Every day was filled with love and companionship. Even Lady Gray had taken to the new man, often preferring his lap to Cass's. The traitor. But Cass didn't blame her. She was rather fond of sitting on his lap herself.

"I'm surprised you had time for this," Charley teased when the girls gathered for their chick-flick night. "Now that you're with Grant, we hardly ever see you."

"At least not without him," Cecily added. "But that's a good thing. You two are perfect together."

"Dan says he hasn't seen his dad this happy in years," Charley said as she filled her bowl with popcorn.

"I haven't been this happy in years," Cass said. Being with Grant felt so right. "Sometimes I think I've been waiting my whole life for this man."

"Now he needs to make an honest woman out of you and propose," Charley said.

"Oh, I don't know."

"Just because you didn't see the bride," Samantha said.

"I don't blame her for hiding. I'm not a good candidate. I didn't do marriage well."

"You didn't do marriage with the right man," Charley told her. "Trust me, it's better the second time around."

Still, she wasn't going to push it. She and Grant were fine the way they were.

But maybe he wasn't so happy. She tried to hide her surprise when they gathered at Zelda's bar with all their friends for the restaurant's annual Halloween party and he announced, "I'm thinking I might want to get a place."

Black-and-orange crepe paper streamers hung everywhere, carved pumpkins sat on the bar, and patrons dressed as everything from pirates to princesses sat around chatting and laughing and enjoying crazy Halloween specialty drinks, waiting for the band to set up.

The festive atmosphere turned to a blurred background as Cass stared at him in shock. "You want to move out?"

He shrugged. "I thought I might build something. I found a lot on the river."

"I saw it," Dan confirmed. "Great place."

It was all Cass could do not to glare at him and say, "Traitor."

"Sounds good," said Samantha.

Cass was still stuck on the idea of him moving out. This was the first she'd heard of it. If he'd wanted her to move out with him, surely he'd have said something. Now, instead, here he was, making a public announcement. They'd get back to her place and he'd drop the bomb. *Sorry, Cass. It's been fun but I don't see it lasting.* Or whatever his cowardly excuse would be.

She barely saw the drink when Rita Reyes, Charley's pal and best cocktail waitress, set it in front of her. This *had* all been too good to last. She should have known.

Grant turned to her. "What do you think? Would you be open to starting over in a mountain cabin?"

"Together? With you?"

"Did you have somebody else in mind?"

Relief flooded her. "Oh, my gosh, I thought…"

He looked at her, obviously confused.

"She thought that you were dumping her," Samantha guessed.

He shook his head at Cass. "Really?"

"What can I say?" The old self-confidence still needed some boosting.

"You crazy woman."

"That's me." *Crazy about you.*

"So how about it? I know you love your house."

She grinned and slipped her arms around his neck. "I love you more."

"Look in your drink," urged Charley.

There was something glinting in all that orangey froth and it wasn't ice. Cass fished out a ring.

"My daughter-in-law thinks we should be setting a better example for the children," Grant said.

"And the grandkid," Dan added, placing an arm around his very pregnant wife.

Cass stared at the ring. The diamond was huge. "Best Cracker Jack ring I've ever seen," she said, trying not to blubber.

He took it from her and slid it on her finger. "You can't have the ring unless you take me, too. I hope you can keep up with me."

Half laughing, half crying, she said, "I'll sure try," and kissed him as their friends hooted and applauded.

Dan stood up on his chair. "My dad just got engaged. Drinks are on the house."

"Thanks, bigmouth," Charley said, but she was smiling.

Cass turned to Grant. "When you first talked about getting a place, I thought you wanted to move out."

"No, just to move on. I think it's time, for both of us. Don't you?"

"Absolutely. You know what this means, don't you?"

"That I have to put up with your ex at Christmas?"

"That, too."

"Okay, what else?"

"We have to take another hike up Lost Bride Trail."

He chuckled. "Fine by me. But we're getting married whether or not you see the bride."

She could live with that.

EPILOGUE

Griffin came back to Icicle Falls for the holidays, sporting an engagement ring. It wasn't the world's biggest diamond, but to her it was priceless. Matt was happily working in a high-end restaurant and she was beginning to get some work herself. She was glad she'd gotten up the courage to leave her comfort zone and start over.

And what fun to be in town for a bridal shower, this time for Cass.

Stef was pregnant and experiencing what she referred to as all-day sickness, but she'd still begged for the privilege of hosting. Now her new great room was packed with Cass's family and friends. Dani had left her Spokane bakery in the care of her most trusted employee and come over early to help Bailey with the food, and the refreshment table was laden with appetizers and all manner of baked treats.

Presents and gift bags had been piled high around the guest of honor's chair and it had taken Cass nearly an hour to get through all of them. She'd received everything from perfume to lingerie. Samantha, Cecily, Bailey and their mom had given her and Grant a weekend at the Four Seasons in Seattle, and Stacy Thomas,

who owned Timeless Treasures, had left everyone oohing and
aahing appreciatively with her present—two crystal wineglasses
engraved with Grant's and Cass's names. Dot had gotten laughs
with her gift—his-and-hers aprons. Grant's said Kiss the Chef
and Cass's suggested Let's Get Hot in the Kitchen.

"I bet they're getting hot all over the house," Charley had
cracked, making Cass blush and everyone else laugh. Not to be
outdone, Charley had given Cass and Grant a gift card for dinner
at the Space Needle. The gift tag had been signed from Charley, Dan and Ethan (the newest member of the Masters family).

"Thank you," Cass said to Stef as everyone milled around,
chatting and eating.

"You're welcome," Stef said. "And thanks for letting me host,"
she said to Samantha, who was standing next to her, along with
Cass's daughter Dani.

"No problem. The important thing is getting to celebrate,"
Samantha said, smiling at Cass. "Anyway, I knew you wanted
people to see the new-and-improved great room."

"Yes, it's so nice to have my house all put together and that
stupid curtain gone."

"Rather symbolic," said Muriel.

"How so?" asked Stef.

"Because the curtain's gone up on new lives for all three of
you."

How right she was.

★ ★ ★ ★ ★

Recipes

Beth Mallow's cookbook is finally complete. You'll want to try these yummy offerings from it.

APPLE STIR-FRY

Ingredients:

2 extra-large apples
¼ cup butter
¼ cup brown sugar
2 tablespoons water
¼ cup slivered almonds
a handful of raisins
a pinch of cinnamon

Directions:

Peel apples and cut into slices, then "stir-fry" in butter on medium heat in a large frying pan for about five minutes. (Don't get it too hot or you'll burn the butter.) Add the brown sugar and other goodies along with the water, then cover the pan, turn the heat down a little and let the apples steam until tender (about ten minutes). Serve warm over ice cream.

STRAWBERRY-RHUBARB CRISP

Ingredients:

(for filling)
3 cups strawberries, hulled and halved
1 cup cut-up rhubarb
½ cup sugar
2 tablespoons cornstarch

(for topping)
¾ cup flour
1 cup sugar
½ cup butter

Directions:

Combine the strawberries and rhubarb, then add the sugar and cornstarch. Cook over medium heat just until thick. Put in a 9-inch pie pan. Mix the topping ingredients and pour over the filling. Bake at 350°F for 30 minutes. Delicious either warm or cold. Serve with whipped cream.

APPLE SCONES

Ingredients:

2 cups flour
½ cup sugar
1 tablespoon baking powder
1½ teaspoons cinnamon
½ teaspoon salt
½ cup butter, room temperature
½ cup peeled and finely chopped apple
6 tablespoons milk

Directions:

Sift dry ingredients together into a bowl, then cut in butter as for piecrust. When thoroughly mixed add cut-up apple and then milk. Knead slightly and form into two balls. Roll each out on a floured surface into circles about six inches wide and about four inches high. Cut each circle into quarters. Put on an ungreased cookie sheet and bake at 350°F for 20 to 25 minutes. Best when served warm!